Brush WITH FAME

It doesn't take a fine-arts degree to slap on superglue.

Andrene Low

All names, characters, places, and incidents in this publication are fictitious or are used fictitiously. Any resemblance to real persons, living or dead, events or locales is entirely coincidental.

Previously published as Mounted and Hung © Andrene Low 2015 - ISBN 13-978-0692423899

ISBN: 978-0-9951235-1-9

1

Standing next to Samantha, her life-long friend, Jennie rubs her finger where an engagement ring should sit. From what she's seen of it so far, Steve would have loved London and while Sam's a brilliant travelling companion, it isn't the same without him.

"Wow, it's a nice looking place. We definitely got lucky here," says Sam.

Coming out of her reverie, Jennie realises she's looking down at a ragged parting in Sam's normally tidy hair. She's looking down on everything and everyone. To avoid paying excess baggage when they'd left, she's wearing her heaviest, calf-muscle-cramping platform shoes: a pair of wooden wedges, each weighing as much as a newborn. Sam calls them glorified firewood.

Focussing on the house sitting at the end of a short, intricately tiled pathway, Jennie can see that Sam is right. They're lucky. Damned lucky.

Dark red brick is layered three stories high and topped with a roof so steep, it has to be a Santa-free zone. Bay windows either side of the glass front door gives the place a look of wide-eyed innocence. While the house is immaculate, the same can't be said for the garden that's sporting a spectacular showing of weeds. Any flowers brave enough to survive, peep warily from a profusion of yellow dandelions.

"I guess Eadie can't garden with arthritis." Jennie flexes her fingers in sympathy. They're still aching from hefting her suitcase from the back of the minicab. Their driver, after loading the huge bag at the station, wanted nothing more to do with it.

Peering over the low wall, Sam says, "If the rent's as cheap as your workmate was saying, then maybe we can do some weeding for her."

Sam's long blonde hair is blinding in the reflected morning sunlight. Jennie would kill for hair like that instead of the short curly auburn locks she's stuck with. Her height – and lack of action on the boob front – means that if it weren't for a lot of hair product, people would think she was a bloke. "We can pitch in with the housework too."

A lace curtain twitches at the bay window to their right and Sam drags her two-wheeled suitcases up the tiled path, before helping Jennie manhandle the beast, as it's been named, up to the front door. Jennie now hates her huge suitcase with a passion. It had seemed a good idea when she bought it and while she can fit everything in, it's a nightmare to move.

"Well, knock on the door then," says Jennie.

"No, you knock, you know her."

"I don't know her."

Jennie had told Sam that Eadie is a workmate's auntie. She's actually Mark's auntie; Mark is Chris's best mate in Melbourne. Chris is Sam's ex-boyfriend. It was so convoluted that Jennie had to think twice before speaking about it, in case she got it wrong. It was better Sam didn't know. No point in getting her hopes up again after it had taken weeks and weeks for her to get over the worst of her break-up with Chris. Jennie doesn't want to pick at that particular scab anytime soon.

"Oh, for goodness sake, I need to get in and lie down." Sam's hand is poised to knock when she spots a doorbell.

Jennie hears a loud *brinnggg* echoing around inside the house. When there isn't an immediate response, she puts her ear to the door and is rewarded with faint sounds. Someone is moving, the increase in volume proving they're getting closer, albeit incredibly slowly.

The door opening at the speed of your average glacier, gives Jennie time to remove her sunglasses out of politeness before looking down at someone she assumes is Eadie. The description Mark gave most certainly matches the woman standing in front of them dressed in a flowery housecoat and fluffy slippers. She's lacking in height and girth and her legs are dandelion stems in all but colour. The main thing about her of any substance is her hair. There's at least double the requirement for such a small woman. Her face is surprisingly free of wrinkles.

Mark said Eadie was tiny but Jennie assumed this was in relation to his six foot three. He even made Jennie feel petite and she's five ten without her platforms.

Ever confident, Sam puts her hand out to shake that of the little woman and they get confirmation that it is indeed Eadie, their new landlady.

Seeing Eadie wince during her greeting with Sam, Jennie makes a mental note not to squeeze too hard when it's her turn to shake.

"And this is Jennie."

Sam deliberately keeps hold of Eadie's hand, avoiding Jennie having to shake it too.

Instead, Jennie waves her fingers in greeting. "Hi."

"I've so been looking forward to meeting you both," says Eadie, her hands now held limply in front of her. "Come in, girls. Can I help you with anything?"

Both Sam and Jennie refuse this well-mannered offer.

Jennie suspects her bag is equal to four Eadies, so the chances of the diminutive woman being able to help move are laughable, if it weren't so sad.

"Why don't you go and sit back down while we bring our stuff in," says Jennie. "We can re-lock the front door and join you then if you like."

"That'd be lovely, but best you don't lock the door. It's stiff and if it's locked, I can't open it." Jennie is further saddened by this no-nonsense approach to the crippling arthritis that has taken over this woman's life, if what Mark said is right.

Eadie moves unhurriedly into a room on the right of the hallway, leaving Jennie and Sam to drag their cases inside. Jennie's relieved to see the hall is tiled. The beast has a tendency to munch on carpet as though it's a giant moth.

She's leaning the beast carefully against the side of the staircase when she hears Sam say "Wow, what a monster!"

Jennie follows the direction of Sam's nod and spots a humungous black-and-white cat staring at them from the first landing.

"Shoot, he's bigger than some of your clients back in Aussie."

Sam had developed a successful business making clothes for small yappy lap dogs during their nine months of living in Melbourne. Doggs' Toggs she'd called it. Sam is planning on setting up a similar business here in London, but it will all depend on whether the little old ladies of London are as batty as the little old ladies of Melbourne when it comes to their canine companions.

The cat gives the girls a good eyeballing, stands, and then dismisses them by showing them his bum, flicking his tail and sashaying out of sight.

Feeling the heat creeping out of the room Eadie had disappeared into, Jennie removes a couple of layers of sweaty 'excess baggage' and hangs the lot on the coat rack inside the front door. Even standing in the relatively cool hallway, she's fighting the sleep that's plotting an invasion of her body.

Waiting while Sam does a similar strip, Jennie stares at the wall opposite until one of the beautiful paintings hanging there swims into focus out of the heavily textured wallpaper. Walking over, Jennie is surprised to see Eadie's name in the bottom right-hand corner. The Eadie who signed this fantastic painting was without argument more capable of holding a brush than the shell sitting in the front room waiting for them. Walking along the hallway she sees that all of the paintings are by Eadie.

"Her stuff's amazing," whispers Jennie, absently, while studying them. "So sad she can't paint anymore."

Jennie already knows a lot about Eadie from Mark and while he'd said she was an amazing artist, Jennie is surprised at how good she was.

Trailing behind Sam into the front room, Jennie's sleep-deprived eyes try their hardest to implode: the room is lovely, but so bright. She wipes at her watering eyes until she can make out Eadie, sitting in a large, overstuffed armchair. Mahogany tables sit sentinel on either side, cluttered with the necessities of everyday life. Small lips around their edges are all that stop some items from tumbling to the plush carpet.

The table to the right of Eadie is mostly taken up with an ornate silver tray that holds a large decanter full of some amber brew and a collection of wine glasses of varying sizes and styles. The table to her left holds a pair of glasses, a collection of precisely folded hankies, a small transistor radio and a hair brush. Most worrying of all is the large family-size tube of haemorrhoid cream. Jenny reminds herself never to walk in here unannounced.

"Please sit down, girls, you must be exhausted." Eadie's grotesquely knuckled hand flutters in the direction of the couch.

Backing up to it, Jennie drops fluidly into its upholstered bliss, sinking deep into its embrace.

Eadie asks about their flight, their plans for London and a long list of other questions. Given the detail Eadie goes into, it's obvious that Mark has briefed her fully on them too. They try their best to answer although Jennie finds it difficult as her brain now has the cognitive capabilities of overcooked cauliflower.

When she's slow to respond to a question about her art background, Eadie says, "You look like you could use a sherry."

Without waiting for a 'yes', Eadie leans over the wide, curved arm of her chair and attempts to pick up the decanter sitting on the table. She isn't up to the task and the decanter wobbles backwards and forwards a couple of times before settling again. Jennie releases the lungful she's been hanging onto.

"Oh, for fu ... goodness sake. Perhaps one of you would do the honours?"

Jennie clambers out of the depths of the couch and pours two miniscule glasses of sherry. She's replacing the decanter stopper when Eadie says, "I'll have one, too."

Jennie's stomach drops when she realises she'll have to drink a glass to be polite. She reluctantly pours a third. She doesn't even like sherry; the only stuff she's ever tried has been sickly sweet and made her teeth go furry. Jennie hands the others their glasses and then picks up her own before slipping back down into the couch.

She's about to take what she hopes is her one sip of the sticky brew, when Eadie proposes a toast. "Here's mud in your eye," is so at odds with the gentility of their small hostess that both Jennie and Sam laugh loudly before adding their own "Mud in your eye" response. Jennie takes a small sip of the pale liquid and is surprised to find it isn't so sweet after all. She takes a couple more sips, and then runs her tongue experimentally over her teeth. She's relieved to find them furry, but only twenty-eight-hours-in-a-plane furry.

Three glasses later and Jennie is no longer able to keep up with the conversation and leaves Eadie and Sam to carry on. Jennie notes that Sam's slurring her words but doubts this is to do with alcohol consumption. Sam can put away a couple of bottles of wine when she's on form, so three sherries wouldn't come close to taking her out.

"Oh dear, I've just realised you girls must be pooped and here I am chattering away." Eadie's face is creased with concern. "Would you like to have a lie-down?"

"That'd be lovely," say Jennie and Sam in unison.

A small widening of Jennie's eyes is prompt enough for the location of their beds to be forthcoming.

"Oh, right. Samantha, you're on the next floor up, the door to the left of the landing. The room at the back. Jennie you're up on the top floor. Follow the stairs as far as they go and the door is at the end of the hall, off to the right.

Before leaving, Jennie pours Eadie a fourth sherry. They leave her sipping this as they drag themselves off to bed.

While Sam pulls the sitting room door closed behind them, Jennie stares at her suitcase, the mountain of clothes on the bamboo coat rack and then the stairs.

She's back staring blindly at her bag when Sam says, "Stuff it. I'm going to collect everything once I've had a sleep."

Jennie agrees wholeheartedly. Dragging the beast up to the top of the house in her current condition would be the end of her. Dragging herself up there is challenge enough.

On reaching the Everest that is the first landing, Sam says, "Spot ya later," before opening the door to her assigned bedroom.

"Yeah, I think it's going to be a few hours before I surface," says Jennie, eyeing the second flight of stairs that turns back on itself. She's about to add that she'll knock on Sam's door later, but the door in question has already closed.

Jennie trudges over to the next flight and takes a deep breath in readiness for the climb. She's about to start the ascent, when a nudge from her bladder stops her with a foot in mid-air. Scouting around for a bathroom, she's relieved when she spies gleaming tiles through a door at the back of the landing.

Hands washed and dried and bladder echoing, she finds herself back at the foot of the next flight. Once happy her oxygen levels are up to it, she lifts her left foot and places it on the first step, then hoists her body up to join it. The balustrade creaks alarmingly, so does the step.

She achieves the next step in a similar fashion, conscious her legs are moving like Lady Penelope's in *Thunderbirds*. She might well have spent the past twenty-eight hours sitting on a plane but Jennie feels as tired as if she'd walked all the way from Aussie to London. Any excitement she'd felt at heading toward England waned around the eighteen-hour mark.

She and Sam lived in Melbourne for eight months and now her home back in Auckland feels like a lifetime away. Jennie has no regrets about moving on from Melbourne because, to her, it had always been a stopping-off point on the trip to London. Sam, on the other hand, had been sad to leave.

Faced with the final flight, she keeps going, thanks to momentum and adrenalin. Up here the air thins at the same rate as the carpet until both are threadbare. After planting an imaginary flag on the summit, Jennie is faced with a short landing, the door at the end open a squeeze, an arrow of light darting toward her in greeting.

She walks stiff-legged toward the door, feeling more *Thunderbirds* than ever, and pushes. It swings open to reveal a room as bright as heaven. It's even brighter than the sitting room. The only things missing are angels and harp music. Her eyes close to slits in response, staying open only enough for her to take in a sliver of her surroundings. Seeing the sunshine streaming in through skylights on both sides of the pitched roof makes her long for her sunglasses, safely tucked in her handbag three floors below. As well as these portals to paradise there is a huge window at the end of the room, with smaller ones low down on the side walls.

The room is overwhelmingly white. The furnishings, ceiling and even the wide, wooden floor boards are all painted this angelic hue. The furniture scattered around the room matches. The dark iron curtain rods atop each of the windows don't. They sit like pissed-off eyebrows, crouching menacingly as though waiting to be even more annoyed. If there had been any curtains hanging from them, Jennie is sure these would have been white too.

The unadorned nature of the bedroom is so at odds with what she has seen of the house, that Jennie believes she must be in the wrong room. She backtracks to the landing but the only other bedroom she can see on the top floor appears occupied.

Back in the white room, it takes a second for her to spot the bed, tucked away as it is in an alcove under the large end window. Jennie staggers over to it, turns her back to the white bedspread and lets her legs collapse as they've wanted to since she started her ascent. Dropping into the middle of the mattress, she's immediately enveloped by a large cloud of dust that puffs up around her, making her sneeze and her eyes water.

Dusty or not, the mattress feels like a family of marshmallows, together for a reunion and even though she's not related, they allow her to join in with festivities.

Jennie wakes up later confused about where she is but on seeing the room bathed in bright moonlight, memories beam back in. Holding her hand close to her face she tries focussing on the watch still strapped firmly around her wrist, but try as she might, she can't make out the hands. She likes to know what time it is, day or night, but not enough on this occasion to get up and turn the light on. It'll have to wait until morning.

She unbuckles the practical stainless-steel Citizen and drops it to the floor beside the bed, wincing at the loud *clunk* it makes as it hits the wooden boards. Painted white as they are, her tired mind had thought they'd be softer.

While massaging the watchstrap dents out of her wrist, Jennie stares at the room, with shapes revealing themselves only when she focuses hard on them. The thing standing in the corner reveals itself to be an artist's easel. It's big and old by the looks of things and the wooden pegs sticking out from the front support a large canvas, blank but for a couple of crooked sweeps of paint. As she focuses on them, the streaks blur and then disappear. "Well, that explains all the white," mumbles Jennie.

She's closing her eyes again when she realises the bedroom door is still open and knows she'll feel happier with it shut, even if it's not locked. She's sure she closed it the night before.

She's fighting to get to her feet when the door slowly shuts.

2

Bright whiteness wakes Jennie the next day by working its way through her eyelids and turning them bright pink. She covers her eyes with her hand before opening them a hint. Even with them shaded, it's still painfully bright. If this really is her room and she wants to sleep in during the summer months, she'll to need to invest in a welding mask.

Looking at her wrist and finding it bare, Jennie snakes her hand over the side of the bed and fumbles around until she locates the watch she dropped the night before. Staring at it through a gap in her fingers she can see it's only five-thirty and far too early for breakfast when you're living in someone else's house.

As her eyes adjust to the ten thousand lumens of visible light, her hand drops away and she takes a good look around at what she hopes isn't her new room. Her gaze eventually settles on a note pinned to the lamp on the bedside table at the head of the bed with her name at the top. "Was that there when I went to bed?" She doubts Eadie left the note. Surely it would be a physical impossibility for their landlady to make it up all those stairs.

One thing it does do though is confirm for her that she's in the right room. Given the furnishings in the room she's seen downstairs, she's a little disappointed that she's been stuffed up in the servants' quarters. Not that she can complain given the cheapness of the rent.

Sitting up and spinning around to position herself correctly on the bed, Jennie reads the note. It gives directions to the kitchen, where she is to help herself to breakfast. It also tells her where the bathroom is up here. Mention of the facilities and her bladder is suddenly full to bursting and Jennie is glad she's still dressed. Getting gingerly to her feet to stop any internal sloshing about, she opens her bedroom door. "Did I dream that?"

She faces the hallway, its darkness absolute after the blinding white of the bedroom. It takes a few moments till her pupils dilate and she can make out the bathroom door off to the right of the landing. She tries the handle, and although it moves, the door doesn't open. Now she really, really needs the toilet. She gives the handle a good rattle but the only response is from inside the bathroom, when a man yells out, "Won't be a sec."

To avoid being caught hanging around outside the bathroom when whoever it is exits, Jennie walks woodenly back to her room, trying to think of things other than her close-to-overflowing bladder. She's not sure she's comfortable being up here on her own with some strange man. If it was him who closed her door last night, then she's doubly uneasy, especially so given there's no lock on her door. She's sitting stiffly on the side of her bed when she hears a door open and the words, "It's all yours," yelled at her.

Thinking arid thoughts, Jennie walks the short distance from her bed to the door and opens it, relieved to see the mystery male isn't in the hallway. She shoots into the bathroom, slams the bolt home and while hopping with crossed legs toward the Victorian-looking toilet, manages to get her belt undone. Her jeans and undies are heading kneeward when she spins and drops herself onto the ornate mahogany seat.

The relief reduces her to tears, as does the feeling that she's peeing razor blades. "Oh, great, a bladder infection, just what I need."

Following a distressingly long time on the toilet, Jennie heads back to her room but it doesn't take long for her to realise there's nothing of hers in there. She's desperate to change out of her travel- and sleep-weary clothes but to do that, she has to drag the beast up from the ground floor. It's either that or lug everything up in several small loads. Even that option would be painful, given the number of stairs involved. Drag the bag it is.

Walking down the final flight she sees a man standing next to her case. He's looking at it with hands on hips, shaking his head and *tsk*-ing

"Can I help you?" says Jennie, causing him to turn in her direction. "Mark?"

She's surprised she hasn't recognised him. His height alone is unusual and his mop of sandy blond hair has always reminded her of the guy from *Scooby Do*. The Shaggy guy not the Ken Doll lookalike.

"What are you doing here?"

He bends over and grabs the handle of the beast. "About to give myself a hernia by the looks of things."

After he straightens and takes the full weight of the case, his eyes widen. "Jeez, what have you got in here, I've moved fridges that weigh less." He drops it back down but still keeps a firm grip on the handle.

Jennie runs down the rest of the stairs and tries to disengage his hand. "Leave it be, I'll sort it out."

"Oh, no you don't." Mark angles his shoulder to keep her

away from the suitcase. "If Eadie catches you moving it with me looking on, she'll give me hell."

Grunting, Mark leans to one side allowing the beast to clear the tiles and starts marching his way over toward the stairs. His other arm is held wide to the side in an effort to balance himself.

"But what are you doing here?" Jennie follows him up the stairs.

"Chris said there are heaps of engineering jobs here and 'cause everyone else had left town, I thought I might as well, too."

His reply is interspersed with grunts, as he picks up the case again after each mini break.

"You know where Chris is?"

"He's in there." Mark nods his head to the side as they make their way past Sam's room on the first floor.

A burst of Sam's laughter reassures Jennie that her friend is obviously happy with this arrangement. It will be interesting to see how living in the same house works out for the two of them. Hopefully, with fewer fireworks than back in Melbourne.

Realising Mark is getting ahead of her, Jennie runs up a few steps.

"Have you been planning this all along?" says Jennie.

Dropping the case on the next landing and flexing his hand, Mark turns. "I might have had something to do with it."

The smile that lights up his face confirms this and Jennie experiences unwelcome tummy flutters. So far as she's concerned that part of her life is on hold and if she were to contemplate another relationship it certainly wouldn't be with someone as blokey as Mark. Steve had been such a gentleman and when they'd made love it had been special, whereas Mark views sex as some sort of recreational pursuit if what Sam said is right. Thoughts of Mark and sex don't sit comfortably and she does her best to scrub them loose.

Changing hands, Mark once again lifts the beast to scale the third and final flight. It's only after he reaches the small landing at the top of the house that he points out his bedroom to Jennie, wriggling his eyebrows suggestively.

She doesn't respond, thinking he's only fooling around, but his, "Worth a try," makes her revise this opinion and shake her head in an unspoken 'no'.

Dropping the beast inside the door of her room, Jennie notices his breathing is laboured and he looks dangerously red in the face. "I think you'd better sit down for a second, you don't look so good." Only after she suggests this, does she realises the single place to sit down in the room is on her bed.

Mark responds by throwing himself on it full-length and putting his hands behind his head. "Hmmm, comfortable, and it doesn't squeak."

She looks down at him with chagrin when he proves it by bouncing up and down vigorously, causing Jennie to shake her head again from side-to-side in rejection of his thinly-veiled suggestion.

Given he made a big point of letting her know back in Melbourne that they were nothing more than mates, his flirting with her now is disconcerting. Certainly she's never given him any encouragement.

Eager to distance herself from him, and aware of the dreadful sensation that she's about to wet her pants, Jennie mutters, "Excuse me," before fleeing to the bathroom.

When she pulls the chain, all she's managed is a teaspoonful of pee and another packet of razor blades. She needs to find a chemist pronto.

Looking through the wide open door of her room, Jennie's relieved to see Mark is no longer in sight, although her bed is still messed up after being used as a trampoline.

She unlocks the combination padlocks that secure the beast before dropping it onto its side and unzipping it. Even though she's just been to the toilet, she can already feel her bladder whinging again. As the urgency to pee increases, so does the speed with which she rummages through her case, grabbing everything she'll need for the shower.

She's surrounded by untidy piles of clothes when Mark speaks from right behind her, scaring the shit, and nearly the pee, out of her. The box of tampons she'd been about to stow back in her case goes flying, with each small white missile trying to put as much distance as possible between itself and its box-mates.

"This was the last thing Eadie ever attempted."

Jennie looks briefly in his direction and is relieved to see he's got his back to her. She scrambles to scoop up all the tampons before Mark can see them, pleased when she manages this without having an accident.

"She couldn't even bring herself to pack it up, just walked away."

Clambering inelegantly to her feet, Jennie can see the canvas with its two red smears as well as a couple of tubes of paint and a paintbrush abandoned on the small shelf beneath the canvas. The floor splattered with a confetti of colour, is all that remains of some paintings.

"That's so sad. I can understand not wanting to paint ... but not being able to. That's awful."

"It's worse than that." Mark walks along throwing open the floor-to-ceiling cupboards that line the back wall of the room.

Jennie's eyes widen at the array of brushes, paints and pastels. At the bottom of the largest cupboard stands a stack of half-finished paintings. "Such a waste." Jennie's conscious that her own lack of action on the painting front is possibly as big a waste, but that's her choice.

Right?

"It doesn't have to be like that," says Mark, as though answering the question she's posed to herself. He flips through the incomplete works before pulling out a watercolour and clicking the cupboard doors shut.

"What do you mean?" says Jennie, although she suspects what might be coming.

"Eadie would like you to finish this." Mark plonks a small board down in front of the large canvas on the easel. The masking tape that was supposed to hold the piece of paper in place on the backing board has long since curled away, leaving the paper floppy and lacking commitment. Certainly Jennie couldn't finish it without the whole thing being re-stretched. Not that saggy paper would be her main hurdle.

The nearly completed painting is incredible with the level of skill shown, way beyond her abilities. She'd dropped out halfway through art school to look after Steve and hadn't been shown some of the techniques she's looking at now. Jennie stutters for an appropriate response.

"Eadie said she'd be happy to help. In fact, I think you'd be helping her by letting her show you some of the more advanced stuff."

Damn it all.

Jennie didn't feel ready to paint again. The only blank canvas she'd looked at after Steve died had immediately filled with images of his face, ravaged and hollow like a Dachau victim. His eyes dead long before the rest of his body gave up. She'd tried to press on and ended up covering the whole canvas in black paint in a futile attempt to obliterate the slide show that had chronicled Steve's awful last days. It kept flickering to life long after she'd burned the canvas.

She couldn't face that again.

"Great, I'll set everything up for you in Eadie's sitting room." Mark doesn't bother waiting for a formal answer. "You can bring down all the arty bits and pieces."

Jennie's shoulders drop when she twigs she's been treed. She'd feel like a complete jerk if she says no to art lessons from

Eadie, which is undoubtedly as Mark and his auntie have planned it.

With Mark out of her room, Jennie scrubs her forehead violently to rid it of any residual images of Steve, although this doesn't stop a few stray tears and the odd sniffle from popping up unbidden. She's annoyed, given how long it had taken her to stop these in the first place.

Pulling herself mostly together, she rummages through the piles of clothes that surround her bag, looking for something to change into. The yellow brightness of the room indicates another summery day and so she digs out something appropriate. It's only when she searches for shampoo and conditioner that she remembers they're stuffed in a rubbish bin at the International Terminal in Melbourne.

Damned excess baggage charges.

She and Sam had been faced with either forking out a ridiculously high excess baggage fee or ditching anything weighty that they couldn't wear. Jennie's legs and feet are still sore from the heavy wooden platform shoes she'd been forced to wear on the plane.

Because Sam had also ditched her toiletries, Jennie knows there's no point asking to borrow any. Hoping there's something in the bathroom, she picks up her clothes and a soft pink, extra fluffy towel from the dressing table. She's relieved to see the bathroom's empty as she now really, really needs to pee. Again.

Standing under the dinner-plate sized shower head, positioned centrally above the large iron, claw-foot bath, Jennie marvels at the difference water can make with any residual tiredness being washed away with the grime of travel. The light streaming in through the skylight high above is also energising. To top off the good feelings circulating around her, she strikes it lucky on the hair products front too, although the scent floating inside the shower-curtained space is masculine.

She's doing a final rinse when she hears the bathroom door open. The squeak that escapes her is involuntary.

"Sorry. I can use the bog downstairs if you like," says Mark.

"Ah, yeah. That'd be great." Jennie turns off the taps. "I won't be long." It's not until she hears the door firmly close that she peeks her head around the end of the shower curtain. Mark's leaning against the closed door, smiling.

"Damn, I was hoping you'd flick the shower curtain back."

"Get out!" Jennie's going to make darn sure she remembers to lock the door in future.

"It was worth a shot." Mark's laughing as he opens the door and leaves.

Jennie's about to pull the shower curtain to one side when the door swings open again.

"Darn it, Mark, will you stop it."

"Okay, I'm going." He pulls the door closed behind him.

Not wanting to avoid flashing her bits again, Jennie reaches out under the bottom of the shower curtain and manages to nab her towel. Safely wrapped, she climbs out of the bath at the end and then whips the shower curtain to one side. Sure enough, the door swings open again, but this time Jennie's ready and throws her full weight against it. She's rewarded with the sound of cranium connecting with oak before the door slams shut.

Followed by the sound of a body hitting the ground.

Regretting her hasty action, she opens the door a crack to see Mark lying prostrate in the hall.

He's conscious, but there's already a large bump forming on his forehead. All that's missing are those little bluebirds flitting around his noggin, tweeting delightedly.

"It's your own fault for winding me up." Jennie looks down at him and marvels at how calm she is after hurting someone. But after shutting the door, she starts shaking. She's never lost control like that, but then she's never been teased like that either. Steve had respected her privacy too much to carry on as Mark did.

What is it about the great lump that riles me so?

Hearing him moving, Jennie slams the bolt shut and after helping herself to some Brut 33 deodorant, she dresses, brushes her teeth and tidies up the bathroom. She's cautious when she opens the door but is relieved to see the hall is free of bodies.

Even though there's no immediate sign of Mark in her room, she doesn't take it for granted this time. After confirming she truly is alone, she closes the door and unpacks her suitcase of everything she can.

Jennie hates living out of a bag, so the more she can put in the small dressing table and hang in the large antique, free-standing wardrobe, the better. She hopes the clothes still smothering the coat rack downstairs will fit in too.

She stows the suitcase under the bed with a few unwanted bits and pieces still inside and lines up her shoes regimentally in front of it before standing back to admire her handiwork. The room is immaculate, which is how she likes it.

Feeling in control again, Jennie heads down to breakfast, amazed at what she missed in her previous trips up and down the stairs. First, because of exhaustion and then concentrating on what Mark was saying. Plus his butt being at eye level didn't exactly help, not that she liked admitting that, even if only to herself.

There's not much to see on the second landing, with all the doors shut. Jennie doubts there's anything behind them either, as the air smells musty and the small half-round table leaning drunkenly against one wall hasn't seen polish in years. The dried flower arrangement sitting on top of it is close to disintegration. Jennie suspects the flowers were fresh when first put there.

Skipping down the next flight to the half landing, Jennie gets a proper look out of the window. Yesterday, all she'd been aware of was trees. Now she can see the houses opposite, as well as glimpses of the surrounding area between the angled rooftops.

The next floor down is where the room that Sam shares with Chris is. Their door is closed and by the sounds of things, they're still in bed. The door to the room opposite is ajar and the large black and white cat stares balefully through the gap. Jennie loves cats but this one scares her, given he appears to be part cougar by the size of him. He doesn't look cuddly at all; if he curled up on her lap, her legs would go numb.

Reaching the front hallway Jennie makes a mental note to ensure she's organised when it comes to bringing things down from her room and vice versa. If she forgot something, it would be a mission to go back and get it. Perhaps she should ask Eadie if she can move into one of the spare rooms on the same floor as Sam and Chris. That's if they are even spare.

Jennie takes her time walking along the hall to the kitchen. The paintings are even more magnetic now she's had some sleep and the level of skill shown is incredible. The subject matter jumps off the paper, be it a bowl of fruit or a dead rabbit.

It takes Jennie a good ten minutes to make her way down the hallway, stopping in front of each painting to give it the attention it deserves. Still appraising Eadie's remarkable talent as she opens the door to the kitchen, her reflective mood disperses when she spots Mark and Eadie sitting at the large pine table, mugs of tea and toast in front of them.

"Good morning," says Eadie, with a chirp in her voice. "I hope you slept well."

"Morning," mumbles Mark, keeping his back to her.

"Morning," says Jennie, to the room in general. "I did sleep well. I can't believe I slept through 'til five-thirty. That makes it over eighteen hours, I think. I've never slept that long before."

"Help yourself to everything. You'll need to boil the kettle again though," says Eadie. Jennie fills it and pops it onto the hob, then follows instructions from Eadie on how to light the gas. With that underway, she puts some toast on and checks out the line-up of jars on the counter, opting for a home-made plum jam.

It's not until she's sitting at the table with her breakfast that she notices Mark is keeping his face turned away from her.

"Come on, Mark, it's nothing to be embarrassed about," says Eadie.

Jennie's still trying to work out what this means when he turns to face her. Recognising the beginnings of a black eye, she spits out the small mouthful of tea she's just taken.

"Silly boy walked into a door this morning," says Eadie.

"That is silly," Jennie hopes she doesn't give herself away in front of her new landlady.

"Yes, I'm going to have to be far more careful in future." Mark's current expression says far more than his words.

"Yes. You will." Jennie hopes he gets the message. If he's going to keep up the sort of behaviour he exhibited this morning then it won't be fun living here. First off she needs to put some distance between the two of them. "Eadie, I don't suppose there's another bedroom on the first floor that I could use?"

"Of course there is, but you'll need to tidy it up. Hasn't been used in years." Eadie looks intently at Jennie. "But what's wrong with the room you've got now? I love that room ... I thought you would, too."

The sadness showing in Eadie's eyes makes Jennie feel terrible for bringing this up. "The room's lovely, but it's such a long way up. I was thinking the first floor would be more convenient is all."

"Are you sure that's the reason?" Mark's tone is sly.

"Yes, I am." Jennie smashes the sly ball straight back at him. "Why do you ask?"

"No reason." Mark stands, and then picks up his cup and plate to take them over to the sink. Walking past Jennie, he stops and sniffs her hair. "Hmmm, nice shampoo. Smells familiar."

Of course, the stuff she used this morning is his; there isn't anyone else up on the top floor. She'd stock up on toiletries at the chemist when she picked up something for her cystitis. With Mark gone, she and Eadie have a good catch up on Eadie's paintings in the hallway. Jennie is surprised to find that Eadie doesn't consider any of them to be her best work. "All the paintings I'm most proud of disappeared long ago."

Jennie's finished breakfast and rinsed off her plate and cup, when Chris and Sam arrive. Her friend glows with happiness and good sex, making Jennie jealous even though she merely wishes good things for the two of them.

Sam is bubbling out of her skin. "Morning!"

"Morning," says Chris, although his eyes don't leave Sam.

"Sam, I'm going to the chemist this morning. You need anything?"

"I'll come with you. Need to see what's available."

"Mark can drop you all down there," says Eadie.

"Jennie, can you let him know we need a lift?" says Chris, giving her a task she could well do without.

3

Systematically removing her clothes from the coat rack, Jennie puts them on as this is easier than carrying everything, especially if she wants to see where she's walking. Luckily the day hasn't heated up yet, otherwise she'd be blinded by sweat well before reaching her bedroom.

At the first floor, she pops her head through the open door of the bedroom opposite Chris and Sam's to check it out as a potential bedroom. She'd much prefer being down here and well away from Mark. His coming on to her all the time is something she'd like to avoid.

Golly, I can tick this bedroom off right now.

Charlie, the monster cat, is dead centre of the large double bed. The depth of cat fur on the counterpane testament to the fact that this is his room and there's no way he's moving anytime soon.

Every flat surface in the room is similarly coated, giving the room a feeling of soft focus. Sensing her presence, he pops up his head and stares her down. Jennie pulls her head out of the room smoothly, scared of spooking the cat into something she'd regret.

Safely back on the landing, Jennie opens the door to one of the front rooms and immediately crosses it off the list of potential bedrooms. Apart from some moth-eaten curtains and a square of carpet, the room is bare and dragging furniture from other parts of the house would be a pain. Unfortunately, the other front room is similarly bare.

She doesn't hold out much hope for the next floor up, given the general air of decay there. A quick peek into all four rooms confirms they're all empty. There isn't even any carpet, although Jennie can see the faded outline of where large floor rugs once lay on the wooden floorboards. Even the moths have given up in these rooms.

Short of ousting Charlie on the first floor, Jennie is stuck in the attic. With Mark.

Jennie brushes her teeth, grabs a cardie and her handbag and makes her way down, down, down to the front hallway. Mark's there, but there's no sign of Sam and Chris.

"Where are the others?" Jennie checks her watch.

"They decided they were still, ah, tired." Mark grins broadly. "They've gone back to bed."

Unable to stop herself tensing up, Jennie isn't surprised when Mark reacts.

"Relax for God's sake. If you're not interested, you're not interested." His hand explores the swelling around his left eye.

"Good, as long as you get we're just mates."

Certainly, Jennie isn't interested in anything else and especially not with him. While she has reacted to losing her fiancé by retreating into herself, Mark has done the exact opposite after losing Stacey. He's seemingly happy to shag anything that moves, if Sam has the right of it.

"Sorry about the eye," says Jennie, unable to fight her good manners any longer.

"Yeah, it's not going to look good for my date tonight, that's for damn sure." He opens the front door, stands aside and gestures for Jennie to go ahead of him.

"Should have thought of that."

Jennie strides past him, stopping in her tracks when she reaches the pavement. She starts moving again after Mark directs her to the left. A little farther along the pavement she spots a stand-alone garage sitting squatly next to the house. It's sufficiently away from the pavement that a car can park there. The space in front is empty.

Overtaking her, Mark heads for one side of the wooden panelled door and opens the large padlock that secures it. The multi-panelled door opens smoothly, which is surprising given the dilapidated look of the building. Jennie had expected the door to squeal and graunch its way open rather than glide as it has. There's a car parked inside but she's unsure of the model as it's covered with a large dust sheet.

Pocketing his keys, Mark stands beside the car and eases off the cover. Jennie thinks his care is overkill until she sees the sparkling, dark green Jag revealed. It's an older model but the condition is still showroom perfect. Jennie can see herself reflected in the gleaming chrome back bumper. "Wow, she's gorgeous," says Jennie, reverently.

"She is, isn't she? Eadie's had her from new but hardly ever takes her out."

"She can still drive?" Jennie imagines that manhandling a beast like this would be well beyond the capabilities of the frail little old lady.

"No. She likes to think she can still take it out for a spin but that she chooses not to. She loves the car too much to sell it."

Jennie nods her head in understanding then stands to one

side to allow Mark to back the car ever so carefully out of the garage.

Settling herself into the plush leather seat, Jennie can see why Eadie loves the Jag. It's so luxurious that it's more like sitting in a small, graciously appointed lounge than in a car. The walnut of the dashboard is polished to a high sheen and interspersed with chrome-trimmed instruments and cream leather upholstered sections. The steering wheel is also clad in leather, with the cover lashed into place by fine cords in a herringbone pattern.

"It looks as if it's never been used." Jennie trails her hand over the arm rest at her side. "How many times did she drive it?"

"No more than six or seven, I'd say. She bought it in defiance when the arthritis kicked in. Everyone tried to talk her out of it but she felt if she didn't buy it, she'd be giving in." Mark guns the engine after getting it to start. A soft purr follows some initial coughing and spluttering.

"That's so sad and courageous."

As they slip backwards past the sitting-room window, Jennie can see Eadie standing and looking out at them. She responds to the wave from the small woman with one of her own. "Does she even like to go for a drive in the car?"

"We don't like to ask." Mark concentrates on backing the car out onto the narrow road.

The trip down to the shops is carried out in relative silence. Jennie looks away from Mark, focussing instead on all the buildings as they glide past. Everything is so different from Melbourne where she's spent the past eight months and from back home in New Zealand. The buildings are a lot older, the roads a good deal narrower and the mix of nationalities peopling the streets, much broader. Jennie takes care to check on landmarks because her plan is to walk home.

She imparts this to Mark while he's stationary at a zebra

crossing, when rather than respond to his arguments, she hops out and slams the door shut. Because he's still in traffic, he has no option but to move along when the car behind him beeps politely. Jennie swings around and walks in the opposite direction and is soon swallowed up by shoppers. First stop, Boots the Chemist.

An hour later and Jennie is loaded down with bags. She hadn't planned on buying as much as she has and knows she's going to regret her spree when she's about halfway back to the house. Stopping next to a park bench on the edge of Turnham Green, Jennie puts all her purchases in a pile on the seat and sits next to them. Rummaging in the assortment of plastic bags, she finds what she's after.

Eadie had said the first purchase should be a copy of the London A-Z. Jennie checks the directory at the back then finds the right map and confirms the co-ordinates. She's still got a hike in front of her but running her finger over the grey shading of Turnham Green, she sees she can save quite a distance with a shortcut directly across it. Putting the A-Z back into a bag, near the top, Jennie stands and picks up all the bags, making sure to distribute the weight between both hands.

It's while she's trudging over the Green that Jennie sees a commotion outside a church that's smack bang in the middle. A tumble of grey stone, with spires aplenty and a mob forming outside the front doors. Curiosity getting the better of her, Jennie veers in their direction. On walking between the turreted pillars that edge the front path, the mob shows itself to be mainly older women with the ratio of twinsets and tweed skirts plainly out of kilter with national averages.

The excitement in the air firmly rules out a church service and anyway, it's Saturday. Jennie asks the woman standing next to her what's happening.

'It's a jumble, dearie." The woman's eyes are alight with some inner flame.

None the wiser, Jennie looks down at the chattering ladies who surround her, checking for an escape route. She's no longer on the edge of the mob but now firmly clasped to the matronly bosom of a much larger group. The chatter of jumble and bargains reaches fever pitch as the large front doors, sitting under an impressive arch, are opened by a minister in full garb. He's part way through his welcoming speech when the crowd moves as one. Rather than going through the doors behind the minister as Jennie's expected, the ladies stream around to the right of the church.

Her arms are pinned to her side; her feet take tiny steps in the small amount of space allotted to them. "This is crazy."

"In'tit, though," comes back a reply from somewhere next to her, followed by a cackle of gleeful laughter.

Jennie has no trouble seeing over the heads of the ladies surrounding her, the tight perms all sitting around elbow height. This does, however, give her a good view of the small hall that's nestling up to the church like an extremely poor relation. That it's a late addition is obvious, with any architectural merit eschewed in favour of frugality. It's an ugly, utilitarian brute and out of keeping with its gracious forebear.

Eventually, the crowd funnels its way through ridiculously narrow doors and into the hall proper. The scene is one of chaos with enough of the crowd getting there before her that the contents of the trestle tables have already been picked apart with any semblance of order destroyed.

Jennie's eyes widen when she spots what looks like a brand new backpack on sale for a pound. It's perfect for carrying all her purchases on the walk home, even if it is a hideous shade of green.

Struggling, she manages to get all her carrier bags into her left hand to free up the right. She's reaching over the front row of ladies and making a grab for the backpack when she's firmly elbowed in the side.

"Oy, I saw that first," is hissed at her. A liver-spotted claw snatches the backpack from under her outstretched hand. The backpack disappears from sight when it's shoved in one of the wheeled shopping trolleys that have been spiking Jennie's feet at regular intervals since she joined the jumble mob.

Jennie's about to give up when a gap opens in front of her and she's pushed into the open space by the ladies behind her. She's hard up against the trestle with a good view of anything not already picked over by the crows. She can't believe her luck when she spots another backpack, this one a nice black and silver model. She grabs it seconds before another liver-spotted claw and fighting every manner she's ever had drummed into her, hisses, "I saw that first," clutching it to her chest.

"There yer go, now yer getting the 'ang of it," says the owner of the claw.

Jennie also manages to score a set of single sheets – perfect for curtains in the studio, meaning she can get dressed in the morning without having to scoot into the back corner to avoid flashing the neighbours. She'd ask Eadie if she had some, but if, as she suspects, the reason the room at the top is devoid of furnishings is due to a lack of funds, she's not about to draw attention to it.

Jennie staggers out of the church, across the small road and back into the park; her fingers close to being chopped off by the dental-floss-like handles of her numerous carrier bags. She slumps onto a park bench and after a short breather, crams all her purchases into the backpack before hefting it onto her shoulders. She strides off toward the corner of the Green, a spring in her step, her hands opening and closing at her sides to get the blood flowing again.

4

Sam stands panting in the doorway of Jennie's room. "Bloody hell, you need oxygen up here."

Jennie looks at her friend's reflection in the small mirror sitting on top of her dressing table, before putting down the hair dryer and turning toward her. "Tell me about it."

"It's a little basic," says Sam, looking around the room.

"I looked for a spare room on your floor but it's no go."

"I thought the other bedroom at the back was empty."

"Nope. That's Charlie the Cougar's room and there's no way I'm ousting him. He looks mean enough to plan a revenge attack, plus the room's knee-deep in old cat hair."

"Gross. Hey, I've got my first Doggs' Toggs fitting this morning. Want to come?"

"Already?"

"Yeah, it's with Mrs Farquhar's cousin, Barbara Harrow." Sam looks at the piece of paper she's holding. "We need to go to Sloane Square on the tube."

Mrs Farquhar had been Sam's best client in Melbourne and the reason she'd ended up with such a successful hound couture business. Mrs Farquhar has been left in charge of the

Melbourne business, with Sam promising to send Sapphire, Mrs Farquhar's blue poodle, a new outfit every month by way of payment for services rendered.

"When are you going?" says Jennie, continuing to tidy her dressing table methodically.

"In about five minutes. The appointment's ages away but I'd rather arrive early and kill time than be late. You know how these old battle-axes are."

Jennie realises that Sam's dressed up. "Five minutes!"

Sam opens the doors to the free-standing wardrobe.

"Oh my goodness, what on earth am I ...?"

Sam pulls a couple of items off their hangers and throws them on the bed.

"There you go. That'll be perfect."

"going to wear?" finishes Jennie, unnecessarily.

With Sam hurrying her along, Jennie is changed and downstairs within five minutes, the A-Z stuffed in her handbag. They also get directions from Eadie, who knows Sloane Square well.

At Gunnersbury Station, they buy tickets and are walking down the stairs when the tube pulls in. They clamber down the stairs as fast as their platforms will allow and arrive in time to hear the guard blast his whistle to announce the doors are closing. Panicked, they barrel through the nearest set of doors.

It's not until those doors close that they realise it's a smoking carriage. Thick cigarette smoke throws the carriage into soft focus and is acrid enough to burn nostrils. Stomped-out butts litter the floor, while the nylon upholstery is liberally pocked with melted spots. The windows and walls are tinted sepia.

The train lurches forward and Jennie grabs hold of an upright pole. It's sticky with nicotine; instinctively she lets go. "This is revolting." She comes close to falling as the train starts a slow right-hand turn, forcing her to grab the pole again. She's unable to stop her lip twisting in disgust.

"I can't believe they're allowed to leave it this gross." Sam keeps her balance by delicately putting one finger on the upholstered back of the adjacent seat, swaying in time to the movement of the carriage.

The soundtrack to this visual and olfactory feast is the hacking and coughing of their fellow travellers. The noises emanating from one old guy nearby indicate he's about to produce a lung, his lunch or both.

At the next station, they jump off, run along the platform, board a non-smoking carriage and are lucky enough to get a seat. Jennie examines her hand for gunge. There's nothing visible but if she forms a fist, her hand sticks to itself.

"Tell me more about Mrs Farquhar's cousin," says Jennie, hoping to take her mind off her 'soiled' hand.

"Not much to tell. She's younger than Mrs Farquhar and married to Earl someone."

"That his first name, or his title?"

"I didn't ask. Guess we'll find out. Eadie knows her though. Old school mates apparently."

"Just like in Melbourne."

"Yeah. Incestuous as all get out," says Sam, commenting on how small the gene pool is when it comes to the rich.

"What sort of dog does she own?"

"It's a poodle, a blue ribbon winner at Crufts apparently."

"What's that?"

"Some high-faluting dog show. It's supposed to be a big deal over here."

"Name?"

"Quincy."

"Biter?"

"Hope not."

They continue in this verbal shorthand; the privilege of those who know each other so well that partial sentences suffice, and because there are no train changes involved, they relax knowing they've got six stops before they have to get off at Sloane Square.

Their conversation follows the rhythm of the train and centres mostly on what they can see out of the window. It's all so different from Melbourne and back home in Auckland. The houses are narrower and taller, their backyards – where they even exist – are miniscule with no room for weekend rugby games or barbeques. They're surprised at how green the city is, with large trees planted in impossibly small holes in the pavement, their boughs overshadowing houses and roads alike. After Baron's Court, the view is replaced by tunnel walls. Their conversation is similarly restrained.

When the tube leaves South Kensington station, the girls get up and move to stand next to the doors. They're not sure what side they'll be getting off, but at least they're closer than they would be if they were still sitting down. Sloane Square looks close on the map painted on the curved bulkhead above them and they're not about to risk being taken unawares.

Safely off the tube and up on the street, Sam pulls the directions from her pocket while Jennie stands with A-Z at the ready.

"Okay, they're on the corner of Cliveden Place and Eaton Terrace." Sam folds the instructions before stuffing them back in her large shoulder bag.

"You mean Eaton Place don't you? As in *Upstairs Downstairs* Eaton Place?" Jennie's voice is brimful with excitement. It's her favourite TV show of all time. Being near the actual location is too good an opportunity.

Sam retrieves their instructions to double check. "Nope, definitely says Eaton Terrace. Not Place. But check the A to Z."

Flicking hurriedly through the street guide, Jennie says, "We've got to go and see the house. Once you've measured Quincy, of course," Unfortunately a quick look in the index at the back confirms that Eaton Terrace and Eaton Place are two different locations. There's more frantic page turning before Jennie has both locations sorted out.

"It's only around the corner from Mrs Harrow's. Can we still go?"

Yeah, sure, why not. Do you remember what number it is in Eaton Place?"

The front of Lady Marjorie Bellamy's house is soon cobbled together in Jennie's mind. "One, six, five." She's mentally positioning the columns on either side of the front door when she realises Sam is walking away. "Wait for me."

They find Mrs Harrow's place easily enough. It's hard to miss something this big. Eadie's house looks like servants' accommodation in comparison and the heavy construction appears to be bomb proof. Large expanses of red brick are sliced and diced with soft grey stone, outlining where one floor finishes and the next starts. Stone also snakes its way around all the windows, like grey kohl. To give the front of the building some relief, every second column of windows juts out, suggesting window seats stuffed full of Sanderson linen covered bolsters, dozens of satin rolls and pillows, the preferred spot of some pampered pet. "It can't be all theirs. Can it?" Jennie tilts her head right back so she can take everything in.

"No, thank goodness. If it were all one place, it'd take a week to find the sodding dog. No, they're on the sixth floor." Sam counts off floors in the air with her finger. "Top floor, by the looks of things."

Sam straightens, before marching up the steps and between the columns that guard the entrance. Jennie follows, hoping she too looks like she belongs. She's glad Sam thought to dress nicely. Chances of them getting in here wearing shorts and a t-shirt would be zip.

"That's odd." Sam looks at the front door and to either side. "There's only one doorbell. How is Mrs Harrow supposed to know we're even here?"

"Maybe ring it and see what happens?"

"Guess there's no other option." Sam pushes the porcelain button that's surrounded by gleaming brass. A bell rings inside the front door, surprising them. There's no response, so Sam rings it again, longer this time.

"Can I 'elp you girls?" comes a man's voice from beside them but below ground level. Looking up at them he pulls on his braces causing his pants to jiggle up and down.

"We're here to see Mrs Harrow." Sam walks to the edge of the step and looks down at their interrogator.

"You mean Lady 'arrow, dontcha?"

"I suppose so. We've got an appointment with her."

"'ave ya now. And 'ow am I supposed to know yer legit? I don't have no visitors on my list for today."

Looking hard at them, his eyes go squinty. Jennie feels as though they've been found wanting and, maybe channelling a little Lady Bellamy, she bristles.

"Excuse me, but we do have an appointment. The Countess will be most put out if you don't let us in." Jennie stops short of finishing with 'my good man'. Jumped up little twit is anything but.

"Yes, so if you'd open the door, we can be on our way," says Sam, in a similar tone.

"Or at least ring the Countess and let her know we're here to measure Quincy for a new coat."

"Why didn't you say," says Cellar Man, before disappearing through a door and into the bowels of the building.

Moments later the door opens and it's as though he's been given a personality transplant, so different is his demeanour.

"Jack's my name." He stands aside to let them enter. "Sorry about the interrogation but we get some funny types around 'ere. Can't be none too careful."

"Ah, right." Jennie wants to point out to Jack that she and

Sam hardly look like homicidal maniacs, or worse, Amway reps looking for two friends to sign up.

He escorts them across the marble-lined foyer and presses the button by the lift doors. They can hear it rattling far above them; the speed it's travelling leaves them in no doubt that the stairs would be a much faster option but not one that's open to them for security reasons. Not that Jennie is complaining. There are enough stairs in her life already. It arrives and the doors trundle jerkily open. Jennie's concerned that it appears original to the building and sized to carry one person at a time. It will be a snug fit with both her and Sam in there.

Jack swings his arm wide in invitation for the girls to enter. Once they're in, he joins them, disproving Jennie's theory on how many adults can fit into the lift at once. When the doors shut, it's difficult for Jack to get his arm up to press the button for floor number six. Sam's sharp intake of breath has Jennie looking at her, brows knotted in question. Sam gives a small shake of her head and mouths 'later'.

Following an agonisingly slow climb, in which Jennie realises she might suffer from claustrophobia, the doors rattle open and they escape. Jennie breathes in as they follow Jack to an imposing front door opposite the lift. He knocks and then waits with them for the door to be answered.

They all stare at the large brass 6A sitting smack bang in the middle. The silence is eventually broken by someone inside the apartment walking toward the door. The dark blue door swings open to reveal a woman in her thirties, hair scraped back close to her head and disappearing into a no-nonsense bun. Her dark grey dress is crease-free and plain; low-heeled court shoes finish the look of professional starchiness. She stares at both Jennie and Sam in turn, and then looks pointedly at Jack.

"These young ladies say they 'ave an appointment with the Countess," stammers Jack, nervously.

"We're here to measure Quincy for a coat," says Sam, causing the woman's gaze to swing in her direction and Jack to shuffle his feet.

Jennie realises she's standing at attention in response to some unspoken command and has to consciously relax her stance, her back is starting to hurt. The woman's gaze swings over to her before, once again, impaling Sam for having the audacity to speak.

Jennie is waiting for the blast she feels sure they're about to receive, when a plummy voice drifts down the hallway. "Is that the girl about Quincy's coat?"

The change in the grey Gorgon is instant. "Um, yes it is," she says, over her shoulder, already more approachable in her manner toward the girls. Jennie no longer feels as though she's about to be grabbed by the scruff of the neck and shown the pavement. "I'm Vivienne. You'd better come in." She steps to one side allowing the girls to enter. Jack tries to follow but the look she gives him sends him backtracking all the way to the lift. He stabs at the down button without looking.

Vivienne closes the door on him. "Insufferable little cretin. Did he manage to cop a feel in the lift coming up?"

"Just a slight boob graze," says Sam.

"Tries it all the bloody time. You're lucky there were two of you."

They follow Vivienne along a wide hallway that's split down the middle by an Oriental runner. Intricate parquet flooring borders each side, polished and darkly nutty. Occasional tables mill about, the holders of antique vases and bowls of over-blown pink roses. Sunlight streams across the floor in wide bands, stolen from the rooms that sit along its length while chandeliers twinkle their light down on what would otherwise be dark spots.

Vivienne swings to the left at the end of the hall and leads the girls into a lounge that wouldn't be out of place in *Pride and*

Prejudice. Staunchly Georgian, from the moulded ceilings, through the overly ornate furniture with legs like a Staffordshire bull terrier, down to a large oriental-patterned Aubusson rug and more parquet flooring.

Jennie's surprised by the approachability of the small, rounded woman sitting on a straight-backed seat, upholstered in a self-stripe gold fabric. The woodwork is gilded to match. She can't be Mrs Farquhar's cousin: she doesn't look snotty enough and lacks the racehorse grooming they're familiar with. Her twinset looks to be less mohair and more Quincy, or maybe it's a combination of the two. The tweed skirt is sporting more than its fair share of dog hair.

The small poodle in question is a doppelganger for Sapphire, Mrs Farquhar's beloved pet back in Melbourne, right down to the colour of the fur. Sapphire was spoilt rotten and blue in colour because of a rigorous beauty regime undertaken by Cynthia Farquhar and Sapphire's stylist. Jennie still finds it hard to believe how human-like Sapphire's regimen had been and probably still was.

With the girls in her mistress's care, Vivienne leaves them to it. Apparently refreshments aren't on offer today.

Barbara Harrow's face creases with a smile, the laughter lines forming swiftly, familiar with the expression. "Now, which of you is Samantha?"

Sam holds her hand up and waves, "And this is Jennie, who I'm travelling with."

"Lovely to meet you both. This is Quincy." She pats the small blue dog fondly on the top of his head, firmly enough that it bobs up and down. "Please, do sit down."

Jennie and Sam perch themselves on the edge of the golden couch. The upholstered seat gives little, having the resistance of a sandbag. Good posture and bruised buttocks are guaranteed. Jennie pulls her tummy muscles in, straightens her back and squirms until her cheeks conform to the upholstered bag of builders' mix she's perched on. Sam is similarly engaged next to her.

"I've heard such good things about your designs. Cynthia raved about some of the ensembles you created for Sapphire."

"What sort of thing do you have in mind for Quincy?"

Jennie waits for a description of an outfit that involves velvet and lace but is surprised by Lady Harrow's answer.

"It would need to be something sturdy. Quincy does like to get amongst it when we head down to the country place and I can't afford for his hair to get too dirty with Crufts coming up."

"I did make an oilskin outfit for one of my clients in Melbourne. Fully lined, of course."

While Sam explains the construction of the piece, Jennie's gaze roves around the room, taking in all the swirly twirlies on the ceiling, the chandelier and then over to the fireplace. The cream marble is even discoloured at the centre top, showing it actually gets some use. The mantle holds a couple of large trophies and an ornately framed oil painting of Quincy, mimicking the style of Rembrandt. Jennie's standing in front of it; examining it closely before she's even aware she's stood up and walked across the room.

"Isn't it fabulous? My nephew, Rupert, completed it for me. He's trained at all the best schools. It's cost me a fortune, but one does like to support the arts."

"It's, ah, very interesting." Jennie desperately searches for more superlatives to describe the paint-by-numbers atrocity in front of her. "He's faithfully recreated the, ah, style of the Master."

"Hasn't he though? My friends are very envious." Lady Harrow smiles ever so smugly.

Half an hour later, the visit is over. Sam has all Quincy's measurements and a full brief from Lady Harrow as to what outfits she wants and in which order. Sam has also taken photos of Quincy with the Polaroid camera she bought in duty-free on the way over. Jennie's pleased about this as she was always getting the dogs mixed up back in Melbourne, especially when there were several mutts of the same breed. To her, one Maltese looks pretty much like another.

Sam throws her arm around Jennie as they make their way to Eaton Place. "Looks like I'll have to get a sewing machine bloody fast. I mean six outfits. In one go."

Jennie's abruptly nudged out of her daydreaming. "What?"

"What's with you, you've been a zillion miles away since we left?"

"It was that painting."

"What about it?"

"It was dreadful. I could do better with a toothbrush and ten-year-old house paint."

"Why don't you? You could use one of the photos I took for reference." Sam pulls one from her shoulder bag. "Here you go, use this one."

Crossing the road, they start their search for 165 Eaton Place, fictional home to the Bellamy's of *Upstairs Downstairs*. It doesn't take long to realise the house numbers don't go up that far. Jennie's disappointed. It would be nice to see the actual home of some of her favourite TV characters.

Sam looks up and down the street. "Are you sure it was one six five?"

Jennie closes her eyes for a second, "Yes, I can see it clearly."

"Not sixty-five?"

Jennie kicks a small white pebble out into the middle of the road. "No. I'm sure it was one six five."

"If it's the Bellamy place you're after, it is sixty-five," says a small woman trudging past them, weighed down by a string bag full of cleaning products. A thin black raincoat swings forlornly from her shoulders. She doesn't pause but keeps walking, eventually adding "They painted the one on for the telly," over her shoulder.

"Thanks," says Jennie, as the old woman disappears around a corner.

Finding the famous domicile, they stand in front of it but Jennie feels let down. She thought it would be exciting but it's just a house.

"Maybe if you look at it from across the street," says Sam, noting Jennie's lack of enthusiasm now that they've located the grail.

"Hmmm, maybe."

They check for traffic, cross the road and once on the other pavement, turn and look over at the house. It doesn't do any good. Without Marjorie and Richard Bellamy standing side by side out front, and all the servants lined up behind them, it's only a house.

5

Lying on her bed the next afternoon, Jennie can't help but see the awful painting of Quincy every time she closes her eyes. Not even jet lag can blot out that monstrosity. She hopes the beloved nephew doesn't have any artistic aspirations.

Jennie knows she could produce something a whole sight better, but the thought of picking up a brush again fills her with trepidation. She's managed to avoid the dreaded training sessions with Eadie by continually 'forgetting' to take any art supplies down to the old lady's sitting room, although she knows she can't stall for much longer. It's not that Eadie's been pushing her; it's more that Jennie is finding it increasingly difficult to ignore the look of disappointment every time she enters the sitting room empty-handed.

Maybe a painting of Quincy will help unplug her creativity? She's hardly likely to see Steve's face when she's concentrating on painting whiskers. This thought has her chuckling quietly to herself although it's still not from deep down.

Only one way to find out. Swinging herself to her feet, she crosses her room and opens one of the large cupboards, still crammed with all of Eadie's art supplies.

By the time she's unable to squeeze the fifth tube, it's clear to Jennie that all the paint has long since solidified. Still-lifes in their own right. She'll have to ask Eadie where the nearest art shop is so she can pick up the basics. Of course, this will mean she'll also have to commit to starting her lessons downstairs.

While the paint might be past it, luckily all the brushes apart from the one left on the easel have been washed off and stored properly so no need to buy any of those. There are also dozens of canvases of different sizes for her to choose from, along with reams of watercolour paper. Jennie picks one of the smaller canvases, walks over and places it on the easel in the corner. Eadie's large, unfinished canvas, with its two sad smears of red paint, now leans face-in to the wall behind the dressing table. It's too big for the cupboard.

She selects brushes, spatulas and rags and arranges them regimentally on the easel shelf, before picking up her handbag and going downstairs to find Eadie. As she crosses the landing on the first floor, she hears Sam's sewing machine chattering away in one of the front rooms. Sewing is another thing Eadie is no longer capable of. Chris has dragged the machine out of storage, given it a good clean, oiled it, and then set up on a temporary trestle table. Sam is making good progress on Quincy's first outfit after visiting a fabric merchant on the way home from Lady Harrow's the day before.

Eadie's in her usual spot in the front sitting room, feet up on a pouffe, book propped on a pillow that's balanced on her tummy, hands limp on either side of the typeset pages. She looks up when Jennie enters the room, "Hello there."

"Hey, Eadie." Jennie sits on the couch

She's thinking about how best to broach the subject of painting when Eadie says, "I expect you'll want to know where to buy some art supplies?"

"I, ah, yes." How on earth does she know that? Maybe she's psychic?

"Sam said you were thinking of undertaking a painting of Quincy Harrow."

"I thought I'd have a go." Jennie expects Eadie to wax lyrical about her own heyday.

"I think that's an excellent idea. You can't do any worse than that painting Barbara displays with such pride on the drawing room mantle. I can't abide the way she always puts guests on the couch, so they have to face the damned thing.

"You've seen it?" Jennie diplomatically desists from any mention of the skill of the artist.

"The way Barbara tells it, the boy is an undiscovered artistic genius. Long may he remain so is all I can say," says Eadie, dismissively.

Jennie smiles in relief. "It is pretty bad, isn't it?"

"I've seen better renderings in the bottom of a budgie cage."

With directions to Eadie's favourite art supply shop, Jennie sets off for the train station. This is the first time she's travelled on the tube on her own, but with the A-Z stowed in her handbag she feels confident she won't get lost. She does have one or two wrong turns along the way, but finds the shop half an hour before it's due to close for the day. The sign above the door proudly announces that they've been in business since 1885. So Dickensian is the establishment, that Jennie's surprised there aren't quills displayed in the bay window. But when the tinkling of a small bell above her head announces her entrance, she's relieved to see many familiar products and brands.

After making herself known to the elderly gent behind the counter as instructed by Eadie, Jennie retrieves a crumpled list from her bag and works her way around the shop, collecting everything she'll need. This involves several trips to and from the counter and serious hunting to find a tube of blue acrylic in the right shade. Once finished, there's a large pile of items sitting next to the old-fashioned cash register.

On seeing the total that pops up in the little glass window on the register, Jennie's eyes also pop. "Wow, that's quite a bit, isn't it?"

"That's all right, Eadie said to put it on her account," says the clerk.

"Oh, but I couldn't."

"Eadie said if you weren't willing to put it on the account then we weren't to sell anything to you."

"But that's ridiculous."

The clerk shrugs his shoulders in answer. Given it's taken Jennie close to two hours to get to the shop, she yields. She can repay Eadie soon enough. Her packages are wrapped in brown paper yanked from a large spindle at one end of the counter, before being secured with tape pulled noisily from a large steel dispenser that looks to be original to the shop. She's relieved when the package also has twine criss-crossed around it, forming a handle of sorts.

Leaving the shop feeling like a shoplifter, Jennie juggles to organise her new paper 'briefcase' and handbag while also referring to the A-Z. She's still outside the shop when the 'open' sign hanging in the glass panelled door flips to 'closed'. Organised, she heads in the right direction for Tottenham Court Road station. From there it's a simple matter of changing at Embankment before a straight run through to Gunnersbury.

The tube station is heaving like a fly-blown carcass. Ticket in hand, she stands looking at a solid block of commuters, wondering if she should wait until later, when she's pressured into moving. She automatically lifts her package of art supplies to avoid it being crushed, and totters to keep her feet in line with the rest of her body. This tsunami of serge, briefcases and brollies carries her toward the escalator and down. She makes sure to stand to the left, so the commuters hooning down the 'walk' side of the escalator don't take her out in their haste.

Reaching the platform Jennie manages to break away from

the bulk of people, toward the curved back wall so she can regroup. She's not even sure which platform she's on and needs to check her A-Z before jumping on a train willy-nilly. It's gone. It must have dropped from the safety of her armpit when she lifted her package to stop it being squashed. Panic presents itself in Jennie's stomach, deep down and oily. She sinks onto the bench next to her, empty because none of the hundreds around her is prepared to wait, even a minute; their evening commute akin to lemmings heading for a cliff.

It takes an hour for the crowds to thin enough for her to stand again. An hour spent looking straight at the crinkled bums of the pants and skirts of her fellow travellers as they stand in front of her, staring blankly at the tunnel wall opposite. Making her way along the platform she's relieved to find a poster with the entire tube map. Following a lot of finger skimming, she spots Tottenham Court Road station. If she can find the platform with the train for Morden, she'll be set.

Looking at the illuminated display overhead she can see this platform services trains to Epping. Epping? When she finds it, so on the edge of the tube map, Jennie thinks it must be somewhere near the English Channel.

She leaves the platform and worms her way through round tunnels to another platform where a straggle of commuters seem to be looking in the right direction. Sure enough, when Jennie looks up, the next train due is heading for Morden. Some of the darkness leaves her stomach.

Moments later a stiff breeze starts, whipping itself up to a gale by the time the tube shoots out of the tunnel and into the station. It pulls to a stop with a squeal, the doors open and Jennie's feet are stomped on by exiting commuters, blindly intent on making connections.

It's a rumpled and tired Jennie who enters the house an hour later. She's pounced on by Mark, who appears to have been loitering in the hallway.

"Where the hell have you been? I've been worried sick!"

"I-I got lo—" Jennie takes an involuntary step backwards.

"Why didn't you call? I would have come and picked you up."

"I'm sorry." Jennie feels her eyes filling and looks skyward in an effort to staunch them.

"You can't wander off on your own like that." Mark shakes her gently by the shoulders.

This slight action proves too much for Jennie's paper briefcase; the bottom of it breaks and art supplies tumble down around her ankles. As she gives into the tears that have been threatening for the past couple of hours, Mark drags her into his arms. While she initially stiffens, she soon relents and allows him to hold her until the sobs run their course.

6

Squinting in concentration, Jennie floods the paint onto the wet paper as instructed by Eadie. Jennie had been confident she'd cope okay with watercolour lessons as she's already studied this at art school; Eadie's instructions soon lets her know she has a lot to learn.

"That's right, let the paint find its own path." Eadie peers at the paper that Jennie has masking-taped to an old paint-splattered piece of hardboard.

"But what if it's not going where it's supposed to?" Jennie is confused by this *Zen and the Art of Motorcycle Maintenance* philosophical approach to painting.

"You can tilt the board slightly." Eadie's hands flutter up to move an imaginary board sitting on her lap.

Jennie tilts the board ever so slightly and is horrified to see the small pool of pale green paint take off at a rate of knots toward one of the masking tape borders. "Ohhh, no, I've ruined it."

"Tilt it back, tilt it back. Quickly."

Jennie does as instructed, overcorrects and sends the little bead of paint streaking for the border opposite. She overcorrects a couple more times, so that when she's finished there's a large pale green, irregular cross on the piece of watercolour paper. Jennie can feel a scream of frustration welling, but this dissipates when she hears Eadie laughing.

"It's not funny. I've ruined this piece of paper."

"Jennie, it's simply a piece of paper," says Eadie, through her laughter. "You need to relax more. It'll show in your work. You need a sherry."

Jennie gives a slight shake of her head but Eadie banjaxes her by adding "Well, I need one and I hate drinking alone."

Knowing she's in for at least three or four glasses, Jennie drops the paintbrush into a jar of water standing at the ready and then puts the board down on the small table that's been set up in Eadie's sitting room. She picks up the crystal decanter that's full to bursting with the pale liquid, pulls the stopper and pours two glasses. She half fills her own but while Eadie's hands no longer work, her eyesight is in the eagle category. "No half measures," says Eadie, nodding toward Jennie's glass. Jennie grudgingly tops it up.

Once she's downed the regulation four glasses, Jennie doesn't feel like painting anymore. She feels like a nap. Eadie is unaffected by the alcohol and keen for Jennie to get on with her lesson.

By the time she's ruined half a dozen sheets of paper, Jennie is finally getting the hang of letting the paint find its own way. The technique is so vague it's not a technique at all. The sherry has helped, although Jennie worries that when she's attained Eadie's level of skill, her liver will be shot.

"Right, that'll do for today," says Eadie, quietly.

Such has Jennie's concentration been on her watercolour lesson, that she hadn't been aware of the old lady's energy flagging and is therefore shocked by the slackness of Eadie's face.

"I hadn't realised," Jennie gives her brush a good swish in

water and leaves it to dry, before giving Eadie her full attention, "would you like to have a lie down before dinner?"

Eadie's mouth is drooping from fatigue, disgust and sherry. "I'd like anything but, but that's what I'm stuck with."

"Would you like some help?" Jennie's not sure where Eadie's bedroom is but assumes it is on this floor. Despite the old lady's strength of spirit, she's not up to climbing stairs.

"That'd be lovely. My room's through there." Eadie nods toward a white panel door to the left of the marble fireplace that dominates the room.

Leaning over Eadie's chair, Jennie places her hand in the middle of the woman's back and helps her inch forward to the edge of the seat. Eadie's spine feels hard against Jennie's palm, with nothing to cushion it but overly thin skin and her floral housedress. Jennie then moves in front of Eadie and sliding her hands under the old lady's arms, she hooks them together at the back and helps Eadie to stand. Progress to the bedroom is slow and as painful for Jennie as it is for Eadie.

The room is like something straight out of the twenties and a tribute to art deco, with mirrored furniture and geometric patterns prevalent. Jennie can see a small bathroom opening off the back of the room and guesses this is the add-on she's seen from the kitchen.

Settled on her bed with a throw rug over her legs, Eadie looks boneless. Jennie takes the empty water glass off the bedside table and nips into the bathroom to fill it. If Eadie wakes up with the dry horrors, then the glass will be ready for her. Jennie's not surprised to see the bathroom is set up for someone with a disability. There are handrails everywhere and it also has a walk-in shower with a small seat.

Clearing up her painting gear, Jennie's mind is full of all she's learned that morning and the horror of what life must be like for Eadie, crippled with arthritis.

"How'd you get on?" says Mark, from right behind her,

causing her to slosh water from the jar all over the stack of papers in the middle of the table. "Oh, jeez, sorry." Mark looks over her shoulder at the soggy mess, "didn't mean to startle you."

"No loss, might even be an improvement." Jennie puts down the jar, shakily.

"You need to learn to relax more." Mark massages Jennie's shoulders. "So tense."

"If I were any more 'relaxed', I wouldn't be able to walk." Jennie takes a small step back toward Mark.

"Are you drunk?" Mark spins her around to face him.

Jennie takes a quick left and right step to keep her balance. "No. Of course not."

"How many have you had?" Mark leans over, sniffing.

"Three, or, four."

"Yeah, sure it was. I filled the decanter this morning." Mark looks down at it and back at Jennie, his eyes wide.

Sneaking a look at it, Jennie's eyes widen too. All that's left in the decanter are dregs and fumes.

"Where's Eadie?"

"I put her to bed. She looked tired."

"Hah, tired." Mark's chuckle rapidly turns into a belly laugh.

"Shhhh," says Jennie, managing to centre her index figure over her pursed lips. "You'll waken her."

"Not a snowball's chance in hell." Mark laughs harder.

Jennie has her hand clamped firmly over his mouth to stop this outpouring of mirth when he leans in and throws her over his shoulder. "Let's get you up to bed."

When Mark swings around and heads toward the door, the spinning in Jennie's head has her worried she's going to throw up. She shakes her head to clear the dizziness but this only makes it worse. Once they're in the hallway and away from Eadie, Jennie shouts at Mark to put her down and wildly swinging her legs around. She pinches his bum as hard as she can when this doesn't have the desired effect.

"Owww. Stop that!"

"Well, put me down then," says Jennie, to Mark's bum.

"No."

"I'm gonna be sick." This is followed by a couple of involuntary hurps and Mark can't rid himself of her fast enough.

"Here, put your head between your knees and take some deep breaths." Mark's hand is planted firmly on the back of her head, forcing it down into the required position.

Staring fixedly at the tiles under her feet, Jennie does as instructed and the nausea recedes. "God, that was awful." She lifts her head experimentally, relieved the spins don't return.

"You still look green around the gills. Come on, you should have a lie-down."

"Don't pick me up though." Jennie's hands are raised to ward off any assistance.

"Chill, will ya. I'll help you up the stairs."

They climb for what seems like hours before they reach the top floor. Without Mark's constant prompting, Jennie is sure she'd now be asleep on a landing farther down. If anything she's drunker now than she was when she twigged she and Eadie had drained the decanter. Talk about a slow burn.

Dropping onto her bed, the spins start up again, although they slow when her head hits the pillow. Her legs hang boneless over the side of the bed and she's relieved when Mark undoes her shoes and swings her legs up onto the bed and straightens her out.

"You are smashed, aren't you?"

"Didn't think sheeeeery was that strong." Jennie giggles at her slurring.

"It's not if you stop after a couple of glasses," says Mark, walking out the door. He's back not long after, carrying a bright red bucket that he plonks down next to the head of the bed. "Just in case."

Jennie's giving in to sleep, when she feels him climb over her and drop on to the mattress next to her. She struggles to wake but the sherry wins out. Her last thought is that it'll serve him right if she's sick all over him.

Jennie swallows hard. Someone's replaced her tongue with a piece of felt. The rest of her mouth is similarly lined. The one thing that's not fuzzy is the pain behind her eyes. She opens them experimentally and the light from the bedside lamp attacks them viciously. She slams her lids shut and her hand swoops up to add further protection.

Jennie's brain is futile in its efforts to track down any coherent memories. "Oh god, what happened?"

"You were amazing," says Mark, from right next to her.

Jennie's eyes open and she jolts into an upright position. This is too much for her. She leans over the side of the bed and is relieved to see an empty bucket sitting at the ready.

"Poor baby." Mark strokes her back, causing Jennie to yank herself away from him and nearly miss the bucket with the next heave. The contents of her stomach purged and her mortification complete. "Excuse me." Jennie throws back the covers and gains some relief when she sees she's still dressed. Distressingly it also reveals Mark is down to his undies. "Oh, god!" Jennie stands unsteadily before grabbing the bucket and fleeing for the safety of the bathroom.

Jennie empties the bucket and rinses it clean before looking fixedly at herself in the mirror. She stares back, no recognition lights her eyes. She doesn't know this person at all. Making sure the door is locked securely, Jennie strips off and climbs into the shower. Her tears blend with the water sluicing down her body and she only snaps out of it when there's rapid knocking on the door.

"I know the size of that cylinder and figure you've got to be bloody cold by now," says Mark through the door.

"Go away!" yells Jennie, at the cream shower curtain hanging limply in front of her face.

"Chill out, will ya. Nothing happened."

"Hah, it's not all about you, you know." Jennie roughly turns off the taps. A shiver works its way up from her core and shudders out through her limbs. He is right about one thing though, she is bloody cold, although she feels a lot lighter. It's the first real cry she's had in ages and holding in the sadness is exhausting. Jennie scrubs away at herself with the super-sized, hard, white towel, the only one available in the bathroom. The roughness of the texture liberating in its abrasiveness as it works away at her protective outer shell.

Dressed again, she unlocks the bathroom door and opens it expecting to find Mark still loitering, but he's nowhere in sight. God, that means he's back in her bed for the night. Well, stuff him; she'd rather sleep with Charlie the Cougar than have to deal with ousting Mark out of her bed. She tiptoes along the length of the landing and then ninja-quiet down the two flights of stairs to the one bedroom not occupied. By humans.

Pushing the door open, a pair of glowing yellow orbs confront Jennie. As her eyes adjust to the moonlight, she can see Charlie is smack bang in the middle of the bed. "Hey, buddy, is there room in here for me?"

Jennie hopes the answer is affirmative. She needs the cat's permission, otherwise she's likely to wake up mid-shred.

Charlie blinks before settling his head back on his front paws and closing his eyes. Jennie takes this as a positive sign and moves gingerly toward the bed. His eyes open and he follows her, but in the absence of any hissing and growling

Jennie's confidence grows. Thank goodness the bed's as big as it is, or she'd have to move the cat and she isn't feeling that lucky.

Looking down at the covers she's once again aware of the fine matting of cat hair that has to be quarter of an inch thick. "Here's hoping the bedspread has protected the sheets," she mutters and eases the covers back, relieved to see pristine white sheets below. The pillow has a few hairs showing but after she turns it over she's faced with a Charlie-free surface. Jennie thinks briefly about ditching her clothes and sleeping in her undies, but worries Charlie might chuck her out in the middle of the night.

Jennie inches her way in, all the while keeping a wary eye on her bed-mate. He's doing the same. Safely under the covers, she lies there stiffly, scared to roll onto her side in case Charlie takes this as a sign to attack. He's a big boy and would do a lot of damage. Her back begins to cramp before she hears his gentle snoring. She then eases onto her side, her preferred sleeping position, facing away from Charlie to avoid threatening him.

Waking up the next morning, Jennie's sure she must be having an asthma attack. Her breathing is laboured and she worries that a latent cat allergy has manifested. Maybe it's because she's lying on her back? That's not usual for her.

Her eyes open and immediately cross, so close are the golden yellow eyes staring back at her. Charlie is sitting on her chest and examining her minutely. "Hey there, boy, thanks for letting me share your bed," says Jennie, softly.

Charlie purrs in response, the deep rumble making itself at home in Jennie's chest cavity.

She lifts her hand from under the covers and after letting Charlie sniff it, scratches him behind one ear. His purr goes into overdrive, with the whole bed rumbling away. Feeling bolder, Jennie lifts her other hand out and scratches behind the other ear at the same time. Charlie's eyes roll back in his head and his mouth drops open revealing some large teeth. He's in cat heaven. He inches his way up Jennie's chest until his head is jammed in under her chin. Cat breath warms the side of her neck. "Oh, you're gorgeous." Jennie drops a small kiss on the top of his head. When he gives her neck a small lick in return, a few tears escape Jennie's eyes and make their way down to mingle with cat fur.

This moment of mutual bliss comes to a sharp stop, when the door opens and Mark walks in.

"I was only joking, you know."

Jennie doesn't know. What doesn't he get about them only being mates? Even if he is only joking, as he says, why does he keep doing it when she obviously doesn't find it funny?

"I went back to my own room while you were undergoing the self-inflicted water torture. You sure as hell don't need to sleep down here with that mangy hunk of fur."

As though realising he's been insulted, Charlie's head snaps up and he growls deep in his throat, causing Mark to take a sharp step back. Jennie lies where she is. All that raw power so close to her face is more than a little unnerving. Charlie gets to his feet, doing real damage to one of Jennie's boobs. His back arches and the hackles on his neck stand up. He hisses at Mark and Jennie knows the cat's about to launch himself.

"Mark. Please leave." Even though Jennie's voice is low, Charlie snaps his head around to look at her. Jennie can't help but gulp.

"Fine, I'm going." Mark walks backwards, his eyes never leaving the cat.

When the door pulls closed after him, Charlie settles himself again, in the same spot. It's as though the altercation with Mark never happened. "Would it be okay with you if I moved down here?"

Jennie scratches away at the hard-to-reach spot on the back of his head and is rewarded with a rumbling purr in answer.

"Okay, then. But I'm going to have to vacuum first."

By the end of that day, Jennie has emptied the vacuum cleaner bag nine times and the room still feels out of focus. It's going to take a while to get it habitable enough to suit both herself and Charlie. "It's no good, I'll to have to take all the curtains down and wash them."

Charlie doesn't raise any objections to this and so Jennie drags a chair over and unhooks the light grey curtains from their track. They drop to the ground enveloping Jennie in a billowing cloud of cat hair. Hard to believe there's still so much hair in them given the number of times she's gone over them with the vacuum cleaner.

She's coughing and spluttering by the time she drapes the curtains over the clothesline at the far end of the backyard. She attacks them with an old tennis racket she's found in the wardrobe of her new room and is mid-swing when Sam walks out with a couple of mugs of tea. "Here you go ... looks like you could use this." Sam holds a steaming mug toward Jennie but pulls it back, spilling some tea, when she realises how much cat hair is floating about in the air. "I'll leave it over here." Sam puts the mug down on a wrought-iron table a safe distance from the clothesline.

"Thanks for that." The thump of a tennis racquet against the curtains intersperses Jennie's words. "I need to get rid of the worst of this before I can put them in the machine, otherwise I'll clog all the pipes."

"Is that all from Charlie's room?"

"Our room, now." Jennie puts the racquet down on the table before picking up her tea. "I'm moving in with him."

"And he's letting you?"

"We've come to an understanding."

"What's wrong with the room you're in now?"

"Too close to Mark. He says he's joking, but I've had a gutful."

"From what Chris was saying, he doesn't hear the word 'no' too often."

"Well, he's hearing it now. I'm going to keep the top room as a studio but I'm moving everything down to Charlie's room later today. Once I get rid of most of the cat hair."

"There seems to be heaps of it." Sam eyes the layer of cat hair sitting on top of the recently mown grass. "It's a wonder the cat's not bald."

7

Jennie sniffs appreciatively at the whiff of acrylic paint in the air in the studio. She a lot more comfortable with these than water colours. After looking at the Polaroid of Quincy, then the postcard of Gainsborough's Blue Boy, her pencil makes light strokes on the canvas as she works on the composition before committing any paint to the canvas. It needs to be enough like the original that people will know what she was trying to achieve.

Her hand flies, so different from the cautious movements of the morning's water colour session with Eadie. No sherry this time though. Mark had refused to top up the decanter, much to Eadie's disgust. If this painting of Quincy works out as Eadie says it will, then Jennie needn't worry about looking for work. Sam is fully employed making doggie outfits with an endless supply of clients and so if Jennie can establish herself as the painter of said mutts, she'll be onto a good thing too. It should pay better than working in an office and also be a lot more fun.

"I can't believe you've moved downstairs." Mark's voice is tinged with disgust and disbelief, in equal parts. His abrupt arrival makes Jennie's hand jerk, adding a small appendage to

Quincy's head that isn't featured on either the Polaroid or the dog. Jennie puts down her pencil, grabs an eraser from the small tray at the front of the easel and rubs at the unwanted pencil marks, careful not to leave a smooth patch on the canvas.

"I was kidding around the other night. Nothing happened."

"Fine, but I don't like looking over my shoulder all the time, waiting for you to pounce." Jennie wipes the eraser up and down the leg of her jeans to rid it of debris before putting it back in the tray.

"Pounce? Are you serious?"

"That's what it feels like." Jennie looks down when she feels Charlie butt his head against her leg.

Mark spots the cat. "What the hell is *that* doing up here?"

Charlie looks up at Mark and assumes his attack-cat stance with tail doubled in size and growl building at the back of his throat. A solid hiss escapes his wide mouth. Jennie's also sure Charlie's claws are more prominent than they were earlier.

"All right, all right. I'm going." Arms raised in surrender, Mark walks slowly backwards out of the room, pulling the door shut after him.

"Good boy." Jennie bends down and scratches Charlie along the length of his spine, before smoothing his tail down to its usual thickness. The cat puffs up every time he sees Mark. Obviously some history there.

With their territory clear of intruders, Charlie saunters back to the bed, jumps up and after turning half a dozen times, settles into a ball a lot smaller than the cat is when he's stretched out.

Confident of no more interruptions, Jennie turns back to her painting, only becoming aware of her surroundings again when her stomach grumbles. Looking at her watch she's shocked to see it's after 7 p.m.

"The light lasts so long here, it only feels like four," says

Jennie to Charlie. He twitches his ear in acknowledgement but doesn't move otherwise.

After dropping her brush into a jar of water sitting on the table next to the easel, Jennie has a good stretch. Her back feels like someone's kicked it. "I'm out of practice." She twists and turns until she's worked out the worst of the kinks and feels human again. She swishes the brush backwards and forwards in the water before washing it with brush soap. Following careful examination of the base of the bristles, she gives it a final rinse before drying it on a soft cloth.

"Come on, Charlie, let's go see if we can rustle up something to eat." He opens one eye and looks at her as if to say 'you must be joking', but when she starts down the stairs, he's shadowing her, demonstrating an ability to walk and stretch at the same time. When they get to the final flight, he runs ahead of her down the stairs and round the corner at the bottom without slowing down. He trots up to the swinging door into the kitchen where he stops and looks back at her. Jennie expects him to wait for her but he reaches up on back legs and leans against the door, swinging it open and disappearing through the gap before she can reach it.

Jennie pushes the still swinging door wide open and walks in to the kitchen to find everyone sitting at the big table about to dig in.

"Good, you're here," says Sam, "I was about to yell out to you."

"Sorry, I'm late," says Jennie, to the table at large "I got lost in the painting."

"What are you working on?" Eadie waits while Mark cuts up the pieces of meat on her plate to save her the trouble.

"A painting of Quincy in the style of Gainsborough's *Blue Boy*." Jennie pulls out her chair and sits opposite Mark. She'd rather not spend the meal facing him, but it's the only seat left.

"Barbara will love that. But how are you adapting it to watercolour?" Eadie's brow is furrowed in confusion.

"I'm going with acrylics on this one." Jennie swiftly adds, "For speed," when Eadie's expression drops into disappointment territory. "It'll look like an oil painting but I'll be able to finish it in a week. Any slower and it wouldn't be worth it."

"I suppose that makes sense."

"I will try a water colour when I get more practice in," says Jennie, hoping to cheer up Eadie, and is relieved when the corners of the old lady's mouth lift.

Her signature complete, Jennie steps back and looks critically at the painting of Quincy. It's turned out a lot better than she expected, it being her first completed painting for over two and a half years. She keeps looking at it while soaping her brushes and laying them out to dry. Jennie appreciates the quality of the gear Eadie is letting her use and isn't about to risk any damaged bristles or paint-choked heads.

Picking up her hairdryer, she turns it to a low-heat, low-blow setting and sweeps it gingerly back and forth over the surface of the painting. Starting at the top, she works her way down in nice, even strokes. She repeats this until any shiny spots dry out to match the paint surrounding them. She touches one raised spot of paint and is satisfied that it's dry enough for her to take the painting down to show Eadie. She knows if Eadie gives the painting her nod of approval then it's good enough to deliver.

"Come on, Charlie," says Jennie, to the black and white mound in the middle of the fur-covered bedspread. "Let's open ourselves up to some criticism."

Charlie's eyes slit open and his head lifts a fraction, but his body stays resolutely where it is. His head drops back down to the covers in defeat, and sleep once again claims him.

"Suit yourself." Jennie walks down the short hallway holding the painting to one side so she can see where she's going and makes her way to the ground floor. Walking into Eadie's sitting room, she holds the painting facing her chest.

"You've finished?" Eadie's expression is a mix of query and anticipation.

"I have." Jennie doesn't move to swing the painting around, shying away from what might be negative feedback, however nicely put by Eadie.

"Let's have a look then." Eadie pushes her reading glasses down her nose to clear her eyes for distance work.

Jennie turns the canvas toward Eadie, walking forward to make it easier for the older women to focus on it. She's holding the canvas in such a way that she can't see Eadie's face; her breathing is shallow as she waits for the verbal assessment of her talent or lack thereof. When there's nothing forthcoming, Jennie lowers the canvas so she can peek over the top. Eadie's face gives nothing away although Jennie takes comfort that it's not set in a grimace, or creased with helpless laughter.

"So?" Jennie is unable to take the suspense anymore.

"It's—"

"Amateurish?"

"No, it's—"

"Really bad?"

"Fabulous."

"Really? You're not just saying that?" Jennie finds it hard to receive a good review without nit-picking it to death.

"I wouldn't do that," says Eadie, her expression aghast. "I respect you too much as an artist not to be totally honest."

"Oh, all right." Jennie feels chastised.

"Put it on the mantelpiece so I can see it in a proper setting."

Jennie does as instructed and then sits on the couch to contemplate the painting with Eadie. Still no sherry on offer though, with Mark working on drying out his aunt. They're sitting in companionable silence when he walks in, although his presence doesn't break their concentration. He wanders over and picking up one of the small sherry glasses from the drinks table, sniffs it, prompting a disgusted, "Relax boy, we're sober," from Eadie. "Instead of skulking around here, why don't you make yourself useful and pop down to the cellar and retrieve that painting of a water jug and lemons."

"I thought you hated it? Wasn't that why you got me to put it down there last week?"

"Good point, take the painting out. Just bring the frame."

"What for?" Mark requires more background before completing this random task.

"For Jennie's painting." Eadie gestures toward the mantle.

Mark walks over to the fireplace, where he stands and examines the painting, moving to the side when Eadie suggests he'd make a better door than a window. "You've finished it already?"

"Yes." Jennie readies herself for the joke she's sure he's about to make at her expense. Since her open rebuffing of him, he's been less than friendly to her and particularly Charlie, her permanent guard cat.

"It's good. It's really good," says Mark, sounding surprised.

"Thank you."

"Well, hurry and get the frame. I think it'd be perfect for the painting," says Eadie.

Rather than hurry as instructed, Mark saunters and Jennie suspects his lack of haste is on purpose, although it's hard to tell with Mark. She doesn't understand him at all.

"Cheeky monkey," says Eadie, a reluctant smile popping up.

A good twenty minutes pass before he returns with the

frame. "Bloody hell, whoever put that canvas into the frame had shares in a blasted nail company."

"Jennie, see how it fits, hold it up against the frame. It's got to be close."

Jennie gets to her feet and retrieves the canvas from the mantle before unenthusiastically walking over to stand next to Mark. He holds the frame up next to the canvas and it doesn't take long to realise the frame will need trimming down. "That's a shame," says Jennie, on her way back to the mantle. "I'm sure I can get it framed somewhere."

"Give me a day or two and I can sort it out for you."

Mark must see something in Jennie's expression that this isn't fast enough for her.

"I've got a couple of job interviews lined up for tomorrow. Okay?"

"I did wonder." Jennie's unable to keep surprise from colouring her reply. For all he'd talked of lots of engineering jobs being on offer, this is the first she's seen of him actually trying to secure one. She'd welcome seeing him out of the house for a good portion of each day.

Mark's response is to snort, although this simple nasal retort is enough to have Jennie's hackles go all Charlie on her. If Eadie wasn't in the room, Jennie's sure she'd be hissing at Mark by now. The slight raise of his eyebrows has her claws popping out one by one, but rather than give him the satisfaction of reacting to his baiting, she leaves on the pretence of having to clean some brushes. Walking passed him, she's unable to miss the whispered, "Chickennnnn," he singsongs in her direction.

Back in the studio with the door shut, Jennie paces, while talking to Charlie. She knows he's listening by the flick of his ears and the odd swish of his tail. It's reaction enough for her to continue venting.

"He's done it again. What is it about him that drives me up

the EFFING wall?" Jennie finishes this sentence by slapping her hand over her mouth.

"And now he's got me swearing. That ... that ... ah ... ratbag."

Charlie doesn't comment, although when she runs out of steam, his head pops up at the unaccustomed quiet.

"I need to go out for a walk."

Her pacing leads her to the door and, after removing her flip-flop doorstop, out and down to her room to change into something suitable for a good, brisk, head-clearing walk.

"Sam, you want to come for a walk down by the river?" Jennie pops her head around the door of Sam's sewing room. "Scratch that. Sam, you need to come for a walk."

"What?" Sam looks at Jennie through bloodshot eyes.

"How long have you been at it today?"

"Not sure. What's the time now?" Sam stretches her arms high above her, shaking her hands loosely.

"Time you had a break. Come on, it'll be a quick one."

8

They complete a lot of zigging and zagging before the waters of the Thames slide into view across the end of the narrow street they're on. Reaching the open area along its banks, Jennie is disappointed. She'd expected the water to be right to the edge of the path. Instead, there are wide swathes of mud on each side of the river. Skimming stones, or simply throwing them into the water, is no longer on the agenda. Jennie's arm isn't that good.

Sam shields her eyes from the sunlight bouncing off slick mud. "It's so dirty."

"It's hardly majestic, is it? Still it's nice to get some fresh air." Jennie sucks in a lungful only to be assaulted by the smell of shellfish baking in the hot sun. "That's weird, why would there be shellfish this far up river?"

Arbitrarily, they set out to the left and away from the city, although they're so far from both the centre of town and the country, it doesn't make much difference which direction they head in. Unless they're up to walking for a very long time.

"How's it going with you and Chris?"

"It's great."

Sam's smile backs this up. Jennie's never seen her friend looking so happy. Even when things were going well with Darren, the scumbag, back in Auckland, Sam hadn't seemed this content. "I'm so glad. I hope you didn't mind me telling fibs about who Eadie was?"

"Hah, no. I don't blame you. I was a mess wasn't I?" says Sam, laughing.

"Just a bit." Jennie's relieved Sam isn't angry about all the lies. She'd told the fibs as she wasn't sure Chris would even be in London when they arrived and so didn't want to get her friend's hopes up.

"What about you and Mark? He seems keen on you."

"Me and Mark?" Jennie bristles. "He's driving me nuts. He makes me swear!"

Sam doesn't say anything. She doesn't have to.

"I know. Right," says Jennie, as though Sam shares this opinion of Mark.

Once Jennie has finished listing everything about Mark that annoys her, they've been walking for half an hour. It's only when Jennie stops for breath that she realises Sam is looking at her, gaping. "What?"

"But nothing you've said is that bad. Why should any of it irritate you so much?"

"I don't know," wails Jennie. "But it does." Jennie knows it doesn't make sense. She has no idea why Mark, or even the thought of him, winds her up so much.

"Fancy a wine?"

"I'm so sorry, I don't mean to. You don't need to hear me going on."

"Not whine, wine." Sam nods over Jennie's shoulder to the pub they've passed that Jennie hadn't even been aware of.

"Yes. Yes, I do."

The walk back to Eadie's takes longer with her new copy of the A-Z making a lot less sense after their stop at the pub. A couple of goes and they manage to open the front door.

Jennie's laughter stumbles to a halt when she sees who's walking down the stairs. How could he bring her here? To his auntie's house.

"Sammy, hello." Sonja jiggles her way down the last few steps. Her boobs threatening to escape at any second, her shorts so short they're more of a belt with a crotch.

"Sam, not Sammy." Sam corrects her sharply.

Jennie's annoyed at being ignored but when Sonja turns toward her and waits to be introduced, it dawns on her that Sonja and she haven't met before. Jennie only knows what the hussy looks like because she's seen Sam's photos of the lecherous Dalmatian draped all over Mark. But those photos were taken back in Australia, what on earth is she doing here?

"This is Jennie, my friend." Sam introduces her.

Jennie's teeth are clenched so tight that all she can manage is a small nod.

There's an awkward silence before Sam grabs Jennie's hand and says "Okay then, we'll catch you later."

Sam drags Jennie toward the stairs but when Jennie trips on the first step, it prompts her to concentrate on the task. When they reach the first landing and peer over the banister, there's no sign of Sonja.

"How on earth can he think of bringing her here?" Jennie spits out once they're safely in her room.

"Beats me. I wouldn't have thought he'd want a bar of her in this house. But why should that bother you?"

"Eadie shouldn't have to deal with some tramp flouncing around in outfits like that."

"I doubt it would bother Eadie. She strikes me as fairly worldly-wise with a murky past from what Chris was saying."

Sam leaves to have a shower before dinner, while Jennie

lies on her bed stewing. She's joined by Charlie but he picks up on her bad mood and after trying, unsuccessfully, to find a comfortable spot, he jumps down and leaves her to it. He spends his time equally between here and the studio. When Sam calls through the door that the bathroom is empty, Jennie has to consciously unclench her fists before getting up. If this is how it's going to be, game on.

Jennie stands outside the swinging door to the large kitchen and wills her nerves to settle so she can push the door open as nonchalantly as possible. Charlie gets sick of waiting and throws his weight against it before she can arrange her features appropriately. She's relieved to find the room empty. That's odd, she can smell dinner, but there are no people or food to be seen. Stilling herself in the middle of the room she's aware of noises coming from a door off to the left of the room. She's seen it before but never bothered to find out where it went. Getting closer to it, she can hear Eadie talking animatedly.

Jennie's about to push on the door when it swings toward her, almost collecting her in the process. A quick step back is all that saves her from a broken nose, or worse.

"There you are," says Mark. "We're in the formal dining room tonight seeing we've got a special guest."

Jennie is tempted to wipe the smug grin off his face as she watches him walk briskly across the room, slide on an oven glove and then open the front of the range. The aroma of roast beef that swirls out to fill the room has her stomach gurgling alarmingly. It might be best to pick a fight with him after dinner. She's about to walk into the dining room, when Mark asks her to carry the veggies in for him. As if she's his lackey. Blooming cheek of it.

Pasting a smile in place, Jennie walks over to the counter

and, after testing the heat of the crockery dish with her finger, deems it cool enough to pick up and carry into the dining room. Turning her back to the swinging door, she reverses into the room which gives her the satisfaction of seeing the door swing crazily toward Mark, with the large roasting dish held out in front of him. From the language she hears, it was a close call, prompting a smug smile of her own.

To this background of cussing, Jennie gets her first look at the formal dining room. It hasn't been dusted in a long time. Although the long mahogany table glitters with polish under the overhead lights, every other surface has a matt finish and the room smells musty.

Looking at the ceremonially set table, Jennie thinks about the best seat of the two available on either side of Eadie, who's at the head of the table. One is next to Sonja, the other next to Sam. A second's decision and Jennie sits herself down next to the Yugoslavian strumpet. The downside is she'll have to make conversation with her; the upside is she won't have to watch Sonja making googly eyes at Mark throughout the meal.

Jennie gets a small flush of satisfaction at seeing the look of annoyance on Mark's face when she puts the veggies down by her plate and takes her seat. Sending a look of studied innocence in his direction, she's rewarded with his jaw tightening.

Once they're all sitting down, Eadie says her own version of grace which is, as far as Jennie can tell, an elegant version of 'two, four, six, eight, bog in, don't wait'. Jennie serves some vegetables onto Eadie's plate, then her own before putting the dish down next to Sonja. Mark serves Eadie with potatoes, meat and gravy, then stands and takes the platter around the table to allow Sonja to help herself, he then does the same with Sam and Chris, before returning to his seat and loading his own plate.

Rather than rise to this obvious bait, Jennie asks Sam to pass the platter over to her. She then concentrates on conversing with Eadie, ignoring Mark and Sonja alike. Feeling a foot on her left knee, she drops her cutlery with a loud clatter.

The size of the foot means it has to belong to Mark, but given he's not even looking at her, Jennie suspects he thinks he's got his grubby toes all over Sonja. The foot starts to inch up her leg, so Jennie calmly drops her hands to her lap and gives the little toe a good twist. A satisfying bounce of everything on the table follows, with Mark glaring daggers at Sonja. Unaware of what's going on, the poor woman looks confused, her face scrunched in question at this look from Mark.

Jennie casually picks up her cutlery and carries on with her meal. Thankfully there are no further instances of footsy during the meal although when Mark stands and starts collecting the dirty plates from the table, Sonja jumps to help him. They disappear one, two through the swinging door and heated words can be heard coming from the kitchen shortly after. When the door swings partly open again, Jennie can see Mark impaling her with a look that makes her nervous.

The door closes again and laughter is heard soon afterwards, Chris says, "I guess we're on our own for dessert." This is confirmed when they hear two sets of feet thundering up the stairs.

Jennie's jaw starts to tic.

9

Laying the painting of quincy atop the pile of tissue paper sitting on her bed, Jennie wraps several sheets around it, before securing it with tape. Brown paper and string follow. Lots of it. She still has no idea how the painting will go down with Lady Harrow. She hopes she isn't seen as trying to upstage the woman's nephew.

"You ready?" says Sam, walking into Jennie's room.

"As I'll ever be. Did the first outfit turn out okay?"

"I like to think so." Sam pulls a small tweed jacket from her shoulder bag and holds it up for Jennie to see. There's one of Jennie's handmade Doggs' Toggs' tags hanging from the garment. "Can I use some of that tissue to wrap it?"

"Sure can." Jennie hands a few sheets of tissue to Sam, who wraps the small garment. "Shame we didn't have room in our bags for some Doggs' Toggs' wrapping paper, but I can make you some more."

"That'd be cool."

"Easy-peasy, now I've got my own studio."

Jennie holds the painting anxiously for the whole trip to Lady Harrow's, worried someone will knock it, or worse put a hole through it. After she's lugged it from the station to the house and up the front steps, she makes the decision that the next painting will be handed over without a frame. While in keeping with the style of Gainsborough, the ornate frame weighs a ton. The one plus is that it means Jack is unable to jam himself in the lift with them with Jennie holding the painting as a shield between them as the door rattles closed.

The lift grinds to a halt somewhere between the third and fourth floors letting them know they haven't escaped unscathed. Damn that blasted man.

"I will not give him the satisfaction of calling out for help." Sam's arms are folded and her expression is mutinous. "The little shit."

Jennie slides the frame down her body until it rests on the ground between her and the doors. She flicks her arms to get some blood flowing, wishing she had more blood in her head. She's sure it's her imagination but the lift seems smaller than their last visit, even without Jack in there with them.

"Are you sure, what if no one knows we're stuck in here?" Jennie optimistically pushes the sixth floor button. It clicks back out, but there's no other movement.

Obviously not sharing Jennie's concerns, Sam leans nonchalantly against the wall of the lift. "Someone has to use it at some stage. He'll have to start it up again then. Won't he?"

Jennie forcefully pushes the large sixth floor button, several times in a row. Nothing.

"Oh, this is ridiculous." Sam looks at her watch. "We're going to be late for our appointment and from what I've heard, the Countess doesn't like to be kept waiting." Sam bounces on her toes, getting a good deal of movement out of the small elevator.

"Don't do that," says Jennie, in a voice that's shrill and

squeaky. Wiping her face, she's able to taste salt on her top lip. She stabs repeatedly at the button and when that results in no movement, she stabs all the buttons. The control panel is lit up like a night bus which is something of a relief when the feeble light above them flickers and dies.

"For God's sake, breathe." Jennie can feel Sam's hand on her shoulder, squeezing, trying to bring her back to reality. Jennie continues to pant, forcing Sam to squeeze harder until the pain cuts through Jennie's panic.

"Ouch, that hurts, stop it." Jennie bats Sam's hand away, but in the process notices that her breathing has slowed.

"Bloody hell, I thought you were going to faint and we don't have room."

The girls are readying themselves to make an almighty din, when the light overhead winks back on and the elevator stumbles into action. After it stops on the fourth floor, they both stumble from the elevator, startling the small man waiting there.

"Going down?" he says.

"No, up." Sam stands to one side to allow him to enter.

"I wouldn't go in there if I were you, we've been stuck for hours." Jennie can't stand by and let someone else suffer the terror they've been subjected to.

"Hours?" Sam looks at her and Jennie can tell her friend is trying not to smile. It's okay for her.

"Blasted thing's always on the fritz. Stairs it is." He opens an unmarked door to the left of the lift and disappears through it.

It's puffing shut when Jennie reaches it and she looks through the tiny safety glass panel at eye height. "There's no way I'm going back inside that moving coffin." She shoves the door open and turns back toward Sam. "Come on, it's only two flights."

When they knock on the dark blue door, both girls are panting. "Those weren't normal flights of stairs were they?"

Jennie hugs the painting to her chest and tries to calm her breathing.

"No, they were not. Guess it's something to do with the ceiling height." Sam looks up at the ornate mouldings well above their heads.

The door swings open and Vivienne gives them a warning. "She does not like to be kept waiting. You'd better have a bloody good excuse, even if you have to fabricate one."

They enter the room and the Countess's eyebrows are so scrunched in annoyance it looks like she's sporting a monobrow. Sam doesn't break stride before putting on a performance that Jennie feels should be worthy of at least a nomination for an Oscar. Given all the hand-wringing going on, you'd think it was Sam who'd been freaking out. The credits are rolling before the Countess relents and admits they do have a good reason for being late. With equilibrium restored, Sam retrieves the outfit for Quincy and proceeds to try it on the dog. It fits perfectly and the Countess is now on best friend terms with Sam.

With the outfit removed and folded, Jennie takes the opportunity to present her painting of Quincy to the Countess. The response is underwhelming.

"That's so, ah, sweet. Gainsborough's *Boy Blue*," says The Countess, doing a lousy job of faking enthusiasm. No metal on the mantelpiece for her. She gives the painting a cursory glance, and then calls for Vivienne. Jennie has no option but to give the painting into the woman's care. The maid is leaving the room when the Countess instructs, "Vivienne, perhaps you'd like that darling painting in your room."

Vivienne's shoulders stiffen perceptibly before she turns and leaves the room.

"Right, that's settled then." The Countess all but dusts her hands, much to Jennie's annoyance. Even she knows her painting is far and away superior to the glorified colour chart above the fireplace. Blasted nepotism.

They're walking down the hallway when they see Vivienne come out of a room on their right. She no longer has the painting. "You can give the painting back to me if you don't want it in your room," says Jennie, quietly.

"Are you kidding? It's so much better than that piece of tat I have to dust every other day. There's no way it's being hidden in a back room."

"What are you going to do with it?" says Sam.

"I've hung it in the guest bathroom, that's the perfect spot."

Jennie straightens. "I'd rather have it back, if you don't mind." She knows she sounds snippy, but can't help it. That painting took days and days of hard work.

"I think you'd better see the guest bathroom before you make up your mind." Vivienne beckons for them to follow her back into the room she's just exited.

"Whoa." Jennie's eyes widen as she takes in the décor of the guest bathroom.

"Bloody Norah." Sam runs her hands over the marble vanity top.

The guest bathroom is the size of the best dining room at Eadie's and a study of gilt fittings and porcelain. The wallpaper is Laura Ashley in style and liberally dotted with small, dark blue fleurs-de-lis. The curtains looping and swirling beside and over the frosted window are royal velvet.

The painting of Quincy hangs above a bath big enough to swim lengths in.

"It looks amazing, but why here?" Jennie is confused as to why this spot is so right.

"Yeah, why in here?" says Sam.

Vivienne ushers them out of the bathroom and is closing the door before she answers, "Because she doesn't go in there, but all her guests do."

Jennie puts her hand on the door to stop it closing. “But, won’t you get into trouble?”

“Once her guests are raving about it, she’ll be chock-full of herself for having discovered you. That and she has a memory like a sieve.”

10

Looking at the canvas with her hand poised, Jennie grimaces in concentration. Decided, she adds more swift pencil strokes. It's to be in the style of Warhol with the canvas split into nine panels, each featuring Colin, a pug from Richmond, in a different colour way. It's un-commissioned, but if what Eadie says is right, it won't be long before Jennie's being paid to paint.

"Jennie ... phone ... for ... you." Sam leans against the doorway, breathing deeply. "We have got to sort out a ... bell system. Didn't you hear me? I started yelling on the bottom step."

"Sorry, when I'm concentrating I don't notice." Jennie pops her pencil onto the shelf on the easel. "Who is it?"

"Not sure. But if she had any more marbles stuffed in her mouth, she'd choke."

This, at least, discounts the call being from anyone at home. Leaving Sam sitting on the top step to get her breath, Jennie skips down the stairs to the hall, where the old-fashioned phone usually sits on a small console table, looking like a large green toad. It's not there but by following the cord across the hallway and into the sitting room, Jennie finds phone and receiver sitting on the sideboard.

"Jennifer speaking."

"Oh, good. It's Wendy Leicester speaking. I was around at Bunty's place for dinner last night and saw your work."

"Bunty?"

"Sorry, school days' nickname. Lady Harrow."

"Right, the painting of Quincy."

"I'm inspired. I must commission a painting of Peanut, my chihuahua."

Jennie scribbles down a time and address, and then rings off.

"Told you so."

It's obvious to Jennie that Eadie was listening to her conversation throughout. The old lady's face is alight with glee.

"How much do you think I should charge?"

"These gals can afford it, so one hundred and fifty at least."

"Pounds!"

"Of course. What did you think I meant, pence?"

On her way back upstairs, Jennie runs figures on how long it would take her to complete a painting of a chihuahua. Not long if she makes it life-size. One thing's obvious, she'll have to get herself a diary if her little business takes off in the same way as Sam's. Jennie swings into Sam's sewing room and finds her friend once again hunched over the sewing machine, working on a lurid purple paisley outfit.

"I've got my first real commission." Jennie still can't get her head around the price tag. Surely Mrs Leicester won't pay that much for it? "I have to go around there in the morning to discuss it with her, you want to come?"

"Sure thing. Might get an order for some clobber out of it, although, to be honest, I've got enough on my plate already."

Looking at the newly-installed second trestle table sitting against the back wall, Jennie can see a pile of orders awaiting

Sam's attention, with each order's material, pattern and specifics bagged up together. There are a lot of bags on that table and Jennie hopes she's not that successful. While Sam can get other people to sew for her, with paintings, everything will come down to Jennie completing them personally.

"Stop fussing, you look fine." Sam bats at Jennie's hands, stopping them mid-tug.

Jennie has one final look at herself in the mirror, her face crumpling into a grimace. "In that case, I'm as ready as I'll ever be."

A large handbag slung over her shoulder, Jennie follows Sam down the stairs, but is unable to resist a couple more tugs. She hates how her skirt is sitting. It keeps bunching up at the front, although she finds if she takes little steps, it hangs perfectly. Great, I'll look like a Geisha, but at least my skirt will sit straight. "I can't visit a new client like this. I need to change." Jennie baulks at the bottom of the steps.

"No. You don't." Sam grasps Jennie's hand and pulls her out of the front door.

This bunches her skirt alarmingly. Her knickers must be showing. She tugs it down into place again, holding it flat for the duration of their walk to the tube. It's not until they're sitting on the tube that she relaxes enough to take the A-Z from her bag to confirm their journey. Mrs Leicester lives around the corner from Lady Harrow, so they'll be in familiar territory.

Jennie looks at the gate spanning the gap in the immaculately clipped hedge guarding the Georgian house that is home to Peanut Leicester and his mistress. "It must be lovely to be this rich."

With the gate unclasped, they walk through the arboreal arch into another world. Like the hedge, every tree in the front garden has been clipped to within an inch of its life, although here, the lines are anything but straight.

Topiary elephants squabble for space with urns, dogs and there's even a giant hand lying passively palm-up, waiting to grab the unwary visitor.

"Whoa, it's rather *Alice in Wonderland* isn't it?" Jennie's gaze scans in both directions as they crunch their way up the blindingly white gravel path.

The swivelling of Sam's head from side to side is accompanied by a stream of constant chatter as she points out different animals, poking Jennie in the side if she fails to look fast enough.

Jennie's sure she's seen movement from the corner of her eye a couple of times now, but every time she turns, all is still. "I'd hate to walk through this lot at night." She can't stop a shudder in her core and is relieved when they reach the security of the marble steps leading up to an imposing burgundy door. Topiary pompom trees stand guard on either side.

Looking in vain for a doorbell, Jennie gives up and forcefully raps the large ring that's held firmly in the mouth of a brass lion glaring at them from eye-height. Jennie's brass on brass knock is startlingly loud but soon has the desired effect when a small man answers the door in a politely quiet suit. His words are clipped and no-nonsense. He's been expecting them. They are to call him Brian.

Silent messages pass between the girls as they mutely follow Brian upstairs and into a sitting room that overlooks the front garden. "I'll let Lady Leicester know you're here." He leaves them to wait.

Jennie checks out the room and once confident there's no one there says, "Do you reckon that's her husband?" Her voice is low. "A husband wouldn't use her title. Would he?"

"Doubt it. Plus he's too subservient." Sam's voice, at normal volume, sounds loud amongst the subdued colours of the room.

Jennie's lungs are full in readiness for a prolonged "Ssssh" when their hostess enters, followed by a long-haired, peanut-sized chihuahua. Jennie noiselessly empties her lungs through pursed lips.

"Jennifer?" Lady Leicester looks at both of them in turn, until Jennie waves her hand to confirm her identity. The woman is class personified. Her hair is professionally styled in a shoulder length bob, her make-up artfully applied and not too heavy, the shirt dress she's wearing is in a gorgeous aqua silk. Jennie's examination of the woman comes to a jarring halt when she spots the slippers. They're sheepskin and not dissimilar to a pair Jennie has at home.

"This is, ah, this is Sam," Jennie nods toward her friend. "And this must be Peanut." Jennie bends down to let the small dog sniff her hand, but not slowly enough given how hard he trembles and backs up. Jennie retracts her hand and the dog settles. His long hair, styled in a way that makes him look like Farrah Fawcett, sweeps out to the sides down the length of his body. His fur is a mix of blond and light blond, his tail is as fluffy as a pissed-off cat, while his mouth curls up to the sides, making him appear perpetually amused.

"Hardly guard dog material, are you?" says Lady Leicester to the small canine. "But we love you anyway. Please, girls, do have a seat."

Lady Leicester waves them to the couch and takes a large, comfortable looking chair for herself. Jennie can tell by the way the woman sinks into the chair that this is a favourite spot. While formal, the room is also welcoming and comfy. Perhaps it's the large multi-paned windows that take up most of the wall overlooking the garden. Even sitting on the couch, Jennie can still see the tops of topiary heads and a trunk. That elephant has to be close to life-size.

Securely ensconced in the large, overstuffed couch, Jennie rummages in her handbag for her sketchbook. Sam is similarly occupied retrieving the Polaroid camera. While Jennie chats to their hostess and gets a feel for the style of painting she's after, Sam takes some Polaroids of Peanut.

This proves difficult when the micro dog explodes into a fluffed-up, bouncing, yapping mess each time the flash goes off and a photo pops out of the front of the camera. Sam gives up after three attempts and the small dog calms down. The trembling subsides and he bounces up onto Mrs Leicester's knee by way of a footstool, before settling himself into a small ball. Lady Leicester proceeds to absently stroke his head.

Sam flaps the photos a couple of times and checks them. She then stuffs them in her armpit to speed up development.

"That's all right, those photos should give me enough reference." Jennie makes notes on the page headed up 'Peanut', including the names of artists whose work hangs on the wall behind Lady Leicester. The mix is eclectic, which is good. It would have been awkward if all the paintings were by someone like Jackson Pollock.

Back through the topiary gauntlet and out of the gate, Sam pulls the Polaroids out from under her arm and hands them over. "I hope you've got a bloody good memory."

"What do you mean?" When there's no response, Jennie looks at the photos. "Oh, blinking heck." She flicks through the photos until she's looked at each one at least three times. It doesn't make them any sharper. The dog looks like a powder puff with teeth in every shot. "I'll need to make sketches of him." Jennie's shoulders drop and she turns and re-opens the recently closed gate.

11

Squeezing a second blob of paint on the mixing board, Jennie tries to block her ears to the sounds emanating from the room across the hallway. It's like the soundtrack from a nature documentary. If the woman doesn't climax soon, Jennie will be the one screaming and loud enough to be heard over Sonja, who hasn't shut up since she and Mark hit the sack. Putting the lid back on the tube, Jennie's hand trembles.

"Arrrgh, I can't stand it." Throwing down the tube and leaving the mixing board where it is, Jennie storms out of the studio. She thinks about hammering on Mark's door and telling them to stow it, but the idea of being that close to wild-man sex doesn't sit well with her. She swings around the top newel post and races down the stairs.

Eadie looks up from her crossword, her face shocked. The door swings open quicker than Jennie's expecting and it bangs hard against the end of the couch. "I'm so sorry." Jennie rubs the end of the couch to check there's no damage.

"What's got you so riled?"

"It's ah, Mark and Sonja." Jennie isn't sure how to broach the subject.

Eadie's mouth quirks up at one corner. "Going at it like rabbits, are they?"

"For hours! It sounds terrible. I can't concentrate. But how did you know? You can't hear them down here can you?" Jennie is aghast that Eadie should have to put up with this in her own home.

"Hardly. No, it's that Sonja has the look of a right one about her. I don't need a soundtrack to work out what's going on. Did you tell them to knock it off?"

"I ... I can't just ... I, no." Jennie's shoulders slump after this stuttered reply. "I'd stuff my fingers in my ears but then I can't paint. I'd move but the top room has the best light."

"What about earplugs?"

"They'd need to be industrial strength."

"Really?"

"She's a screamer." Jennie can't believe she's discussing someone's sex life with an octogenarian. Her hands feel cold as she holds them against her cheeks.

"Ah, right. You could always wear the earmuffs that the chap who mows the lawns uses. They're out in the garage somewhere."

Standing at the top of the stairs, Jennie pulls one of the earmuffs away from her head. The damned woman is *still* on the brink of climax! Snapping the earpiece back into place, the silence is blessed. These could work. Singing to herself, Jennie gets back to her painting. The trip downstairs has been quick enough that the paint she'd squeezed earlier is still okay. She mixes the two paints, checks the finished colour against the blurry Polaroid of Peanut and gets to work. Painting fur is tricky but at least she's managed to mix the right shade of blond.

Jennie's so immersed in the painting that it takes a couple of seconds for her to realise there's a half-naked man standing next to her. Spinning wildly, she doesn't relax when she faces Mark. If anything, this has her even more wound up, especially given he's only wearing an incredibly small towel. Noticing the conspicuous smear of blond acrylic paint across the middle of his muscled chest, she staggers backwards to put some space between them, her brush held out in front of her like a sword.

His mouth is moving but he's not saying anything. She wrinkles her brow at him and tilts her head to the side and he steps nearer and removes her earmuffs. "Jeez, do you have any idea of the racket you've been making?" he shouts.

"Me?" says Jennie, indignantly.

"That god awful hymn you've been singing off-key and at the top of your lungs for the past half hour. Bloody near impossible to stay hard when it sounds like a small furry animal is being tortured to death next door."

"Hah, that's rich coming from you," says Jennie, stabbing him in the chest with the paint brush.

"What do you mean?"

"You and her. Talk about small furry animals being killed. It's disgusting." Jennie puts her hand up to her jaw to quench the tic that appears whenever Mark is near. Her teeth hurt, she's trying so hard to hold in her anger.

"Oh, come on. You're a big girl. You sure you're not enjoying it?" Mark moves perceptibly closer, causing Jennie to back up again. Being faced with this much testosterone plays havoc with her peace of mind.

When she's hard up against the bed, she leans down and pokes Charlie whose head pops up. On seeing Mark, he assumes his attack position in seconds. On all fours, back arched and hair blow-waved to double its standard volume, a deep growl forms in the back of his throat. Stepping to the side and looking down, Jennie's in time to see Charlie wiggling his bum in readiness to launch himself at his nemesis.

Mark legs it, followed out of the room by Jennie's laughter.

Charlie gets a good, long cat massage before Jennie gets on with her painting. She hasn't had to put the headphones back on but has them snug around her neck ready to be donned at the smallest squeak from the bedroom on the other side of the landing. She's thinking about stopping for the day when she hears movement out in the hallway.

Mark is dragging an enormous suitcase across the landing. Jennie's relieved to see he's dressed, although he's roughly put together. Wonder where he's off to?

Sonja stumbles out of the room after him and attempts to drag the bag back into the bedroom. A tug of war ensues, with the top of the case tipping backwards and forwards between them, depending on who is winning. Either Sonja is incredibly strong or Mark isn't giving it his all.

"But where am I to go?" Sonja has another attempt at gaining control of the suitcase.

"There are plenty of hotels." Mark's jaw is tight, the words forced through clenched teeth.

"It could happen to anyone. I did not mean to laugh."

Seeing Jennie listening to this interaction, Mark's hands drop so suddenly that Sonja flies backwards when the full weight of the bag is left to her insistent tugging. She missteps and for a horrifying second Jennie thinks the woman's going to take a header down the stairs. Mark makes a grab for her and manages to stop her taking a fall, although she still gives her head a decent crack on the newel post. She then sinks gracefully in a heap, taking Mark with her.

Jennie drops her paintbrush and races out to check for damages. Mark's fine but Sonja has a decent bump on the back of her head with blood showing through her blonde hair. "Is she okay?" Jennie answers herself, "She doesn't look okay. You need to get a doctor, she might need stitches."

"Shit, it was an accident. You saw, it was an accident. I'd never hurt anyone."

"Mark, it wasn't your fault. Go sort out a doctor."

With Mark flying down the stairs to phone for a doctor, Jennie shoves the huge suitcase to one side, having to use her legs given the dead weight of the thing. She lays Sonja on her side in the recovery position and once happy the woman isn't going to roll backwards and spill down the stairs, she runs into the bathroom and grabs a towel. Gently lifting Sonja's head, Jennie slides this underneath. The carpet up here hasn't been vacuumed in living memory. No need to risk the doc having to pull carpet fluff out of the wound.

Sonja is moaning and coming around when Mark gets back upstairs. "Doctor's on his way. Eadie knows a chap who isn't averse to making house calls. Otherwise, we'd have had to get her to the emergency room. How's she doing?"

"Coming around."

"What happened?" Sonja's voice is thick and full of confusion.

"You're all right. Doctor's on his way. Just lie still." Jennie puts a calming hand on Sonja's shoulder and pushes her back down to the carpet.

"Why does my head hurt?"

"You had a nasty fall." Mark crawls over Sonja's legs and sits on the ground in front of her. He grabs her hand and gives it a reassuring squeeze.

She pulls her hand free. "Who are you?"

"It's Mark." Jennie's voice is low as she looks at Mark over Sonja.

"Oh? Then who am I?"

"Are you sure she's telling the truth?" Sam peers round the dinner table, her comment causing knives and forks to be abandoned.

"Sam. She has a lump the size of an egg." Jennie's hand strays unconsciously to the back of her own head.

"She did look fairly spaced out when I took her dinner up to her," says Mark.

He isn't the only one who's been roped in on room service duty although he's taking it more seriously than anyone else, putting his search for work on hold until the girl is back on her feet. While Sonja is tucked up in his bed on the top floor, Mark has taken to sleeping in the bed in Jennie's studio. It has to be awkward for him because he'd obviously been trying to get rid of Sonja when the accident happened. Jennie still isn't one hundred percent sure what the fight had been about, although she has a fairly good idea.

The doctor who stitched Sonja's head hadn't seemed too concerned that his newest patient seemed to have knocked something loose in the memory department. "She'll come right. Give it a day or so." Jennie suspects this to be the psychiatric equivalent of 'take two and see me in the morning'. It has been days since the accident and Sonja appears no closer to getting her memory back. Maybe Sam is onto something?

"It has been four days." All faces swing to look at Chris. "Well, it has. That's enough time for her marbles to have sorted themselves out."

"Tricky things head injuries." Eadie plays devil's advocate.

Following much discussion it's decided to leave it a couple more days and then get the doctor back in.

"Time to get up!" Jennie rips the pillow off the bed in the studio, causing Mark's head to thump abruptly onto the mattress. She drops the pillow on his face and groans soon seep from under it. "Come on, Mark, move it. I need to get painting." Jennie puts her foot against the side of the bed and nudges it violently. "That was our agreement. You could sleep in here but you needed to be up and out of bed by eight."

There's a mumbled, "Okay, you asked for it," before Mark's hand drops down to the covers and grips them.

Jennie spins and marches over to the front window to stare at the street until she hears him stumble out of the room. She kicks his abandoned undies beneath the bed, picks his clothes up off the bedspread and marches with them at arm's length to the door where she throws them out in the hallway. She closes the door soundly and jams her flip-flops one on top of the other under it as a makeshift doorstop. She's hoping this will give her some peace and quiet and stop Mark popping up next to her buck-naked.

"Hey, where are my grots?" comes through the door.

"Under the bed. Get a clean pair." Jennie doesn't hear if he responds to this as she's already slapped the lawn mower man's earmuffs on. Harmony descends with the silence.

It's hours later when Jennie clocks that her bladder is so full it's hurting. She drops her paintbrush into the jar of water and takes off the earmuffs. She shouldn't wait so long to pee, it's asking for another bout of cystitis. Kicking her flip-flops free from the bottom of the door she opens it. Stepping over Mark's clothes on her way to the bathroom, she hopes he's wearing something.

Post pit stop, Jennie checks on Sonja to see that she has everything she needs. The woman is lying on her side facing away from the door. "You got everything you need?"

There's the sound of paper rustling before Sonja rolls over to look at Jennie. "I am good, ah?"

"Jennie."

"Yes, that's right. My head, it hurts so much. I forget." Sonja drapes a limp hand artfully over her forehead and sighs.

What a ham. Leaving Sonja to the accompaniment of an orchestra of very small violins, Jennie goes back to work on the painting of Peanut, chihuahua extraordinaire. She should be able to finish it in a couple of days and hopes Lady Leicester likes it. She still has trouble believing the woman accepted the one hundred and fifty quid price tag without a quibble. This alone makes Jennie nervous about making the painting the best she can. Not that she'd ever hand over anything she wasn't altogether happy with.

The next morning, Jennie walks back into her bedroom after the world's fastest shower. She's in time to turn off her alarm clock. Funny that when faced with a day in front of the easel, she has no trouble getting up early. That hadn't been the case when she was working at her parent's plumbing supply shop back home, or the insurance office job from hell in Melbourne. Both of those had her continually hitting the snooze button until she risked being late.

Dressing hastily, she pulls on the second-hand clothes she's picked up from a local charity shop. No point getting paint all over her good gear. Even so, she still checks herself in the mirror before leaving the bedroom. This results in some hair fluffing and the application of lip gloss.

Swinging into the kitchen with Charlie hard on her heels, Jennie is surprised to find it empty. Looking at her watch, she realises she's breakfasting earlier than normal this morning. Chris would usually be around at this time but he's away in Germany for an interview with BMW for a job in their design studio. Lord knows what will happen if he gets the job; Sam's on tenterhooks waiting for him to return.

Much as she gets on well with Chris, it's nice having this time alone with no need for conversation, although Charlie keeps up a constant monologue until she shakes some kibble onto his special plate and tops up the milk in his bowl. "There you go, big guy." Jennie pats the top of his head as he crunches away, his concentration on the task saying more than meows about how good those little biscuits taste.

Jennie also makes quick work of her breakfast and has rinsed and stacked before she thinks to check the roster on the inside of the pantry door. Damn, she's on breakfast duty for Sonja. "No time for toast, that's for sure." Charlie looks at her, realises she's not talking to him, and goes back to his breakfast.

Arms out in front of her, Jennie carries the laden tray up the stairs. Shame they couldn't move the head-case downstairs. It's slow going when you're making sure not to spill tea or trip on a step. Reaching the top landing, the muscles in her arms are screaming. Backing up to the door of Mark's room, Jennie pushes it open with her bum and reverses into the bedroom.

Swinging around, a cheery greeting at the ready, she is surprised to find the bed empty. With no patient in sight, Jennie balances the tray on one of the bedside tables, moving a magazine to the side to clear a flat space. The magazine slips, crashing to the floor; an aerogram swooping down after it. Checking the tray is secure, Jennie picks them both up and drops them on the bed.

Walking back across the landing, Jennie can see the bathroom door is shut and someone is moving around inside. Presumably Sonja. Jennie knocks on the door to the studio and when there's no reply, she pushes the door open a nudge. There's no way she wants to catch Mark unawares. The bed is empty. It's also made. Well, as made as Mark ever manages. That's good, it's been wearing thin kicking him out of bed every morning so she can get on with her painting. Not that she can start now, not without water to rinse her brushes.

Jennie is walking back up the stairs from filling her water jar when she sees Sonja skip across the landing and into Mark's bedroom, with Mark right on her heels.

Squealing and laughter starts not long after the door is slammed shut.

Barnyard noises follow.

Jennie slaps on the earmuffs and sets about finishing her painting of Peanut in the style of Botticelli's *Birth of Venus*. Jennie's had to play around with the proportions and swap the angels for cherubs to avoid Peanut looking ginormous.

She stands back and examines the canvas. Walking from to side to side, she checks it from every angle, and then walks to the far side of the room to take it in from a distance. A few more daubs of paint are added before she's satisfied enough to add her signature to the bottom left-hand corner of the canvas. Dropping her brush into the water jar, she pulls the earmuffs down in time to hear Sonja screaming Mark's name over and over again.

Jennie grimaces at the image that's popped up in her head. "She's either got her memory back, or he's wearing a name tag."

12

Shutting the gate and incarcerating herself in her private topiary nightmare, Jennie rushes down the gravel path, gaze swivelling from side to side checking for movement. She reaches the front porch with a sigh of relief and gives the lion's head knocker a couple of good *thunks*.

Brian ushers her into a room on the ground floor, to wait for Lady Leicester. While small, the room is exquisitely furnished although it lacks the warmth of the sitting room upstairs. The floor is a chequerboard of black and white tiles, great for dirty shoes but hard and unforgiving. The two chairs that sit on either side of a small mahogany table look to be similarly lacking in any softness.

Jennie leans the painting against one chair and sits gingerly on the other, confirming it's padded with the same brand of builder's mix as the chairs at Lady Harrow's, with Jennie's cheeks flattening to suit the profile. Luckily she doesn't have to wait long before Lady Leicester enters. "I'm so looking forward to seeing it." When she doesn't make a move to pick up the painting, Jennie does so, putting it on the table so she can undo the wrapping.

With the final piece of tissue folded back, the painting of Peanut is revealed and Jennie holds it up for inspection. She also holds her breath. She hates this. It's not until she hears the clap of hands that she breathes out evenly, releasing the reef knot in her stomach.

"It's fabulous. I love it." Lady Leicester claps her hands again. "Come, we've got to go and show it to Caroline."

Jennie dutifully follows Lady Leicester up the stairs and into the sitting room of her previous visit to the residence.

"Caroline, I'd like you to meet Jennie Farrell. Jennie this is Caroline Michaels. You must see this fabulous painting that young Jennie has completed of Peanut." She swings it around and proudly holds it up for Caroline to inspect.

The hands that stretch out to take the painting are beautifully, although not ostentatiously, manicured, with the nails buffed rather than painted. Jennie looks at Lady Leicester's visitor with an artist's eye, noting that everything about the woman is understated but exceptionally elegant.

She has a look of old money about her, as though anything that had to be proven was sorted out long ago. The dark chocolate-brown jacket, white shirt and hound's-tooth pants sit casually on the woman's frame. Her hair is coiffed into a gleaming bob of dark brunette perfection. Not a stray hair wavering from its allotted location.

The woman is quiet, nerve-rackingly so for Jennie. She stands and peers at the painting before taking it from Lady Leicester and walking over to one of the large windows. She bravely turns her back on the topiary beasts outside and holds the painting up to the light.

By the time she says anything, Jennie is transferring her weight from one foot to the other, unable to centre herself.

"This is good." The woman's voice tends toward surprise.

"I know, isn't it? She's caught the expression on my little darling's face perfectly." Lady Leicester is beaming when she bends over to pat the subject matter. He's lying fast asleep on the couch. Curled up next to him is a Maltese Terrier, whose snowy white and finely combed hair makes Peanut look positively down-and-out.

"This isn't just good. It's gallery good." Caroline looks over at Jennie. "You painted this?" The woman's face hides her disbelief, although not well.

"Yes."

"Without help?" Caroline looks at Jennie as if to gauge the truth of her answer.

"Yes." Jennie tries to keep her tone smooth and even, although this is hard when you're on the guilty-until-presumed-innocent end of the third-degree look that Caroline's giving her. It's strange enough for Jennie to have another woman looking her straight in the eye. Caroline Michaels may even be taller than she is.

"Hmmmm." Caroline's tone doesn't convey her belief, or otherwise, of Jennie's response.

Jennie is about to question this seeming lack of belief, when Caroline continues. "I'd like you to paint Monroe for me." Putting the painting of Peanut on a dark mahogany, pedestal table, she walks over and picks up the limp and sleepy pooch. Monroe hardly rouses, draping herself limply over Caroline's arm. The little face is clear of a fringe, the hair pulled back tight and held in place with a pale pink bow. The eyes, nose and mouth look dark in comparison with the pure white fur. If it weren't for those features and the bow, the dog would be borderline albino.

"What sort of thing would you be after?" Jennie risks patting the small dog's head and comes close to losing a finger. Time she learned: the smaller the dog, the shittier their disposition. She should have learnt her lesson back in Melbourne with Honey Bun the killer corgi.

"I'm in your hands on that front. In fact, I'd be interested to see what you come up with. Would you be able to produce something in say four weeks? My husband's birthday is coming up."

Jennie feels she's been set a test, although what for she's not certain. "Of course. Four weeks should be fine. Would it be all right if I took some reference photos and sketches now?"

Given the go-ahead, Jennie gets her sketchbook and the Polaroid out of her bag. Caroline puts the floppy dog back on the couch, having to resort to holding it up for Jennie to take a Polaroid. No sooner has the flash gone off than Peanut explodes into a yelping bouncing fury. His yelps are ear-splitting.

"I'm so sorry, I forgot Peanut doesn't like the camera." Jennie puts it down on the chair next to her bag. "I can take sketches if it's going to upset him." From her experience of dog owners in Melbourne, Jennie knows any further photos will be out of the question. She's surprised therefore when Lady Leicester puts Peanut out in the hallway and shuts the door on him.

The doggie equivalent of 'let me in, let me in, let me in' is constant with no sign of let-up. Jennie grabs the camera and snaps four more shots of Monroe in quick succession.

"Okay, all done."

Lady Leicester opens the door and Peanut explodes back into the room, still barking and pissed off at being locked out for what was less than a minute. After an ankle-threatening growl in Jennie's direction, he hops back up on the couch via the footstool, turns a couple of times and settles back down into a little ball.

Jennie completes some sketches of Monroe although they lack detail, given the dog has subsided back into a white powder puff. Jennie asks Caroline Michaels a couple questions before feeling confident she has enough information to get started on a painting of the Maltese terrier. An idea has formulated while she's been working on the sketches. Let's hope Monroe's mum and dad think it's a good idea, too.

Jennie's leaving the room with a cream Basildon Bond envelope full of crisp ten pound notes, when she overhears Caroline saying to Lady Leicester "You don't mind if I show Peanut's portrait to David, do you.

Closing the gate between her and the topiary beasts, Jennie breathes a small sigh of relief. She doesn't know what the hell it is about the shaped trees but they give her the heebie-jeebies.

Rather than head back the way she'd come that morning, she continues on her way aiming for the middle of the underground map. Her destination is the art supply shop. If Eadie doesn't know she's going there, she won't be able to phone ahead and get the staff to put Jennie's purchases on her landlady's account. Jennie likes to pay her way and if she's got to be sneaky, then so be it.

Baseball cap stuffed on her head, A-Z in her hand and backpack cinched tight, Jennie heads in the direction of the station to catch the tube into Oxford Circus. It means a longish walk at the other end but also means she won't have to change trains. She'd rather walk than get lost on the underground.

Tinkling her way into the shop, Jennie pulls the cap snugly down into place and looks sideways at the shop assistant standing behind the original Dickensian glass-topped counter. It's not the same guy as before, allowing her to relax and pull her cap off to remove the risk of looking like a shoplifter. She completes her selection a lot faster this time, having a better idea of where everything is. When she dumps four tubes of white acrylic onto the counter, the assistant's eyes widen. "Winter scene, is it?"

At Jennie's wrinkled brow, he adds "Snow," nodding toward the tubes on the counter.

"Something like that." Much easier to go along with his suggestion than try to explain what she's really doing. He'd never believe her anyway. In less than ten minutes, Jennie is back on the pavement with the paint supplies stowed in her backpack. No way is she going to get caught like last time. She shrugs and jiggles until the backpack finds a comfortable spot, squares her shoulders and heads toward the tube station. If those commuters think they are going to push and shove her around again, they have another think coming.

13

Pushing herself up against the metal edge of the bed frame, Jennie shuffles back until she's hard up against the window frame in the studio. Even here, there are varying degrees of brightness and it's good to get as much light as possible onto the pages of the library book she's skimming through. She's had this book, plus a pile of others, out for what feels like weeks without being any closer to selecting the perfect reference for Monroe's painting.

Jennie flips over to the inside cover and checks the date stamped on the sheet of paper glued to the back page. She's still got ages before she needs to take them back. What she doesn't have ages for is finishing the painting in time for David Michaels' birthday party. At least she's narrowed it down to a couple of options.

Jennie waves to get Sam's attention. Her friend's ears are stuffed with offcuts of the purple velvet she's stitching. Jennie is sporting the earmuffs that are the only thing between her and Mark's love life. Holding up the book, she shows Sam first one photo and then the other; flipping the pages backwards and forwards until she gets a thumbs-up symbol. Jennie turns the book and checks the photo, nodding in agreement with Sam's choice. It's the one she's been leaning toward, too.

Seeing Sam's lips moving, Jennie pulls the earmuffs down around her neck in time to hear "... photographic?"

"What?" Jennie mouths this, underscoring the question with knotting brows.

Sam pulls the velvet stoppers from her ears before continuing. "Are you going for something photographic?"

"Haven't decided. That'd sure as heck be the easiest option, but I get the impression Mrs Michaels is after something a mite edgier. I feel I've been set a test on this one."

"How so?"

Jennie's still wracking her brain for an answer when the strains of what sounds like monkeys moving bags of concrete, bounces across the landing from Mark's room and in under the door.

"Never mind." Sam stuffs the offcuts of velvet back into her ears before shouting, "I'm back off downstairs. My ears are starting to hurt." She piles all her sewing into a small basket and is at the door not long after. "Ready?"

Confused as to what she should be ready for, Jennie stares vacantly, although this vaporises when Sam puts her hand on the door handle. "Oh, right." Jennie snaps the earmuffs back into place although not speedily enough to stop her ears from being assaulted by monkeys hefting heavy bags whilst jumping excitedly on a bed.

Using the book on her lap as reference Jennie spends the remainder of the morning sketching various layouts for the painting of Monroe. She checks through all the library books for the style of painting she's after. Closing her eyes, the finished piece is tantalisingly close, although not in focus enough for her to break out the paints. It's only after the bed is strewn with open books and half-finished sketches that Jennie finally comes to a decision. She snaps closed all the books whose styles haven't made the cut. When finished, there are two books and one sketch left on the bed. She transfers the books to the table beside the easel, well clear of any paint, and tapes the sketch to one of the easel uprights.

A quick trip to the bathroom to fill the water jar and she can get started. She opens her door at the same time as Mark opens his on the other side of the landing. He's wearing a smile and attempting to drag a towel around his middle. He appears 'perky' given all the bags of cement he's recently moved. Jennie squeaks, shuts her eyes and then the door. Pulling her earmuffs down, she hears the bathroom door slamming. This is followed by a deafening fart and what sounds like a horse peeing on concrete. "Good lord, does he do anything quietly?"

With Mark out of the way, Jennie nips downstairs to the bathroom below and fills her water jar. She runs back up the stairs as fast as the sloshingly full jar of water will allow. She's almost back in her room, when she cannons into Mark coming out of the bathroom. The contents of the jar slosh up toward his shoulders then down his bare chest and into places Jennie doesn't want to think about.

"Argh, bloody hell, that's freezing!"

"Sorry." Jennie struggles to hold on to the slippery jar, holding it against her chest to stabilise it. She twists her body away from him and backs into her studio. With the damp towel clinging to him, Jennie can see he's no longer as perky as he was and she's dismayed to feel a smile coming on. She's never found bodily functions funny before. *What the hell is wrong with me?*

After shutting the door, she moves to one side so he won't see her shadow and listens intently. A lot of muttering and cursing and Mark stomps back to his room, slamming the door.

Jennie holds the jar up and groans when she sees the small amount of water left in the bottom.

Back after topping it up, Jennie snaps the earmuffs into place. Even though there are no wildlife noises emanating from across the landing, she finds the lack of outside influence frees her mind to concentrate on her painting. Peering at the sketch, Jennie makes a few tentative pencil strokes. She stands back to survey them, and then adds more. Her movements gain in confidence until the pencil is flying, with the strokes so light at times that the pencil loses contact with the canvas. It will be that lightness of touch that will make the painting work.

As soon as everything is sketched to her satisfaction, Jennie drops the pencil. Texture will be the key with this portrait as there won't be a lot of colour. She mixes acrylic gel and modelling paste on a piece of greaseproof paper. Looking as scrumptious as almond icing, she applies it to some of the fine pencil lines using a small palette knife. Standing to the side from time to time, Jennie checks the overall shape she's creating.

At her nod of approval, she wipes the palette knife clean and bins the leftover 'icing'. It will take a couple of hours for this lot to dry, if not longer.

With everything cleaned up, Jennie puts her ear to the door to check the coast is clear and then goes in search of Sam. As she walks down the stairs, she stretches her arms over her head and gives them a good shake on each landing until she reaches the first floor. Locating Sam is easy, with the sewing machine chattering away like an audible neon sign. Jennie's still twisting and turning when she walks into Sam's workroom.

"Lunch time."

"Thank God. My back is killing me." Sam takes her foot off the pedal, leaving the small coat she's working on where it is, half in, half out of the machine. "You thinking of going out for something?" Sam rolls her shoulders first one way, then the other.

"Don't have time." Jennie confirms this by looking at her watch. "Nope, don't have time. There's heaps of stuff in the fridge."

"Picnic?"

"Yeah, why not?" Jennie admires the startlingly blue sky visible between the branches crowding the side window of the room. The front window, with its heavily detailed lace curtains, doesn't allow for the observation of much at all. "It's looking nice out there."

There's an in-depth discussion about sandwich fillings as they wander downstairs and into the kitchen. The conversation peters out when they see Sonja sitting at the table with Mark working their way through a pile of doorstop sandwiches.

"You're up and about. How are you feeling?" Jennie hopes she's put enough concern into her voice. Inside, she's happy that the room service days are over.

"Have you remembered anything yet?" Sam eyes Sonja while waiting for a response.

"I, ah, I have ... no." The Yugoslavian girl's face is a picture of distress.

Jennie's not buying it. That look is too contrived and has her gut screaming 'Liar, liar, pants on fire' at her subconscious. Mark's eyebrows hitch up on his forehead at her non-committal "Hmmm," and she consciously fights the sympathetic response that would be her usual fare. Keen to get away from his scrutiny, Jennie gets stuck in helping Sam with sandwich assembly. At the speed Sam is working, it would seem she's keen to escape, too. Their task is aided by all the sandwich makings still being on the counter top.

Jennie settles herself into the garden chair opposite Sam, before pulling the plate and her sandwich off the table and into her lap. "She's lying through her teeth."

"What makes you say that?" Sam's voice is muffled by a mouthful of ham and bread.

"Don't know. But something's *off*."

A soft breeze from Jennie's travel dryer makes its way backwards and forwards across the canvas. She has to dry each layer of paint as she goes to get the effect she wants. After it's firm to the touch, she pulls an old sheet over the top of it. Anyone seeing the piece at this stage, other than Eadie, would wonder what she was up to. The white cotton is still fluttering into place when her stomach gurgles in an alarming fashion. Looking at her wrist, it becomes obvious why. She jumps when there's a loud banging on the door.

"Dinner's ready." Mark sounds annoyed at having been sent to collect her.

Leaving her tools to soak, Jennie 'unlocks' the door. Rather than being halfway back to the ground floor, Mark is leaning against the newel post. Jennie baulks, then gestures to him to precede her down the stairs. He shakes his head and indicates that she should go first. Conscious of having Mark right on her heels, Jennie makes her way downstairs with him following so closely, she's sure she can feel his blooming breath on the back of her neck.

Jennie stops on the first floor, and pushes open the door to her bedroom. "Come on, Charlie. Dinner time." She can't help but smile at the intake of breath behind her.

Charlie saunters out of her bedroom, stretching the afternoon nap out of his tight muscles. Who'd have believed sleeping could be so stressful? His left front and right back legs are stretched full out in a yoga pose Jennie can't remember the name of, when he spots Mark standing behind Jennie. His extended limbs snap back into their locked and loaded position. This is followed by a deep growl, Jennie doesn't even need to indicate Mark should go ahead of her. He's off down the stairs three at a time. Jennie leans over and smooths Charlie's eyebrow whiskers back over the top of his head. "Good boy."

Without Mark shadowing her, Jennie is a lot more relaxed for the final flight although her feet slow as she nears the kitchen door. The idea of sharing another evening meal with Mark and Sonja is already giving her indigestion.

14

Holding tight onto the painting of Monroe, Jennie walks down the stairs carefully. Very, very carefully. Her free hand slides down the bannister, ensuring stability. She wants a second opinion before finishing the piece and short of slinging Eadie over one shoulder and lugging her up to the top floor, this is the next best thing.

Jennie's heart has a good old crack at exploding out of her mouth when her foot slips off the bottom step, sending her in a body-jarring thump to terra firma. She waits until her breathing evens out, and the glut of adrenalin is reabsorbed before continuing into Eadie's sitting room.

Eadie's not there, bringing Jennie to a standstill. Once she lets silence descend, she becomes aware of faint snoring coming from Eadie's bedroom. Jennie looks around the sitting room but can't see a sherry glass in sight. That's usually the reason for a mid-afternoon nap.

Propping the painting up on the mantle, Jennie puts her head around the door of Eadie's room. The snoring is much louder in here and more than likely the result of the rather large, but damn near empty tumbler sitting on the bedside table. The golden dregs in the bottom are familiar. Eadie does love a tipple.

Sniggering to herself, Jennie is backing out of the room when she cannons straight into Mark, causing him to grab her firmly by both shoulders.

"What are you laughing about?" He still sounds annoyed. He hasn't spoken to her, apart from the occasional grunt, for days after their last scrap.

Jennie turns toward him, her finger pressed to her lips. The other hand grabs the handle of Eadie's bedroom door and pulls it quietly shut. She stands in front of it, guarding it. "Eadie's tired, she's having a nap."

"Tired or drunk?" Mark doesn't bother lowering his voice, Eadie's tonsils still flapping in the breeze more than a match for him.

"Tired." Jennie hopes her face stays straight, although she has trouble looking Mark in the eye. Not that this has anything to do with lying to protect Eadie's afternoon session on the sherry.

Mark doesn't say anything and because his face also remains straight, Jennie has no way of knowing if he's swallowed her line or not. Giving him as wide a berth as she can, Jennie collects the painting and gets out of his presence. Hearing him on the stairs behind her, she increases her speed. By the time she reaches the top floor, she's running. She makes short work of putting the canvas back on the easel and jamming her flip-flops under the door. She also leans all her weight against it for insurance.

She can hear him breathing outside the door, but he doesn't attempt to push his way in. Pressed against the wood as she is, Jennie has no trouble hearing the "Gutless wonder" muttered through the door.

She relaxes when she hears the door to Mark's bedroom shut. "Zoo soundtrack coming right up." She takes the earmuffs off the upright of the easel and wastes no time in snapping them into place. She looks at the painting and wonders whether she should continue or wait for Eadie to sober up. She moves to get the paintbrush out of the jar of milky water but is only halfway there before her hand drops back to her side.

Unmoving, she continues to examine the painting minutely. "You can do this. You know what Eadie would say. You're capable of this." Jennie knows she's spoken aloud, even though she hasn't been able to physically hear the words. And anyway if the room's empty does she make any sound at all? She pulls the earmuffs down to see if there's any reaction to her pep talk, but all is quiet. Strangely so. Jennie tiptoes over to the doorway and presses her ear hard against the dark wood. Not even heavy breathing.

Twisting her flip-flops out from under the door, Jennie inches the handle around and opens the door in millimetre increments. It takes ages before she's able to look through the gap with both eyes at the same time. The door of Mark's room is wide open, but a quick looksee around the corner confirms the bathroom door is shut tight. Jennie closes the door with the same laborious speed and feels lucky to have everything secure when distinctly masculine footsteps echo outside.

Jennie leans into the door, expecting another onslaught against the door, and almost has an accident when Mark's, "I can see your shadow under the door," slips through the wood and worms its way into her ear.

She stumbles away, trips over the mat and lands hard on her knees. Her mortification is complete when she hears a deep rumble of laughter from out in the hallway. This only gets louder after Jennie bangs her feet on the ground in frustration.

Rolling over, Jennie forces Charlie off her chest. It's made difficult by the large black and white cat hanging on like he's riding a bike. Jennie's lying on top of him before he pulls his claws clear of the bedclothes.

"Sorry, big guy, it's time to get up."

Charlie doesn't agree. He stays where he is, lying on his back. Tucking up his back legs, he flips his tail between them for modesty then crosses his front paws over his chest in a pose reminiscent of Jennie's grandad.

Easing out of bed, Jennie takes her camera off the hook on the back of the door and snaps off a couple of shots; the flash is bright in the still dim bedroom. Charlie's only reaction is a slight opening of one eye, his gaze benign. Encouraged, Jennie puts the camera down on the end of the bed and pulls the curtains wide, flooding the room in early morning light.

Charlie stretches limbs in all directions before drawing them back in. His front paws now cover his eyes rather than his chest. "Oh, that's so cute." Winding the film on for another shot, Jennie sees she's sitting on thirty-three. "Okay, mister. Photo session coming up." She walks around the bed taking pics of Charlie until the film is out. Much easier to change it now than when she's out sightseeing.

During her David Bailey impersonation, Jennie's been conscious of the sewing machine chattering away through the wall in the front room. It's early for Sam to be up and sewing. She usually doesn't start until mid-morning at the earliest.

Post ablutions and dressed for another day at the easel, Jennie checks in on her friend.

"You're up early." Jennie picks up a piece of leopard print Lycra and rubs it between her fingers.

"Yeah, I've got to finish this lot today, so I'm free for the weekend."

Jennie drops the fabric, her face a study of concentration. "What day is it today?"

"Friday. Chris is back tonight."

"I wonder how he got on." For Sam's sake, Jennie is hoping it hasn't worked out. Sure a job at BMW in Germany is what any auto-design engineer would give a non-required limb for, but it would mean a difficult decision for Sam. If she went with him, she'd have to give up her dog-clobber business, move countries, and learn another language. Everyone is avoiding the other option like it's a contagious disease. Especially Sam.

"Lousily, I hope. I know it's selfish but ..." the rest of Sam's reply peters out.

"Maybe he'll get something else. This hasn't been his only interview."

"Fingers crossed he gets something close to here." Sam snips the threads on the just-completed seam.

"You had breakfast? I'm heading down now."

"No time if I want to be free and clear when Chris walks in the door."

"I'll get you something. Peanut butter or vegemite?" Jennie's already on her way.

"Vegemite, please. And I'd kill for a coffee."

"Coming right up," sings Jennie from the top step where she's paused to hear Sam's order. She skips down the stairs and into the kitchen.

Her skipping is brought up short when she spots Mark and Sonja sitting at the table. Jennie can feel the tension in the room when she sets about making breakfast, her concentration torn between her culinary undertaking and their conversation. The tones are low and muttered, causing her ears to swing like radar in their effort to pick up at least a snippet; when she walks over to the table to grab the milk for her and Sam's coffees, the conversation slams shut. Sonja's mouth is down at the corners and her arms crossed firmly across her low-cut tube top, pushing her nipples alarmingly close to the edge.

Jennie wastes no time in slopping milk into two mugs and

heading back to the toaster. There's now more noise coming from the toasting bread than the two breakfasters.

"Whoa, that was awkward." Jennie places the tray on Sam's cutting-out table.

"What was?"

"Mark and Sonja. Don't know what they were discussing, but Sonja's not a happy bunny."

Sam moves her chair over to sit with Jennie. "She still making out she can't remember anything?"

"I think so. But how are we supposed to know for sure?" Jennie talks through her mouthful of peanut buttery toast knowing she's breaking a cardinal mother-rule.

Sam licks a smear of vegemite off the end of a finger. "There must be some way of trapping her."

Dishes washed and put away and breakfast taken into Eadie, Jennie makes her way back up to her studio. With any luck, she'll finish the painting of Monroe today. Eadie has confirmed she's bang on with her treatment of the portrait and that confirmation has added a much-needed confidence to her palette work. Jennie can see the completed piece sharp in her mind and is eager to finish it to see if her imagination and reality are in agreement.

Swinging around the post at the top of the stairs she's aware of angry voices coming from Mark's room, making her shoulders drop. It's better than noisy lovemaking but still not conducive to the creative process. Jennie shuts the door of the studio, slaps on the earmuffs and lets her body relax into the silence that descends.

That's one good thing to come out of all this; she'd never realised before how much the silence helps. Now she embraces it, the exclusion of external stimuli allowing her to concentrate on her work.

She's nearing signature in the corner time when she becomes aware of the easel trembling. "That's odd." The earmuffs have dropped to her shoulders when the bathroom door is slammed with such gusto that it causes ripples in the water jar. Shouting by Mark follows. Sonja's screamed responses are even louder. "Jeez, not again." The fights are a pain in the butt. Jennie creeps up next to the door to see if she can pick up anything else.

"Suit yourself. You can bloody stay in there for all I care." Mark stomps back to his room.

The door to his room has no sooner slammed shut that Sonja explodes out of the bathroom. The door has been opened with such force that it's smashed back into the wall to her room, right next to where she's standing. "That must have been one doozy of a swing." Jennie drops down and peers through the keyhole, making sure to keep herself off to the side. She doesn't want any tell-tale shadows giving her position away.

Sonja is standing outside Mark's room, her body language shouting 'fight, fight, fight'. She shakes the tension free from her body before gripping the door handle and wrenching at it. The door doesn't budge. "Mark! Let me in!" It isn't a quiet request. It's screamed at the door. Jennie's sure if she were closer she'd be able to see the spit that must be flecked all over the door, given the vehemence in the woman's voice.

The door doesn't open, so Sonja hammers at it with her fists and then kicks the bottom of it. Mark refuses to answer and Sonja's attack on the door escalates to the point Jennie opens her own.

"Ah, do you think you should be doing that?"

When there's no reaction from Sonja, she repeats herself, loud enough to be heard over the assault on the solid oak door.

The girl whips round in Jennie's direction, her eyes glazed over like a junk-yard dog or a psychopath. Her breathing is laboured and she's fighting to get enough air.

Jennie doesn't understand what's screamed at her, but the intonation and facial expressions leave her in no doubt as to the message. It's enough to have her closing her door to escape the fury.

The relief she feels, when she sees Mark's door opening, is short-lived and Jennie can't help a sharp intake of breath. Catching her staring open-mouthed in his direction, Mark's only reaction is to quirk an eyebrow.

He's a little naked. Actually, he's a lot naked. He's not even wearing a smile, although some bits of him seem happy enough.

Sonja turns back in his direction and also sucks in some air.

"You are magnificent!"

She throws herself at Mark, climbing up his body like it's a jungle gym. When he swings her around, her extended foot slams the door shut, cutting off Jennie's view of proceedings. Not that Jennie needs to see what's going on to know what's going on.

She slaps the earmuffs back into place and is about to ever so carefully put her signature on the bottom of the painting of Monroe when the easel starts to shake. "For pity's sake." Jennie tosses her brush into water in disgust. "He so needs to use the big head rather than the little head."

15

Jennie flicks the sheet over the ninety-nine percent completed painting with a muttered, "Pain in the arse." She collects everything that needs cleaning and stalks into the bathroom. It takes longer to rinse the sink afterwards. She stomps back into the studio, unceremoniously dumps the cleaned items onto the table, and then tosses her earmuffs in the direction of the bed. With fingers stuffed in her ears, she tramps along the landing.

She can still hear them but if she pushes her fingers in any further, she's going to risk self-inflicted brain surgery. Humming to block the still-audible grunting and moaning, she leaves them to it, dropping her hands to her sides only when she reaches the first floor.

The sooner the nymphomaniac admits to having her memory back, the sooner Mark can get out of bed and get himself a job. At least then the monkey sounds would be restricted to the nights when Jennie is safely tucked up, two floors below. And why does the blasted girl need round-the-clock care anyway? It's not like she's in danger of popping off if the effort she devotes to sex is any indication.

Jennie looks in on Sam. "You done for the day?"

"Just finished." Sam is folding up a small leopard print coat with an alarmingly long train.

"I feel like a sherry. Forget that. I NEED a sherry."

Sam stops folding the small coat, her face full of concern. "What happened?"

"The rabbits were going at it so hard the place was shaking. I couldn't even sign my painting."

Jennie gradually opens the door to Eadie's sitting room; you never knew what state the old lady would be in. Eadie is stretched over the side of her chair attempting to grab the decanter of sherry from the table next to her.

Sam, who's right on Jennie's heels, pushes past and grabs the decanter before it topples over. "Here let me get that for you."

"That'd be lovely. Help yourself, too." A gnarled hand indicates some spare glasses on the tray. All of them a lot smaller than the one Eadie's selected for herself.

Once they're all settled and the common 'here's mud in your eye' toast is out of the way, Eadie takes a healthy swig from her glass. "How's the painting going?"

"Complete apart from the signature."

Eadie takes another healthy swig. "Waiting for the paint to dry enough?"

"She wishes. More like waiting for the house to stop shaking." Sam's comment is punctuated with small sips of the golden brew.

Following an initial crease of concentration, enlightenment dawns on Eadie's face. "Ah, right. She does strike me as being a goer."

"I don't know what he sees in her." The other two look at

her incredulously. "Well, apart from that." Jennie is annoyed that she's so annoyed.

"I don't think I've seen the gal since she bonked her noggin. Memory back yet?"

"Not yet," say Jennie and Sam in unison.

The room falls silent as the three of them mull over the issue of Sonja and her faulty memory. Jennie would love nothing more than to prove to Mark that the floozy is having him on, that's there's more to life than sex on tap. She doesn't like her chances if this afternoon's session is anything to go by, although the fights did seem to be happening on a more regular basis. Unfortunately, they're always followed by rowdy make-up sex.

"I'll bet you any money you like, she's found out about the boy's trust fund."

Jennie and Sam look at each other. "What trust fund?" they ask.

"Didn't you know? The boy's loaded."

The thought hung AND loaded flits across Jennie's mind before she can snaffle it under control. It's a while before she has it safely jammed into a little-used corner, allowing her to get her mind back on the conversation.

"No wonder he isn't in a hurry to get a job," says Jennie.

"Don't think he's not a worker because of the trust fund. He's never been one to sit around twiddling his thumbs," says Eadie, looking up thoughtfully.

"He's definitely not idle," says Sam, snorting.

"No twiddling jokes, please," pleads Jennie, causing the other two to break into loud guffaws.

"If she does know, he's done for," says Sam, once she's got her laughter under control.

"What if?" It's only when the other two look at her that Jennie realises she's said this aloud.

"Yes?"

Both pairs of eyes stay on her.

"What if he was to lose the money?" At their reaction, Jennie explains. "Not genuinely lose it, make out he's lost it."

"Might be the jolt the gal's memory needs." Eadie rubs her hands together as enthusiastically as someone with arthritis can. "Oh, yes." Her eyes squint in concentration before she snorts and takes another ladylike sip of her sherry.

Before Eadie can elaborate, the front door opens.

"I'm back!" is shouted to the house in general.

Sam runs out of the room, appearing with Chris ten minutes later. They look soggy around the mouth and Chris's hair has had a good ruffling.

"How did you get on, boy?" Eadie puts her finished glass down noisily on the small table to her right. Jennie takes the hint and tops it up.

"It went well, I think."

Chris drops into one of the oversized arm chairs; his lap is soon full of Sam. He manoeuvres around her to open the first envelope from a pile that has been collecting on the table in the hallway, awaiting his return from Germany.

"I got it, I bloody got it," he says, his voice full of surprise.

He stares fixedly at the partially opened letter for a few seconds before flipping down the bottom third. He crushes the letter into his embrace of Sam and his face breaks into a wide grin. "It was a long shot. But I got it."

"You did?" Sam squirms around in his arms so she can look at him.

Jennie can tell Sam's trying to inject some enthusiasm into her voice, but failing miserably. Able to tell her friend is fighting to get the next question out, Jennie comes to her rescue. "When do you start?"

"Next week." Chris is shaking his head as though even he can't believe the speed with which things are moving.

"Next week! How long for?" Sam's tone is one of constraint.

"At least through until Christmas time. It's a contract for now, but they're hinting that if it works out, I could go permanent."

"Permanent? Oh ..." Anything else Sam has to say dies in her throat.

"Does that mean you'll be moving?" Jennie takes up the questioning given Sam has been struck mute.

"Yes. And soon."

"Soon?" Sam chokes out this one-word question before collapsing back against Chris.

"You don't have to sound so happy." Chris looks crestfallen at Sam not celebrating his momentous news.

"But I won't see you for months if you move to Germany." Sam swipes at her eyes.

"Germany? Hardly." Chris wipes Sam's tears away. "I got the contract at the Rolls-Royce factory at Crewe. Remember I went for the interview before I left?"

While Jennie is starting to feel comfortable in London, she doesn't know if she wants to be left on her own yet. "Crewe? How far away is that?"

"Less than two hours on the train." Chris looks at Jennie over Sam's shoulder. "I'd have to stay there Monday through Thursday nights ... it's only a contract, so no point in moving permanently."

Sam and Chris disappear for a proper catch-up, leaving Eadie and Jennie to fall into a companionable silence. This is broken by the occasional slurp or sound of a sherry glass being put down onto a mahogany table. It's mainly Jennie putting the glass down, with Eadie finding it easier to keep hold of her glass until it's empty.

"I know how we can sort that girl out." Eadie holds out her glass to Jennie, presumably for a refill, but when Jennie takes the top off the decanter she's told not to bother in a voice that's all business.

Jennie takes the three glasses to the kitchen to rinse them. She stares into space while waiting for the hot water to come through the antiquated plumbing, and can still see the look of contemplation on Eadie's face. What's she planning?

"Take that ya little buggers." Jennie holds the glasses under the hot tap one at a time, washing off a fair few free-loading ants in the process. It's a wonder Eadie doesn't suck a few of them down given she works away at one glass over the course of the day. That sitting room must have the drunkest ants in London.

"So, what were you thinking of?" says Jennie, when she puts the clean glasses back on their silver tray. She squishes a couple of ants with her thumb and wipes their bodies onto the leg of her jeans, then reclaims her previous spot on the couch.

"Well ..." Eadie pauses for dramatic effect.

Jennie unconsciously leans forward in her chair.

"In fact, best you don't know."

Jennie slumps back, strangely deflated. "I'm happy to help."

"Excellent. Will you trail the phone in here for me, please?"

Jennie returns with the phone from the hallway, paying out cord as she goes, and can't believe it when Eadie dismisses her. She contemplates eavesdropping at the door, but can't bring herself to do it. Integrity sucks at times.

Subsequent to being ever-so-politely kicked out of Eadie's sitting room, Jennie drags the front doormat over to cover the phone cord, to stop anyone tripping over it. She's flattening it into place when a giggling Mark and Sonja stumble down the stairs and out the front door without so much as a hello in her direction.

It worries Jennie that even looking at Mark fully clothed, all she can see is him without a stitch on. "That will make dinner interesting." Jennie goes rigid in annoyance with herself and a *grrrrrr* escapes her clamped-down teeth.

Shaking her head hard in an effort to rid it of images of

Mark in the buff, Jennie storms upstairs. She's puffed by the time she's back in the studio but doesn't muck about. She flips the sheet clear of the painting of Monroe, takes off the top of the tube of mid-grey paint and dips one of her finest brushes into it. No point in squeezing any onto her paint board for this job.

Signature in place, Jennie puts the top back on the tube and carries the brush into the bathroom to clean it. She then allows herself a critical look at the totally finished painting. She thinks it's good, but you never knew for sure, but chances are if Eadie likes it, then so will Mrs Michaels.

With a distinct sense of déjà vu, Jennie walks downstairs; one hand holding the painting, the other sliding down the bannister. The harder she concentrates on the stairs, the less steady she is. Giving herself a mental slap one flight down, she continues with more confidence. It does the trick and she arrives outside the door to Eadie's sitting room without mishap.

Seeing the telephone cord snaking its way into the room makes her pause. Putting her ear close to the door, she can hear Eadie talking animatedly. "Damn." She's hanging around wondering whether she should return the painting to her studio when Mark and Sonja walk back in.

"What are you doing skulking around in the hallway?" Mark looks at her as though she's trying to flog something.

"Nothing."

Mark's about to take it further when Sonja's hand slithers around his waist from behind. Where it slithers next has both Mark and Jennie's eyes widening. Jennie knows her nostrils have flared but she's unable to help it.

"C'mon, let's get you to bed."

Mark's eyes are dark with passion and Jennie takes a small step back and her mouth drops open, until she sees Mark is talking to Sonja. The back of her free hand finds its way first to one cheek then the other, coming away a little warmer for it.

Mark smirks at her, before dragging Sonja's hand out of his jeans and pulling on it to lead the tart up the stairs. Jennie can feel his gaze on her until he's out of sight but it takes longer than that for her heart to slow down and her to stop feeling unsullied enough to face Eadie.

She listens again at the door; this time rewarded with Eadie wrapping up her conversation. Rather than walk in the second the phone is hung up, Jennie waits a minute longer and then makes her entrance as though she's just come down the stairs.

She's about to swing the painting around for Eadie's inspection when she sees the grin on Eadie's face. It's positively evil. "Everything all right?"

"Excellent. Couldn't be better. Is that the painting of Monroe?"

In answer, Jennie turns the canvas and holds it up. By the time Jennie's explained the third different reason for something, Eadie holds her hand up to silence her.

The silence stretches out, to the point Jennie's arms are starting to ache. Her forearms are knotted before Eadie speaks.

"Jennie, it's wonderful."

"You think so?"

Eadie snorts. "You won't hear false flattery from me, young lady."

Suitably chastised, Jennie drops to the couch and props the painting next to her.

"Are you going to frame this one?"

"I thought I'd leave it. I've never been to Mrs Michael's place, so I'm not sure what she'd like."

"They're such minimalists, they'd probably prefer it without a frame."

Looking up at the front of the Michaels' house on Monday

morning, Jennie can't imagine the couple being minimal about anything. The house reminds Jennie of an over-blown wedding cake with whoever was in charge using every nozzle in their icing kit. As far as Jennie can see, the only thing missing is a bride and groom cemented in place on the roof. Swapping the heavily wrapped painting to her other hand, Jennie knocks on the ornate front door. She doesn't have long to wait before it's answered by Caroline Michaels herself. The light coming from inside the house is bright, giving the woman an angelic aura.

"Please, come in." Mrs Michaels stands back to allow Jennie to enter without bumping the painting. "I can't wait to see what you've come up with." Without warning, she takes the painting out of Jennie's hands.

Jennie's mouth is opening and closing as she mutely follows Mrs Michaels over to a grouping of white, industrial-looking leather couches. The woman drops onto one of these, indicating Jennie should sit on another, and sets about unwrapping the painting of Monroe.

The interior of the house couldn't be a greater contrast to the exterior. It's art gallery empty; all white walls and shiny wooden floors interspersed with the occasional column. The room they're in runs from the front of the house right through to the back, giving Jennie the impression that it was once a series of smaller spaces. The walls are over-populated with artworks of every era and style, and more than a few famous names amongst them. There doesn't seem to be any logic to the collection.

After it's orbited the room, Jennie's gaze settles on the couch opposite her. Mrs Michaels matches the room. Dressed in white from head to toe, she matches Monroe, who morphs into focus at one end of the couch. The dog has everything dark tucked away under that mountain of silky white fur and without dark eyes, nose and toes on view, the dog blends in.

The sound of ripping paper rattles Jennie's nerves. She'd

much rather have presented the painting formally than have it torn open like this. The woman's nails are long enough that they could do some real damage. Jennie is unable to keep quiet. "Just be careful of the surface as there are some prominent areas. I've used a different technique for this one." She's relieved to see Mrs Michaels slow down her flurry of opening.

After the final layer of paper is pulled back, Mrs Michaels stills and all movement stops as she stares fixedly at the painting on her lap. Moments later, she lifts it reverently from its nest of tissue, the wrapping fluttering to the floor as she rises. She carries it over to the nearest mantel and places it in the middle before spinning on her heel and walking a few metres back. She turns again, and then thoughtfully examines the painting. She still hasn't said a word.

What if she doesn't like it?

There's a few quid's worth of paint and gel on that canvas. The woman opens her mouth to speak, but then clams up, walking off to one side to view the portrait from another angle. She walks first to one side, then the other, still without commenting. Backwards and forwards until Jennie is fit to scream.

"Don't you like it?" Jennie doesn't know if she wants to hear the response to this.

What if she doesn't like it?

"It's—"

"Yes?"

"It's interesting."

"You don't like it?" Interesting didn't sound good. It was one of those things you said when you hated something but didn't want to hurt someone's feelings.

"No, I do. I'm not sure what to make of it. It's different."

Different. It was another one of *those* words.

"Different good or different bad?" Jennie doesn't like interrogating people but it's as though this is going to be the only way she'll get any sense out of the woman.

"Good. Very good. I can't wait to give this to David." Mrs Michaels retrieves the painting and does a poor job of re-wrapping it with the shredded pile of paper. It's so bad that Jennie is unable to stop herself offering to take over. She doesn't want the painting damaged before David receives it for his birthday.

"You'll have to come, of course."

"Excuse me?" Jennie looks up from the neatly closed package on her lap.

"To David's party. This coming Saturday. Only right you should be there."

Jennie can see Mrs Michaels' lips moving but nothing is reaching her ears. They're full of the rush of pounding surf. The woman disappears and all Jennie can see is the contents of her wardrobe flashing by in a kaleidoscope of hangers and outfits totally inappropriate for a London society party. Turning up at Sapphire's fifth birthday party in Melbourne dressed as a cat was a memory that couldn't be erased. How the hell were they supposed to know the fancy dress was only for the dogs? Jennie's hatred of going out 'in society' has been formed with good cause.

Clawing her way back out of the imaginary wardrobe, she finds herself on the front steps, holding a stiff cream envelope. It holds a thick wad of twenty-pound notes. Crisp and new. There's also a heavily gold-embossed invitation with Jenny & Partner scrawled untidily along the thin black line in the middle. "Partner?"

Jennie stumbles down the short, cobbled drive to the pavement, Steve, her late fiancé, at her side. Visible only to her heart.

16

Steve sits next to jennie on the tube home, he walks up the path with her, and he even follows her in the front door. His image dissolves when Jennie hears Eadie calling out to her. The last traces of her late fiancé falling away, Jennie pushes open the door to Eadie's sitting room only vaguely aware when she drops onto the couch.

Without Steve to distract her, the nightmare of what to wear the following Saturday starts up again. "I'll have to say no."

"What's that?"

"I can't go."

"To what?" Eadie's face is a study of 'oh my god, I'm experiencing a senior moment', snapping Jennie out of her introspection.

"Mrs Michaels has invited me to her husband's birthday this Saturday. But I can't go."

"Why?"

"Nothing to wear, no partner and I haven't exactly had a good time at that sort of affair in the past."

"Are you out of your tiny mind? Do you know who David

Michaels is?"

What follows is tantamount to a lecture. According to Eadie, David Michaels' gallery in Mayfair is the rich person's equivalent of Athena.

"As in Athena the Tennis Girl calendars?" says Jennie, causing Eadie to scowl at her for interrupting the lecture.

"David's gallery sells nice artworks to nice ladies to hang in their nice homes. Complementary colours, of course. But there's also a serious side and David Michaels' has launched many a career."

"But what's that got to do with me. I'm not serious about my painting. It's a hobby."

"Psssh. You've got a natural talent that you should bloody well develop. You are going to that party." This last is said with conviction, revealing a steely personality.

"But I haven't got anything to wear. I can't spend money on clothes I'll never wear again."

Eadie doesn't say a word. Edging her bum forwards on the seat, she pushes herself to her feet, her hands then transferring from the arms of the chair to the canes propped on either side. "Come with me."

Jennie gives Eadie a head start before also getting to her feet. Even taking her time it isn't long before she catches up. An eternity of frail movements later, they're standing next to a large carved chest that sits squatly at the end of Eadie's bed.

"Open that for me, would you?" Eadie looks down at the Eastern landscape depicted on top of the wooden box.

Jennie kneels in front of it and lifts the creaking lid. The smell of moth balls is aggressive in its attack of Jennie's airways. Her lungs do their best to empty themselves of the noxious brew, coughing and hacking so badly that she's forced back onto her heels. Even Eadie's moved away.

"I used to love that outfit." In response to a confused look from Jennie, she adds “Slide that tray to the left. The dress I’m after is beneath it, wrapped in tissue.”

Jennie does as told and sure enough a securely wrapped parcel is revealed when she moves the tray. The paper is similar in appearance to Eadie’s skin. Parchment thin and with a lot of age spots. Surely whatever is in it will have long since disintegrated, never mind the damage inflicted by the plutonium-grade mothballs. With the package out, Jennie wastes no time in getting the lid of the chest back down. The smell of camphor subsides somewhat, but the air is anything but clear. Even moths out in the hallway should be getting nervous.

Eadie sits on her bed and pats the counterpane beside her. Jennie accepts the invitation, laying the package between them.

“Open it.”

Jennie folds the first layer of tissue back and is somewhat heartened to see the next layer is looking a little perkier, a little less spotty. The closer she gets to the contents, the better the quality of the paper. With the last layer peeled back, Jennie feels her eyes widen at the sparkling jewel that is revealed.

“It’s vintage Worth. Wore it to many a party when I was younger.”

“But …” the rest of the sentence dies. How do you explain to an octogenarian that you’re a foot taller than they are? And that if you wear their beloved dress you won’t even need to bend over to show your bits to the world?

“It was calf length on me and I used to be a good deal wider than I am now.” Eadie looks down at her chest with a *moue* of disgust. “Now I’m more in need of a belt with cups than a bra.”

“Oh, right.”

“Close the door, try it on.”

The silver and black twenties-style shift dress shimmies into place and Jennie is delighted to find that not only is it a perfect fit, the length is spot on too, finishing not too far above her knees. The beaded dress feels amazing, the weight of it clinging to her tall form.

"Look in the mirror."

"Wow." The dress is gorgeous, highlighting all the right places and – Jennie twirls for effect – none of the wrong.

"The coat I used to wear with it is hanging in the wardrobe."

Following instructions from Eadie, Jennie locates a beautiful black satin swing coat with a wide collar.

"Are you sure?"

"Absolutely. They're all yours."

"Thank you so much." Jennie removes the coat before folding Eadie into the gentlest embrace possible. She'd love to squeeze her tight but worries about breaking bones.

After Jennie pulls away, Eadie sneezes. "You might need to air it out."

"Just a bit." Jennie twirls and is again assailed by the smell of camphor. She lets her coughing subside before removing the dress with care not to snag any of the beads. There are a couple coming loose that she'll need to get Sam to look at. Jennie's folding it back in amongst the tissue when she remembers the other obstacle to her attending the party. "But I can't go on my own and Sam won't want to. It'll be the last weekend before Chris moves up to Crewe."

"What about Mark?"

"What about him?"

"He'd make a wonderful partner. Do him good to get out of the house without that floozie in tow."

"Good luck with that."

"This Saturday you say." At Jennie's unwilling nod, Eadie carries on. "By the way, what did Caroline think of the painting of Monroe?"

"She loved it. I think. Let's hope Mr Michaels does, too."

After helping Eadie back to her chair and getting her all set up with everything, Jennie collects the re-wrapped dress and the coat. She's leaving the sitting room when she spots the phone cable worming its way under the door. "Do you want me to put the phone back?"

"No, leave it there. I have some calls I need to make."

Both arms cradling her new clothes, Jennie heads up to her room. She's walking across the landing when Sam comes out of her sewing room, arms stretched high above her head and hands shaking.

"What the hell is that smell?" Sam drops her arms and sniffs at Jennie's package before pulling back sharply. "It reminds me of the old biddies in Melbourne."

"Hah, I'd forgotten about that." Jennie and Sam had been undecided as to whether the money smelled of moth balls because the old ladies didn't trust banks, or they were dodging the tax man. Either way, their money had reeked.

"What is it?"

"Nothing. Just a dress and coat that Eadie gave to me."

"C'mon, let's have a gander."

Jennie reluctantly follows Sam back into the sewing room, where she places the clothes on the end of the cutting table, causing a large moth to beat a hasty retreat from the nearby curtains. After the coat gets a general nod, Jennie opens the tissue and holds the dress up for Sam to see. She swings it backwards and forwards it to demonstrate the live nature of the material.

"That's incredible. Why'd she give it to you?"

"I've been invited to Mr Michael's birthday party this coming Saturday."

"You know what would go amazingly with it?" Not waiting for an answer, Sam skips out of the room. "My silver platforms," drifts back from the hallway. Sam is back with the shoes a minute later, holding them by the straps. She hands them over to Jennie.

"You don't have to do that. I don't even know if I'm going yet."

"Of course you are. Let's have a closer look at the dress. I think it needs mending in a few places."

"Honestly, you don't have to do that. I don't think I'm going."

"Of course you are." Sam spreads the dress out on the table and examines it minutely, tutting and pinning in turn. "Leave it with me. I need a break from that outfit I'm making for Colin Wells."

"The pug?" Jennie looks at the totally uninspiring beige vinyl that's half gobbled up by the sewing machine.

"Yeah. He reminds me a little of John-John but with a lot less slobber."

"Here's hoping you don't need to end up making a burial shroud for this one." Jennie shudders before continuing. "I've had a great idea for a painting of him. Do you reckon Mrs Wells would be interested?"

"What've you got in mind?"

"Warhol. Like his self-portrait. The one that's split into squares."

17

"Can someone pass me the marmalade, please?" Jennie looks hopefully down the table. It's unusual to have everyone at breakfast together, and being the last to arrive, she's stuck right at the end. It's far more common to eat your toast standing up while waiting for a second batch.

"Here you go." Chris picks the jar up from right in front of Mark and hands it to Sam to who hands it to Jennie.

No assistance has been forthcoming from Mark and Sonja's side of the table. Jennie scowls in Mark's direction without reaction. He and the Dalmatian seem to be in their usual state of pre- or maybe even post-coital foreplay. It makes her blood boil and it's not exactly conducive to eating either; although Eadie sitting at the other end of the table is oblivious.

"Jeez, you two, get a room."

Jennie's head snaps up from her clinical examination of her piece of jammy toast. Obviously Chris has no issues with saying something.

"Good. I'm glad I'm not the only one." Eadie demonstrates she's not as unaware as Jennie had thought.

Mark's face colours and he moves away from Sonja. She

follows him as though joined at the hip and other more reproductive areas. Mark retrieves her hand from his lap and puts it on the table, patting it into place.

Everyone's concentration breaks when they hear what sounds like a stack of mail being shoved through the slot in the front door. This is followed by a large crash. "Damn, I've been meaning to fix that basket." Mark stands, ostensibly to collect the mail, but Jennie wonders if it's also a way to distance himself from Sonja's roaming digits.

Swinging back through the kitchen door he appears to be holding a week's worth of mail. Everyone at the table receives something with the exception of Jennie. Even Sonja is holding a crisp, expensive-looking envelope. She looks mystified when she flips it over to read who it's from. Maybe she isn't faking that memory loss after all. "I do not know this person. Do I?" She hands the envelope to Mark, who's now dished out all the other mail.

"Not sure. Sam got one the same. Open it up."

Sam looks at her matching cream envelope. "I don't know who it's from either."

"You could both solve this by opening the blasted envelopes." Eadie's agog with anticipation and close to bouncing.

Sonja's blood-red talon is making short work of the seal on her envelope while Sam has resorted to a knife to open hers. They pull familiar, heavily embossed invitations out at the same time. "That's nice. Chris and I have been invited to David Michaels' party this Saturday night."

"We too have been invited." Sonja waves the invitation at Mark as he sits back down.

"We can all go together."

Sam isn't able to hide her grimace as she looks at Jennie. Sam's about as keen on Sonja as Jennie is.

"I haven't decided that I'm going yet."

"Of course you are. I've already RSVP-d for you." Eadie is smugness personified.

"Oh boy, I'm going to have to hurry to whip something up in time for this Saturday." Sam's eyes take on a faraway look as she goes about designing a new outfit in her head.

"You will buy me dress." Sonja emphasises this command by poking Mark in the chest with one of her bright-red letter openers.

Jennie's mouth pops opens. She expects Mark to react, but all he does is sling his arm around the back of Sonja's chair and give her a brief squeeze. This isn't confirmation enough for Sonja, who has a thorough rummage in the vicinity of his wallet, repeating "Promise," until Mark does so much to everyone else's relief.

Eadie's eyes are alight with excitement and taking a closer look at their landlady, Jennie wonders if this excitement isn't also laced with a dash of deviousness.

Leaving Mark and Sonja with the dishes – it's about time they pulled their weight around the place – Jennie helps Eadie into her sitting room before following the others upstairs. Chris is organising himself for his move north the following Sunday and Sam is sewing. Jennie's about to walk into her room when Sam calls out, causing a change in direction.

"It's all finished." Sam indicates the dress hanging from the picture rail that bisects the walls two-thirds of the way up. "I fixed those loose beads and strengthened all the seams. A couple were about to die."

"I don't want to go. The dress is beautiful and all, but you know how much I hate these things."

"But we'll all be there. It'll be fun."

Jennie retrieves the dress without further comment. Everyone else's idea of fun is her idea of hell. Events like this make her miss Steve and feel like a second-class citizen.

"I'm off to the Wells' place to deliver Colin's trench coat if you want to come. See if you can get another commission."

Any thoughts of her late fiancé and social ineptitude are promptly replaced by images of the small pug dressed in a beige vinyl trench coat. Even if she doesn't get a commission, it will be worth tagging along to see that alone.

"Sure, I'll hang this up, throw on some shoes and I'm good to go."

Ticket to Richmond in hand, Jennie clatters down the stairs ahead of Sam and onto the platform at Gunnersbury station. She automatically heads to the right and looks down the track to see if a train is on its way.

"Wrong side." Sam stands on the opposite side of the tarmacked expanse, occasionally looking in the other direction.

"I thought the Wells'd live in the same area as all the others. They slumming it?"

"The Green at Richmond is *not* slumming it."

The trip is a short one, with Richmond a mere two stops away. They travel high above the Thames on their way and despite looking long and hard; they're unable to spy the famous greenhouse at Kew Gardens. Ironically, there are too many trees in the way.

At Richmond, Sam strikes out confidently: she's been here before. A couple of wrong turns and she has to take a quick look at the A-Z. "All these streets look the same. If it wasn't for the pubs, how the hell would you know where you were?" She folds the corner of the page over and returns it to Jennie's handbag.

The Green is beautiful. "I see what you mean about not slumming it." Jennie stops and scans the wide expanse of grass spreading out on the other side of the road. The perimeter is an unbroken line of trees, protection from the sun during cricket matches and home to a multitude of squirrels.

"Here we are." Sam starts confidently up the path, and then stops so abruptly that Jennie comes close to walking into her. "Wrong colour door." Sam swings around and makes her way back to the pavement, shadowed by Jennie. Sam takes a small address book out of her handbag and flips through to the Ws. "Ah, twenty-seven, not seventeen."

Farther along the street, they find the right house, which proves to be identical to number twenty-seven, apart from the colour of the door. It's Georgian with large six-panel sash windows at regular intervals on every floor, while four dormers crowd the edge of the roof, like eyebrows.

No wonder Sam had mixed them up. Who'd have thought they'd have group housing in the 1800s? The gleaming scarlet front door is answered immediately, leading Jennie to suspect the lady of the house has been hovering in the hallway.

"Come in. I can't wait to see his coat."

Mrs Wells is fizzing with excitement, her hands clasped together to stop them fluttering. She's a fluttery type of woman, well-frilled in the clothing department, with the tones the only muted thing about the ensemble. Peach would be one of Jennie's least favourite colours and should, she felt, only be seen on fruit. On the plus side, it at least matches the tight curls scattered atop the woman's head.

Mrs Wells flutters alongside them into a front sitting room that she's indicated they should enter. Jennie looks at a bright-green cushion, covered in dog hair, sitting at one end of the heavily buttoned black leather couch that dominates the room. It's the largest couch she's seen outside of a hotel reception area.

"Colin's out for his walkies, with George, my husband. George loves all that fresh air. Out every morning. Rain, hail or shine."

Jennie and Sam haven't been perched on the edge of the couch for long before they hear the front door open. They also discern a lot of unclipped toenails on parquet flooring. Presumably Colin's.

A small, and surprisingly cute, pug thunders into the room ahead of George and makes straight for Mrs Wells. George is like an extra out of *It Ain't Half Hot Mum* and looks at home in his safari suit. All that's missing is a Pimms, a *punkawallah* and that short Welsh bloke with the great voice.

He drops the empty leash onto a sideboard and looks enquiringly at Jennie and Sam. Mrs Wells goes through the introductions, stumbling over Jennie's name. After it becomes obvious he wants to shake hands, both Sam and Jennie stand.

It's while her hand is pumped up and down, that Jennie gets a good whiff of the old man. Any fresh air he gets while out on his morning constitutional is cancelled out by all the cigarettes. He smells reminiscent of an ashtray that's a week overdue for cleaning. His wife makes no reaction when he dutifully kisses her on both cheeks. Mrs Wells is either a hay fever sufferer or so used to the aroma that she no longer notices.

Greetings over, he leaves them to it, muttering something about looking at his hedges. More likely his Benson & Hedges thinks Jennie with an inconspicuous chuckle to herself.

The small black pug is still bouncing. It's like watching a superball lose momentum, with each *boing* a little lower than the one before. He finally subsides; Sam pounces on him and the porridge-coloured trench coat is buckled up minutes later. A silver-haired pug wouldn't have been able to pull it off, but the beige coat looks good on Colin, especially with its duck-egg blue satin lining.

Colin's mummy is bubbling with excitement. Jennie never thought she'd see a woman in her seventies squealing, but never say never. Sam ignores it and gets on with taking some Polaroids to keep on file. After flapping one to develop it, she shows it to Mrs Wells. The woman clasps the Polaroid to her chest as though it's on a par with some of the modernist paintings Jennie has seen dotted around the walls. The Mondrian is easy to spot and Jennie's sure that's a Braque above the grand piano.

"May I keep this?" Mrs Wells pulls the photo away from her chest to look again, even going so far as to kiss the bottom of it.

"Of course you can. But you should get Jennie to paint a portrait of him."

Mrs Wells looks up from the photo. "A portrait." She looks at Jennie, focussing on her properly for the first time during the visit.

"Yes, that's right." Jennie delves into the side pocket of her handbag and pulls out photos of Peanut the Chihuahua as *Venus Rising* and Quincy as Gainsborough's *Blue Boy*. She doesn't show the Polaroid of Monroe's portrait to Mrs Wells as it doesn't show up well in photos.

"You painted this?" Mrs Wells holds up the photo of Quincy's portrait. When Jennie nods, she continues. "I asked the Countess who'd painted it, but she wouldn't tell me. Kept trying to get me to commission her nephew." The woman's lip is curled so tightly, Jennie and Sam burst out laughing. It's not long before Mrs Wells joins in.

"I saw the Polaroid of Colin in his file and I thought perhaps he'd look good painted in the style of Andy Warhol's self-portrait. A grid, with each image in a different colour."

"Yes." Mrs Wells' initial response is decidedly tepid but after a few moments looking at Colin, now comfortable on his green cushion, then up at some of the art on the walls, it warms up. "Yes, you're right. It would look perfect above my desk."

18

The tube is pulling into Kew Station on their way home from Richmond before conversation starts up again. Jennie has been working out her weekly takings, based on the number of weeks they've been in London and how much she's already been paid. Forgetting the portrait of Quincy that Lady Harrow hadn't offered to pay for, it works out to around seventy-five pounds a week. That's more than enough to live on with Eadie yet to charge them any rent. Even paying for the utilities has had them close to blows, but since getting her bank account number from Mark, they'd been depositing money every week without saying anything.

The only thing Eadie hadn't argued about was the housework and a roster had been drawn up with each of them taking turns at the manky task of cleaning the toilets. The only areas not on the roster are Eadie's sitting room, bedroom and bathroom because she has a char. Flo comes twice weekly and helps Eadie with her shower while she's there. When this phantom visits is anyone's guess because none of the others have ever seen her.

"Are you okay if we go through to Shepherd's Bush?" says

Sam, "I want to go to the market and get some fabric for my dress. For Saturday."

"Yeah, sure. Do you know where it is?"

"Yep, Eadie gave me directions to a place. I need to check it out for Doggs' Toggs anyway. Has to be closer than the current shop."

"I wonder what Sonja will wear? I still can't believe she ordered Mark to buy her a dress like that." Jennie knows her lip is curling *à la* Mrs Wells but is unable to stop it. She'd never treat a guy like that. It makes her feel sorry for Mark. Almost.

"Yeah, looks as though she knows about the trust fund, all right."

Their conversation halts when the conductor walks through the train. It amazes Jennie that they can tell who's new on the train and who already has a ticket. Never hesitating when approaching new passengers ready to hand out tickets and snap change out of their coin holder.

After transferring at Hammersmith, the girls arrive at Shepherds Bush Market in reasonably short order. It's an odd mix of complete tat and some good buys. There's even a vintage clothing shop with a green and black dress in the window that stops Jennie in her tracks. Sam keeps walking. "Sam, you've gotta see this."

Sam executes a neat turn and makes her way back. "See what?"

Jennie points at the tiny front window of the shop, where the dress hangs forlornly on a bent and battered, thin metal dry cleaner's hanger. Even in the dim of the market, the dress exudes style.

"Wow." Sam walks up to the window, her face so close the glass clouds. A second later a buzzer announces their arrival.

"Can I please have a closer look at the dress in the window?"

The West Indian woman behind the counter beams at

them. "It's a gorgeous dress that one." The strong Cockney accent makes Jennie shake her head to clear her ears. That can't be right. Jennie had been expecting the singsong tones more common to the West Indians living in London. This is pure Bow Bells.

Sliding off the bar stool she's perched on, the woman sashays from behind the counter and over to the front window. It only takes a couple of steps to accomplish this although she has to squeeze past Jennie and Sam to do so. She unhooks the hanger using a broom handle with a nail in the end and swings it over to Sam to remove. Sam holds up the dress, looking at it from every angle, checking the brocade fabric, checking the zip, checking the large bow on the front.

"Can I try it on?" Sam is looking around the shop for a changing room.

"Sure you can." Using the same broom handle, the woman slides a curtain across the front window and door. "There you go."

Jennie can't stop a gurgle of laughter. The curtain has turned the whole shop into a changing room, making it incredibly claustrophobic in the process. Sam shrugs, hands Jennie her handbag and starts stripping. When it comes to zipping up the dress, Sam turns her back to the shop owner in an unspoken plea for assistance. Jennie doesn't have any free hands and there's no floor space to put their bags down.

"How does it look?" Sam runs her hands down the sides of the dress and attempts to look down, then behind herself to get a feeling for the fit.

"Amazing," says Jennie.

"Here you go." The owner plunges a hand into the middle of the only rail of clothes in the store and, like a magic trick, produces a full-length mirror. She holds it up so Sam can see herself.

"Wow." Sam looks at the front, twists side on one way, then

the other. "What's the back look like?"

"Even better than the front," says Jennie.

"Use the hand mirror beside the cash register," says the owner, nodding toward the museum piece that takes up most of the counter.

Sam looks away from the full-length mirror and swings the hand mirror up so she can see for herself. "Wow."

Despite it being summer, Jennie knows it can get cool in the evenings, prompting her to ask, "Do you have any coats that'd go with it?"

"Good point. Do you?" Sam stops twirling long enough to look at the shop owner.

By the time Jennie and Sam have looked at every coat the woman has flicked their way, the counter is close to buckling under the weight. Sam holds up a dark pewter-grey silk coat that's decidedly flapper in style. "You know what?"

"What?" Jennie peers at the coat in the gloom before pulling the curtain to one side so she can have a closer look at it.

"This'd go perfectly with your dress and ..."

"and you could wear the black coat," says Jennie, finishing Sam's sentence before dropping all the bags she's holding onto their feet, grabbing the coat and putting it on.

"Brilliant," they say in unison before bursting into laughter. The shop owner looks from one to the other before shaking her head in amusement.

Once they sit down on the tube for the trip home, Sam immediately opens the top of the large paper bag and looks at the dress. "I feel bad that it was so cheap. Sure, I'll have to replace the zip, but, wow."

"It was made for you. And I love the coat."

Sam is still uttering the occasional "Wow" when they unlock the front door.

"Yoo-hoo!" is warbled at them from the sitting room.

Neither of them resents time spent with Eadie. Apart from being a first-class old lady, there's the whole rent-free thing going on.

"So, what have you girls been up to?" Eadie's eyes are sparkling with anticipation as she looks first at Jennie, then Sam.

"We went to see Mrs Wells out at Richmond to deliver Colin's trench coat. Jennie's been commissioned to paint a portrait of him."

"And then we went to Shepherd's Bush and Sam got an amazing dress."

"You did? Let's see it."

Sam drags the dress from the large, brown bag and gives it a good shake in an attempt to get rid of some of the wrinkles. Even so, it looks tired. "It needs some work and a wash, but I think it'll look gorgeous."

Sam drapes it softly over Eadie's lap so the old lady can have a closer look. An arthritic hand strokes the fabric and lifts the large bow sewn under the bodice. "Looks to be designer."

Seeing Eadie attempting to open the dress up to check for labels, Sam retrieves the frock. "Here, let's see if there are any labels. I didn't see any when I was trying it on in the shop but after she'd pulled the curtains, it was fairly dim." Sam unzips the dress and flips it inside out before placing it back in Eadie's lap.

"I thought so." Eadie points to a label in the back of the dress, hardly visible due to age and vintage sweat. "Dior. Very dirty Dior."

"No wonder it looks so amazing on." Jennie is fashion savvy enough to know that designer always looks better. It's all down to the quality of the fabrics and the cut. "Look at what else we got." Jennie retrieves a matching paper bag from her backpack, unrolls the top and pulls out the dark pewter coat. Shaking it, she holds it up for Eadie's appraisal. Jennie's relieved to see the coat is clean; washing it would have been a nightmare, especially with the embroidery.

"Oh Jennie, that's beautiful. It would look lovely with the beaded dress. You should let Sam wear the black one."

"Are you sure?" Jennie feels mortified that Eadie has solved this issue without them even bringing it up.

The raising of one grey eyebrow is answer enough.

"I'm gonna have to wash the dress pronto." Sam picks it up from Eadie's lap, using her thumb and forefinger. "If I'd seen how filthy it was in the shop, I wouldn't have bought it."

"Soap and water will fix that. Perhaps you should wash it this afternoon, so you know what you're dealing with."

When Sam exits in search of cool water and lots and lots of washing powder; Charlie wanders in looking for company.

"What style are you going for with Flouncy's boy?"

"Who?" Jennie absently tugs on Charlie's ear as he rubs himself against her shin.

"Hah, sorry. Francis Wells. We called her Flouncy when we were all debs together. So many ruffles on her dress that she looked like a flamenco-dancing sea anemone."

"She was very flouncy." At Eadie's questioning look, Jennie is prompted to continue. "Oh, right. I'm thinking of painting Colin in the style of Warhol's self-portrait, with lots of different colour-ways."

Jennie stays with Eadie a while longer discussing options for the portrait, until Jennie is firm in her mind as to how to start. She tops up Eadie's glass before leaving her in Charlie's company. Jennie had been concerned when Charlie jumped up onto the arm of Eadie's chair but the big bruiser seemed to know he couldn't drop onto that particular lap, instead contenting himself with staying on the arm.

19

"Why are we eating so much?" Jennie looks at the formal dining table, groaning under the weight of a large roast lunch with all the trimmings.

"Because the Michaels have a bad habit of under-catering." Eadie spears another pre-cut, ladylike-sized piece of beef, swirls it through some gravy and pops it into her mouth.

"This Yorkshire pud is amazing." Mark manages to get a whole one in his mouth. The meat juices running down his chin make him look like a well-done Dracula.

By the time all the serving platters have been emptied, there's a lot of groaning around the table and a few belts have to be undone. The only person who doesn't seem to have stuffed themselves silly is Sonja.

"Was there something wrong with the food, dear?" Eadie looks at Sonja, who's sitting to her left.

"It was nice. My dress though, it is ... ah ..."

"Skin tight," says Jennie, under her breath to Sam.

"A couple of sizes too small," says Sam, meaning Jennie has to slap her hand over her mouth.

"Fitted," says Eadie, glaring at both Jennie and Sam.

"Yes, fitted." Sonja looks at them, confused as to what they're finding so funny.

"Mark, would you be a dear and get me that box of chocolates off the sideboard, please?"

He groans before getting to his feet, pausing to do up his belt, and then retrieving the box. He places it next to Eadie where Jennie can see the Cadbury logo. She's so full, even the thought of chocolate makes her nauseous.

Eadie manages to get the top off the box with some difficulty then folds the dark purple paper back to reveal the glistening chocolates nestled in their individual paper cases. She holds it out to Sonja. The box is trembling alarmingly by the time Sonja takes two and pops them both into her mouth. Jennie tries in vain to rid herself of the image of a couple of chocolate-shaped lumps sticking out of the gut region of Sonja's fitted dress. Like twin outie bellybuttons.

Eadie swings the box to her right to offer them to Sam but her grip isn't up to the task and the box falls drunkenly to the floor, chocolates scattering far and wide onto the dusty carpet. Charlie is on them with impressive speed given he'd been deep asleep when they hit the ground. He sniffs a few, gives Eadie a funny look and then stalks back to his spot on the chaise longue in the corner. He's asleep again with equally impressive speed, leaving Sam to retrieve the ruined chocolates.

Because Jennie, Sam and Chris had cooked lunch, they leave Sonja and Mark with a mountain of dishes to work their way through. Chris will spend the afternoon sorting through everything he'll be taking north with him on Monday. Jennie and Sam will primp and preen, hoping to give Sonja and her *fitted* dress a good run for their money.

After Sam finishes doing her make-up for her, Jennie looks in the mirror and hardly recognises herself. Her skin looks smoother, her eyes bigger and her lips fuller. Sam has even managed to beat Jennie's curls into submission, so they don't look like a freak electrical experiment gone wrong. "Oh Sam, that's ..." Unable to find the right words, Jennie hugs Sam firmly. "Thank you."

"No worries. I'll grab Eadie's coat and finish getting ready in my room."

The door clicks closed behind Sam and Jennie looks at the silver beaded dress lying on her bed. Even having everything perfect doesn't make her feel any better prepared for the evening ahead. She's never been a social animal and after a couple of disastrous evenings in Melbourne, she's less assured than ever. If she's lucky, her outfit will show itself to have the properties of chainmail and protect her from social hurt.

When dressed, she does feel better. Certainly she's never scrubbed up this well before, although the glamorous clothes make her even more of a stranger to herself. She double checks the contents of her small evening bag, does up every button on the coat and squares her shoulders before leaving her room.

Jennie walks into the sitting room to find Eadie seated in her usual spot. Jennie has to undo all the coat buttons, take it off and give Eadie a twirl before putting everything back as it was. Even though it's still early, Eadie is rugged up from head to toe in a winter-weight dressing gown.

Chris and Sam arrive next. Sam's coat is also buttoned tight, meaning she too has to go through the rigmarole of taking it off so Eadie can look at the dress underneath. The coat drops from Sam's shoulders and both Eadie and Jennie squeal, "It's turquoise!"

"I had to wash it three times."

Jennie can't help but look at her watch again.

Chris too is looking at his watch. "We'll be late if we don't leave soon."

"Do you want to see where they are?" Sam rests her hand on the sleeve of his tuxedo. "Our shoes aren't up to a quick trip."

They hear him hurtle up to the first landing before yelling Mark's name a couple of times. They hear him take on another flight, the calling of Mark's name getting fainter all the time. Waiting, Jennie is aware of twitching, her watch constantly turned toward her face. It's a good five minutes before he's back with Mark in tow

"Where's Sonja," says Sam.

"Suffering from a ripping dose of Montezuma's Revenge," says Mark.

"That's no good," says Eadie, her face suspiciously bereft of any expression.

"Yeah, she's running out of ammo, but isn't in any state to go out. Wants me to go though," says Mark, explaining his suit.

"Off you go then, have a lovely time." Eadie beams at them all in turn, smiling brightly in Mark's direction.

"You should come with us, now we're short one," says Mark.

"I couldn't."

"Why not?" is chorused by all.

"Well, I suppose."

"Come on, let me help you get ready." Jennie stands next to Eadie, her arm held out for support. Once in the bedroom, Jennie helps the old lady sit on the side of her bed before going over to the wardrobe and throwing the doors wide. "What would you like to wear?"

"What about this?"

"What about what?" Jennie turns toward Eadie. Any other words fail her. The old lady has pushed her dressing gown back to reveal she's already dressed for the evening.

"If you could hand me that pair of cream pumps."

Aware her mouth is open, Jennie walks across the room with the requested shoes. "But how did you—"

"And if you could get my pearls off the dressing table."

"But how ...?"

When Eadie pastes on a look of innocence, Jennie blurts out, "The chocolates!"

"I think we've got time for a quick sherry, don't you?" Eadie nods toward her bedside table. "Can't go back out there too soon."

Filling glasses for both of them and then taking a good belt of her own, Jennie pops her head out the bedroom door. "Won't be too much longer." She moves around the room, opening and closing doors and drawers while sipping her sherry.

"Right, let's go." Eadie puts down her empty glass on the bedside table and struggles to her feet.

Jennie sculls the rest of her glass and pops it down next to Eadie's.

"Oh, and my evening purse." Eadie points toward a small ivory-satin bag sitting ready on the trunk at the end of her bed.

Getting out of the black cab at the Michaels' house is like rebirth. It had been a squeeze fitting the five of them in with a lot of care taken not to squish Eadie for fear of popping a hip, or worse.

Staying inside, Mark helps Eadie out and into the care of Chris, who supports the old lady as she steps down from the cab. Even though Chris is gentle, Jennie is worried to see a brief flicker of pain mar Eadie's otherwise serene face. Hard to believe the mischief the old lady had been up to earlier in the day.

Mark pays for the cab and they regroup, prepared to enter what Jennie now thinks of as the cake house. She hears, "Bloody blancmange," float up from next to her, confirming

Eadie's obviously not keen on the architectural style of the place either.

Compensating for Eadie's walking pace, extra slow because she refused to bring her canes, the trip up the front path to the house is sluggish. At the top step, Jennie looks back to see there's a retinue building up behind them. Some of its members' eyes are rolling so violently at the hold-up that they look like starters for the Grand National. Their aristocratic, horsey features only help with this impression.

Safely inside the entrance, invitations and coats are handed over for checking and safe keeping. The horsey crowd swirl around them, unable to wait any longer. Eager to get at the free food and wine.

Dropping her coat from her shoulders, Jennie hears a sharp intake of breath from behind her and is unable to stop turning to see what's going on. She's heard the saying of someone's eyes being out like organ stops, but this is the first time she's seen it in action. If she had a hanky, she'd be tempted to wipe away the imaginary drool collecting on Mark's bottom lip.

"What?"

"Nothing." Mark looks annoyed at having been caught out, giving Jennie the satisfaction of knowing she's not the only one who doesn't have full control of their feelings

"Come on, Eadie, let's find you somewhere comfy to sit." Jennie holds her arm out at her side offering it as a support that is gratefully accepted.

Walking into the front room, Jennie's conscious of blocking Eadie from any jostling. She's relieved to see Mark has stepped in on the other side. Between them, they cleave a path through the bejewelled guests, heading toward a large chair with a stupidly tall back sitting next to a white plastic, pedestal table. The chair is upholstered in white with a multitude of silver studs highlighting every edge of every plane. It's not until Jennie hears the breath expelled forcefully out of Eadie's lungs that Jennie examines the chair more closely. What she'd taken for leather appears to be man-made. Very shiny, very white, unforgiving plastic and not actually padded at all.

"Can I get you something to drink?" Jennie crouches down next to Eadie to match head heights but when she feels the back of her dress give, she promptly stands, her hand straying to check she's not flashing her knickers to the world. She's sure it feels different. "Eadie, is the back of the dress okay?" Nervously, Jennie turns her back so Eadie can check it.

The strangled sound she hears doesn't give Jennie any confidence and she edges her way around the back of the chair and up against the wall. It's then she realises Eadie is oblivious, looking straight ahead, her posture rigid. Jennie tries to work out who, what or why Eadie is so alarmed, but it's impossible when faced with a sea of people, all sporting a homogenous Kensington sense of style.

Jennie scans the crowd looking for Sam. Neither she nor Chris is in sight, only Mark. "Damn!"

"Mark," Jennie hisses in his direction, in vain. "Mark." Jennie calls as loudly as she dares and is rewarded when he looks away from the filly he's chatting to and over at her. He looks at her in query but doesn't move, forcing her to beckon desperately. His exhalation is easy to spot but he excuses himself from his conversation and moves over to her side.

"What?"

"I need help." Jennie's aware her jaw is locked so tightly that her words are forced out through her teeth like a ventriloquist. Not waiting for him to confirm he'll help, she pushes on. "Can you please check the back of my dress? I think I might have ripped it."

"Turn around," says Mark, his tone resigned.

With him effectively blocking her from the rest of the room, Jennie turns. The "Nice undies," from Mark sees her swing back and press hard against the wall.

"Oh no, you have got to be kidding me." The extra air she gulps in is making her dizzy.

"Of course I am." He waits until he sees Jennie relaxing, before adding, "Or maybe not." Mark wiggles his eyebrows before making his way back to the woman who's been glaring at Jennie for stealing Mark away from her.

By the time Jennie realises that she still doesn't know if he's teasing or not, he's out of handbag range. She fingers the back of the dress again. She's sure she can feel an opening in the seam. She won't be happy until someone else has had a chance to have a proper look at the dress. She's only just wedged herself between the wall and Eadie's chair when Eadie struggles out of the chair and walks away.

Without her canes, Eadie's gait is wobbly and her grasp on remaining vertical tenuous at best. Normally, Jennie would be the first to offer assistance but the thought of her pink undies peering out the back of her torn dress glues her to the spot.

Feeling marooned and ridiculous jammed in behind the chair on her own, she knows she looks silly because of how hard Mark is laughing; his companion turns to see what all the hilarity is about. The woman's forehead creases so heavily that she's more pug-like than is common amongst the Kensington set.

Jennie desperately scans the crowd, looking for Sam. Even on tiptoes, she's unable to see any sign of her friend. The only thing for it is to get her coat back; it's satin and so she won't look out of place wearing it. Certainly a few other women are sporting coats of a similar style.

Hurrying across the room with her hands crossed behind her, her posture ramrod straight, Jennie hears her name called. Pretending not to hear it, she keeps walking toward the door but has to stop when she feels a hand on her back. Looking over her shoulder she sees it's Mark who has stopped her. "Jennie, Caroline Michaels would like a word." His face is creased in a smile that borders on manic.

Keeping her hands in place, Jennie turns to face their hostess. "Oh, hello, Mrs Michaels, sorry, I didn't hear you."

"Come, Jennie, I'm about to give David the painting."

Inwardly groaning, Jennie has no option but to follow Caroline Michaels to stand in front of the fireplace, which is filled to overflowing courtesy of a large vase of dark red roses. David Michaels is waiting there.

Caroline Michaels claps her hands. "Excuse me! Can I please have everyone's attention?"

It's no longer Jennie's imagination that every eye in the room is on her. It's a fact. She presses her crossed hands in tighter against the back of her dress and hopes she can stay where she is until this hell is over.

"First of all, thank you, everyone, for coming along and sharing our special evening. As you'll know, David's reached an important *milestone*." This proclamation from Mrs Michaels is met with titters from around the room and a groan from David. Mrs Michaels hands the ostentatiously wrapped present to David, then gives him a quick peck on the cheek.

"Thank you, there's nothing like celebrating impending old age with friends and family." David Michaels' tone is wry. At several prompts of "Open it", he works away at the large black bow, handing it to Jennie, forcing her to move a hand from behind her. He hands her the wrapping paper and a mountain of tissue paper, compelling her to use both hands to hold everything. She steps back until she trips over the hearth, causing David Michaels to look away from the painting momentarily.

Seeing him peering at the painting makes Jennie forget her ruined dress. She hopes to hell he likes it, because if he doesn't, she can kiss goodbye to any more commissions. These people were like lemmings when it came to what was 'in' and what was 'out'. Holding the painting at arm's length, David continues to examine it.

"Thank you, darling." He holds onto the painting with one hand and awkwardly hugs his wife with the other before swinging in Jennie's direction taking her by surprise.

"You did this?"

"Yes?" Jennie wishes she had a free hand to wipe at the perspiration forming on her top lip like a shonky fake moustache.

"It's very good." At the calls for him to let others have a look, he swings the painting around and places it on the mantle behind them. The crowd hurries in and Jennie feels like she's in the middle of an upmarket game of bull-rush.

Pushing Jennie to one side to avoid her being bowled over, David Michaels asks, "Where are you exhibiting?"

"I'm not," stammers Jennie, all the time trying to keep her back to the room. This is made difficult when she has to dodge a small occasional table. Without a free hand, it's impossible for her to cover any draughty bits in her dress.

"Here, let's get rid of that." David Michaels relieves Jennie of discarded ribbons and wrapping paper, screwing them all into a tight ball and dropping them on the ground behind them. Jennie immediately crosses her hands behind her. "I've seen a few of your paintings now. You're wasting your time on the chocolate box tat that most of these old toadies want." His voice drops as he finishes this sentiment, but even so a couple of matrons look sharply at him.

Jennie is torn between being outraged at having her work described as chocolate box tat and agreeing with him because deep down she knows he's right. "It pays the bills."

"Yes, well," he says, before adding quietly, "I've been known to flog the odd monstrosity myself."

Jennie can't help but like David Michaels and his disconcerting honesty.

Once she's promised she'll visit him at his gallery, she manages to escape to the reception area, almost crying with relief when she gets her coat on. Suitably covered, she goes in search of Sam and Chris, tracking them down on the dance floor. When a waiter walks up with a tray of champagne, Jennie takes a glass and downs half of it before he has time to move off.

"Bad night?" he says.

In answer, Jennie finishes the glass, puts it back and collects two more.

20

Jennie makes quick work of the second glass of champagne, placing the empty on the tray of another passing waiter. With the edge of her distress softened, she sips a third, enjoying the buzz created by the previous two. After watching Sam and Chris dancing for a minute or two, she moves on, not wanting to look like a wallflower.

She spots Eadie sitting on an unforgiving leather couch. Jennie starts toward her when she realises Eadie is deep in what looks like a heated conversation with the old gent sitting next to her. Jennie veers off into another room, realises she's finished her third glass and remedies this next time a waiter passes. The Michaels might not provide a lot of food, but Jennie's never seen so much champagne in her life.

She's standing out of the flow of foot traffic, watching life pass her by when she becomes aware of a conversation taking place on the other side of the pillar.

"It's complete rubbish, of course." The voice is plummy English schoolboy, full of spite and jealousy. "Someone, as talented as I, can see that."

With nothing better to do, Jennie relaxes against the pillar and settles in to eavesdrop. Her body tenses up at the next slice of spleen. "Anyone with a tub of Polyfilla could have come up with that garbage. I can't believe she's so full of herself."

Jennie leans back to take a peek around the pillar and falls off Sam's borrowed platforms. The man holding court sees her and clams up, leaving Jennie in no doubt that she's the subject of the conversation. His audience has the decency to colour and disband, leaving her tormentor on his own.

Any hope of Jennie's that he'll leave too, is crushed. "You'll never make a go of it. I'll ruin you. Your stuff is rubbish."

Jennie moves away from him, the venom in his voice and his spittle-foamed mouth. Unable to deal with the open hate on the guy's face, she pushes through the nearest doorway, desperate to get away before the threatening tears make an appearance. She's relieved to see she's in a deserted back hallway. Not much chance of anyone coming in here. It's not meant for public viewing with the paint on the walls peeling in places and the floor carpeted in an ugly floral explosion.

Jennie walks to the end of the hallway where a staircase disappears toward what must be the cellar. Checking the ground, she sits gingerly on the top step and surrenders to the tears.

Why on earth has he got it in for me for? How can someone I don't even know hate me so much?

Jennie jumps when she feels the floorboards under her creaking. She hadn't even been aware of anyone walking into the hallway.

"The dress is fine, you know," says Mark, standing behind her.

Oh great, just what I need.

"Thanks," mumbles Jennie, deliberately keeping her back to him. Although any chance of avoiding him is quashed when Mark plonks himself down on the step next to her. He slings his arm around her shoulder and she shrinks away from contact with him, but this only makes him hug her tighter and she's unable to stop the tears flowing in earnest. She hiccoughs to a stop. "It wasn't that. It was ..."

"Yes."

"Some guy was really mean to me. About my painting of Monroe."

"If you mean the pudgy Hooray Henry with the missing chin, I wouldn't worry too much."

"Hooray Henry?"

"A jumped-up English twat who wouldn't know a proper day's work if it bit him on the arse."

Jennie can't help a small teary burst of laughter. "But he said he'd ruin me."

"Are you serious? You know who he is, don't you?" At the shake of her head, he carries on. "Rupert Smythe-Brown, Bunty Harrow's nephew."

"But he's a talentless git."

"With no chin."

Jennie giggles again before taking the crumpled serviette Mark hands her. She dabs under her eyes trying not to smear her mascara too much. It's waterproof but not bulletproof. Mark helps her to her feet and they leave the hallway through a different door from the one Jennie used before. This takes them into the kitchen.

None of the uniformed staff pays them the least attention as they zigzag their way through and out the other side. They're now in a reception room Jennie hasn't visited before. She's relieved to see Chris and Sam sitting side by side on a couch set in the wide bay window.

"Are you leaving?" Sam gestures toward Jennie's coat.

"What? Oh, no." Jennie turns and punches Mark in the arm.

"Ow, what the hell was that for?"

"For you making me thinking my bum was hanging out the back of my dress."

Mark rubs absently at this arm. "Mightn't be a bad idea if we leave now. Eadie's all done in. Been arguing with Wallace Smythe-Brown most of the evening."

"Smythe-Brown?" Jennie's swings in his direction.

"Father."

"Chinless?"

"Chinless," confirms Mark.

Sam and Chris look on with interest at this verbal shorthand.

"Long story," says Jennie.

Jennie throws the bedspread back the following morning, getting a pissed-off and muffled *miaow* from Charlie for her efforts. "Sorry, can't sleep." She uncovers him before dragging on her dressing gown. The bedside clock shows it's still far too early for anyone other than Eadie to be up and about.

Jennie's head thumps in time to her heartbeat as she walks down the stairs in search of dry toast. She'd only had four glasses of champagne but, coupled with a sleepless night, she feels as if she's been on a real bender.

Walking across the sitting room to Eadie's bedroom, confirms that Eadie is already awake. Otherwise, she would have been able to hear snoring by now.

"Good morning, hope you slept well." Jennie tries hard to sprinkle her voice with enthusiasm.

"Oh, I hardly ever sleep." Eadie is propped up in bed with a mountain of pillows behind her. "I could kill a cup of tea."

"Toast, too?"

"That'd be lovely. Marmalade, please."

Order confirmed Jennie makes her way back to the sitting

room, down the hall and into the kitchen. She's surprised to find Mark already there, hunched over the table, his back to her. His hair is styled like a toilet brush and he's wearing a worryingly short, ugly, mustard towelling bathrobe that she's been lucky enough to never have seen before.

"Morning."

Rather than reply, he waves his hand sloppily in the air without turning. Jennie watches as he takes a tentative sip of coffee, the aroma of which fills the kitchen. She's banging around setting a tray for Eadie and herself, when she sees Mark put his hands over his ears. Strange, he'd been reasonably sober on the way home.

Leaning against the counter waiting for the second round of toast to pop, she says, "Why are you hungover?"

When there's no reaction from him, she asks again, slightly louder.

"Huh? Oh, had a couple of snorts when I got home."

"How's Sonja feeling this morning?" Jennie wouldn't like to think Eadie had done any lasting damage to the girl, courtesy of the dodgy chocolates.

"Fine. She was feeling okay when we got in last night."

"Memory back?"

"The odd snatch." Mark snorts at some personal joke before taking another, larger, sip of his coffee.

The toast pops and Jennie swings into action completing the laying of the tray. It weighs a ton and the full pot of tea only adds to this. She manoeuvres her way backwards out of the kitchen, before turning and making her way through to Eadie's bedroom.

With Eadie set up with her tea and toast, Jennie drags the dressing table chair across to the blanket box and takes a seat, ready to eat her breakfast. Her first bite of toast is safely in her mouth when Eadie's comment stops her chewing; the toast sits forgotten in her mouth.

"We need to plan on how we're going to kibosh that little toerag, Rupert Smythe-Brown."

"How do you know about that?" As far as Jennie is aware, Mark's the only one to be aware of the incident last night. The little old lady borders on the psychic at times.

"We need to take him seriously. If he's anything like that pillock, his father, he'll fight dirty."

"But why?"

"Because by painting a decent portrait of Quincy, you've made him a laughing stock."

"Oh." Jennie once again becomes aware of the piece of toast in her hand, puts it down on the plate and licks the butter that has pooled in her palm.

"But does it even matter? I'm as happy sticking to the dog paintings. That's not going to bother him, is it?

Jennie hopes to hell Eadie answers no. She's still not sure she can handle painting anything more emotionally challenging than her doggie stuff. Even the Monroe piece had been a trial, with Steve's eyes staring out at her from the painting on more than one occasion.

"Of course it'll bother him. Again, if Rupert is anything like his jackass of a father, he'll be vindictive and petty. He'll take it as a personal affront if you doodle something halfway decent on a used serviette."

"Oh," says Jennie, before taking a sip of her rapidly cooling tea, which she then has trouble swallowing.

"Yes, 'oh'. I don't think your Steve would have wanted you to give up art on his account."

This comment comes out of nowhere and Jennie puts her cup back down on the saucer with enough force that she may as well have simply dropped it. She's filling her lungs to respond when Eadie holds her hand up to silence her.

"I know you don't want to talk about it, but promise me you'll at least think about it. That piece you did of Monroe is the first thing I've seen you complete that's actually got some heart and soul in it. Your other pieces have been technically competent, but a little lacking. You have to stop burying that part of yourself if you want to have a career in art."

"A career?" says Jennie, packing up the tray in readiness to make her escape.

"Yes. A career. David Michaels spoke highly of that painting of yours."

"I thought he was simply being polite."

"On the contrary, he thinks you've got a bright future in front of you. But that means you need to start working on non-commissioned pieces. Hold on the pooches."

"But what about Chinless, won't he poison everyone against me?"

"Yes, but only if you sign them."

21

A sob escapes sam's tightly pressed lips prompting Jennie to drape an arm over her friend's shoulder and pulls her in close. "You'll be seeing him soon."

"I know, but we've only just found each other again."

They stand on the pavement until the cab taking Chris to the station, turns at the end of the street.

"He'll be back on Friday night." Jennie squeezes Sam harder, before releasing her. "The week'll pass quickly."

"I suppose."

With Sam soothed and safely tucked behind her sewing machine, Jennie readies herself for another day at the easel, the plan being to make serious headway on her Warhol-inspired portrait of Colin Wells. Jennie's using its completion as an excuse not to deal with the whole Rupert-serious-painting issue. Surely he can't be as big a jerk as Eadie is making out.

Taking her earmuffs off the door handle of her bedroom, she slaps them on before heading up to her studio. She's glad she's taken this precaution when she realises the whole top floor is shaking. After running the coital gauntlet, she jams her flip-flops under the door ensuring she's left in peace for the morning. A rubbery 'Do Not Disturb' sign of sorts.

She tries concentrating on the painting of Colin, but it's made difficult by thoughts of Mark and Sonja not so far away. Worse than that, if she stands still, she's aware of movement in the floorboards.

"Animals!" she yells, followed by, "Did I say that out loud?"

She doesn't need these distractions and needs to work hard on the painting for a good few days to make progress. Because of the grid nature of the portrait, it's more like nine little portraits and that's a lot of work.

Jennie jumps, nearly sending the easel toppling when a broken flip-flop is held right under her nose. It's damn near ripped in half. Jennie spins around to face an irate Mark.

"You broke them! You could have knocked."

She's glaring back at him, when he yanks her earmuffs off and flings them in the general direction of the bed. "I did bloody knock. And I don't appreciate being called an animal either." He signals an end to their discussion by slamming the door hard behind him.

"Hey, if the collar fits!" Jennie screams after him, before running at the door and throwing her whole weight against it, only managing to hold it closed when he tries to get back in. Fuelled by indignation and adrenalin, Jennie withstands the onslaught, even risking a yelled, "Go and take a cold shower."

She hears him stomp down the stairs and realises her heart is thumping, loud and strong, in her chest and her arm and leg muscles are hurting from prolonged straining. Jennie straightens and wobbles the cramp out of her legs. "What the hell is his problem?"

Even with an absence of primate sounds, she retrieves the headphones. The isolation works so well with her art, helping her focus.

She jumps again when Sam pops up right next to her.

Luckily it doesn't result in any extra paint on the canvas. Jennie pulls the earmuffs down around her neck in time to hear Sam's, "... looking amazing."

"Yeah, I'm really pleased with it." Jennie drops her brush into water, swishes it rapidly backwards and forwards, and then plonks it onto a rag lying on the table. "Lunch time?"

"And some. It's gone two."

"You eaten?"

"Was just going to."

They're walking down the final flight when Jennie spots Mark in the hallway below. When he sees her, she feels the temperature drop. She pastes a matching look on her own face, glaring back at him; when they pass each other, the air becomes even cooler. Jennie's glad Mark is making his way back upstairs. No way in hell would she be able to eat with him working on a shitty mood like that.

"What the hell was that about?" Sam looks closely at Jennie.

"Who knows? Chicken or ham?" This last is said from the depths of the fridge where Jennie is foraging for sandwich fillings, with the added benefit of hiding any expression on her face.

"Ham."

Doorstop sarnies constructed, the girls sit at the table, cooled by a slight breeze coming through the french doors, open to the garden. Only crumbs remain when they hear knocking on the kitchen door. Jennie jumps up and opens it wide, so Eadie can make her way in. By the time Eadie reaches the table, Sam already has a chair pulled out and waiting for her.

"Cup of tea?" says Sam.

"That'd be lovely."

"Have you had lunch?" Jennie readies herself to knock

together another sandwich, although maybe not of the jaw-dislocating proportions of those hoovered by her and Sam.

"Yes. Mark made me something earlier."

Jennie stiffens. Hard to believe the guy who'd been so nice to her on Saturday night could have turned into the arsehole of earlier that morning.

With Sam bustling around making a pot of tea for Eadie, Jennie sits back down and using a dampened finger, makes quick work on the final few crumbs left on her plate.

"I've started on the Colin Wells' Warhol portrait."

"And?"

"It's going well. I've worked out the colours for each section. I'm going to work across then down."

Eadie nods her assent to this process. "When are you catching up with David Michaels?"

"How did—? Ah, I need to phone him and arrange a time." For someone who's more or less house-bound, the woman misses nothing.

"Why don't you do that today? Get in as fast as you can."

"There's no rush." Jennie stacks the plates on the table to make room for Sam with a tray full of tea stuff.

"There might be." Eadie's eyes have gone all Mata Hari, prompting Jennie's forehead to crumple in a non-verbal question. The old lady, keeping equally quiet, simply flutters her hands in the international gesture for 'I couldn't possibly say'.

Sam's gaze alternates between the two of them, her forehead knotted, but mainly because she has no idea what is taking place. Realising neither of them is going to come clean, Sam turns the pot around three times before pouring a cup of tea for Eadie, taking care not to over-fill it. Eadie's tea intake is limited to half cups, although she can sink an awful lot of those.

Leaving Eadie with the dregs of the pot in her cup, the girls head back to their respective projects, propping the kitchen door open to make it easier for Eadie to get back to her beloved sitting room. Jennie's foot is on the first stair when, "Don't forget to call David Michaels," warbles through from the kitchen. "Number's by the phone."

Jennie's foot drops reluctantly back to the ground floor and she breaths in deeply before walking over to the small table that holds the phone. Sure enough, there on a small piece of paper, written in caterpillar lettering, is David Michaels' name and a number. Her hand is paused to dial the first number when, "Let me know how you get on," echoes its way down the hall. Eadie's like a dog with a bone.

Jennie hasn't organised her thoughts properly when the phone is answered. "David Michaels' Gallery." The voice has enough plums to make a lot of jam.

"May I speak to Mr Michaels, please?"

"I'm afraid he's very busy right now." The answer is so automatic that Jennie knows David Michaels is either genuinely busy, or Jennie's voice is too low-brow for her to even rate speaking to the man. More than likely the latter. She's tempted to say she'll call back but knows only too well that Eadie is earwigging from the kitchen and will give her grief if she tries it.

"Would you let him know that Jennie Farrell called?"

"Oh, oh, just a moment, I believe he's become free." This response is nowhere near as well-rehearsed.

"Jennie, I've been expecting your call."

"You have?" Jennie's eyes narrow as she looks toward the kitchen.

"How about you pop in and see me at the gallery tomorrow. Say ten o'clock?"

Jennie jots down notes on how to get to there, with David Michaels going into great detail. Tube stations, landmarks, corner pubs and statues. He effectively paints a picture in Jennie's head of the journey to his gallery.

Hanging up, she follows the autocratic, "Well, how did you get on?" down the hall, wondering if there's any point in answering Eadie, when the old lady doubtless knows more about it than she does herself. The inquisition continues as she wanders into the kitchen. "When are you going in?"

"Ten o'clock tomorrow."

Nodding in a satisfied manner, Eadie rubs her hands together. All that's missing is an evil laugh.

Leaving Eadie to her machinations, Jennie is still shaking her head when she walks into Sam's sewing room. "She is unbelievable."

"Who? Sonja?"

"Hah, no. Eadie. I feel like I'm a pawn in some game she's overseeing."

At Sam's prompting, Jennie outlines everything that has happened around Eadie's involvement in her fledgling painting career. "But surely, that's all good." Sam looks mystified as to why Jennie would be indignant over someone looking out for her.

"I don't know if I'm ready for anything serious. Painting the dogs is fun. Sure there's pressure as to whether the mums will like the portraits, but exhibiting in a gallery is a whole different story."

"It can't be that bad."

"It can if someone like the Chinless Wonder is gunning for you."

Jennie rubs at the skin on her ring finger, taking no comfort from Sam's constant repetition of, "You'll be fine."

22

A feeling of dread creeps in under the covers with Jennie, making her uncomfortable and forcing the sleep from her body. She lies still, wondering if it's the remnants of a nightmare, then she remembers. Being pressured into painting seriously again is more like a daymare and something she'd rather avoid.

"C'mon bozo, time to get up." Jennie pushes gently at Charlie at the same time as sliding from underneath him. No need for an electric blanket with him around. He gives her the evils even though she's taken as much care as possible not to disturb him.

Dragging on her dressing gown, she walks over to the large free-standing wardrobe that dominates one wall. Staring at the clothes hanging from the carved trim around the top of the mahogany tomb, a frown skims across her forehead before deepening. Taking today's outfit down and draping it over the end of the bed, she opens the doors and stares fixedly at the contents. Her gaze swings back at the dress and jacket on the bed, then returns to the wardrobe.

"They'll have to do." She closes the doors, turning the handle to signal an end to her outfit indecision. For now.

Opening the door to her bedroom, she stands still for a moment. Relieved to be the only person up and about, she slips quietly downstairs for a solitary breakfast.

She's safely in the kitchen, staring out of the window at the peace of the garden when a noise behind her nearly causes her to have an accident.

Jennie hadn't even seen Mark over by the toaster when she walked in. "You're up early. I'll leave you in peace," she says, already on her way back to her room.

"For God's sake, relax will ya. I'm leaving." He steams toward her with a fully laden breakfast tray, forcing her to jump to the side. She steps forward to pull the door open for him, but his growled, "Leave it," stops her cold.

Watching his progress through the wildly swinging door, she expects him to head toward Eadie's room, but he turns and starts up the stairs. "Boy, she's really got him wrapped around her little finger," says Jennie to Charlie, who's finally made it down. He doesn't seem to care, and is only interested in his empty bowl. The simple yowl enough of a message for her to take down his biscuits from the Charlie-free zone on top of the fridge.

To an accompaniment of loud crunching, Jennie sets about getting her breakfast. She doubles up on everything knowing Eadie will want breakfast at some stage. She's relaxing with a first sip of tea, when Mark swings back into the kitchen. He opens the fridge door more forcibly than is good for the hinges, grabs a jar of jam and then stalks out again. "Forget wrapped around her little finger, he's firmly under her thumb," says Jennie to Charlie, who's now rubbing himself against her legs and nudging her in hopes of a small piece of crust. Jennie's happy to give him more than a crust, with every mouthful sticking in her throat and no amount of tea helping.

She looks over at the tray sitting on the counter next to the toaster. The only problem with taking Eadie's breakfast into her is that Jennie will get a grilling on what she hopes to get out of the meeting with David Michaels that morning. She's lifted it clear of the counter when Mark returns. Without bothering to speak to her, he drops the tray he's holding onto the counter, grabs Eadie's tray out of her hands and swings back out of the kitchen.

Jennie looks briefly at the remnants of Sonja's tray and then, fighting every instinct, leaves it sitting there before walking out of the kitchen without looking back. Her right foot's reaching for the third step, when Mark walks out of Eadie's sitting room. "She wants to speak to you."

Jennie stops, one foot mid-air, before walking backwards down the stairs until she's on the ground floor. She swings, expecting Mark to move but he doesn't and she has to wend her way around him. Jennie's feet drag their way across the sitting room carpet.

"Jennie, is that you?"

"Yeah." Jennie leans through Eadie's door hoping to make it brief by not fully committing herself to the room.

"Come in, sit down." Eadie pats the coverlet.

Jennie perches on the end of the bed and waits. She doesn't have to wait long.

"So, what's the plan for this morning?" Eadie's level of anticipation is evident from the woman's small frame trembling.

"Plan?"

"You must have some idea what you want out of it."

"I'm not sure. Maybe I can do the occasional painting. Between portraits," says Jennie, being vague and non-committal.

The snort that issues from Eadie is worthy of a bloke twice

her size. Ladylike it most certainly is not. "I know they pay the bills, but you're wasting your talent on them."

"Talent." Now it's Jennie's turn to snort.

"Yes. Talent." Eadie thumps her hands on the bedspread in exasperation, and then winces. The language that follows surprises Jennie. She doesn't even know what some of those words mean. She doubts Brenda, their profanity-loving flatmate from Melbourne, would either.

"Oh, my goodness, is that the time." Jennie peers pointedly at the small alarm clock sitting on the bedside table. "I need to get going." This last is said when Jennie is well on her way to the door. Her premature escape has more bad words issuing from Eadie and Jennie knows she'll have to deal with the situation sooner or later.

Eadie's swearing is still audible when Jennie flies through the sitting room door and straight into Mark, who doesn't appear to have moved from earlier. "What on earth did you do to her?" The anger on his face tilts Jennie more off-balance than ever.

"Nothing! Go and see for yourself." She throws her arm in the direction of the door and takes the opportunity to steady herself on the wall.

Mark hestitates between staying and berating Jennie and going to check and see if Eadie is all right. The unceasing swearing and muttering coming from the direction of Eadie's bedroom wins out and Jennie makes her escape. She doesn't bother going into her bedroom, instead heading straight into the bathroom. She's locking the door when she hears heavy footsteps on the stairs. Still, she waits until he's well on his way to the top of the house before stripping off and getting into the shower.

Re-checking the piece of paper in her hand, Jennie looks up at the ornate Fox & Firkin sign swinging above the pub's front door, and ticks it off her list. No way is she getting lost with the directions David Michaels has given her.

With a few more landmarks crossed off, she stands across the road from the glass-fronted Michaels Gallery. Purveyors of Fine Art the sign says, but Jennie has her doubts given the butt-ugly painting on an easel in the main window. She's waiting for a break in traffic when she spots who's about to open the glass door to leave. Jennie swings around so abruptly that the lady, who had been about to pass her, fumbles to keep hold of her Harrods' bag. "Oh sorry," mutters Jennie, moving out of the woman's way. She then closes in and examines the window display of the shop directly in front of her. Given it's a shoe repair shop, even Jennie's aware this looks odd.

Checking the reflection, she's able to see when the coast is clear; although by the time Rupert Smythe-Brown has finished admiring the glorified paint chart in the window of the gallery, the proprietor of the shoe repair shop is looking ready to call the cops. Jennie waves weakly to him before turning back toward the road.

As she's crossing it, she can see David Michaels removing the unpleasant painting and replacing it with something that shows the artist has talent. Jennie opens the door in time to hear, "... out the back." He hands the offensive piece to an assistant who is close to running when she disappears through the double swing doors at the back of the gallery.

"Was that ...?"

"Unfortunately, yes," says David Michaels, dusting his hands before moving one toward Jennie.

She dutifully shakes it, although she finds the formality a tad strange.

"Come, let's have a cup of tea." This offer also acts as an order to the assistant who's reappeared through the double doors. Without pause, he turns straight around and disappears again.

Jennie follows the gallery owner over to a pair of black leather couches and seeing him sit, she follows suit so she's facing him, the glass coffee table all that stands between them. Seeing what's hanging on the wall behind him, her mouth drops open. She knows she must look gormless, but is helpless to correct her gape.

"You seem surprised."

"I'm-I'm-I'm ..." Jennie gives up trying to think of a sensible response. She can't get over how it feels to see her painting of Monroe hanging in pride of place in a gallery.

"I don't think you realise how good it is. I've already had a couple of offers."

"You have?"

"But it's decidedly not for sale."

Jennie's digesting this when he adds "Unless, of course, someone offers me silly money," showing a decidedly commercial side to his personality.

"And Mrs Michaels would be all right with that?"

"Good God, no! She'd kill me."

With the tea delivered, Michaels gets down to the real purpose of her visit, which is good, because Jennie suspects she's knows what it is and is dreading it.

"I've got an exhibition coming up. I'd like to include some of your work."

"But haven't you already got enough?" Jennie's head swivels, taking in the walls of the gallery.

"Hah. No, this is a special exhibition I hold twice a year."

"I'm really not ready to paint properly again. I'm really not." It's not until she looks down that she sees she's wringing her hands together in terror.

"Eadie explained the situation to me," says David Michaels,

hurrying on when he sees her expression darken. "Yes, well. Sometimes you need to get back in the saddle."

"And flog a dead horse," spits out Jennie, before she can catch herself.

"Not dead. Only resting," says David Michaels, with more than a nod to Monty Python.

"But what about Rupert Smythe-Brown? He said he'd ruin me."

"You should have seen the look on his face when he sat where you are now." David Michaels's laughter starts off politely enough but rapidly progresses to loud guffaws causing one or two heads in the gallery to turn in his direction. He snorts to a stop before adding, "He has no idea how bloody awful his stuff is."

Much as Jennie would like to agree, she sits quietly. No way does she want to tempt fate by talking about Chinless in public.

Jerking his thumb back to indicate the painting of Monroe, he says, "You wouldn't be so reserved if you'd heard what he said about that piece earlier."

Jennie remains quiet with difficulty.

Michaels grunts before continuing, "Eadie and I think you should paint under a pseudonym, that way your work will be looked at for its own merits."

Jennie nods. None of this is news to her.

"Maybe a man's name. Really throw him off the scent."

"A man's name? No way." Jennie repeats the mantra that has accompanied her home on the tube. She opens the front door although she has difficulty getting it open far enough for her to squeeze her way in. The door is partially blocked by a suitcase that could double up as a coffin. The only things missing are handles on the sides and a brass plaque on top. Curiosity getting the better of her, Jennie flips over the tag tied to the handle. It takes her a moment to realise the reason she can't read it is because it's in another language, rather than handwriting worthy of a doctor as she'd first thought. "Sonja," whispers Jennie, to herself and the hallway. She hadn't taken that much notice of the bag last time it was outside Mark's room, obscured by a comatose Sonja.

She flies up the stairs to Sam's sewing room, screeching to a halt in front of the large table where Sam is sitting. "Is Sonja leaving?" Jennie's voice is low.

"Not that I'm aware of. Why?"

"Her suitcase is in the hall."

"Maybe she's going to store it in the cellar." Sam clips the threads of the outfit she's working on, before sweeping them into a rubbish bin that she puts back under the table.

"Not if the weight was anything to go by."

"Maybe she's stuffed Mark in there."

"Physically impossible."

"How'd it go at the gallery?"

Jennie stops her pacing; the carpet in front of Sam's sewing table has taken enough of a beating. "They want me to paint using a guy's name."

"It would confuse old Chinless." Sam's foot lifts off the pedal as she finishes a seam.

"I saw him this morning. At the gallery."

"Did he see you?"

"No, I hid across the road. Although I'm not sure why." Jennie's brow knots over this.

"When's the exhibition?"

"Only eight weeks away," says Jennie, pacing again.

"Great, that's heaps of time."

Jennie staggers to a stop, her expression incredulous. "He wants four paintings from me!"

"Two weeks each should be plenty, shouldn't it?"

Jennie supposes from Sam's point of view that eight weeks is plenty of time but, if she's supposed to keep painting doggie portraits as suggested by both David Michaels and Eadie, eight weeks is nothing. She wipes her hands down the side of her jeans transferring their clamminess to the solid fabric. "Oh, my God, I haven't bloody got time to bloody chat now."

Leaving an open-mouthed Sam, Jennie legs it up the stairs to the studio. She's relieved to find the top floor strangely silent and the door to Mark's bedroom slightly ajar. If anyone were inside, it would be hermetically sealed. Excellent, with the whole floor to herself, any distractions will be of her own making.

Part of her realises one good thing about the pressure is that it will help keep her emotions in check. When this clicks, she staggers to a halt. "They wouldn't! Would they?" While Jennie isn't sure of David Michael's Machiavellian side, she wouldn't put anything past Eadie. Still, if it worked?

Getting everything prepared for a solid afternoon of painting doesn't take long with every movement precise, planned and logical. Only minutes have passed before Jennie slides a brand new wooden stopper under the door to her studio and snaps on her earmuffs. A couple of deep steadying breaths, and she picks up her paint brush and gets on with the painting of Colin the Pug. Her creative heart rebels at this new no-nonsense approach, but if she's going to have even one painting ready for the exhibition, then this is how it has to be.

Only when her bladder is close to exploding does Jennie stop for a break. It hasn't all been solid painting though. Now and then she puts her brush down to make notes on a small pad about ideas for her exhibition pieces. Only subject matter at this stage as she's still not sure what medium she'll use, although she's tending toward watercolours. With Eadie on hand for advice, this makes the most sense. Possible pseudonyms are also littered on the pad, none of them any good.

Jennie's experiencing great difficulty deciding on a boy's name.

Ablutions complete, she's closing the door of her studio when she looks across at the still-open door to the bedroom on the other side of the landing. "That is just plain weird."

Charlie, who's appeared on the top step, miaows his agreement, before squeezing his way through the gap and disappearing into Mark and Sonja's room.

"Charlie," Jennie hisses at him, "you can't go in there." She snorts, "What am I saying? You can go anywhere you damn well like."

Jennie crosses the landing and stands outside Mark's door, when curiosity gets the better of her. Apart from when Sonja had been holed up in bed with a banged head, the door to the room has been firmly closed. Looking into the room through the gap left by the partially open door, she can see the room is a tip. Pushing the door *accidentally* with her foot, the chaos widens. Clothes litter every flat surface, including the floor. The door to the wardrobe is wide open, revealing the ludicrously empty interior.

It's only after looking more closely at the clothes Charlie is stomping around on, does Jennie realise they're all Mark's. Not one slinky, sexy, too-small outfit among the lot of them. "That's odd." Her voice sounds loud amid the unaccustomed silence currently experienced on the top floor. It's quiet enough that she can hear footsteps on the stairs, a couple of flights down.

"Charlie, out of there now," she hisses at the large black and white cat who's concentrating on sucking a pale yellow t-shirt into submission. He ignores her, the goofy look on his face proving beyond doubt that he's entered his catnip zone.

With the footsteps getting nearer and louder, Jennie runs Pink Panther-style back to the studio. She doesn't fully close the door as she suspects Charlie will be making a dramatic entrance soon. Hopefully before Mark gets back upstairs.

"Get out of there, you mangy piece of shit!"

The deep-throated growl coming from the direction of Mark's room says clearly what the large black and white cat thinks of this demand. Jennie can't resist peeping through the gap to see what's going on. Mark is standing outside his room with the door wide open. He keeps pointing toward the stairs and yelling "Out!" For all the good it's doing.

Knowing she won't be able to concentrate on her painting, while this stand-off is going on, Jennie opens the studio door wide. "Need some help?" It's the first time she's spoken unbidden to Mark since the animal comment and the words stick in her throat.

Mark doesn't answer her verbally, simply standing to the side and indicating she can enter his room to collect Charlie.

Jennie inches her way through the collage of clothing and bends over to pick up the cat. Remembering his bulk, she bends her knees, although a grunt still pops out when she takes his full weight. There's also the added load of the t-shirt he's refusing to let go of. She is walking past Mark when he spots it. His nostrils flare, prompting her to lean Charlie toward Mark so he can unhook the t-shirt. A deep growl from the feline indicates this isn't a good idea. "I'll bring it back in a second."

Placing Charlie on the bed in the studio, Jennie gets the t-shirt away from the cat but only by replacing it with one of her fluffy slippers. The t-shirt will never be the same. "You bad, bad boy." Her tone makes Charlie's ears flatten and his head dip as though she's going to strike him. She instantly feels contrition and strokes his head until he settles.

"I'm really sorry, but, ah ..." Jennie holds out the t-shirt to Mark, who's standing in the middle of his horizontal wardrobe. "I can't believe he could destroy it like that."

Mark takes the shirt from Jennie and holds it up. There's a suspiciously damp patch surrounded by several large, jagged holes. “Hmmm, he’s good, but he’s not that good.” Mark tosses the t-shirt in the general direction of a small, plastic latticework rubbish bin. It’s a direct hit, but the weight of the shirt is too much for the fragile receptacle and it topples.

Jennie’s still looking at the bin when, “Bitch!” comes vehemently from behind her. She swings, ready to retaliate, but he’s looking at a dark khaki jacket that he’s holding. It’s missing a sleeve and all its buttons. Her gaze swings from that ruined garment to the rest of Mark’s clothes on the floor. It doesn’t look as though anything is still intact.

“Sonja?”

“Yes.” Mark’s reply has a flat tone to it, his jaw clenched so tightly, that this single word has trouble escaping. He places his hand in the middle of Jennie’s back and pushes her toward the door. She gives up trying to stand on carpet and simply ploughs on through all the clothes. She’s only just achieved the landing, when the door shuts loudly behind her, smacking her on the bum.

Jennie takes a step toward her studio, before swinging to the right and hurrying downstairs. “You are not going to believe it,” she says, bursting into Sam’s sewing room. It’s empty, meaning the rest of her gossip has to shudder to a halt. Busting to share, Jennie searches for Sam, eventually finding her in the kitchen with Eadie. “You are not going to believe it.” Jennie’s ready to launch into a detailed description, when she becomes aware of a third presence in the large room. Sonja’s stands forlorn, by the stove, her eyes rimmed red. Gone is the polished, superior creature.

“You’ve finished the painting?” Eadie’s suggestion is thrown at her like a lifebelt. One Jennie grabs and clings onto with relief.

23

To a background of Sonja emptying her sinuses into a paper towel, Eadie, Jennie and Sam carry on a non-verbal conversation. But no amount of head-nodding and eye-widening can convey the full story.

"Would anyone like a cup of tea?" Jennie looks at the other occupants of the table who nod their assent. She looks over at Sonja, who also nods yes through the shredded, soggy ball of paper.

Glad to have something to do, Jennie sets everything up, with the roar of the kettle in the quiet room, making conversation impossible. Tea brewed, cups and saucers, sugar and milk sorted, they settle for a cuppa including Sonja, who's joined them at the table. Jennie's grossed out by the ball of slimy kitchen paper that Sonja continues to grip as though her life depends on it. She tries hard not to look at it, but the soggy blob has magnetic properties. It's when her gaze is yet again skittering away from focussing that she notices the printing. Not the veggies, fish or cooking paraphernalia commonly seen on kitchen paper towels, but an official looking logo.

She manages with a nudge and nod to bring it to Sam's

attention. Not one to hold back, Sam blurts out "Should you be scrunching that letter like that?"

Sam's question brings Sonja out of her funk. "No, you are right. This is evidence!" She pulls the letter out of the grip of the snottered paper towel and slams it down on the table. The typing has smeared in places but not so much that Jennie and Sam can't understand it.

Sam's eyes widen as she finishes reading. "Whoa."

"That must be a shock." Jennie looks at Sonja trying to see what emotion the woman is experiencing. She's certainly feeling shock herself given the contents of the letter reek of Eadie's interference. For Mark's trust fund to be frozen like this, seemingly out of the blue, is too much of a coincidence. Continuing to look at Sonja, Jennie realises it's not shock the woman is exhibiting, but pure, blind rage. The kind that would have you shredding the entire contents of someone's wardrobe. But why would she be so angry about Mark being cut off? That part in proceedings makes no sense at all.

"What?" demands Eadie, from the end of the table, prompting Sam to pick the letter up delicately by the corner and move it down the table to where Eadie can see for herself.

Jennie can hear the words as Eadie reads quietly through the letter as though seeing it for the first time, something Jennie now doubts more than ever. Sonja, too, is listening intently.

"He know! He say nothing! I turn down others!" Sonja's hands slam down on the table, rattling the tea things and causing Eadie's hand to fly shakily to her chest in the region of her heart. "I get even!" A promise added in tones that are cold and hard-edged.

Jennie's thinking through a response to this accusation when she hears the doorbell.

"I go now. But he will hear from me. I will show him."

Sonja jumps so abruptly to her feet that she knocks the

table sending the milk jug rolling drunkenly onto its side, and emptying its contents all over the table. Jennie's tempted to use the paper towel abandoned by Sonja to mop up the milk, but it'd do more damage than good. She drops a couple of clean towels over the spill as she listens to Sonja arguing with whoever it is at the front door. As Jennie blots away, Sam walks over and pushes the kitchen door open a gnat's whisker, evoking hisses of, "Sam!" from both Jennie and Eadie.

She waves behind her in their general direction, to shush them, but then she's rapidly retracing her steps, running backwards to accomplish this. She's only regained her seat, when Sonja storms back into the kitchen.

"You must help me," she says, looking at Jennie and Sam in turn.

It's not a request: it's an order and Jennie bristles. A responding salvo is readied, but is put away when Eadie says, "Yes, Jennie, Sam. You must help her."

Walking into the hall, their steps slow when they see the Samsonite coffin still in pride of place in the centre of the hall and a cab driver hurrying down the front path. It's when they attempt to pick it up that Jennie wishes it really did have handles on the sides. She'd be happier moving it if there were six of them lifting it, with a wreath on top and Sonja inside.

Sam tries to get Sonja to help, but she responds, "I am too upset."

A couple of suspected hernias, a lot of swearing and even more sweat later, and the coffin is safely stowed in the back of the cab. Jennie and Sam wait until Sonja's hearse disappears from view before performing an impromptu dance, left arms hooked as they whoop around in a small circle, right arms waving wildly above their heads.

They're laughing, their arms still hooked, as they dance back into the kitchen.

"Where's the letter?" says Jennie, looking at the table in front of Eadie.

With a look of pasted-on innocence, Eadie looks up from the cup of tea shaking against her bottom lip. "What letter?" Eadie's face is free of expression when she takes a small, careful sip of tea.

A line of questioning forming in her head, Jennie's cross-examination is interrupted by loud hammering on the front door. "I'll get it." Walking toward the front door, Jennie hears Sam asking the same questions she's been planning herself.

Opening the door with a pasted-on smile, Jennie is trampled by Sonja, who pushes past her without a word. The words start loudly enough in the kitchen, though when Sonja sees the letter is no longer on the table, Eastern European accusations are flying in all directions when Jennie gets back to the kitchen.

The hint of a smile that flutters to life on Eadie's face does nothing to quieten Sonja. After the tirade moves to focus on Eadie, Jennie steps in. "Shut up! How dare you speak to Eadie like that?"

She's ignored and the screaming continues, so Jennie worms her way between the two of them and physically pushes Sonja back. While Jennie might always have thought of Sonja as being tall, she's not much taller than Jennie herself and Jennie's a lot stronger.

This is something Sonja finds out for herself when her hands fly toward Jennie's face, presumably in preparation for scratching out eyes. Jennie's head snaps back out of range, her hands grip hard onto one of Sonja's and with a quick twist, Sonja is facing away from Jennie with her hand jammed halfway up her back. "Sam, can you help me here, please?"

"With pleasure." Sam grips Sonja's other arm and together the two of them push the kicking and screaming girl out of the kitchen, simply shoving their squirming captive against the swinging kitchen door to open it. "Nose job," splutters Sam, laughing and trying to keep her grip.

They screech to a halt when they see Mark swing his way around the newel post and land in the hallway. Relief swamps Jennie, when rather than yell at her and Sam, he turns and opens the front door. His face is rigor-straight as the three girls stumble past. Sonja aims a vicious kick in his direction that he manages to avoid, and then enrages her further by *tsk*-ing and shaking his finger.

With a good shove, they get Sonja out onto the doorstep, jump back and lock the door on her.

"Do you think the glass will hold?" says Jennie, concerned the current constant hammering will prove too much for it.

"If she breaks it, she pays for it." Mark herds Sam and Jennie away from the door and the pounding to stop.

They're all traipsing through to the kitchen when, "I will get you for this!" is screamed through the letter flap.

"Is she gone?" Eadie face is creased with concern.

"Hopefully, for good." Sam dusts off her hands in a business-like manner.

"I feel mean now. Will she be okay on her own if she's still suffering from amnesia?" Jennie knows she's a softy, but there are moral responsibilities at stake.

"She suffered a head-on collision with the gravy train and miraculously got her memory back," says Mark.

Eadie laughs uproariously at this ditty and is soon joined by Sam and Jennie.

"You don't seem too upset by it," says Jennie, her tone deliberately neutral.

"Hardly. The lawyers who handle my trust are Melbourne-based, so when I saw the letter was from a London company I'd never heard of, I knew it was a have." Mark looks pointedly at Eadie.

“You’re not too upset?” Eadie has the good grace to look guilty over her meddling.

“Hell, no! I wasn’t sure how I was going to get rid of her,” says Mark, with relief.

This throwaway line has unwanted thoughts popping up in Jennie’s brain. The feelings that accompany them make themselves known in the region of her heart, and she has to thump her chest to dislodge them. Unfortunately, this makes those feelings drop down her body and cause a sharp intake of breath that has Mark looking in her direction.

“I still don’t get why she wants to get even with you?” says Sam, catching Mark’s attention.

“She was expecting a marriage proposal.”

Eadie’s cup clatters back into its saucer. “Never mind gold digger, that girl is more of a mining company.”

A late lunch and Jennie is back up in her studio working on another row of Colins. Even though the top floor is blessedly empty, she puts on her earmuffs and slides the recently purchased doorstop into place. With Sonja gone, she doesn’t want to have to deal with Mark’s attentions again. That had been one good thing about having the Slavic nympho on the premises. Not that Jennie will miss the simian concrete crew.

While working, she ponders possible subject matter for her exhibition pieces but her mind keeps sweeping back to the same one. She gives up the fight and concentrates on it with the piece of her brain not working on her current painting.

Hours later, her back feels as though it’s been kicked hard, her eyes hurt and the light is starting to fail, meaning she’s certainly missed dinner. Jennie stretches out kinks while examining the painting in front of her. She removes the earmuffs and kicking the doorstop aside, goes in search of food and company, not encountering either until she's in the kitchen.

Sam is bustling around the cooker, with Mark acting as her apprentice. There's a lot of slicing and dicing going on and the kitchen is filled to bursting with the aroma of garlic.

Eadie doesn't appear to have moved from her spot at the end of the table. "How'd you get on?"

"Great, I reckon a few more hours and I'll be close to finished."

"Goodness, that's fast." The surprise is writ so strong on Eadie's face that Jennie instinctively knows Eadie's thinking 'too fast'.

"Once I got into the swing of things, I really sped up. They're effectively all the same, just different colours."

Eadie's slow nodding confirms her understanding of the process.

"Dinner'll be ready in ten." Sam calls over her shoulder while standing to the side to let Mark scrape a chopping board's worth of vegetables into the family-sized wok sitting over the largest flame. Jennie can see a big pot on the back element, presumably with rice boiling inside it.

The platter that Mark drops into the middle of the table eleven minutes later is the size of a baby's bath. It's piled high with rice and a chicken stir fry. Everything is glistening with sauce.

"It's sweet and sour," says Sam.

Jennie helps herself to a small serving. "How come it's not orange?"

"Not sure. I think the takeaway must add colour to theirs. I followed the recipe to the letter."

"I'm sure it will be lovely." Eadie waits patiently while Mark fills a bowl for her.

Once Sam has served herself, Mark gets stuck in and fills his own bowl to the point of overflowing.

Jennie spears a piece of chicken and pops it into her mouth, chewing tentatively for a start and then with more enthusiasm. “Wow, this is good.”

There’s a chorus of ‘*mmm*’ from around the table that confirms they’re all in agreement. For a while, the only sounds in the kitchen are of cutlery on crockery, chewing and sighing.

With the edge of her appetite filed smooth, Jennie’s eating slows. “I’ve been thinking about what I’m going to paint for the exhibition.”

“And?” prompts Eadie.

“I’m thinking a day in the life of Chicken George.”

“Who?” comes back at her from the other three.

“The homeless guy who lives at the end of the street. His face is amazing.”

“I don’t think he’s the full quid.” Mark’s face forms a portrait of concern. “Don’t you go seeing him on your own.”

“That doesn’t mean he’s dangerous.” Jennie’s wishing she hadn’t said anything. No way would Chicken George agree to being painted if she had Mark hovering over her. “It was just an idea.”

“If you’re going to see him, I need to go with you.” Mark’s tone indicates this isn’t negotiable. Eadie and Sam are nodding in agreement.

“Fine, I’ll think of something else then.”

24

Letting herself quietly out of the back door the following morning, Jennie walks briskly down the side path, pulling on the straps of her backpack when she turns onto the pavement. She can't help the occasional nervous peek over her shoulder.

When she reaches the greasy spoon in Chiswick High Road, the smell of bacon and her tummy rumbling is a prominent reminder that she hasn't had breakfast yet.

"Can I please have two bacon butties and a couple of cups of tea?" Jennie counts out the exact change onto the pale yellow Formica flap that separates her from the cooking side of the enterprise.

"Eat in or takeaway, luv?"

"Takeaway."

Do I really look piggy enough that I'd sit here and hoover my way through two sandwiches and two teas?

Apparently so.

Her stomach continues to rumble as she watches the large woman behind the counter assemble the sandwiches. An artery-clogging amount of butter is slathered onto four slabs of white bread before half a pig's worth of bacon is piled on two slices and the others then slapped on top. The sandwiches are wrapped in necessary greaseproof paper and then shoved into a small plastic bag that struggles with their combined bulk.

Two polystyrene cups are filled from a large aluminium teapot before everything is handed to her. Slipping one arm through the handle of the bag, Jennie carries a cup in each hand. She's standing next to the door wondering how on earth she's supposed to open it, when another customer arrives.

Jennie puts her head out and checks in both directions, before allowing her body to exit the shop. She walks briskly toward their street, where she peers around the large hedge that borders the vacant section on the corner. The coast is clear as far as she can see. She nips through the gap in the hedge without anyone calling her name. Then she slows, not sure how to go from here, it being a difficult situation to plan for.

Walking toward to the shanty hugging the trunk of the large tree that dominates the section, she's hoping Chicken George is at home.

"Hello!" Her voice cracks, meaning anyone inside won't be able to hear her, even if the walls are paper thin. "Hello!" The loudness of this second greeting, gives Jennie a start. Rustling from inside lets her knows that George is indeed in for callers. He crawls out of the small doorway, looking frightened. Allowing her voice to drop to a more soothing level, Jennie adds, "I'm so sorry, I didn't mean to startle you."

He doesn't speak, even after he's staggered to his feet. Jennie hadn't realised how big he is, only having seen him in the distance. Maybe Mark was right?

His hair adds to his height, dreadlocked simply through not having been washed for a long time. Every crease on his dark, weathered face is filled with dirt; his nut-brown eyes are full of pain, the likes of which Jennie has only seen before on dogs at the SPCA. His clothing is also brown, maybe not by design but certainly from the dirt that has rubbed smooth on every surface giving the heavy fabric the appearance of leather. His feet are wrapped in sacks held in place with cheap twine. Pieces of newspaper poke out of the tops, presumably there for padding and warmth.

"I need your help." Jennie holds out one of the cups of tea.

He looks at it, but still doesn't speak; she's relieved when he tentatively takes the cup from her. His hands are even grubbier than his face, the nails black with dirt. With a hand free, she delves into the plastic carrier bag to retrieve one of the bacon butties.

His nostrils flare as the aroma of bacon hits them. Jennie sees him swallow and knows saliva must be pooling in his mouth too. He takes it but doesn't move to open the package.

"Can we talk?"

"What about?" His voice is beautiful. Deep and melodious and certainly not what she expected.

"I'd like to paint a portrait of you." His visage crumples in confusion, prompting Jennie to add, "A painting." Her subject matter snorts and a small smile flits nervously across his face.

"I'd pay you, of course," says Jennie, but when she sees the look of affront on his face, adds quickly, "Not charity, wages." The gossip that he's a proud man appears spot on. She's relieved when he kicks a log of wood in her direction and plonks himself down on the ground, not worrying about a seat for himself.

Jennie perches herself carefully on the log, puts her cup of tea on the ground beside her then grabs the other bacon sandwich and takes a large unladylike bite out of it. If she acts normally then hopefully this will help him relax. She demolishes half her sandwich before she risks a peek in his direction.

He's finished his butty and is looking longingly at the remains of hers. Given she's had to force the last couple of mouthfuls down, she wraps the rest of hers up and puts it back in the bag. "I'm full. Are you okay to throw this out for me?" At his nod, Jennie tosses the bag gently in his direction.

"Why would you want to paint me?" The deep rumble of his voice tugs at a memory of Jennie's, until she works out what it is. He sounds exactly like the guy on the *Black and White Minstrel Show* on the telly. This is something Jennie had grown up watching with her parents.

"Your face is interesting. And I love your chicken." Jennie moves her feet out of the way as the chicken responsible for George's street name pecks at the ground between her feet. The bird is making short work of any crumbs there when Jennie risks patting the back of its neck. She's rewarded with the chicken leaning into her hand in obvious enjoyment.

"Peggy likes you," rumbles across the rough ground between her and Chicken George. Silence settles on the three of them, eventually broken when he asks "What would I need to do?"

"It's easy really. I can take some photos of you and use those as reference. That's it."

"When?" comes back the bald reply.

"Now, if you like." When there's no negative reaction to this suggestion, Jennie shrugs off her backpack, being careful not to squash Peggy when she puts it down on the ground. George is watching her movements so intently that Jennie has to force herself to slow down. She doesn't want to spook him. He looks apprehensive when she removes the Polaroid camera from the depths of the bag. "It's a Polaroid camera."

"What do I need to

"Just be yourself." Jennie snaps off a photo of his head and shoulders and watches him freeze in alarm when the photo pops out of the front of the camera. "The photos are instant." Jennie shoves the still-grey photo under her arm to speed up processing before taking a photograph of George's shoes, his hands and then a couple of Peggy. Finally, she takes a shot of the two of them together.

With all the shots developed, Jennie checks she has everything she needs. The two photos of the chicken are so close to being identical, that Jennie offers one of them to George as a keepsake. She feels genuine warmth from the tramp when his face splits in a wide grin, revealing teeth that are surprisingly straight and white. "Look, Peggy, it's you." He drops a heavy pat on the head of the chicken that is pecking at the Polaroid of itself.

With promises to take photos of the finished paintings, Jennie packs up and before leaving George and Peggy to their thoughts, she hands over eight, well-used five-pound notes. George's reaction shows it's a lot more than he's been expecting but rather than get into an argument, she waves briefly and walks away. Pushing through the gap in the hedge and glancing back, she's pleased to see George carefully fold the notes and slip them in a pocket, before delving into the plastic bag for her leftovers.

Jennie wastes no time getting home. She's eager to get on with the paintings but also hopes to be back inside before anyone realises she's even been out. Far easier than dealing with the third degree she'd get from Mark and Eadie. Sam would understand, but the other two were far too protective by half. She's thought about using the back door again, but if there is anyone about, they'll be in the kitchen for sure.

It's not until she's concentrating on easing the front door shut that Mark asks, "What are you up to?" from right behind her.

Jennie's spins in his direction and thinks briefly about faking that she's leaving to go out but isn't sure how much he's seen. She's still considering an answer when he sniffs at her and before she can react, drags his finger from the side of her mouth and down her chin. He slowly sucks on it while looking her dead in the eye; her heart flutters erratically along with other parts of her body that she'd long since thought dead.

"Bacon! Where have you been that you're sneaking back in?"

Mark follows Jennie into the kitchen where she dumps her backpack and takes a seat at the table. Sam and Eadie, who are already there, look quizzically at Mark as he continues interrogating Jennie. Not getting a response, he asks the same questions again. Louder.

"You want a cuppa?" Sam raises her voice to be heard.

"That'd be lovely." Jennie's voice is equally loud.

Realising he's not going to get an answer, Mark starts guessing.

Jennie's blasé "nopes" stumble when he correctly guesses that she's been to see Chicken George. No sooner has the strangled "Nope" left her lips than he pounces.

"I told you not to see him on your own. The guy's bloody nuts."

"You really shouldn't have been alone with him, Jennie," says Eadie.

"For goodness sake, the guy's harmless. And anyway, it was worth it." Jennie pushes herself to her feet, stomps over to her backpack and retrieves the photos. Without another word in her defence she tosses them onto the table before retreating to lean against the counter, arms crossed, face defiant.

Mark picks up one of the Polaroids. "No sane person has a bloody chicken for a pet!"

"Peggy."

"What?" Mark's tone is terse.

"The chicken's called Peggy." Jennie doesn't look in Mark's direction when she flings this back at him. She's too interested in watching Eadie's reaction to the photos. When the old lady lifts a trembling hand to cover her lips, Jennie can't help some cross-examination of her own. "What, Eadie?"

"That face." Eadie's hand gently strokes the photo she's still holding.

Jennie pushes herself off the counter and walks over to see which of the photos Eadie is looking at. "That's my favourite, too." Jennie looks at the picture of George with Peggy clasped firmly beneath his arm. Both man and chicken are staring straight down the barrel of the camera.

"What marvellous subject matter." Eadie swaps the photo for another.

"I'm thinking watercolours." Jennie waits for Eadie's response to this and isn't disappointed when the old lady looks up, her eyes brimming with tears. "Will you be able to help me with the technique side of things?"

"Of course I will," whispers Eadie, beaming.

It's only when Jennie realises she's heard this reply easily does it dawn on her that Mark has finally shut up. Seeing the look of grudging respect on his face, she raises an eyebrow. It's enough to elicit another forceful, "You still shouldn't have gone to see him on your own. Promise you won't again."

"Fine." Jennie's teeth are clenched together so hard, she's surprised the word's managed to squeak out. "Eadie, I'm going to get my sketchbook. Won't be long."

Suspicious that she's capitulated too easily, Mark launches into another lecture, but rather than stay and listen, she closes the kitchen door on him. Stomping up the first flight of stairs, she can hear him still ranting.

"God, you're not my blasted husband," Jennie yells out before slapping her hand over her mouth, hoping she hasn't said this as loudly as it sounds in her head.

Her hopes are smacked about severely when she hears, "You wish!" shouted back at her from the kitchen.

"Damn him." The higher she goes, the louder her stomping gets. It feels good, although by the time she reaches her studio she's feeling silly, even if it has released the frustration from her system. She makes short work of collecting sketch pad and pencils before racing back downstairs. She reaches the first floor landing at the same time as Sam, who's walking up. Mark starts up the stairs too, so Jennie nips into Sam's sewing room before he can see her.

Once Sam is safely in the room too, Jennie pushes the door shut. "What are you working on at the moment?"

"Have a look." Sam rummages around on the large table that holds her sewing machine and holds up a partially completed woollen jacket in a serious hunter green. "It's for Garth Fogle."

"What *make* is he?"

"Shih Tzu."

"No, I meant what *breed*."

"He's a Shih Tzu," Sam says, slower this time allowing Jennie to realise Shih Tzu is a breed, rather than a description of the dog's temperament.

"Do you think his owner would be interested in a portrait?"

"Don't you have enough on your plate with the Chicken George paintings?"

"Yeah, but if I suddenly stop the doggie portraits, Chinless might smell a rat."

Sam drops the small, green coat back onto her table. "I'll check when I do the final fitting."

Checking the way is clear, Jennie belts down the rest of the stairs and through to the kitchen. "Oh." Eadie's no longer there and neither are the photos of Chicken George and Peggy. Swinging around, Jennie retraces her steps in the direction of Eadie's sitting room.

Eadie is shuffling through the Polaroids sitting on a tray on her lap. "I'd love to paint this sort of subject matter."

"He's wonderful isn't he?" Jennie drops onto the couch and flips open her sketch pad. She waits patiently for the old lady to get her fill of them before retrieving the photos, tray and all, from Eadie. "I was thinking a big painting of Chicken George and Peggy together, then smaller pieces that concentrate on his hands and feet and maybe one of the hovel itself?

"That'd work beautifully as a collection."

Jennie sketches away furiously, the pencil flitting over the pristine white pages. Now and then she pauses to check one of the photos for reference. When the pencil finally stills, she places the sketch pad on Eadie's lap and sits back to await critique.

"You have a fabulous eye." Eadie taps the sketchbook gently. "These'll look magnificent as watercolours."

"I only hope I can pull it off."

Back up in her studio, Jennie looks at the pencil drafts in her sketchbook. They're surrounded by a mass of scribbled notes that cover everything from colour to technique and other general pointers. Jennie will have a go on her own first and then get feedback from Eadie. Otherwise, it would be too much like painting by numbers.

One thing that's patently obvious though is that Jennie will have to stock up big time at the art supply shop.

25

Her rotating ears resembling the dish on a sonar tower, Jennie listens for the sound of Mark closing the front door after him. It's ridiculous sneaking around but she doesn't want him tagging along to the art shop, because he's worried she'll nip in to see Chicken George and Peggy on the way to or from the station.

The door shuts with a resounding echo up through the stairwell letting her know it's safe to leave her room and creep up to the half landing to check which direction he's gone in.

She's halfway there and inching her way up each tread when Sam's voice catches her unawares.

"What on earth are you up to?" Sam's voice is loud in the quiet of the hallway.

"Shhhh." Jennie still isn't a hundred percent sure it was Mark who left. It could as easily have been someone arriving. She skulks her way up and peeks out of the window. There's no sign of him on the doorstep or the front path. Angling her head first one way and then the other, she can't spot him on the street either. "Damn."

She turns away from the window and leans against the

wall. Not knowing which way he's gone makes it bloody hard to avoid him. The odds are fifty-fifty she'll stumble into him. On the bright side, the odds are also fifty-fifty she won't. Looking down, she's aware Sam is still standing outside her sewing room, staring at her.

"I'm trying to avoid running into Mark," says Jennie, walking back down the stairs toward the first floor. "He's still giving me so much grief about Chicken George, that I'd rather dodge him."

"Ah, gotcha. Have a look out the window of the sewing room. You can see the garage from there."

"Of course!" Jennie speeds up, motoring as she passes Sam. With no lace curtains on the window overlooking the drive, she's surreptitious in her sticky-beaking and stands well back from the glass. The dark green Jag reverses out of the garage and Mark hops out to close the door, resulting in Jennie jumping back yet further into the room, even though, the chances of him seeing her are slim. He gets into the Jag, backs onto the road, and roars off in the direction of Chiswick High Road. Her trip to the tube station is fast and she's happy when she makes it there without being spotted by Mark. It's perhaps later in the day than she likes for a trip into town but Mark took ages to leave for his job interview.

"Hi, there Roger," says Jennie, while the bell tinkling her arrival at the art supply shop is still in full swing. "I'm in a hurry today." She throws her backpack on the glass-topped counter, grabs one of the old wire baskets and sets off collecting her supplies like the winner in a 'grab and go' shopping competition. She has to ask directions on a couple of items and at one stage Roger has to pop out the back for her.

"You are a woman on a mission," says Roger.

"Limited time." Jennie is unable to stop her fingers tapping on the counter, she hopes Roger will match the tempo of her rat-tat-tat, but it's in vain. He moves at his own speed and is wrapping yet another parcel of paints when Jennie puts up her hand to halt him. "That's not necessary. I can pop everything straight into my backpack, that's why I brought it with me.

"Let me finish this one." Roger continues his laborious taping while Jennie scoops up everything except the brushes and shoves the lot into her backpack. The brushes she stows carefully in a side pocket.

To avoid their usual argument about her paying rather than Eadie, Jennie throws the required money on the counter, swings the backpack over her shoulders and is through the door seconds later. She can see the 'but' still hovering on Roger's lips when she pulls the door shut behind her. Jennie makes a mental note to tell Eadie she's paid for this lot to avoid any double-dipping.

Jennie reaches the tube station right at rush hour. This time she's not going to be pushed and shoved. She walks tall and strong and this sends out a subtle message that keeps people well out of her way. Surfing her way through the crowds, she has no trouble finding the right platform and is soon on a train that should have her home in half an hour.

Jennie rolls with the motion of the tube train, hanging from one of the handles located at regular intervals along the rails running the length of the carriage. She's surrounded on all sides by sweaty commuters. Some of them are sporting perspiration out of kilter with an office job. One hummy armpit is so close to her face that Jennie feels as though she's wearing it like a gas mask. She swaps hands so she can turn away, but this brings her face up against an armpit that wouldn't know deodorant or soap if they ganged up and attacked. Breathing through her mouth goes some way toward reducing the gag factor.

She's counting the stations until fresh air and freedom when the tube rolls to a sluggish stop, the lights flicker on and off for a few seconds and then give out altogether, plunging them into darkness. It's more than dark: there's a complete absence of light until Jennie's eyes adjust and she can spot weak emergency lights that are nowhere strong enough for her to make out her surroundings. Only the lights themselves are visible making them appear as though they're floating.

As is the British way, no one says a word about this development. Five minutes later and, apart from shuffling, heavy sighing and the occasional fart, the carriage is still quiet, although the smells now wafting about are strong enough to be heard.

"Oh God, how much longer is this going to take?" Jennie's voice echoes around the carriage, startling herself and those around her. One simply does not talk aloud in a position like this.

Jennie's question is answered when a crackling voice emanates from a nearby speaker although most of the message is unintelligible due to static and a strong Indian accent. Summary is they're working on it, but with no indication of when the problem will be rectified.

Jennie holds her watch close to her face and peers at the barely visible luminous dial.

Shit, it's already five-thirty.

Another hour, and the smell in the carriage has reached abattoir levels. This coupled with the temperature increasing steadily is making it more than a little unpleasant. So much so, that even the locals are starting to voice their displeasure. Perhaps they feel safe speaking in the dark.

Jennie swaps arms, yet again flapping the one she's dropped to her side in hopes of getting some blood back to the extremities. Instead, ferocious pins and needles play havoc. With the carriage seemingly not going anywhere soon, she maybe doesn't need to hold on, but worries that if it starts up suddenly she could fall over. She's carrying glass in her backpack and would rather not risk the inside of it resembling a Norman Bluhm when she gets off this godforsaken train.

There's a loud thump from further up the carriage that makes Jennie think someone has finally given up and dropped their briefcase on the ground rather than keep holding onto it. A sigh close to her and the feeling of a fellow commuter sliding down her side and Jennie realises people are fainting. Jennie would be amongst them if she hadn't just spent a hot summer in Melbourne. Sure she's finding it hot, but nothing compared with living in a clapped-out caravan when it's crowding forty degrees Celsius.

She counts five more thumps before the train finally lurches forward. They move several metres before the lights desperately claw their way back to life. Jennie looks around at her fellow inmates. There are some commuters standing, who are as pale as those already stretched out on the floor. She's about to ask the lady next to her if she's okay when the woman's eyes roll back and she sinks gracefully, landing in a heap around Jennie's ankles.

At the next station, it's like the evacuation of Dunkirk. Everyone who's able to gets off the train does so, leaving the prone where they are. Jennie's more than horrified by this cavalier behaviour, until she sees the ambulance teams standing on the platform. They swarm on to kneel beside those poor unfortunates stuck to the floor by chewing gum and God knows what else. Cold compresses and oxygen are administered.

Once the casualties have been carried off the train, all the commuters swarm back on. Jennie's reluctant to join them. She'd rather catch a bus home but wouldn't know which one to catch or even what direction to head in. She's the last one to reboard, with the doors sliding closed worryingly near her face, necessitating some limbo-dancing action to avoid having her face jammed into the angled top of the door. On the bright side, leaning against the glass panel next to the doors she no longer has anyone's armpit shoved right in her face.

Leaving the station, the tube accelerates smoothly, as though it hadn't limped in there ten minutes earlier. Unfortunately, after this promising start, it once again falters and staggers to a halt. Darkness follows.

This time, even the English voice their disapproval before settling down for another smelly sauna.

Emerging from Gunnersbury Station, Jennie's steps are hesitant. It's going on for eight o'clock and she knows the whole house will be in an uproar; her disappearance registered with the local police station by Mark at the least. He's such a panic artist.

Jennie stalls halfway up the front path. She hadn't realised there were that many light bulbs in the place and is sure the house must be visible from space. She squares her shoulders before turning the front door handle and is pounced on seconds after the door shuts. Mark is in the lead, but Sam and Eadie are firing questions at her, too.

"Stop!" Jennie's voice is forceful, her hand held up like a pointsman. With the trip she's endured, she does not need the Spanish Inquisition.

"I'm fine. The bloody tube stopped three bloody times. I'm bloody tired, bloody hungry and my bloody feet bloody hurt."

Because her response has contained more bloodys than she's used in the past six months, mouths drop open and eyes widen. Before they can gather their wits, Jennie swings the backpack off her shoulders and stows it under the coat rack. She marches down the hall to the kitchen and straight arms the door open, nearly collecting Charlie in the process. When it swings closed behind her, they're all still standing in the hallway.

"God, that felt good," whispers Jennie to Charlie who's winding his way around her ankles in the international cat signal for 'top up my biscuits'.

She drops a couple of pieces of bread in the toaster and goes to do his bidding. He follows her at a run, behaving as though he's simply starving, although the mound of biscuits sitting in his bowl belies this. "The fresh ones taste so much better don't they, boy?"

Jennie's putting the box of biscuits away when the kitchen door swings open. Her shoulders tense in response and she stares fixedly at the toaster hoping whoever it is will leave her in peace. It's been a hell of an evening.

"Sounds like you need a cup of tea," says Mark. His tone is conciliatory and Jennie turns in surprise.

"That'd be lovely," says Jennie, her shoulders settling back down. While Mark gets a pot of tea sorted out and Jennie rummages in the fridge for toast toppings, Sam helps Eadie into the kitchen.

"Points failure?" says Eadie.

"I'm not sure. The announcements were so garbled, it could have been a training exercise for World War III for all I know." Jennie is still having trouble believing what she's experienced. "People were dropping like flies."

"What do you mean?" says Sam.

"They were fainting all around me. Don't think the English are used to the temperatures we've experienced, after being stuck in the dark for hours."

"It sounds hideous," says Sam.

"Yeah, not something I'm keen to go through anytime soon."

"I could have driven you there," says Mark, looking somewhat hurt that Jennie hadn't called on him for his assistance.

"For goodness sake, I'm an adult. I can make my own way around London without having to have my hand held all the time." Jennie knows her tone is sharp, but she's feeling especially exasperated after the journey from hell.

"Fine," says Mark, holding up his hands in surrender, his expression shuttered.

"Fine then," says Jennie, calculatedly taking him at face value.

"Excellent, so everyone's fine then," says Eadie, fighting in vain to hide a small smile.

Mark stops what he's doing, drops all the tea-making paraphernalia on the counter in front of Jennie and says, "Fine then. I'll leave you to it." His exit from the room is of the miffed variety.

"I'll make the tea," says Sam, also trying not smile.

Jennie looks from one to the other. "What's so bloody funny?"

"Nothing," say Sam and Eadie in unison.

"Hmmm, you both seem to find 'nothing' very amusing."

Jennie turns her back on them and concentrates on spreading butter and Marmite on her toast. She doesn't particularly like it, but it's as close to Vegemite as she can find. They'd finished the small jar they'd brought with them, and she and Sam had looked for Vegemite at a shop in the city that stocked Aussie products. Pound for pound, it was more expensive than crude oil. Some would say that's what it tastes like, but Jennie loves the flavour. She certainly found it far more palatable than the used engine grease that masquerades as Marmite. Next commission she got, she'd buy a jar of the real deal.

Leaving Sam and Eadie sipping their brew, Jennie takes her tea and toast up to her studio, only stopping briefly at the bottom of the stairs to collect her backpack. It's a balancing act, but she manages to reach the top of the house with no spillages. Charlie's close on her heels, but only because he adores Marmite and toast.

The door to Mark's room is wide open and she can see him pacing backwards and forwards, chewing through energy at a rate of knots. Espying her, his pacing swings toward the door, but rather than come out onto the landing and lecture her on going into town on her own, he slams the door in her face. The solid wood door shuts with a loud bang, but it's not thick enough to stop her hearing him muttering away, even when she's in the studio, albeit she hasn't yet closed her door.

"Boy, he's really ticked off," says Jennie to Charlie, who's circling her, looking for a snack. Jennie puts down her mug and plate on the table next to her easel, then breaks a piece of crust off and holds it out to him. He takes it and settles down to chew on it contentedly while Jennie unpacks her supplies. It's too late to start on anything tonight, but at least this way she'll be ready to go first thing in the morning.

She jumps slightly when Mark's door is thrown open, shattering the calm at the top of the house.

"Here we go," she says quietly to Charlie.

But rather than cross the landing, Mark stares at her for a moment with knotted brows, before swinging around and stomping down the stairs.

Jennie looks down at Charlie, who's ready for another smidgeon of toast. "What, doesn't he care anymore?"

26

The next morning, Jennie is up and dressed early with the studio demanding her presence. After rushing through breakfast and her shower, she goes up to the studio, where a blank piece of water colour paper stares up at her from the table next to the easel. It's taped to a piece of hardboard to keep it flat and is raring to go, although Jennie is now hesitant, her enthusiasm of earlier diminishing.

She moves the chair from in front of the dressing table and plonks it down next to the work table, her mind settling on the painting's composition. It's so different to the daubs she's been completing of the posh dogs of London and while she's done preliminary sketches, the process of putting paint on paper gives her pause.

She settles herself on the hard-backed chair and swivels her gaze between the sketches clipped to the easel and the virgin piece of paper in front of her. She straightens everything around the backing board more than once. Out of distractions, she starts.

The next few days are a blur of paint, hastily eaten sandwiches and lots of cups of iced tea that didn't start out that way. Eventually, the painting is at a stage where Jennie has to get feedback from Eadie. While the temptation is to plough ahead, Jennie's worried she'll progress too far and then have to start again, even if this first painting is more of a practice piece than the real deal.

"Eadie?" says Jennie, walking quietly into the sitting room. It's not super late but if the old lady has already retired for the night, Jennie doesn't want to disturb her. She needn't have worried when Eadie responds from her bedroom sounding very much awake.

"How have you been getting on?" Eadie's expression is one of query, her face lit with anticipation.

"Okay, I think." Jennie places the partially completed watercolour, still attached to the backing board, carefully on the side of the bed.

Eadie doesn't say a thing. She stares fixedly at the painting while Jennie moves her weight from one foot to the other, hopping on the spot. At length, Jennie has to look away and stare at the nearest wall.

Eadie murmurs something and she spins back, waiting for the criticism she knows will be forthcoming.

"Jennie. It's wonderful and I particularly like that you've given the subject matter room to breathe," says Eadie, referring to the goodly amount of white space left on the page. "Yes, there are one or two tricks you've missed and a couple of spots that need fixing, but the overall composition is excellent."

"Do you really think so?" says Jennie, before stumbling on. "Right, I forgot. If you don't mean it, you don't say it." She breaks into a wide grin.

"I never thought it would be possible for a chicken to evoke such emotion."

"Peggy is gorgeous, isn't she?"

"A stunner of the first order. Did you bring your notebook with you?"

"No, I didn't. I wasn't sure you'd still be up. Do you want to do this now? It can wait until the morning," says Jennie, her voice tinged with concern.

"I'm up for it, if you are. I don't sleep much these days. Ah, nights."

Jennie sprints up to the studio, grabs her notebook and legs it back down. She sits on the blanket box, notebook open on her knee, ready for instruction. Half an hour of scribbling and discussing techniques with Eadie, and Jennie is in a quiet state of panic, something the old lady picks up on.

"I know this is a lot to take on, but you're a talented artist. You'll get it."

"I hope so. The exhibition is frighteningly close for this many things to be wrong."

"They're not wrong, just areas that could be improved. You could exhibit this painting as it is now."

"Really?"

"Yes, really. But the more buttoned-down we can make the final pieces, the less room that little upstart Smythe-Brown will have to manoeuvre."

"I don't think I could ever paint something he'd like. He'll hate it on principle."

"Speaking of which, have you decided on your pseudonym yet?"

"I've narrowed it down to a few. Why does it have to be a guy's name?"

"Because Smythe-Brown is a misogynistic little turd. Exactly like his father." Eadie spits this out with such venom that Jennie leans back. "The more we can manipulate him, the better. They both need to be taken down a peg, once and for all. One thing though, when you come to sign it, make sure you incorporate your signature into the composition itself."

"Why's that?"

"Harder for someone to reframe it and claim it as their own."

Jennie doesn't miss the bitterness in this comment, but given the lateness of the hour, doesn't push Eadie to elaborate.

Once she's settled Eadie for the night, Jennie returns the painting to her studio. She's not sure she's going to get a lot of sleep herself. Her mind is whirling with techniques and intrigue. Rupert's dad must have done a real number on Eadie for the woman to be so bitter about him and his offspring.

She's in bed staring at a blank page in her notebook and thinking of possible pseudonyms when she hears someone laboriously mounting the stairs. It has to be Mark. Chris is up north and Eadie never ventures upstairs. Also, the tread is too heavy for Sam. There's some scuffling, following by a loud crash, then agonised groaning, confirming without doubt that it's Mark. While it sounds like he's had a skinful and she'd rather leave him lying there, Jennie is unable to ignore the sound of someone obviously in pain.

Jumping out of bed, her hand is already on the doorknob when she realises she's hardly dressed for an encounter with Mark, especially if he's drunk. She pulls on her dressing gown and ties it securely before opening the door. Staring out into the gloom, she can make out Sam standing in the doorway opposite.

Jennie flicks on the light. Mark's lying in a heap in the middle of the landing. There's a lump already forming on his forehead from where he'd introduced it to the hall table. The pot plant that normally sat innocuously on this piece of furniture lies in pieces close by.

Sam shakes her head and stares down at Mark's unmoving form. "Bloody hell. He's been on a bender."

Jennie nudges Mark with her toe in hopes of eliciting a few

signs of life. "No way can we get him up to his room in this state."

"I vote we leave him there," says Sam. "Goodnight."

Jennie's returned goodnight is to the closed door of Sam's room. She looks back at Mark, who's rubbing his head and groaning.

"Are you okay?"

His response is unintelligible apart from a few choice swearwords. He rolls over onto his stomach and gets unsteadily onto his hands and knees. He doesn't try for any further altitude, before crawling into Jennie's bedroom.

"Hey, that's not your room."

He keeps crawling until his forehead makes contact with the side of the bed. "It'll do."

Jennie watches in horror as he clambers up onto her recently vacated bed, rolls onto his back and passes out. Charlie is not amused but no amount of deep growling will budge the interloper. His expression of disgust at this development is such that Jennie can't help but laugh.

"Come on, buddy. Let's leave him to it." Jennie grabs her notebook from the bedside table and clicks her fingers at Charlie. She's halfway up the first flight of stairs toward the studio before he catches up. He's slower than usual because he's still half asleep, with his legs seemingly not correctly attached to his body.

Jennie's awake early the next morning. She's forgotten how bright it is first thing in the studio. Still, she's got a heap to get on with, working her way through all the notes she'd taken during her session with Eadie the night before.

"I hope he's got the hangover from hell," Jennie says to Charlie. She's only ever shared a double bed with the cat before and the single means his bulk is draped artfully over her legs, stopping her from moving them, or even rolling over. “Come on, ya big lump. Move, so I can get up.”

Opening one eye, he stares at her balefully, before pretending to go back to sleep by going all floppy. His weight increases in direct proportion to this new level of relaxation and forces Jennie to slide her legs out from under him one at a time although she still gets a couple of warning growls.

“Sorry, matey, but I’m not playing pinned-to-the-bed to keep you happy.”

Safely out from under him, Jennie strokes her hand over his head and down the length of his back until she hears his seismic purring, his way of saying she’s been forgiven.

Jennie uses the upstairs bathroom before going back down to her room. Mark’s bedroom had been empty when she passed it, so chances are he’s still sleeping in her bed. Jennie creeps down the last few stairs to the first floor landing; she needs to be as quiet as possible for her plan to work. He’s still in there. His snoring could take on a fully laden freight train and win.

She crosses the landing and knocks on Sam’s door, not bothering to be quiet given the din coming from her own bedroom.

A muffled, “Come in,” makes its way through the heavy wooden door.

Jennie settles herself on the end of Sam’s imposing four-poster bed. With both bedroom doors ajar, Mark’s snoring is audible even from in here.

“If he’s still in there, where did you sleep last night?” The look on Sam’s face tells Jennie that her friend is hoping for developments.

“In the studio,” says Jennie, halting Sam’s aspirations.

“You know, you could stitch him up good and proper,” says Sam, mischief marking her face.

"That's what I was thinking, too."

"C'mon." Sam throws the covers to one side and springs out of bed.

As they walk across the landing, Sam is already trying to undo the belt on Jennie's dressing gown. Jennie slaps her hands away.

Sneaking around the end of the bed, Jennie starts to lie down on top of the covers but a hissed, "No!" from Sam stops her in her tracks.

Her frown of confusion is answered by Sam, who throws imaginary covers to one side, letting Jennie know that on top won't do.

Jennie mouths, "Do I have to?" Sam's head tips to the side and she rolls her eyes.

Jennie eases the covers back gently and is about to slide in under them when there's more arm waving from Sam on the other side of the bed. "What?" whispers Jennie.

Sam tugs wildly at the front of her dressing down. Jennie crosses her arms over her chest protectively, all the while shaking her head from side to side.

Sam crosses her arms mutinously in response before hissing, "You want this to work, don't you?"

Jennie's shoulders drop, she fumbles with the knotted belt at her waist and eventually shrugs out of the dressing gown. She hangs it over the bedpost at the head of the bed, so it's as close to hand as possible without actually being on her body. Running her hands down the front of her heavy lawn nightgown with its lace detailing, she realises she's fairly well covered, even without that extra layer of protection.

Lying down as gently as she can, she then pulls the covers carefully up and pretends to be asleep, although she feels about as relaxed as an ironing board.

Nothing happens and she opens one eye a slit. Sam tiptoes out of the room, although not for long. Her friend fakes a noisy and public entrance that makes both of Jennie's eyes ping wide open. There's no reaction at all from Mark. His snoring continues unabated.

"Jennie! *What* are you doing?" yells Sam, loud enough to be heard over the chugging and squawking of Mark's nasal cavities.

His breathing gymnastics come to a snorty halt and there's a slurred, "What the hell?" from the heap lying next to Jennie.

"What are you doing in here?" says Sam, looking authentically indignant. Jennie's impressed with the acting skills on show and hopes her own will be up to snuff.

"What?" Mark's gaze roams around the room, his confusion evident.

This is perfect, thinks Jennie, he has no bloody idea how he got here.

Mark swipes his hand across his forehead, obviously trying to get his brain to work; the only result is a groan of pain when he encounters the site of his connection to the hall table the night before. His head rolls to the side and he spots Jennie lying next to him.

A look of horror crosses his face and Jennie breathes deeply in readiness for playing her part in this farce. She doesn't get a chance.

His initial horror turns to something altogether more lecherous and he rolls over, bringing himself into close proximity to her. "Now, what do we have here?" says Mark, before emptying his lungs into Jennie's face.

"My God!" She waves her hand in front of her face and pulls back as far as she can. "Your breath is lethal." This is an understatement. His breath is alcoholic enough to warrant an age restriction.

"You didn't say that last night," says Mark, moving even closer.

Panicked, Jennie scuttles rapidly away from him. And falls

out of bed. This development is met with evil laughter from Mark, who rolls back to the other side of the bed and throws the covers back. He stops all movement and another groan escapes him.

He must be nursing one hell of a hangover thinks Jennie, gleefully. With his back toward her, she jumps up, grabs her dressing gown and drags it on, belting it securely before walking around the bed to join Sam.

"Jennie, I thought you said you spent last night in your studio?" Sam's gaze flips between Mark and her.

"I did! He's making it up."

Damn Sam and her warped sense of humour.

"Am I?" says Mark, before struggling to his feet to waver slightly before moving Sam to one side so he can exit the room.

"But nothing happened!" says Jennie, more forcefully now.

"Of course it bloody didn't." Mark's tone is so emphatic that Jennie is surprised to find it's hurtful.

"Well, thank you." Jennie knows she sounds snippy but is unable to put a lid on it.

"Trust me, if something had happened between us, even if I weren't still fully clothed, you sure as hell wouldn't still be wearing that chastity belt of a nightgown." The look he gives her after this bald fact has her double checking the overlap on her dressing gown. It does no good, she still feels naked under his gaze.

With Mark safely out of the room and stumbling noisily up to the top of the house, Sam breaks the silence. "Man, he has seriously got the hots for you."

"What?" squeaks Jennie. "He hates me with a passion."

"Passion yes, hate no," says Sam, as she disappears through her bedroom door.

Despite much head shaking, this comment rattles around in Jennie's brain like a bluebottle caught in a jam-jar trap. It settles every so often, but refuses to die.

27

Jennie is well and truly chained to the studio for a couple of weeks, swapping between acrylic daubs of snotty dogs in the style of the old masters and her real passion, the watercolours for the exhibition. She's faced her late fiancé's steady gaze a few times, looking back at her from Chicken George's eyes. But rather than being upsetting, Jennie's found the encouragement in those familiar eyes helpful.

Working on the painting of the chook, Steve's eyes are full of mischief and Jennie is unable to stop a good burst of laughter escaping.

Her leg muscles get a serious workout with the numerous trips up and down to speak to Eadie. On the plus side, this has helped her back survive all those hours at the easel.

Sam has been similarly tied to her sewing machine, working on a couple of big orders. With Chris still up in Crewe and Mark having landed a contract with a big engineering firm in nearby Hammersmith, the house has felt strangely empty. Jennie feels bad about leaving Eadie on her own so much but when she'd tried to stay down longer than it took to discuss the stage of the latest painting, Eadie had given her a right ticking off and sent her packing back to the studio.

The light fading, Jennie stands back and looks at the painting of Chicken George's boots, if they could be called that. It's been a tricky balance between getting enough detail in to show the newspaper, sacking and twine and ensuring this painting sits comfortably with the simplicity of the others already completed. Leaving it to sit on the easel and in her mind, she washes her brush and puts it on the table to dry.

She collects several half-finished cups of tea and after balancing them, takes them through to the bathroom to empty before going down to the kitchen. Time for a full cup of tea and a hot one at that. She pauses on the first landing to see if Sam's around. She is, but she's obviously in the shower.

Swinging into the kitchen, Jennie has a cheery greeting at the ready, but apart from a cup of tea sitting at Eadie's end of the table, there's no sign of life. Jennie pops the three cups into the sink and fills them with water and washing up liquid. The skim rings are milky and solid and won't give up their rights without a fight.

"Do you think she'd like me to take that through to her," Jennie says to Charlie, who swings into the kitchen shortly after her. "I've got to stop talking to you as though I expect you to answer. People will think I'm barmy." Charlie miaows in response. "Exactly."

Jennie picks up the cup from the table but realises the tea is as cold as those she'd dumped in the bathroom sink upstairs. "Maybe a fresh cup then?"

Charlie agrees. Pushing her way back out of the kitchen, Jennie goes in search of Eadie to see if she'd like a fresh cuppa. Given how little movement the old lady has, this doesn't take long.

"Tea?" says Jennie, walking into the sitting room. Seeing the blank look on Eadie's face and a decanter that's down to half an inch of sticky goodness, adds, “Coffee it is,” before spinning around and heading back to the kitchen.

Eadie’s on her second cup before her face loses the stroke look.

“Don’t let Mark catch you like that,” says Jennie. “He’ll confiscate it again.”

“For god’s sake, I’m an adult. It should be me keeping him in line.”

“It’s only because he cares. He—” Jennie immediately stops her defence of him when she sees the look of hope that pops up on Eadie’s face. To avoid having to speak, Jennie takes a long, slow sip of her coffee.

“I’m close to finishing the last one.”

This sudden change of subject momentarily confuses Eadie. “Oh, the paintings, right. And ...?”

“I think it’s the best one so far. Certainly the most difficult to complete.”

“And with a week to spare, too!” Eadie rubs her hands together carefully before adding an emphatic, “Excellent.” All that’s missing is an evil mastermind laugh.

They’re both making short work of a third coffee when Sam wanders in. She’s carrying a small tartan jacket and her sewing kit. Settling herself in the armchair opposite Eadie’s, she sniffs the air appreciatively. “Is there any left?”

Jennie swills the ancient percolator. “Sorry, don’t think you’ll wring any more out of it.”

“Damn, I’m parched.” Sam stuffs everything down one side her chair before leaping to her feet. She relieves Jennie of the perc on her way to the kitchen.

She rustles up another brew and returns with Mark sniffing over her shoulder. She must have run into him in the kitchen because he’s clinging onto his favourite mug as though it’s a lifeline.

There's contented slurping from all, when the sound of the front door opening echoes around the room. The muffled thump of a suitcase hitting plush carpet follows. Sam puts her cup of coffee on the nearest flat surface and races from the room.

"Ah, young love," says Mark, before ruining the effect by sniggering. This elicits a scowl from Eadie.

Chris is the first to enter the sitting room, with Sam close on his heels. She's waiting for him to sit so she can claim his lap, when there's a restrained knock on the front door.

"I'll get it," says Sam, with resignation. She's the obvious choice being the closest to the front door but she can't help a look of longing in the direction of Chris's lap before she retraces her steps.

While the knocking might have been restrained, the response when Sam opens the door is anything but. The broken English and strident tone of their visitor lets them know that hoping they had seen the last of Sonja when she'd left three weeks back was an empty wish. Her stream of vitriol is interrupted by scuffling and thumping, with someone landing hard against the wall a couple of times. This is punctuated with grunts and more cussing.

The sitting room door flies open, hard, and smashes into the end of the couch, and Jennie jumps. She's lucky not to have had her elbow cracked.

"Mark, I think you should go and smooth things over," instructs Eadie. She looks rattled by all that violence occurring so close to her.

While Mark's face is a vision of 'do I have to?' he gets to his feet promptly, although he's not as eager in actually moving toward the hallway.

He hasn't made any headway at all when Sonja screams from the hallway, "I know you fake money loss. I find letter in rubbish bin." Sounds of her straining ensues, and a lot more foreign cussing, given its tone. Sam's doing a bang-up job of keeping the crazy woman out in the hallway.

"Oh, dear. She must have found the letter my lawyer friend sent to me." Eadie's expression is one of annoyance at herself. "How stupid of me. I should have burned it."

As Sonja strains to crawl her way around the edge of the door and into the room, Chris dives into the inside pocket of his jacket and pulls out something. He hisses, "Mark!" before throwing whatever it is at him. Mark's reactions prove quick enough that he catches it with the smallest of juggles.

Any more hesitation is out of the door when Mark sees what it is he's holding. He's down on one knee in front of Jennie with the lid flipped open before Sonja manages to drag herself into the room on all fours. Sam is riding her like a limpet.

Jennie is unable to prevent a look of surprise and an unwarranted smile at finding Mark on one knee in front of her. Memories of Steve in the same position flood her, although these are soon mopped up by less happy thoughts.

Taking in the tableau before her, Sonja's cussing changes to ear-splitting, spit-lubricated screaming. Sam doesn't stand a chance and is bucked off, hitting the door handle hard enough to have a spot of blood make an appearance on her forehead.

"That's enough!" shouts Chris, loud enough that everyone stops what they're doing.

With Sonja momentarily gobsmacked by the scene in front of her, Chris takes the opportunity to get between her and Sam. He drags Sonja to her feet but soon realises the error of this manoeuvre when she starts kicking out at anything and anyone.

Charlie sidles under Eadie's chair in the nick of time; Sonja misses him but scores a direct hit on the small table next to Eadie's chair. Jennie has to smother a small chuckle at the look of disgust on Eadie's face when the decanter and a couple of glasses go flying. The sweet smell of sherry pervades the room.

"Instead of kneeling there laughing, do you want to give me a hand?" says Chris to Mark, who's still assuming the proposal position in front of Jennie.

"Oh, yeah, sure. Why not?"

Rather than get to his feet, Mark launches himself sideways at Sonja's legs and wraps his arms around them, to stop them doing any further damage.

Sonja spits out, "You marry this bitch?" She's looking at Jennie like something she'd find on the bottom of her shoe after walking a dog.

"I couldn't help myself," says Mark, before turning googly eyes on Jennie.

It's all Jennie can do to stop rolling her own in response. If he lays it on any thicker, there's no way Sonja will buy it. He must have read some of this message in her response because he swiftly tones it down. He grunts out "didn't realise", "snuck up on me" and "match made in heaven," all while trying to keep hold of Sonja's scissoring legs.

Sonja still doesn't look like she's buying it, but she eventually stops her thrashing around.

"You let me go, please. I leave now."

The boys are tentative, but after a non-verbal conversation, they let go simultaneously. Sonja staggers, before pulling herself up straight and strong. The tilt of her chin is an indication of how she's feeling, but she's silent on it. Her departure from the room borders on regal with the sitting room door closing quietly after her. The room stays silent until they hear the front door closing with more force.

The silence lasts for a couple more seconds before the room moves forward again, as though an invisible handbrake has been released. Chris kneels down next to Sam and pushes her fringe back. "Are you okay? That's a nasty bump."

"Never mind that!" Sam swats his hand away and gesticulates wildly between Mark and Jennie. "How on earth did I miss this?"

"Hah, you didn't," says Mark, before rolling back on the floor laughing. "That was priceless. Quick thinking, mate." Mark snaps the lid closed and tosses the ring box back to Chris.

"But, but, but ..." Sam doesn't get any further. "But, but if ..." she tries again with no more success.

"But?" says Chris, this single word dripping with innocence, while he tosses the small blue box from one hand to the other, and then back.

"Oh, my god, oh my god, oh my god," says Jennie, finally twigging. This response is the only nudge Sam needs. Any bump is forgotten with her squealing "Yes, a thousand times yes." Following a lot of fumbling, the engagement ring slides into place.

There follows the usual discussion on "When did you know?" "I love the ring," and a lot of holding the hand out at arm's length for admiring glances for anyone interested in looking.

"I think this calls for a drink," says Eadie, her gaze already turning toward the usual position of the decanter. "Drat, might need to get that cleaned up before the ants carry me away."

Jennie's hand is on the handle of the sitting room door when they all hear the front door slammed, loud enough to have the paintings on the walls rattling.

"God Almighty. Is she back?" Jennie backs away from the door, worried she'll get collected by it when it's thrown open. It stays shut.

"Aww, bloody hell," says Mark, rolling to his feet. He's at the front window and has the lace curtains back moments later. "Shit, that was her leaving. The bitch faked it. I hate to think what she's done to my room.

"Never mind yours. What about mine?" Jennie grabs at the

handle and wrenches the door open. She's on her way upstairs seconds later, with Mark hard on her heels.

A quick look into her bedroom confirms that nothing has been touched, but her relief is short lived. "Shit, the studio."

Sprinting the rest of the way, she catches up with Mark on the final flight and they split at the top of the stairs.

"Oh, thank god. No more damage." Mark's tone is relieved.

Jennie isn't sure Sonja could have done any more damage to anything of Mark's but the Dalmatian has more than made up for this in the studio. Her numbness is rapidly replaced by tears and she's a snivelling mess when he wanders in.

"Shit! This is my fault. I'll help you clean up."

The clean-up is going to take a while, plus a whole lot more work from Jennie. The painting of Chicken George's boots, still sitting on the easel, has taken the brunt of Sonja's venom. The word 'slut' is smeared across it in red paint, although when Jennie looks more closely, she realises it's lipstick.

"That cow," says Jennie, looking at the ruined watercolour. How could she do that to an artwork? Jennie's heartbreak at the destroyed painting is smartly replaced with panic. Even though the other three pieces are safely downstairs in the sitting room, this painting of the boots had been the hardest and taken the longest to complete.

"Oh my god, I've only got a week before the paintings need to go to the framers. I'll never be able to repaint it by then.

"Of course you will!" This emphatic statement is Eadie's, a voice not heard in the studio for a long, long time.

She's cradled in Chris's arms. Sam is behind them. Chris puts the old lady down as gently as he can but her countenance is still marred by a flash of pain.

"Eadie, you shouldn't have come up here," says Jennie, her own worries banished for a moment. She helps the old lady make her way over to the bed where she settles herself as comfortably as she can.

"Don't you make me use bad language, young lady," says Eadie, with forced cheerfulness. "Now what's this about you not having time to finish another painting of the boots?"

"But I've only got a week. That's seven days!" Jennie is unable to stop her voice turning shrill, panic welling up in her throat.

"Yes, and that's to finish a painting you've already completed once before. Remember how much faster you got on the Warhol painting with each subsequent rendition in the grid." Eadie's voice, by comparison, is the epitome of calm and reason.

"That's true," says Jennie. Some of her anxiety dropping away.

"And we can bring meals up to you and take care of everything else," says Sam.

"Yeah, you name it and we'll take care of it," says Mark.

"First thing we're going to do though is get a bloody great lock on that door!" says Chris nodding at it.

With the troops rallying around her, Jennie embraces the sense of relief that floods her. She can do this. She might even show the slut version as a modern art piece. It's the sort of whacky thing that someone with no artistic appreciation would pay big bucks for.

By the end of that day, Eadie is safely back downstairs, the studio is tidy once again and Jennie has started on the preliminary pencil outline for the replacement boots painting. The following morning a locksmith arrives and fits an incredibly large lock on the studio door. He hands the key and a spare to Jennie with the aplomb of an official giving someone the keys to the city. Jennie hasn't received a key with this much ceremony since her uncle handed her a pug-ugly mirrored monstrosity on her 21st birthday.

True to their word, the others take care of everything. Jennie has her washing done for her and she's off dishes and housework duties, too. Even Charlie deigns to let someone else feed him his meals. In truth, he's happy for anyone with opposable thumbs to be on call. The celebration of Chris and Sam's engagement is put on hold until after the exhibition.

Jennie immerses herself in her work and after five long days, manages to replicate the painting of Chicken George's boots. She thinks this version is even better. Something Eadie confirms.

The four paintings still attached to their backing boards, are propped on various surfaces around the sitting room, so she and Eadie can examine them, looking for anything that could or should be tweaked. Jennie is so close to the paintings that she no longer knows if they're any good or not, although she can't see anything glaringly wrong.

Eadie's gaze wanders from painting to painting. She occasionally raises a hand but doesn't say anything for the longest time. Jennie's fit to bust when eventually the old lady breaks her silence.

"Well done, girl!"

The gasp of breath that escapes Jennie's lungs surprises both of them. Jennie is about to ask Eadie if she really thinks so when she remembers the woman's mantra. 'If she doesn't mean it, she doesn't say it.'

"I love the pseudonym by the way. William Charles Flushing sounds highfaluting enough to appeal to both generations of the Smythe-Browns. How did you come up with it?"

"Dad's a plumber. It seemed appropriate."

Jennie's laughter joins Eadie's.

28

Jennie and Eadie have finally subsided into the occasional snort about the pseudonym, when the old lady finally centres her thoughts.

"Right, get these back upstairs and lock them up tight, but don't wrap them until you take them to the framers tomorrow afternoon. Let the paint settle."

"Will overnight be enough?"

"More than enough. I'm playing it belt and braces."

Jennie carries the paintings back up to the studio one at a time so she can keep a hand on the banister on each journey. She re-locks the door after each visit. This is a touch paranoid of her, but she's not about to risk losing all the paintings with the exhibition only a couple of days away.

She's carrying the last one up the final flight when Mark comes out of his room.

"All done?"

"Yep, finished. And been given the Eadie stamp of approval."

Once she's unlocked the door, she holds it open in invitation for Mark to enter.

Propping the last painting on the floor up against the wall with the other three, she waits for comment from him. She's expecting a simple 'nice' or something similarly lame but is surprised when he talks knowledgeably about them. He picks up on her surprise.

"What?"

"Nothing. It's that I'd never picked you as an art-lover."

"Runs in the family."

Jennie's about to push him on this, when he abruptly leaves.

With a small frown of concentration that's tinged with confusion, Jennie goes back to looking at the paintings. She scans the studio. Nothing. Not a thing. Not even a doggie commission. She should feel relief, but all she feels is empty. She can't just stop again. An image of Steve flits across her mind and while it still brings sadness, there's also acceptance now.

Eventually, her gaze settles on the small pile of Polaroids that she's used as reference for the watercolours. She has no need of them now, but rather than trash them, she decides she'll hand them over to the bum along with the Polaroids of the finished paintings.

A quick trip down to Sam's room and Jennie is back in the studio with the camera. She takes photos of the painting of George and Peggy together and the one of Peggy on her own, but doesn't bother with the painting of his boots or his hands as she doubts he'd understand the artistic merit of these. She pops the developed photos, along with the originals, in the side pocket of her handbag.

Rather than risk the ire of the entire household, Jennie locks the studio, and then knocks tentatively on Mark's door.

"Yeah?"

"Mark, will you come with me down to Chicken George's house?"

The door swings open, and Mark looks at her incredulously. "That's not a house, it's a hovel. And what the hell do you need to see him for anyway? I thought you were done with those paintings?"

"I am, but I promised him he could have Polaroids of the paintings when I was finished with them."

Mark looks set to argue this, but before Jennie has her mutinous expression fully in place, he stops, surprising her.

"Okay, let's go." He unhooks a jacket off the back of his bedroom door and drags it on. It's still got both sleeves but the pockets on the front are close to falling off and it's missing half its buttons.

"Wait here for me," says Jennie, when they reach the gap in the hedge. This is the first time either of them has spoken since leaving the house. Again, Mark looks to be readying himself to argue, but when Jennie lays her hand on his arm, he relents.

"I won't be long."

Walking through the long grass, Jennie is confident that George is at home, although he looks to be readying to move on if the fully-laden supermarket trolley that sits next to the door of the hovel is any indication. Peggy is conspicuous by her absence. Jennie can't even hear clucking.

"Hello," says Jennie, careful to keep her tone gentle and non-threatening. There's no response, so she tries again and hears rustling from inside.

George emerges tentatively; his face is streaked with tears, the furrows showing lighter. The grime diluted.

"Are you okay?""

"They took her," he moans.

At Jennie's look of confusion, he continues, "They took my Peggy."

"What!" Jennie only realises she must have yelled when she sees George cower and senses Mark walking up next to her.

"We all right here?" His tone is threatening and George stumbles backwards as though he's been struck.

"Someone stole his chicken."

"God, for a minute, I thought something really bad had happened."

This cavalier attitude to Peggy's disappearance has George keening in distress.

"She's all the family he's got," Jennie hisses at Mark, before forcibly turning him around. "Go wait by the hedge."

"My baby, my baby." George is sitting on the log that constitutes his patio furniture, rocking back and forth, leaving Jennie unsure of what she should do.

George continues his rocking, although now he has the photo of Peggy that Jennie had given him when they'd first met. He's cradling it as gently as if it was the chicken herself. This reminds Jennie of the extras she got with her.

Rather than go through them and explain each one as she had planned to, she hands the pile to him.

"Thank you." George doesn't look up at her as he's too busy shuffling through the Polaroids. When he comes to the photo of him and Peggy, his tears flow unabated.

"I promise I'll keep an eye out for her. If I find her, I'll let you know."

The evening of the exhibition and Jennie is not-so-quietly freaking out. Mark delivered the paintings to the gallery earlier that day, who assured her that David Michaels had taken possession of them personally and that they'd been taken straight out to the back.

Rummaging furiously through the stack of paper and painting paraphernalia on the table next to the easel, Jennie mutters to herself. "I left it here. I'm sure of it." No matter how many times she riffles through everything, the invitation still doesn't show itself. "Maybe it's in my room."

Hurrying downstairs, Jennie's aware of panic rubbing away at her carefully constructed calm. A forage through both bedside tables and all her handbags for the missing invitation doesn't help. She stands next to her bed, eyes closed and replays what she did with it after taking it out of the envelope. This process is interrupted by Mark giving her the hurry up from downstairs where he's waiting in the hall with the others.

"I can't find my invitation," wails Jennie, in the general direction of the others before she walks haltingly downstairs.

"You're one of the featured artists, dear. You're hardly going to be turned away," says Eadie, reasonably.

Despite all of Eadie's assurances, Jennie remains on tenterhooks until she's safely inside the gallery. As in life, she still expects a hand to grip her shoulder any second.

"Wow. So many people." Jennie's hands stick to her sides with nerves and perspiration.

"That's not unusual for this type of event," says Eadie, from her seat next to where Jennie's standing. "Free food and wine."

Firmly glued in place with anxiety, Jennie's unable to move around the gallery and has sent Chris and Sam on a sortie to gauge the feedback on her four pieces. Watching them threading their way through the bejewelled crowd back toward her, her nerves stretch tighter.

She wipes her hands again, pleased she's chosen to wear something dark that's unlikely to show the damp patches on each hip.

"So?" Her question rushes out when they settle next to her.

"Unbelievable," says Sam.

"Unbelievable good or unbelievable bad?"

"Unbelievable amazing," says Chris. "People are raving about your stuff. There are already three sold stickers in place."

"Yeah, and some old biddy was haggling with David over the price of the fourth one," says Sam.

The knot deep in Jennie's chest releases. Even though her name isn't on the paintings, they're still her babies and it would have destroyed her to hear people hated them. She couldn't have asked for a better response really.

"I don't know why you're so surprised," says Eadie. "I told you so."

Jennie is about to reply, when Mark explodes. "What the hell is she doing here?" She's shocked both by his tone and that he's right behind her. She hadn't known he was there, her mind-numbing nerves being her sole focus.

"Who?" comes the response from all of the others.

"Sonja," says Mark, pointing at the woman, who's on the far side of the gallery.

"At least we know where your invitation disappeared to," says Sam.

Jennie's gaze catches that of Sonja's and is stabbed by the look of pure hatred marring the woman's usually attractive face. "Surely she wouldn't attack my paintings here?"

"Not on my watch," says Mark, moving to run interference between his ex and anything painted by Jennie.

Eadie, who has by now struggled to her feet, gasps. "That's not good."

"Are you okay?" says Jennie, immediately thinking Eadie must be in pain.

"Not me. That!" With her hands full of walking sticks, Eadie nods her head emphatically in Sonja's direction along with a small grimace indicating this sudden movement hasn't come easy.

Jennie looks to where Eadie's indicated, to discover that Sonja is no longer on her own. She's with Rupert Smythe-Brown and they're chatting up a storm. There's a lull in their conversation when Sonja points at one of Jennie's paintings and then at Jennie herself, followed by some full-on venting. Smythe-Brown's eyebrows crawl up his forehead like slugs on a lettuce leaf and it's not long before the expression on his face is as rotten as that sported by Sonja.

"Shit," says Jennie.

"Oh, shit indeed," says Eadie. "Even if she doesn't know about the pseudonym, it won't take long for that hideous little cretin she's smarming all over to put two and two together."

Sam and Chris, who've also been watching this exchange, confirm that it is indeed an 'oh shit' situation.

"I'm on it," says Chris. He's only taken one step when the room's attention is gathered in by David Michaels ringing a small brass bell. Those at the corners of the room scrum in, hoping there's more food on offer. This landslide of old money forces Chris back next to them.

"Maybe he won't do anything?" says Jennie, although even she doesn't believe this.

"Excuse me everyone, your full attention, please." David Michaels' voice increases in volume ensuring he receives just that.

His speech consists of lots of 'thank you' and other general toadying before he goes on to introduce the artists one by one. Jennie has already been told that he'll be announcing her last, given it's a reveal. She hadn't banked on the crowd being so unforgiving, making her progress to the low platform at the front of the room ridiculously slow. She's still a couple of rows back when she hears her pseudonym announced. Before she can push through to the front, she hears Rupert Smythe-Brown's nasally-challenged voice, squeaking louder than usual to ensure he's heard over the muttered complaints about meagre rations.

"I know, I know, it was naughty of me to paint under a pseudonym, but I wanted to be accepted for my own talent, rather than simply by my sterling reputation."

Jennie gives up trying to move the mountain of angora in front of her and stares open-mouthed at Rupert, who climbs onto the low podium and stands next to an astonished David Michaels. The gallery owner's mouth is hanging open in the same way as Jennie's, although he soon gets his thoughts together if the look on his face is anything to go by. He re-opens his mouth to speak, but is interrupted by Rupert, who says, "Yes, it was David's idea that I paint under a pseudonym."

"I hardly think ..." starts David Michaels, but he's quickly silenced by an unlikely source.

"That's right," says Barbara Harrow, backing up her nephew with blind loyalty and leaving the gallery owner in an awkward position. He'll have to call both Rupert and Lady Harrow liars if he's to clear things up.

Even Jennie can see that this wouldn't be good for business and if Jennie speaks up and says she's the artist, she'll only look like a spoiled brat. God, she's going to get even with him for this.

"When can we expect to see more of this wonderful work from you?" says Jennie, during a small pause in Rupert's litany of lies. Her pitch ramps up in the middle of the question due to pure rage.

The crowd erupts with calls for answers and also wants to know what his inspiration was for the collection. He squirms but never falters enough to be caught out. Eadie fires a couple of technical questions at him, but while he undoubtedly lacks raw talent, he knows exactly how it should be done. All that dosh his doting auntie spent on lessons seemingly not a complete waste of money after all.

The language in the car on the trip home is colourful, with

most of it blue. Jennie is furious, although not as irate as Eadie who keeps muttering "It's happening again."

David Michaels had been seething when they'd left the gallery not long after Rupert's duplicitous charade and informal question time. Jennie had been unable to stay and watch the odious little shit having praise heaped on him for all her hard work and talent. The smug look on Sonja's face as she'd hung around Rupert's sweaty dough-like neck was also something none of them were keen on looking at for longer than was absolutely necessary.

They're driving down their street and close to home, when Jennie, who's staring into the middle distance out the side window, spots some movement. "Stop the car!"

Maybe something good will come out of this night after all.

Mark's response is immediate, although by the time he's pulled over, they're a good way down the street.

"What's wrong?" he says, twisting around in his seat.

Rather than answer him, or the questioning looks of the others, Jennie ditches her handbag, opens the door and jumps out before running back down the street. Because she'd left her door open, she can hear them pondering what the hell's got into her. Even she realises her actions must look rather bizarre.

Walking along stooped over, Jennie peers into the shadows under the large hedge she's now next to.

"Peggy?" Jennie makes her voice as welcoming as possible. "Is that you, darling?"

There's a small *cluck* in response.

Holding her fingers near the ground, Jennie flicks them together softly and gradually a small beak, then the rest of the chicken, emerges from the dark. Jennie has her hands on both sides of the bird in readiness to grab it. Slowly does it. She can now feel the soft feathers, but doesn't want to spook the bird by moving too quickly.

"What the bloody hell are you doing?"

Concentrating on catching Peggy as she has been, Jennie hadn't even heard Mark approaching. Given the reaction from the chicken, the bird has been unaware too.

"Arrrgh!" Jennie staggers and takes a header into the hedge while Peggy scarpers as fast as her little chickeny legs will carry her.

"At least we know why she crossed the road," says Mark, helping Jennie to disentangle her hair from twigs that currently have it in a death grip.

She's upright in time to see Peggy disappear between a couple of houses on the opposite side of the street. After crossing the road, Jennie looks down the alley but it's closed off at the end by a gate, with the gap at the bottom being no barrier for a chicken.

"At least we know she's still alive," says Jennie, when she rejoins Mark on the pavement.

"Good god, your face!" says Mark, putting his hand under her chin and tilting her face toward the street light.

"What about it?" says Jennie, feeling it with her hand. Her face is damp. "It's only rain water."

"No, it's blood. You're scratched to hell. Sorry I scared you like that."

Deciding the chicken is going to have to wait, they return to the car although they're close enough to home that Jennie could walk.

There's a fuss in the car when they see the state of her face and Jennie isn't sure if it's because everyone is going on about it, but it's stinging like crazy now.

An examination of it in the mirror at home confirms for her that she does look like she's been dragged through a bush backwards. Cleaning the blood away makes a big difference though and after daubing liberal amounts of antiseptic cream on each and every one of the scratches, she joins the others in the sitting room.

The decanter receives constant attention while they go through the evening in detail, wondering if it's possible to reverse things, to stitch up Rupert, whatever. Plans are tabled and rejected or deemed too risky and more than a little illegal. Jennie surprises herself by coming up with the most illegal plan of all but, rather than share it, she decides to wait and discuss it with Eadie in private.

Their swearing and tension is interrupted by the phone ringing. "I'll get it," says Jennie, needing a small break from the energy-sapping atmosphere in the room.

"Edwards' residence. Jennie speaking." She's careful to hold the phone away from her face with its scratches and slavering of cream.

"Jennie, it's David Michaels. I am so sorry about what happened this evening. By the time I gathered my wits, it was too late. I can't believe he stood there and spouted those blatant lies. When his aunt backed him up like she did, I knew we were scuppered."

"Yeah, I couldn't believe that."

"It's left me in a bind. Calling out a Right Honourable for telling porkies is one thing. Fingering a Countess for the same is tantamount to social suicide but I'll have a think about how we can even things up. You should too."

"Trust me, we are. Thanks for calling."

Jennie returns to a room that's flat. The energy's flat, the expressions are flat and so is the mood. The wall of negativity stops her in her tracks and so rather than reclaim her seat, she steps backwards toward the hallway.

"Look, there's nothing we can do about it tonight. You guys can keep working on it, but I'm going to bed."

She's only part way up the first flight of stars when conversation in the room erupts again. If only some of the things they're suggesting be done to Rupert were possible. Surely it wouldn't be that hard to arrange for him to be kidnapped and dropped off an island somewhere? Getting him hammered and shaving his eyebrows off would be a doddle. Wouldn't it?

That thieving little bastard.

Shit, he's making me effing swear.

Following a crap night's sleep, Jennie is up early, finding it hard to sleep-in when she's still seething. The night had been passed in a repeat cycle: she'd manage to calm down when an image of Rupert spouting all those lies flitted, yet again, from one side of her brain to the other. And so the cycle would start afresh.

Rather than continue to stew about the events of the previous evening, Jennie gives Charlie his breakfast, then slips quietly up to the studio where she unlocks the large padlock with the key hanging around her neck on a chain. To ensure she's left uninterrupted, she jams the wooden doorstop in place after she's inside. The locksmith hadn't felt it was necessary for the door to lock from the inside. Jennie hadn't been in agreement but then neither had she been paying his bill. Eadie had brooked no argument on that score.

It's only after she's been working away on her latest doggie painting for several hours that the perfect strategy for revenge comes to her. It's perfect. It's foolproof. It's possibly illegal. But no more so than Rupert claiming her work as his own. She maps it out on a big sheet of paper, looks at it from all angles and can see no minuses, only pluses. Taking her sheet of scribbles down to show Eadie, she knows she's onto a winner when a positively evil grin spreads across the old lady's face.

"Of course, we'll need to wait for the Michaels' next party or until David has another exhibition to put it in place," says Jennie.

"I don't think that'll be a problem. I've never seen David so incensed. I think he'll be delighted to organise something special for this." Eadie taps the paper. "And I can get you the reference material you'll need."

"You can!" Jennie's aware her expression has set hard. Now this, she hadn't expected.

"For goodness sake, don't look so shocked. I wasn't always this old and decrepit."

29

After a brief conversation with David Michaels, Jennie is quickly on her way to the gallery. Mark had offered to drop her off, but as she'd pointed out, traffic would be awful at that time of day, and anyway it was quicker and easier on the tube. It wasn't as if she had to carry a heap of canvases, although she did have a sketch pad and pencils in her backpack.

The gallery owner's opening gambit is, rather than a formal greeting, "Good lord, you look a mess!"

"Yeah, I took a nose dive into a hedge." Jennie hadn't looked in the mirror before leaving the house but realises her scratches, which had already started to crust over, must look appalling. Following her angry start to the day, she's not even sure she remembered to brush her teeth. A quick exploration with her tongue confirms they're feeling grubbier than they should. She pushes herself back on the couch, so she's as far from David as possible. For all she knows, pure spleen might smell really bad.

"A hedge? Ah, no, it's the bags under your eyes I'm talking

about. They're bigger than those I use when I'm travelling abroad," says David, with blunt honesty.

"Oh. I didn't really sleep at all. I was, ah, am, so fu ... furious."

"And with good bloody reason. Still this might help ease some of the pain." He retrieves a neatly folded cheque from the inside pocket of his jacket and hands it over to Jennie. "We sold all of them."

Thanking him, Jennie carefully unfolds the cheque, unsure what the total will be once he's had his cut. Her eyes widen when she spots the total on the cheque. "But that can't be right."

"Do you honestly think I'd take a commission after what happened last night?"

"But, it wasn't your fault."

"Good lord, you are going to have to toughen up if you don't want every gallery owner in London taking advantage of you."

"But three thousand pounds, that's a huge amount of money."

"They got bargains. You are going to be selling your work for a lot more than that in a year or two." Nodding to counteract Jennie's head shaking, he adds "So, what is this plan you've cooked up?"

Jennie pulls her backpack over on the couch and digs inside, before pulling out the now crumpled master plan. She opens it and after smoothing the worst of the creases, lays it on the coffee table in front of her. She spins it around so David can read it.

His finger scans over the page as he reads each of the points in turn, occasionally backtracking and obviously linking ideas together. "Now, this is evil. And bloody brilliant." His booming laughter bounces dangerously off paintings and sculptures, causing heads to turn in their direction. The gallery staff frown until they realise who's behind this uncouth racket.

"How quickly can you finish a dozen paintings?"

"A dozen? I'm thinking I'll only need six for the plan to work."

"But you're forgetting, you'll still need to give paintings to Shit-Brown to sign."

Jennie's so busy giggling at David's bastardisation of Rupert's surname that it takes a second or two before she can answer. "I hadn't thought about it, but it makes sense."

"Of course, you don't need to spend as much time on his six paintings as those of our Mr Flushing."

"Let's see, twelve paintings. Six of them done in four days each and the rest ten days each? That makes twelve weeks. But that's ages."

"Not really. I won't announce the exhibition for another month, so we paint the little shit into a corner. It'll take another week of panic before he admits defeat and has to approach you to bail him out."

"And by then, I'll already have completed three of my paintings."

"I suggest you do one of his and then one of yours in turn. That way if you run out of time, we can still exhibit four or five paintings."

"Do you think he'll bite?"

"I'm going to make it a solo exhibition. No way in hell the pretentious little prat will be able to resist an opportunity like that."

"Right, I'd better get started then. Eadie has said she's going to help with ... ah ... reference material."

"I should imagine she'll do anything to help you get even. Rumour has it that Rupert's father did something similar to her. Her career never really recovered."

On leaving the gallery, rather than heading for home, Jennie makes a quick trip to the bank before calling into the art supply shop. Looking at the pile of large brown parcels sitting on the counter she realises there is no way she can get this lot home on the tube, even allowing for her new ballsy travelling persona.

"Can I use your phone?"

"Not a problem, love."

The assistant shows her to a back room that doesn't look as though it's been updated since the shop opened for business in the 1800s. Certainly there are no modern conveniences like a fax machine or typewriter. Even the phone, which is ancient, looks modern by comparison to its surroundings.

Jennie's only returned to the shop after a cup of tea and a ham sandwich at a local café when Mark pulls up in the dark green Jag.

"Thank you so much for this. I'd never have got this lot home on my own."

"See, you should have let me bring you in here in the first place."

"Yes, Mark, you are so right. I should have asked. It was silly of me. What was I thinking?" says Jennie, managing to keep her face straight throughout. She doesn't feel like an argument right now and would prefer to settle in the comfortable leather passenger's seat and watch the world slide by.

Mark's response stutters to a halt when he realises she's not going to argue about it.

"But ..."

"Yes?" says Jennie, sweetly causing him to frown suspiciously.

"Nothing."

The trip passes in silence other than the occasional remark from Mark on landmarks and everyday London life.

It takes a couple of trips from the car to the house before everything is stacked in the hallway, with Eadie calling out continuously from when they first open the front door.

"With you in a second, got a couple more loads yet," says Jennie, through the door of the sitting room, before returning to the car.

With the final items inside, she calls out again. "We're taking everything up to the studio and I'll catch up with you then."

A snort of frustration is the only response from Eadie to this development, causing a small smile to dance across Jennie's face.

"Come on, we'd better hurry or she'll be fit to bust," says Jennie, quietly to Mark.

With Mark loaded up like a donkey and Jennie lugging a bulging backpack, they stagger up to the top of the house, and then thunder back down for the final load.

"Bloody hell, I know how those Sherpas feel!" says Mark, dropping the final load on the floor of the studio.

"Yeah, I feel the need to plant a flag." Jennie wipes perspiration from her forehead and flaps her top in an effort to cool off before locking the door and trudging back downstairs to update Eadie on developments.

"So?" Eadie's eyebrows are raised as high as physically possible, reinforcing how important the answer to this particular question is.

"Really well. Rupert's in for a surprise in a little over a month when David announces to all and sundry that he'll be the subject of a solo exhibition."

"A solo exhibition. That's the perfect bait. When's it to be?"

"Early January. That way I've got a month to get work underway and it gives Rupert even less time to sort himself out. David reckons it'll take a week before Shit-Brown realises he doesn't have any option but to get my help." Jennie sniggers thinking about this new and perfect surname for Rupert.

"Shit-Brown! Haven't heard that in ages!" Eadie's snort of laughter is not at all ladylike and far louder than such a small frame should be able to produce. "His father hated it."

"So it's been around for a while then?"

"Yes. Someone in the art community came up with it years ago after Rupert's father got away with some rather unscrupulous behaviour."

"Any ideas?" says Jennie, now knowing full well who the originator is.

There's no response from Eadie other than to suggest that this latest development deserves a toast. It only takes the smallest of glances toward the decanter for Jennie to acquiesce.

Once again, everyone in the house promises to support Jennie while she throws herself into the dual creation of two collections. One named for Rupert Shit-Brown and the other attributed to William Charles Flushing. Because of their dodgy content, there is no way Jennie can put her own name on them. To do so would be artistic suicide.

True to her word, Eadie provides the rather dubious reference material needed. Even Mark looks surprised when he takes the collection of books and photographs up to the studio on Eadie's behalf. Jennie is unable to do anything about the colour that floods her face at the look he gives her when she mumbles thanks and takes them from him.

Flicking through them after he leaves, her face flames

afresh. If she'd known what was in them when he handed them over, she wouldn't even have been able to look him in the eye. Jennie's plan had simply been to paint Rupert in racy undies and the like. But this is in another league altogether. How on earth did people get their jollies with this type of thing? It looked painful, if nothing else. There's certainly nothing sexy about it that she can see.

The book she's skimming through flips open to a particularly graphic illustration, and a yelp of surprise escapes unbidden. Where did a guy even find a saddle like that; let alone one that looked to be made to measure? Not the local pet shop that's for damned sure.

Jennie doubts she'll be able to paint the subject matter Eadie's provided. If it makes her feel uncomfortable simply looking at the material, what will it be like to paint them?

It doesn't take long for Jennie to realise that completing what she calls the shadow collection, will be the hardest thing she's ever done. The paintings to be signed by Rupert will be child's play compared with the secret collection.

Sitting with Eadie while they go through the composition of each painting makes her feel as though she's been caught fiddling with herself in public.

Even thinking about it later sends a red flush lewdly groping at her chest and face.

When Mark had walked in on them during that session, Jennie had slammed her sketchbook closed so hard it had hurt her leg. That people get off on this sort of pain is something she still can't grasp.

Locking herself in the studio, complete with masking tape over the keyhole and the sheets over the window that faces the street, Jennie is as ready as she'll ever be to begin. She's already completed the first Rupert painting, a particularly ragged teddy bear sitting next to some chipped and faded building blocks. Entitled '*Little Boy Bear*'. The toy's expression is ambiguous, but is sure to bring back childhood memories for anyone viewing it. Good memories. Bad memories.

With that painting safely propped against the far wall, Jennie looks down at the unsullied canvas sitting nervously on the easel, like a virgin about to be deflowered for the gratification of anyone watching. The purity is soon smudged by numerous soft pencil strokes, with the crude act coming to life under her hand.

The pencil slips from her hand when there's a sharp rap at the door. The lead snaps loudly when it hits the unforgiving wooden floor.

"Who is it?" squeaks Jennie.

"Mark."

"Hang on a second."

Jennie's gaze flickers around the room, desperately looking for something to cover the offending artwork. The sheet she usually uses is in the wash. No way in hell does she want him seeing this! Short of ripping the bed to bits, there's nothing suitable to cover it with. She slides it beneath the bed before going over and removing the wedge from under the door.

"How are you getting on?" says Mark, peering over at the table hoping to see what she's working on.

"I've finished this." Jennie gestures toward the teddy bear painting near his feet.

"Wow. On the face of it you've painted a bear with blocks, but ..."

"Yes?" The painting has already had the thumbs up from Eadie, but feedback from different quarters is always reassuring.

"It's too sodding good for Shit-Brown to put his name to."

"Oh, I see what you mean. Problem is he has to be convinced enough with the quality of the paintings to go ahead with the exhibition. Otherwise, he'll pull the plug."

Mark curses roundly before continuing. "Damn. You're right. Such a bloody waste though."

"I'll be painting lots more in the future. David's already said he'll hold an exhibition of my own work."

"Have you started on any of the second collection yet?"

"Not yet," stammers out Jennie, aware a swathe of red has started spreading from her solar plexus.

"Are you okay? Should I open a window?"

Without touching her face, Jennie can tell the red has reached its mark.

"No, I'm fine. Must be coming down with a cold is all."

"It is bloody hot in here." Mark walks over to the window and Jennie fans herself in an effort to cool off enough that she no longer looks like she's related to a tomato. When he stops next to the bed, his foot is dangerously close to the canvas under it. He leans across the bed, ready to throw a window open when she stops him in his tracks.

"No, don't do that. If the room cools down too much, it can affect the paint."

She knows this is rubbish given people painted outdoors all the time, but he swallows it. Swinging back toward her, he catches the edge of the canvas with his foot, punting it out into the open.

"Excuse me!" Jennie doesn't wait for a response, but dives out of the room, around the corner and straight into the bathroom. No way can she face Mark with that sketch sitting between them with all the subtlety of a value pack of extra-large condoms.

From her spot where she leans against the basin, she can hear him laughing. He doesn't stop. It's a gut-busting belly laugh that goes on and on. Jennie goes from being embarrassed to being irate. "How dare he laugh at my stuff like that," she says, to the reflection in the mirror. After slamming her hands down hard on the rim of the basin, she storms back into the studio.

By now Mark is lying on the bed, rolled double. Tears stream from his eyes. He's holding his stomach.

"It's not that bad."

Physically restraining himself, Mark manages to snort out, "It's not that."

"What then!" Jennie knows her voice has risen, both as a result of her anger and having to be heard over the grunting and guffawing coming from Mark. By comparison, his nightly snoring is positively melodic.

Mark gestures to the canvas now sitting against the side of the bed. "It's how you've portrayed him. How in god's name did you come up with that?"

"Um, books and stuff."

At this revelation, his head snaps up, although the laughter has yet to cease.

Jennie adds, "The ones Eadie loaned me," and his laughter dies. Now it's his turn to look flushed.

30

Stretching tall, Jennie twists first in one direction, then the other, the resulting crackles and pops testament to the hours she's spent in front of the easel over the preceding month. It's all very well the others waiting on her hand and foot, but it means she no longer gets as many breaks as she used to.

Looking at the dregs in the coffee cup and the few crumbs on the plate that are all that's left of lunch, Jennie decides she needs a change of scene. Grabbing them both, she makes her way down to the kitchen. She's stepping off the bottom step when a slew of mail is shoved through the flap in the front door. Most of it makes the basket, but a few slide down the ramp formed by the bottom letters and onto the floor.

The one that lands right next to Jennie's foot is addressed to her. The envelope is heavy duty and cream. "This could be it," says Jennie, to the empty hall.

"Could be what?" comes back from Eadie in her sitting room.

"I think it's the exhibition invitation. Hang on while I dump these dishes in the kitchen."

Jennie strides down the hall and shoves at the swinging door with a shoulder. She's back in the hallway moments later, simply having dumped her dishes on the counter. She scoops the mail off the floor and then empties the basket. Working her way through the pile, she sorts it onto the hall table, before picking up the letter addressed to her and a few for Eadie.

"Here you go," says Jennie, putting the pile of letters for Eadie on the old lady's lap. The envelope on top, matches the one Jennie is already ripping open. Sure enough the substantial gold-embossed card inside announces the solo exhibition of Rupert Smyth-Brown. "I thought there was an 'e' on the end of Smythe."

"Hah, David spelt his name wrong. His father always had a bloody conniption if we forgot the 'e'. We used to spell it wrong on purpose. Pompous little twits, both generations."

"January the 3rd. Two months to go," says Jennie. "Isn't that a little early in the New Year?"

"David Michaels is more than likely hoping some of his best clients won't be able to make it as they'll still be in the country for Christmas."

Jennie looks at the flowery and overly-grandiose invitation. "I wonder how many he sent out."

"Over one hundred and fifty, I believe. This has been a long time coming."

"One hundred and fifty!" Jennie swallows convulsively at the thought of so many people seeing the filth sitting face-in to the studio wall.

Sure enough, only a week goes by before Jennie receives a summons to meet with Rupert. The pub is as east of Kensington as is possible without actually leaving London and manifestly well clear of any of his usual haunts.

"You're not going *there* by yourself," says Mark. His tone indicates that she can debate as much as she likes, but she will not win this particular argument. Eadie backs him up and Jennie gives in.

"The little shit has chosen that place deliberately to unnerve you. You take Mark with you and watch him change his tune when the two of you walk in."

"It can't be that bad?" says Jennie, laughing.

"Don't know what it's like now, but it used to be very bad. Had a hell of a reputation."

Eadie's gaze is hitting somewhere around middle ground in the room but it's easy to see she's looking at some things she'd rather forget. The pain etched on her face stops Jennie's laughter.

"We'll take the tube," says Mark.

"We will?" This confuses Jennie as Mark would always rather drive if he can.

"Hell, yes, if we park the Jag in that area, we'll come back to find anything not screwed down is missing, maybe even the whole damned car."

The farther east the tube takes them, the happier Jennie is to have Mark at her side. The names sliding by are unfamiliar and there are a lot of them before they reach their stop. Things go downhill after they leave the station where at least some standards have been maintained. The smell of urine in the underpass says the station toilets have largely been ignored. The acrid stench stings Jennie's nostrils and she's pleased when they emerge safely from the other side of this busker-free zone.

The pub is a couple of blocks from the station but after several minutes of brisk walking, they stand safely outside, with Jennie puffed from the pace set by Mark. She's had to trot to keep up. The pub's exterior is tatty, having given into gravity and weather years ago. The skin of white paint that covers the majority of the building is currently shedding, rather like a snake coming out of hibernation, while the black woodwork owes its lustre more to a noxious soup of pollution and rampant mould than anything produced by Dulux.

The building is a rotting corpse, in reverse, with black bones and white flesh.

It's only when Mark squeezes her arm reassuringly that Jennie is even aware her hand has inched its way through the crook of his arm. Rather than pull away, she scoots closer and feels safer immediately.

He looks down at her. "You ready?"

"As I'll ever be!" says Jennie, with fake conviction. "Let's get this over with."

They march forward in step, both straight-arming one of the double doors, and striding into the gloomy interior. Jennie is relieved to see the interior is less toxic than the exterior although she still wouldn't feel comfortable eating anything in here.

"Where's the snug, mate?" says Mark, to the furtive-looking individual behind the bar.

No words are forthcoming, but the swing of the barman's head to their left sends them in that direction.

Again, they each straight-arm one of the double doors, although this time with less force given each door is primarily made up of a grime-encrusted pane of glass that hasn't seen any Windex and crumpled newspaper in living memory.

Their dramatic entry has Rupert Smythe-Brown leaning back into the red velvet banquette where he's settled himself. The sneer pasted on his face slithers away and hides in one of his chins. "What's he doing here?"

"Don't talk about me in the third person, mate. I'm right here," says Mark, with forced jocularity.

"Eadie wouldn't let me come on my own."

"That old slag," spits Rupert. "Why she's nothing but a—"

Before Rupert can search for another scathing description for Eadie, Mark gently uncurls Jennie's hand and leans menacingly over the table. "You shut your fucking mouth about Eadie, or I'll shut it for you. We clear?" While Mark's voice is quiet to avoid it carrying to the main bar, his words, delivered as they are so close to Rupert's face, have the desired effect.

Holding his hands up in surrender, Rupert jerks his head up and down in small nods of compliance. This motion shows anything not attached to muscle or bone, to be the consistency of blancmange.

Convinced the odious little man is going to behave, Mark straightens up and pulls out a chair for Jennie, but doesn't sit himself.

"Get up!" says Mark.

Jennie starts to do so, confused because he's just helped her to sit. It's only when his hand drops gently to her shoulder that she realises he's talking to Rupert.

"I'm not going to fight you," says Rupert, his eyes wide, his tone squeaky with fear.

"Relax mate, I wouldn't waste my energy on a little turd like you."

Rupert's arse stays stuck to the velvet, and so Mark walks round the table and drags him to his feet. Rupert tenses, ready to protect himself, but rather than pummel the little weasel, Mark frisks him thoroughly.

He's nearing the end of his search when he uncovers a personal recorder in the front pocket of Shit-Brown's jacket.

"Now, what do we have here?" says Mark, holding up the small device and clicking it off.

Rupert's only response is an ugly sneer although this is soon replaced by a grimace when Mark drops the recorder onto the grimy floorboards and smashes it with the heel of his boot. Rupert breathes in as though to voice a complaint about this wanton destruction but Mark's expression renders him mute.

Mark takes the chair next to Jennie and indicates to Rupert that he should start talking.

Rupert takes a nervous gulp of his Guinness. "Aren't you going to drink something?"

"This isn't social," says Mark, a hard edge to his voice.

Jennie gestures toward the state of Rupert's glass and the grimy table it's sitting on. "Can't afford to get sick, can I?"

"No, I suppose not," concedes Rupert, who doesn't seem to share her worries about catching anything from their surrounds. He's at home, which surprises Jennie, given what a bloody snob he is.

Rupert takes another sip of his drink. "You have to paint six paintings for me by the first of January."

"Have to?" says Mark.

"Well, she's the reason I'm in this predicament," says Rupert, indignantly.

The way Rupert stares at her makes Jennie feel guilty until she remembers the night of the exhibition and a much more appropriate anger replace her guilt.

"Like hell I am. *You* are the only reason you're in this mess you vain-glorious little toad." Jennie is vibrating after this tirade, but it's a feeling she could come to enjoy.

"She's got you there," Mark points out.

Rupert stills for a moment, obviously going over options. "But you'll still complete them, won't you?" says Rupert, looking dangerously sure of himself.

Even though this question is rhetorical, as far as Shit-Brown is concerned, Jennie still feels the need to answer.

"And why is that?" She's genuinely curious as to what he thinks he holds over her.

"Because if you don't, father and I will go public about what Eadie used to get up to in the good old days."

While Jennie is still frowning at this change in direction, Mark jumps in.

"She thought you might try that. Told me to tell you that she doesn't give a rat's arse what you and your dear old dad come out with. She's too damned old to care anymore."

Rupert opens his mouth to reply a couple of times, but no audible response is forthcoming.

Mark goes for the jugular. "She also said that if the pair of you go public, then she's got some excellent mementos of her own."

Mark pulls the front of his jacket away, takes a photo out of his shirt pocket and holds it up for Rupert to see. Rupert pales and his mouth droops open, leaving Jennie in no doubt as to the subject matter. It's doubtless along the lines of some of her more recent 'works of arse'.

Jennie rests her hand on Mark's arm when he starts to put the photo away, but rather than flip it around for her to see, he shakes his head and slides it out of sight.

"One hundred and fifty pounds each it is then," says Rupert, without preamble. "Same as you charge for those ugly mutt daubs."

Jennie's mouth opens to react to this slagging off of her doggie paintings.

He's got a bloody cheek considering the state of that piece of shit that takes pride of place on his aunt's mantelpiece.

Before she can respond, Mark baldly replies to Rupert. "One thousand each or we walk."

"I won't pay that much," splutters Rupert.

Mark retrieves the photo from his pocket at the same time as Jennie says, "Fifteen hundred quid each it is then."

Rupert's gaze swings between then, unsure how he's lost control of the negotiations.

With Rupert sitting open-mouthed like a clown in a sideshow, Jennie outlines the subject matter of each of the six paintings. Every time he tries to interrupt, she simply holds her hand up and ploughs on. When they leave, Jennie has a nine-thousand-pound cheque safely tucked in the inside pocket of her handbag. Rupert also knows she won't start work on any paintings until the cheque has cleared, in case he has any ideas about putting a stop on it.

Safely through the urine gauntlet and on the tube heading west, Jennie is still shaking her head at how well it had gone.

"How did you know to look for a recorder?"

"It was something Sam mentioned. Apparently she used one to nail some creepy boss of hers."

"Of course. I'd forgotten about that." Jennie pauses briefly. "That must be one doozy of a photo you showed him."

Jennie is still desperate to see it but won't ask for a peek now. If the subject matter is as racy as she suspects, she doesn't want to look at it with him holding it out for her to see. Thinking back, she's glad he refused to show it to her in the bar.

No sooner do they shut front door behind them, than Eadie call's out, "How'd you get on? Hurry up, the curiosity is killing me."

They ditch their jackets and join Eadie so they can put her out of her misery. Rather than respond verbally, Jennie pulls out the cheque and casually drops it on Eadie's lap.

"That's a lot more than I thought he'd pay." Her eyes are wide in surprise although they don't take long to crinkle in laughter. She eventually sobers and turns to Mark. "You had to pull out the big guns, didn't you?"

"Yeah, he was being a jerk and threatening to go public."

Mark pulls the photo out of his pocket and puts it inside a cigar box that sits on the small knick-knacks table next to Eadie's chair. Before he closes the lid, Jennie catches a glimpse of the contents. It would seem there are a lot more photos where that one came from. Even thinking about the possible contents of that small wooden box makes her feel pink.

"Right, young lady, you need to get cracking again. The quicker you move ahead, the longer you can have off at Christmas time."

"Of course. I'd forgotten about that."

31

The weeks following the meeting with Rupert swirl by in a swathe of paint, gallons of tea and the occasional break for sleep or showering. Jennie feels like an extra out of the movie *They Shoot Horses, Don't They?*

Sam's been working as hard, trying to rid herself of a backlog of outfits so she can take a couple of weeks off and go up and stay with Chris in Crewe. Her departure is only a few days away. With the hours the two of them have been working, Jennie doubts she'll even realise Sam has left. As it is, they only happen upon each other on the stairs or in the kitchen.

Despite the various offers to take sandwiches up to her, Jennie has stayed firm on coming downstairs to make her own. If nothing else, it gives her body and mind a break. She's enjoying working on the watercolours of the vintage toys for Rupert, but doesn't know how she feels about the acrylics that form the shadow exhibition. For one thing, she's having difficulty painting them as badly as they need to be for the sake of authenticity.

Grinding her teeth, Jennie concentrates on the acrylic currently strapped to the easel. It's not the only thing strapped down. Jennie checks her reference material again and notices something she hadn't seen before. The contrast on the illustrations is appalling, with new monstrosities making themselves apparent when least expected.

"What on earth are they for?" Starting at the pulley, her finger traces a length of rope. "No!" Jennie's face wrinkles in horror and she slams the book shut. "I can't paint that!"

"Can't paint what?" says Sam, from right beside Jennie's left elbow.

"Oh, hell!"

Even without the earmuffs on, Sam has still surprised her. Maybe she should go back to putting the doorstop in place, but as Mark no longer hassles her all the time, it seems like overkill.

Unlike her watercolours, Jennie can't stand the silence while working on what she calls her pain-tings. The less she concentrates on the abomination she's working on, the better. Rather than answer, Jennie flips through the book until she finds the appropriate plate and thrusts the large volume at Sam.

Sam looks at the page and then shrugs. "What?"

"Keep looking."

Jennie can see when Sam spots the items hidden in the overall blackness of the image. She too uses her finger to follow the rope to its eventual hook-up point.

"Bloody Norah. I don't blame you for not wanting to paint *that*!"

"Exactly."

"But you're going to have to paint it if you want to stitch Shit-Brown up good and proper." Jennie bristles and readies herself for an argument on this point but doesn't get any further when Sam continues. "Anyway, I'm off. Just came up to say goodbye."

"Already? I thought it was still a couple of days away," says Jennie.

"Nope, today's the day."

"Say 'hi' to Chris for me, won't you?"

"Will do. Walk me down?"

Jennie is happy to accompany Sam to the front door and take the opportunity to make a sandwich and have a comfort stop before heading back to the studio. Sam's bag is already sitting in the hallway, Mark stands next to it.

At Jennie's questioning look, he says, "I'm taking Sam to Euston Station 'cause I'm heading that way myself."

Sam throws her arms around Jennie, who returns the hug with as much enthusiasm.

"See you in a couple of weeks," says Sam.

"Feels like longer," says Mark, picking up Sam's bag.

Sam doesn't respond to this jibe, other than to punch him in his non-bag-carrying arm. Her hand doesn't slow until it's on the door handle. She's turning the knob when someone announces his or her arrival with a no-nonsense *rat-a-tat-tat* on the wooden strip between the two frosted glass panels.

"Sonja?" they all mouth at each other, before each of them shakes their head in answer.

Sam turns the handle and pulls the door wide. "Brenda!" she shrieks and launches herself at the stunning creature standing on the coir mat.

"Don't do that, you'll crush my suit. It's designer." Brenda peels Sam away and puts space between the two of them.

"Good god," says Jennie. "What are you doing here?"

"Well, thank you very effing much. Call this a bleeding welcome?"

Jennie can tell by the multiple profanities bandied about by Brenda that she's through her not-swearing phase. And even comfortably out the other side it would seem. While Brenda might look gorgeous, her language is a truckie's mum's nightmare.

"We're happy to see you," says Sam, before stepping to one side to let Brenda, their old flatmate from Melbourne, enter the hallway, "We weren't expecting you,"

It's not until she's inside they see the massive trunk adorning the pathway.

"Christ Almighty, is that Louis Vuitton?" says Mark.

"Might be." Brenda is uncharacteristically coy.

"When did you get in? Are you travelling alone? How long are you here for?" Sam fires questions at Brenda in rapid succession.

Rather than be ruffled, Brenda simply answers. "This morning. With Martin. At least a month."

"You can have my room for the next couple of weeks, if it's okay with Eadie. I'm off up north to stay with Chris."

A warbled, "Fine by me," from the sitting room confirms Eadie is on board with this suggestion.

Mark, who has remained silent throughout this mostly high-pitched exchange, taps Sam on the shoulder and holds his watch up for her to see.

"Shit. We'd better get going, or I'll miss my train. Jennie can show you where everything is."

Sam gives Brenda a final gentle squeeze and is out of the door, followed by Mark with her suitcase. They both edge their way around the trunk with Mark instructing Jennie and Brenda to simply drag it inside for now and he'll sort it out when he's back. Because of the wide leather handles at each end, moving the logo-covered case inside is a lot easier than it would have been moving Jennie's beast of a suitcase this distance.

The front door closed again, Jennie turns to Brenda. "Cup of tea?"

Before Brenda can respond, there's an undignified snort from the front sitting room.

"You got anything stronger?" says Brenda, hopefully. "Even in bloody first class, it's been a sodding long trip."

Jennie can hear Eadie's crow of delight at this request and knows these two are going to get on like the proverbial burning building. There'll certainly be enough accelerants around if the two of them have their way.

"Come on, you must meet Eadie."

Jennie pushes the door to the sitting room fully open and Brenda follows her into the room. Jennie is horrified to see Eadie is doing her best to get hold of the sherry by grabbing wildly at it. As a result, the sparkling crystal decanter is wobbling around on the silver tray like a drunk on ice skates.

"Here, let me get that," says Jennie, diving at the neck of the skater when it's close to failing a triple axel.

During the course of the afternoon, Jennie is brought fully up to date on what Brenda has been doing in the preceding four months. Jennie is stunned when Brenda lets it slip that Martin McGowan, the elderly married gent she's having an affair with, is even talking about leaving his wife.

"Wow," is the only response Jennie can come up with, so she repeats it a couple of times for emphasis.

"They all say that," slurs Eadie. "Hope you've got a back-up plan."

"Hell, yes," says Brenda, although she doesn't elaborate.

Before Mark makes it back, Brenda and Jennie discover his stash of bulk-bought sherry and top up the decanter.

Unfortunately, given the state of the three of them, he isn't buying its still-full status.

He helps Eadie to bed before escorting Brenda and Jennie up to their rooms on the first floor. He then trudges back down for Brenda's trunk. Jennie concentrates on the sounds of him lugging the large chest up the stairs in order to stop thinking about the increasing speed of her pillow. But it doesn't matter how much she shakes her head, the damn thing won't stop accelerating.

She only just makes it to the bathroom before all those little glasses of pale liquid are back again. She should know better than to try keeping up with Eadie, let alone Brenda. It doesn't help her feel any better when she hears Mark's laughter from the landing and his crowing, "When will you ever learn?" as it slips under the door and kneels next to her at the porcelain shrine.

It's a while before Jennie gets rid of enough sherry that she feels she can safely leave her spot next to the large Victorian toilet. With her teeth and face scrubbed, she staggers back to her room. Half an hour crouched on the cold tile floor has left her chilled, so she's grateful to see Charlie smack bang in the middle of her, or rather his, bed. She slides in under the covers and jams herself up against his bulk. His heat finally creeps through the thickness of blankets that separates them, her teeth stop chattering and she drops into a deep sleep.

It's dark when she comes around. She reaches over and flicks on the bedside light, illuminating the small alarm clock that's snuggling up to its base. "Eight thirty! What a waste of a day," she says to Charlie, who has inched his way right up on top of her back, effectively pinning her stomach down to the bed. She hears rather than sees him yawn. The clicking of his jaw testament to how wide he's stretched that mouth of his. She rolls smoothly to one side in hopes of dislodging him, but the only response is him holding on tighter and growling menacingly right into her ear.

"Sorry, boy, I need to get up."

Jennie tries a few more experimental wriggles but with no result other than Charlie showing his displeasure with rumbles and claws.

She's attempting to slide out from under him, when there's a knock at the door.

"Come in."

It's Brenda, seemingly unmarred by the quantity of sherry she consumed earlier. Mark peers over her shoulder and Jennie knows she's about to be ribbed again for trying to keep up with the other two.

"What a beauty!" says Brenda, spotting Charlie.

Before either Mark or Jennie can voice a warning, Brenda scoops said beauty off Jennie's back, flips him over so she's holding him like a baby and, after lifting him up to her face, blows raspberries all over his tummy.

Jennie can't decide if it's she, Mark or Charlie who is most astounded by Brenda's actions.

Mark and Jennie keep their looks of surprise when Charlie, obviously deciding he likes this treatment, arches backwards in Brenda's arms and pushes his tummy skyward, letting her know he'd like some more. Brenda obliges.

"I don't believe it," says Jennie.

"Must be a case of evil attracting evil," says Mark.

"What," says Brenda, her voice muffled, her face full of cat.

"You! And that. That – thing!" Mark gesticulates toward Charlie, now tossed over one of Brenda's shoulders. Presumably so she can burp him. Her hand runs up and down his back, none too gently, mussing his fur until it sticks out in all directions. His back legs dangle passively with not a claw in site.

Knowing that if she'd treated Charlie in this cavalier fashion, he'd have shredded her, Jennie simply shakes her head in wonder. Charlie loves it.

"Come on, ya big lump, let's head downstairs and see if Eadie is up and about."

Rather than put the cat down, Brenda leaves the room with a compliant Charlie draped around her neck like a fur stole. She has a firm grip on his front and back legs to keep him steady.

With the feline sandbag no longer on her back, Jennie can roll over. Because Mark's still standing in the doorway, she pauses before throwing back the covers, but then realises she's still fully dressed, although crinkled.

Both she and Mark are on their way down the stairs when they hear a "Good god, what on earth are you doing with Charlie!" from Eadie, in the sitting room.

Brenda's reply of, "But he looks so cute dressed up," sends Jennie and Mark thundering down the stairs. They're not disappointed.

Eadie is standing outside her bedroom, balanced precariously on her two canes. Brenda is on the couch with Charlie, who is sporting a small velvet coat that had until recently been worn by a large china doll that now sits naked and forgotten on the sideboard.

"Sorry, is it an antique?" says Brenda, stroking the nap of the dark blue coat, that's a surprisingly good fit on the cat.

"Never mind the bloody coat. Keep that up and Charlie is likely to disembowel you," says Eadie.

It would seem as though even Eadie has had to handle the monster feline with kid gloves. Certainly the shock on her face replicates that of Mark and Jennie's when Brenda declares he's a sweetheart and proves it by blowing more raspberries on Charlie's straining tummy. If the damned cat could giggle, Jennie thinks, he'd do so now. As it is, his purr is a loud rumble that makes itself at home in the small gap left behind in Jennie's chest by him changing allegiances so readily.

32

Standing back from the easel, Jennie looks objectively at her work. She's particularly proud of this painting of a Victorian skipping rope. Getting the texture of the cord right has been a real challenge and she's infuriated no-one will know she's the artist responsible. Even more annoying is that she won't be able to paint in this style again without being accused of plagiarism.

"Damn that podgy little toe-rag."

"Who's a little toe-rag?" says Brenda, arriving with a mug of coffee in each hand and Charlie hard on her heels. The look of pure adoration on his face is a small thorn in the side of Jennie's psyche.

"Rupert Smythe-Brown."

Brenda puts Jennie's coffee on the edge of the cluttered table next to the easel, then perches herself on the single bed. "More!" She waves her hand in the air, indicating Jennie needs to elaborate.

Jennie picks up her coffee and takes a healthy slurp. "He's the little shit who's paying me to paint these so he can sign them with his name."

"Ooooh, you said shit ... he must have you really pissed off."

Jennie gives a brief outline of what Rupert has done to make her swear, albeit mildly. Brenda punctuates this spiel with multiples of "Screw me!" and by the time Jennie's finished, Brenda's as pissed off as she is.

"I hope you're not letting the little turd get away with it."

Jennie puts her mug on the bedside table and retrieves one of the wall-facing acrylics. "Anything but."

Jennie holds the painting full of ropes and pulleys up for Brenda's inspection.

Brenda snorts so hard that coffee shoots out of her nose and splatters her jeans. "Is that him?"

"Yep!"

After blowing her nose, Brenda peers closely at the painting. "Who's William Charles Flushing?"

"That's the pseudonym I used on the first lot of watercolours. The ones he took the credit for."

"So why sign the slap and tickle lot with that name?"

"Because he's already admitted in public that it's his pseudonym."

A couple of small light bulbs flicker to life in Brenda's eyes. "And if he denies painting the acrylics, then people will start to doubt him painting the first lot."

"Yep. People already think there's something screwy going on given the usual rubbish he cranks out."

"Sodding genius!"

"Thank you," says Jennie, before curtseying deeply to both sides and waving at an imaginary audience.

"Better wipe it for finger prints before you hand it over."

Jennie's stomach drops at this comment. She's well aware what she's doing is borderline criminal, but wiping off finger prints? That makes everything all too real.

"Relax. You're doing no worse to him than the little fucker did to you."

When it's obvious Jennie is twitching to get back to work, Brenda leaves with the empty mugs and Charlie shadowing her.

Jennie once again looks at the painting, this time checking it from a technical standpoint. "Done!" she says, with a healthy dose of satisfaction.

Actually, that's not true. It's not quite done. Rupert still needs to sign it.

Jennie lifts the watercolour and its backing board off the table and leans it face out against the wall by its acrylic counterpart. Both paintings include the skipping rope but whereas the watercolour is all innocence, its acrylic shadow is a sick and twisted depiction of a public school education. Or so Eadie says. The content of the shadow pieces has been a revelation to Jennie, who happily describes herself as straight and even a little on the staid side.

She has trouble understanding people getting their rocks off through pain. The thought of Rupert being hog-tied like that makes her feel uncomfortable. The idea of being the one wielding the whips and clips makes her stomach roil and she flips the bondage acrylic back to face the wall. The less she has to look at it the better.

A quick glance at her watch lets her know she has time to complete the preliminary sketches for her watercolour of a Victorian cup and ball game. What she doesn't have, and isn't keen on seeing, is the reference for the acrylic version. She's thought about the material but doubts it'll be close to the horror Eadie will provide for her.

Might be best to get it over with?

"I'll complete the watercolour sketches first," she says, stalling.

With all delaying tactics exhausted, Jennie realises she'll have to talk to Eadie about the acrylic reference sooner or later. On her way down to the sitting room, she runs into Brenda on the first-floor landing. The sharp cut of Brenda's outfit, the sleekness of hair and perfection of make-up are testament to her being on her way out.

"Wow, where are you off too?"

"I'm catching up with Martin. We're going sightseeing."

"Must be a pain not to be able to stay with him at the Savoy."

"Tedious is what it is. Still, once that old bitch he calls a wife shuffles off back to Melbourne, I'll be able to shack up with him."

"When's that?"

"Not fast enough. She keeps changing her flights."

Jennie follows Brenda downstairs, the beeping of a cab heralding its arrival when they're near the bottom. Jennie waves Brenda off before swinging open the door of the sitting room and shuffling in for a conversation she'd rather not have. Even her sketch book is quivering about being sullied with more porn.

Eadie admits to not having the reference to hand, and Jennie can't help but feel majorly relieved.

"I'm still waiting for the photos," says Eadie, before taking a good swig of the half-finished glass of sherry in her hand. The second Jennie's poured for her.

"Photos?"

Eadie's expression twitches in confirmation that the background material for this painting is the holy grail of dirt. "Yes. Photos." She polishes off the rest of her glass after a toast to the missing snapshots.

Thoughts of what will be in the photos are bad enough to make Jennie stand and pour herself a healthy glass of sherry. She's only vaguely aware of her actions until she's faced with a real full-to-the-brim crystal glass. It's trembling as much as her hand.

This pro-activeness on the drinking front is so out of character for Jennie, that Eadie stops chatting and peers intently at her.

Eadie's face creases with concern. "What on earth is wrong?"

Rather than answer, Jennie polishes off the fortified wine in a couple of large, throat-searing gulps.

"Ah," says Eadie, the penny falling from great height, "not keen on the subject matter?"

"Hardly," chokes out Jennie, before turning to refill her glass. This time it's a deliberate action and she sculls the second glass in the same way. It's not until she's halfway through her third that the tremors soften along with any straight lines in the room.

Subsiding into the couch, Jennie nurses the rest of her sherry. "That's better." She's conscious the edge on her voice is as fuzzy as the room.

"Do you want to talk about it?" offers Eadie.

"Not really. I want this nightmare over. I ... ah ..." Jennie stops herself adding anything further, by putting the glass back up to her lips.

"It might be better if we discussed what's bothering you." Eadie's voice is gentle with a healthy dose of coaxing applied on top.

"It's just that ..."

"Yes," says Eadie, encouragingly.

"It's wrong. It's sick. It's perverted." Jennie is glad the glass she's holding is empty when a shudder of disgust racks her body.

"To some, it might seem like that but we are talking about consenting adults."

Jennie doesn't respond. She'd rather avoid this discussion and certainly doesn't want to get into an argument with Eadie about the rights and wrongs of bondage and discipline. Jennie wouldn't feel comfortable discussing this with Sam, let alone her octogenarian landlady. It's wrong, on so many levels. She hopes her non-committal "Hmmm," is answer enough.

"Well, yes." Eadie looks as if she's about to continue and Jennie can't help but hold her breath. After nothing else ensues, she empties her lungs in a heartfelt sigh that turns into a cough when Mark blasts into the room.

"What the hell is in this?" He drops a Boots' photo envelope into Eadie's lap with disgust. "The whole photo department sniggered like a bunch of thirteen-year-olds after I handed over the docket, and when the girl at the cash register asked if she could tie up the package for me, I thought the guy on the developing machine was going to wee himself."

"Oh dear," says Eadie, trying hard to keep a straight face. And failing.

"So?" says Mark.

"Help yourself." Eadie awkwardly picks up the envelope from her lap and holds it out to him.

He snatches it from her and she's unable to stop a small squeak of pain escaping her tightly pursed lips.

"Shit, sorry," says Mark, his movements slowing as he fights to regain his composure.

His composure is rapidly bent out of shape again when he opens the envelope and flicks through the photos. Jennie's never seen him like this.

"Bloody hell, there's no way I can show my face in that chemist again." He's still shaking his head in denial when he dumps the photos and envelope sloppily onto the coffee table.

"Where the bloody hell did you get them from?" Mark's stance is now unforgiving, his arms crossed and foot tapping impatiently.

It's such a movie pose that Jennie is unable to stop a small giggle escaping, causing Mark's look of disgust to swing in her direction. Any further mirth on her part is quickly swallowed.

"I've had the negatives for years," says Eadie, nonchalantly, "I knew they'd come in handy one day."

"You mean, you took the photos?" Mark's volume is now borderline shouting.

Eadie arches one eyebrow delicately, but doesn't admit to anything.

"Jeez. You know what," Mark holds his hands up as if to ward off any further explanations, "I don't want to know." After dropping his hands to his sides, he leaves the room abruptly.

Unable to help herself, Jennie leans forward in her seat until she can focus on the photo sitting on top of the pile. She knows her eyes have widened to the point her eyeballs are in danger of dropping into her lap but is unable to do anything about it. Jennie blindly puts her empty glass on the small table next to Eadie and retrieves the photos from the coffee table. She flips through them. Slowly at first, then with greater speed until it's like watching a stop-motion movie. Rupert Shit-Brown's ugly mug is grimacing prominently in most of them.

"How, in goodness' sake, did you get these?"

"A protégé of mine took them. Thought I might like them for old times' sake."

Jennie thinks they can't get any worse until she comes across one where something other than his face is showing. The photos fall limply from her hands and slink their way down into the dark places between the cushions.

"I-I-I can't paint Rupert doing this!"

"It's not that bad."

The disbelief in Eadie's voice is strong enough to have Jennie scrambling to retrieve the photos. She double-dips her hand into the Sanderson Linen cracks on either side of her, to make sure she has all of them. Once she's tidied the pile, she leans over and deposits it gently in the middle of Eadie's lap.

"What's wrong with that?" Eadie holds up one of the less offensive photos and turns it for Jennie to see.

It's not until Jennie hears herself say, "Humph, that's nothing," that she realises how inured she's become to this subject matter. It's not something she's happy about. No one should ever feel comfortable about a subject like this. "Keep going." She indicates Eadie should continue working her way through the pile.

Jennie minutely examines her fingernails while Eadie laboriously works her way through the stack of photos. But rather than snorts of disgust, the old lady is chuckling away and Jennie thinks she even hears a whispered, "I loved that one", but it's not clear enough for her to be sure. A belt of unladylike laughter bursts from Eadie, and Jennie's head rockets up in surprise. The laughter continues until there are tears furrowing their way down Eadie's face and she's holding a hand to her side obviously to squash a stitch into submission.

"You don't find it disgusting?"

"Jennie." Eadie wipes gently at her face with a lace hanky. "We can't all be saints."

Jennie's mouth opens to voice a response, but none is forthcoming. Surely she's not the only one to be disgusted by this stuff? Mark didn't seem keen. And what does Eadie mean about saints. Surely the old lady doesn't mean her? She's done bad stuff. Lots of it.

"Shoplifting when you're five doesn't count," says Eadie, out of the blue, arresting Jennie in her analysis of bad stuff.

"How did ..."

Eadie flaps the most offensive photo around as though it's a party invite. "You don't need to paint it exactly as it is here. Inference always works best anyway. Leave it up to the imagination of the audience and all that."

"I suppose." Jennie hesitantly takes the photos back from Eadie. She's still thumbing her way through them when she gets back up to the studio. It took longer than usual because she needed to stop every couple of steps for fear of tripping.

The last thing she wants to do is fall over and squash her face up against any of the subject matter of these particular holiday snaps. That's nightmare territory as far as she's concerned.

Only after flipping through the photos several more times does she formulate a plan for the final painting. It's tricky and will need a lot of imagination on her part to paint the scene at an angle different from that shown in any of the photos.

Her sniggers have turned to laughter when she looks up to find Mark standing in the doorway and regarding her with curiosity. He looks pointedly at the photos and then her before wiggling his eyebrows. His expression is so loaded with innuendo that the photos slip from her nerveless fingers.

From the photos on the floor, he carefully selects one and hands it back to her. "I think you dropped something ... Mistress." His smile is broad and teasing and, for a change, not lecherous.

Jennie doesn't need to look down to know which photo he's handed her.

33

Flipping the reference photo around again, Jennie re-attaches it to the upright of the easel with masking tape. Crossing her arms firmly over her chest, she cocks her head first to one side and then the other, and looks at the photo for a couple of minutes.

"Damn!"

It doesn't matter which way she looks at it, the photo doesn't help with the composition she's decided on. For that, she'll have to get her head right inside the scene and it's something she's been avoiding like the plague. The way Shit-Brown is trussed up in the photo is disturbing enough without imagining what he looks like from all the other angles.

Brenda wanders in with Charlie, both of them stopping next to Jennie as she examines the photo.

Brenda peers closely at the photo. "Jeez, he's got bigger knockers than me!"

While Jennie might roll her eyes at this observation, she has to admit Brenda is spot on and stores this piece of information for use in the final painting.

"I was wondering if you wanted to have a break from this. Do some Christmas shopping."

"Christmas? But it's only ..." Jennie's voice trails off while she tries to decipher exactly what the date is. She's still working on the day of the week, when Brenda interrupts her calculations.

"December."

At the blank look that stays pasted on Jennie's face, she says, "Tuesday."

Following another short break, she adds, "The eleventh."

"Really?" says Jennie, weakly. The year is disappearing and it's not long before she needs to have finished the painting she's about to start working on, along with its less incendiary watercolour counterpart. "I don't know that I've got time. Well, not if I want a break over Christmas."

"Sure you do, we'll only be gone a couple of hours and it looks like you're doing bugger all here anyway." Brenda taps the still pristine canvas sitting on the easel. "But, Jeez, I don't blame you stalling with that as the sodding subject."

The reaction from Brenda surprises Jennie. Her rough-as-guts Ocker mate usually isn't fazed by anything.

Brenda has another look at the photo. "Trussed up like that, he looks like a sodding turkey with his giblets hanging all over the show."

"Don't say that! Not with Christmas coming up."

"Go on. I dare ya to paint him getting a right going over with a turkey baster!"

"Brenda!" Jennie's moral outrage is shattered by a fit of the giggles.

Getting to the end of their street, Jennie naturally turns toward the Chiswick shops.

"Where the hell are you off to?" says Brenda, stopping any forward momentum on Jennie's part.

"I thought we were going shopping in the High Road?"

"Sod off. All right if you only want meat and veg and shit like that."

At the questioning look Jennie is throwing her, she adds, "Regent Street!"

"Regent Street?

"Yeah. Where else?"

After course correction, they waste no time getting to the tube station although Jennie is unable to stop her head swivelling from side to side as she keeps an eye out for the world's most elusive chicken. After that first sighting, she hasn't seen any further trace of it. Even putting flyers in letterboxes hasn't resulted in anything.

Walking up the stairs from the tube to the street, both of them are tightening and re-arranging their coats, scarves, gloves and hats. Despite it being sunny, the weather is cold, hence they're both layered like onions. Jennie fumbles to get the top button of her coat done up, eventually pulling off one of her gloves with her teeth.

While wriggling her hand back into the glove, Jennie's gaze scans from one end of the street to the other. "Look at the lights. There's heaps of them. Shame it's not dark." She'd heard the lights in Regent Street were gorgeous and given the sheer number of them, she knows they'll look amazing when switched on. There are nets of lights shaped like stars suspended across the middle of the street. At night they'll look as if they are hovering there.

"Come on, I need to find Liberty."

"Liberty?"

"Some flash place I've heard about. Want to get something for Martin."

It's not until Brenda is a couple of yards ahead of her that Jennie realises she's stopped walking.

Brenda buying something? For someone else?

Shaking her head to dislodge this anarchic thought, Jennie jogs to catch up.

"Of course, it's his money I'm spending. But it's the thought that counts."

And the earth rights itself on its axis. Jennie had been worried for a minute that she'd stumbled into some alternative reality. Generous is something Brenda, most definitely, is not.

Jennie is astonished to see the Liberty building is similar to the old pub they'd frequented back in Auckland. Of course, this is more likely to be a real deal Tudor building than a cheapo knock-off. She also doubts her feet will stick to the floor in this place, although they do glue her to the spot when the double doors shut behind them.

"Wow, I feel guilty of shoplifting already."

The heat in the place is overwhelming and they remove layers and undo buttons. Jennie stuffs her gloves and hat into the side pockets of her coat with the result that her hips look huge.

"Whaddaya mean?" says Brenda, through a mouthful of glove.

"I hate places like this, they always manage to make me feel as if I've been caught doing something wrong." Jennie knows she's fidgeting but is unable to stop herself, reinforcing her guilty-as-sin demeanour.

"God, relax, would ya."

Brenda doesn't look at all cowed by her surroundings or the staff who undoubtedly went to better schools than either of them. One of these sleek creatures approaches them, her face set in polite 'query. Jennie reads the query as being, 'What on earth are *you* doing in here?'

A string of polished vowels back up the visual request, but

rather than wait for the woman to finish, Brenda holds up her hand. Jennie is uncomfortable at how rude this is, akin to flashing your undies during a Sunday school recital. But it works. The marbles jammed in the woman's mouth spill messily onto the floor.

"Menswear?" says Brenda, in a no-nonsense tone.

The assistant points graciously toward some stairs before going back to rearranging perfectly folded items on a mahogany display case that looks to be original to the building.

They're nearing the bottom of the flight taking them to the basement before Jennie gets up the nerve to speak. "That was rude, wasn't it?"

"They're shop assistants. Pisses me off when they take one look at me and decide which box they're going to jam me in. Snotty bitches the lot of them." She doesn't wait for a response from Jennie, instead stepping into a menswear department that's straight out of *Are You Being Served*.

Jennie is relieved to see that, like Grace Brothers, the assistants down here are all male, with the majority on the wrong side of fifty. Brenda will be in her element.

The selection process is quick, with Brenda knowing exactly what she wants and it is simply a case of the nearest shop assistant finding everything for her. The wad of twenties Brenda pulls from her purse to pay for the pocket square and tie pin smells ever so faintly of mothballs. Jennie is shocked at how many of these Brenda has to hand over for what is a handkerchief-sized square of silk and a tiny piece of jewellery. With that much cash, Sam would be able to buy enough fabric to make coats for most of the lap dogs in Kensington.

Much to Jennie's surprise, this purchase is only the first of many, with Brenda eventually buying gifts for everyone in the house. Brenda even sends Jennie to wait in another department in Selfridges while she buys a gift for her.

Jennie joins in the buying frenzy, it being hard not to get

caught up in the Christmassy excitement of it all. Brenda even goes so far as to buy a belt for Mark at House of Fraser, and Jennie realises she'll have to buy something for him too, or it will look odd on Christmas morning. But what to buy? Clothing made the most sense, given Sonja had trashed damned near everything in his closet. But wasn't that too personal?

They're in WHSmith buying ribbon and wrapping paper when Jennie spots the perfect thing for him. The large book of classic cars is ideal, if the wreck he drove in Melbourne is any indication. She's relieved as she's spent most of the afternoon fretting over what to get him. Certainly she's devoted a lot more nervous energy to that particular gift than any of the others she's purchased.

Staggering out of the last store, the Christmas lights twinkle into life. At last, a plus-side to it getting dark mid-afternoon.

Jennie stares in wonder at the huge star-shaped nets slung out over the middle of the road. There are also lights shaped to look like stars and comets spaced out along the length of the road. "They look beautiful."

They're footsore and shattered when they stagger into the house not long after five. They'd been lucky, managing to catch a tube before the commuters started leaving the city but they'd put in some miles with all that shopping.

The book Jennie bought for Mark had felt like the reasonably slim volume it was when they'd left WHSmith, but as their trip home progressed, Jennie could feel it weighing down the bag more and more. By the time they walk up the path to the front door it feels like she's lugging a complete set of Encyclopaedia Britannica.

Well, maybe a half set.

"I'm knackered," says Brenda, dumping all her bags on the floor in the hall.

Jennie doesn't get much further with her lot. "I'm bushed."

They're stripping off their outer layers when Mark comes in the front door from work. Because of the carrier bag barrier in front of him, he doesn't get much further.

"Bloody hell. Did you leave anything behind?"

Looking down at the mass of bags that surround her, Jennie realises he's got a point.

In an uncharacteristic show of independence, Jennie nods at Brenda "It's her fault."

Brenda snorts before flipping her scarf over a free peg on the hat stand. "Yeah, I twisted your arm to buy that lot."

"Hey, some of it's yours."

Mark pushes a roll of Christmas paper away with his toe, its slippery length having escaped one of the WHSmith bags. "Isn't it early for Christmas shopping?"

"I'll bet you're one of those blokes who panic-buys on Christmas Eve," says Brenda.

Mark smiles and strikes a pose that suggests, 'yes he is and rather proud of it'.

Brenda's voice is smug, when she adds, "And you get stuck with all the crap no one else wants."

"Don't you mean *we* get stuck with all the other crap no one else wants," says Jennie.

Any trace of a smile slips from Mark's face and Jennie sees a small spark of panic make itself at home in his eyes.

34

Jennie squints at the photo taped to her easel. She needs to make sure the details on the harness are spot-on in this final acrylic. If she ignores the biped being held in place, she's able to admire the workmanship of the bridle. It'd be tricky enough making one to fit a horse, let alone one that's a snug fit on the squidgy little Hooray Henry who's the star of the photo.

A couple of hours later and Jennie is happy with her progress. It's a constant battle to hide her innate talent given these paintings are meant to be by Rupert. And even though she's trying hard to paint badly, she worries people are still going to say this is some of his best work.

Brush down, she stands back to check the overall composition. She then walks back and forth in front of the canvas, all the while stretching out kinks in her back and shoulders. She's stronger, with there being far fewer cracks and groans from her body when she goes through loosening up everything after a few hours of painting.

"Hmmm, it's okay. I guess."

She shouldn't be stressing so much over the acrylics, or

even the watercolours. It's not like her name will be on any of the paintings in Rupert's exhibition. Still, it wouldn't pay to make them too awful. If she did that, Rupert was as likely to fall on his sword and *out* her as the artist behind the work even if he took his aunt out in the process. It's a risk she isn't willing to take.

To extend her break, Jennie wraps another Christmas present. She's delighted with the theme she's gone with. The paper is a glossy dark green while the ribbon is bright red with a white polka dot. She has a real aversion to the brightly patterned Christmas paper most people go for. She's even made her own tags rather than clutter up the packages with pug ugly to/from stickers. It's okay for kids, but to her, nothing looks better than a beautifully decorated tree with lots of tastefully wrapped presents underneath.

Not that this will be the case with the monster fir currently sitting naked in the corner of Eadie's sitting room. Rather than strapping it to the top of Eadie's pristine Jag, Mark had arranged for the tree to be delivered. He even coerced the delivery chap into helping him set it up in the large half barrel. Jennie hopes there's some water in there otherwise they will be vacuuming up pine needles for months.

Even though the tree is yet to be trimmed, there are already a few presents scattered around it, wrapped in a hideous mix of snowmen, Santas and nativity scenes. One is even wrapped in newspaper. Jennie suspects Mark might be responsible for that and shudders at thoughts of her beautifully wrapped presents sitting in amongst that lot.

Maybe I can group mine to one side?

Another present completed, with a bow that would do an origami master proud, and Jennie goes back to her 'Whoa Nelly' painting. She works feverishly for the rest of the morning, grabs a quick sandwich and takes it back upstairs to eat while she keeps on working. While she's in the zone, she likes to keep at it. She feels like she's cracked it when the light starts to fail mid-afternoon, reminding her she must look at buying some lamps to lengthen her painting day.

Tidying everything away, she hears Brenda yelling up the stairs for her to get her arse downstairs to the sitting room. There's no urgency in Brenda's tone, so Jennie knows the house isn't on fire and everyone is in good health. She finishes her clean-up and then hastens downstairs as she suspects she knows what's up and it's something she wants control over.

The smell of Christmas tree that Jennie first encounters in the hallway has scenes of Christmases past popping up in her mind. The scene in the sitting room is unfortunately one of chaos. Eadie's face is contorted in disgust, her top lip hiked up and nostrils flared; Brenda is perched on top of a museum piece of a ladder, trying in vain to get a fairy on top of the otherwise bare tree. Looking at the Barbie-in-Drag creation in Brenda's hand, Jennie realises it must be this that's responsible for the look on Eadie's face.

"Stop!" Jennie knows this has come out a lot louder than she meant, but she simply can't allow that, *thing*, to go on top of their beautiful tree. The wrapping paper is bad enough without besmirching the tree, too.

Brenda freezes in place and this puts an end to her naturally balancing the wobble of the ladder, causing her to sway dangerously. Jennie runs across the room and grabs onto the aged wooden and rope beast to steady it and then puts a hand on Brenda's leg to steady her, too.

Knowing an argument is unavoidable, Jennie wades in. "Brenda, can you please come down here. We need to plan what goes on the tree, not throw stuff at it."

"Well, sodding excuse me, Miss Arty Farty."

"Language!" says Eadie, uncharacteristically.

"Shit, sorry."

"Yes, Brenda, we don't use Arty Farty in this house," says Eadie.

With Brenda safely back down on carpet firma, and the drag fairy still in her hand, Jennie starts negotiations.

Jennie looks pointedly at the numerous plastic bags full of baubles and tinsel scattered at random around the room. "So what are our options for a theme?"

Brenda's face scrunches in confusion. "A theme? Why can't we just chuck shit at it?"

"Because then it will look like shit," says Eadie, saving Jennie the trouble.

"Jeez, you two are as bad as each other. Screw this. You do it."

Brenda shoves the fairy hard into Jennie's chest, where one of its wings digs painfully into her left boob.

"Ouch, careful." Jennie moves the fairy away and is annoyed to see it has poked a hole in her sweatshirt.

Rather than apologise, Brenda storms off muttering in unflattering terms about tree snobs. Any negotiations are effectively over when the sitting room door slams behind her.

"Oops," says Jennie.

"It needed to be done. I don't think I could have sat in here with a tree trimmed by 'shit being thrown at it'."

"Me neither." Jennie puts the fairy down on the coffee table, picks up a bulging carrier bag and has a rummage through its contents. "Although looking at this lot, I don't think it will matter how much love we put into it. It's still going to look horrid."

"We don't need to use that lot. I've got a few things in the cellar.

The layout in the cellar appears to have been designed by

rabbits with the warren of corridors and small windowless rooms being perfect for bunnies. Following Eadie's vague instructions, Jennie finds the decorations in the far reaches of the cellar, giving her time to think about her last few Christmases. This will be her third Christmas without Steve. By now they would've been married and might even have had a little one on the way, if not already there. Jennie can't imagine how Mark must have felt on hearing his girlfriend Stacey had been pregnant when she died in their bike accident.

Banging her shin hard on a crate compels her to concentrate on her task, forcing her back to the here and now. On the plus side, it's a lot easier to deal with the festive season when you're so far from home and the past.

By the time she's finished carrying up all the boxes from the cellar, the sitting room looks how she imagines Santa's grotto would. Following Eadie's directions, she puts all Brenda's bags of plastic tat behind the couch, lines up the cartons and then opens them one by one. Their contents are dazzling. Hand-blown glass baubles packed in straw, wooden toys that look to be Victorian and strings and strings of silver and white beads.

"A tree without tinsel? I'm in heaven," says Jennie, letting the slinky beads run through her fingers.

"Have you opened them all?"

"Just one more." Jennie flips the cardboard flaps to the sides and gasps at the contents of this last box. "Oh my God, it's gorgeous." She reverently retrieves the beautiful angel nestled in the bottom of the carton. It's the only thing in there.

"It was my mother's."

Eadie's voice cracks at the end of this statement, causing Jennie to stop looking at the angel and check on the old lady. "You okay?"

"I'm fine. Remembering happier times."

When pressed by Jennie, Eadie recounts her childhood Christmases, full of charades and singing, of happy times and the joy of being part of a large and loving family. This contrasts sharply with the collection of waifs and strays who'll be celebrating Christmas with her this year. Mark is her only living relation as far as Jennie can tell.

"I didn't mean to bring you down," says Eadie.

Jennie sneaks a tear off her cheek and wipes it down the side of her jeans. "That's okay. No reason we can't make this Christmas as fabulous though. Is there?"

"No indeed."

Checking the stability of the tree, and that they can water it, Jennie gets stuck in with the trimming. She starts at the top by putting the angel in place. This is hair-raising because of the rickety ladder, but luckily she's taller than Brenda, and doesn't need to stand on the top step. Steadying herself with one hand on the wall, she puts the antique angel safely atop.

Working her way down, Jennie follows Eadie's instructions and makes a few suggestions of her own. It takes three hours before the tree is trimmed to the satisfaction of both of them, but it looks wonderful and is as good as anything Jennie had seen in the upmarket shops of Regent Street. Better even.

"Right. I'd better go and sort out Brenda now."

The words have no sooner left Jennie's mouth, than there's an impatient tooting out front. Pulling the curtains to one side, Jennie can see it's a black cab. The front door opens and Brenda stomps down the path.

"Or maybe not." Jennie lets the curtain drop back into place.

"She'll come round when she sees the tree."

"I'm not so sure about that."

Brenda's behaviour around the whole Christmas thing is a surprise to Jennie. The girl usually didn't give a damn about anything. Her buying everyone in the house a present being the biggest shock of all.

"I've got it!"

Jennie retrieves the carrier bags of decorations from behind the couch and threads most of them onto one arm before picking up the rest with her free hand.

"Got what?"

"These won't go to waste." Jennie manoeuvres herself out of the room.

The conditions for the next few days are icy, with Brenda freezing everyone out. She refuses to discuss the tree-trimming incident, although she grudgingly admits it looks, "Quite nice, if a little sodding boring."

Jennie is busy for the next few days working on breaking-in the *Whoa, Nelly* acrylic. She gets it to a point she feels reasonably happy with it, and then puts it to one side so she can start on its Victorian rocking horse watercolour counterpart. Any breaks are spent working away in her bedroom on her secret project. A week's concerted effort and the watercolour is complete to her satisfaction. Jennie then pops the equestrian acrylic back on the easel. It's as hideous as she'd hoped, although mostly down to deliberately bad technique. It'll have Rupert ripping out what little hair he has left when he sees it unveiled in all its equine glory.

Declaring it finished. Jennie then carefully signs it *William Charles Flushing*, making her heart quicken.

The next morning, after taking the last load of clothes from her bedroom up to the studio, Jennie is ready for breakfast. She hopes Brenda has started to thaw because eating toast with that type of energy on the other side of the table is not conducive to good digestion.

Swinging into the kitchen, her shoulders drop. A dark cloud of pissed-offedness still swirls above Brenda. Eadie in her place at the end of the table appears oblivious to this heavy weather, as does Mark. The two of them are chatting away about their plans for the day, effectively ignoring Brenda and her persistent bad mood.

Once she's got some toast and checked Eadie has everything she needs, Jennie takes her spot opposite Brenda. The tightness in her throat is slightly eased by a small sip of her tea.

"Ah, Brenda," starts Jennie, tentatively.

"What?" is tossed belligerently across the table.

"Sam and Chris are back this weekend."

"Oh, great, so now I'm going to be chucked out on the street."

Behind this animosity, Jennie spots anxiety. "Goodness me, no!" says Jennie.

"Of course not!" says Eadie.

Even Mark is shaking his head.

Rather than give Brenda time to refute their denials. Jennie presses on.

"Actually, I thought you could move into my room, and I can head back up to the studio," says Jennie. On seeing Mark's gaze swing rapidly in her direction, she adds "And don't you get any blimmin' ideas either."

"A guy can hope. Can't he?"

"No, he can't!" Turning back to Brenda, she continues "Would that work for you?"

"I suppose it'll bloody have to, won't it? The bloody Savoy is off the books until after bloody Christmas."

"Good then, I can help you move after breakfast," says Jennie, with forced enthusiasm.

Jennie gestures toward the door of what is now her old room. "After you. It's all yours."

"I hope you vacuumed," says Brenda, unwilling to accept this olive branch gracefully.

She's nursing her resentment although Jennie suspects this is more for protection.

Jennie is right behind her when she opens the door and bangs straight into Brenda when she stops dead in her tracks. "It's ... It's ... ah ..." Brenda is unable to finish.

"I hope you like it. If not, then I can take it all down."

Brenda walks into the room and spins around so she can take everything in.

"It's wonderful."

Jennie's, "Are you crying?" is out before she can stop herself.

35

Unceremoniously shoved out of the bedroom—now known as Brenda's Tacky Plastic Christmas Grotto—Jennie listens carefully at the door. She's rewarded with a lot of nose-blowing from the other side, confirming that her decorating the bedroom with all the tasteless tinsel and baubles has been well received. She even draped Christmas lights over the headboard of the bed. She thinks it's awful, but Brenda obviously loves it.

"Right then!" Jennie claps her hands together, rubs them vigorously and then clasps them tightly to hold them against her mouth. This gesture is accompanied by an internal pep talk before she hikes up to the studio.

Jennie turns her attention to the chores that have been piling up in the preceding weeks. She also needs to turn the studio back into her bedroom. She wasn't exactly methodical when bringing everything up that morning and the pile of clothes sitting in the middle of her bed and the tumble of shoes next to it mean she has some serious organising to do.

The two-bar heater that has been running at full-belt from first thing that morning has warmed the room enough to make it bearable if she's moving around, but that's about it. Looking at the sheets hanging limply at the windows, Jennie realises she needs to sort out some heavy duty curtains or else freeze her butt off come bedtime. It hadn't been an issue in the middle of summer, but the small heater simply isn't up to the task of keeping the room warm overnight now that it's winter.

"But first, let's sort this lot out."

Once she's obsessively cleaned all the painting gear and put it away in the big cupboards, Jennie works methodically on the rest of the room. She hangs and folds and puts away until the bed is free of clothing and her shoes are once again regimentally lined up under the bed. The room doesn't look lived in and that's how she likes it.

"Okay!" Jennie shrugs into a jacket, grabs her handbag off the bed, slings it over her shoulder and walks out of her room. "Curtains or bust."

Down in the front hallway, she drops her bag on the floor and gets her big coat off its peg on the coat rack, followed by a hat and a scarf. It's freezing outside and the more layers she can pile on the better. Fully wrapped, she has difficulty retrieving her bag, the multiple layers making it difficult to bend over. The bulk of material in her armpits means she can't put her arms down at her sides either. Still, anything is better than being cold.

Her hand is on the front door knob when she looks at Eadie's sitting room door. Rather than leave, she opens the door to that room and pops her head inside.

"Eadie, I'm off out to buy some curtains, is there anything you want from the High Road?"

"Curtains?"

"Yeah, I've been using a set of sheets up in the studio but they're not up to keeping out this cold." Jennie nods her beanie's bobble toward the window.

"Good grief, I thought I'd told Mark to put everything

back." At the look of confusion on Jennie's face, she continues. "I stripped the colour out of the room, preferring things to be stark white when I'm painting. I could have sworn I told Mark to put it back how it was. Must be losing my marbles."

"No worries. I've mostly been in the downstairs room anyway."

"I feel terrible now knowing you've been up there in such Spartan conditions."

For Jennie's who's always felt like the poor relation in the room allocation stakes, this comes as a welcome relief.

"The curtains that used to hang in the studio are down in the cellar. I think there are some other bits and pieces there too."

Jennie makes her way through the kitchen to the cellar, not bothering to remove the many layers she's piled on for a trip to the shops. She knows from collecting the Christmas decorations, that it's blinking cold down there.

If anything, the cellar feels even colder today. Surely they're in line for some snow with the way the temperatures are plummeting? Pulling the cord to turn on the one bare bulb that hangs forlornly from the rafters above, Jennie hunts for the promised curtains.

After a few false starts, she finds the curtains, although not where Eadie had said they were.

The large package is wrapped securely in white plastic and has also been bound with a length of sturdy rope. Its shape and size is reminiscent of props Jennie has seen in murder mysteries, with the spooky atmosphere in the cellar only adding to this impression.

Poking the package experimentally, she is relieved to find the contents feel more curtain-like than cadaveric. Bending her knees, she drags the bulk over one shoulder and then straightens, taking its full weight. A body might well have weighed less.

Sniffing the package, now that it's so close to her nose, she's relieved to find it smells only a little stale. With any luck, the curtains won't be mouldy because it's anyone's guess how long they've been down here.

Back up in the studio, she cuts open the end of the bag and is assailed with a musty aroma. Pulling the first pair of curtains from their packaging, the room reeks of abandoned house. It's something she'll have to put up with because there is no way she's opening any windows. She'll take smelly over freezing any day.

Keeping well away from the small heater, and its valiant efforts to keep winter at bay, Jennie flicks out the first curtain. Stinky it might be, but it's also magnificent. The gorgeous silk is lined with a heavy wool fabric meaning they'll shimmer beautifully, but moreover provide excellent insulation. Their dark ruby red colour will also add some much-needed warmth to the room that is currently looking a touch on the polar side.

Jennie clips the last hook into place with a deal of satisfaction and not a little relief. It's taken hours to unpack the curtains and hang them on the iron rods above the windows. Her arms feel ready to drop off from all that heavy lifting. The effort has been well worth it though, with the room feeling warmer already, if only because of the injection of colour.

Turning on the bedside light, she pulls the curtains firmly closed, overlapping them in the middle to ensure there aren't any gaps. With any luck, closing the curtains will give the heater a chance to warm the room and air the curtains before she goes to bed. It would be good if the room weren't so chilly by then.

She's standing in the middle of the room admiring the general splendour of all that silk, when she hears grunting and thumping behind her. She swings around to see Mark man-handling an enormous carpet along the short hallway outside her room.

"Eadie said you were trying to warm the place up. Thought you could use this."

He drops the rolled-up rug in the middle of the floor, and it lands with a colossal thump. A huge cloud of dust billows up and engulfs both of them and the resultant coughing moves them both out onto the landing while they wait for things to settle down.

"Jeez. Sorry. Didn't realise it was so bloody dusty."

With the air cleared, Mark helps Jennie unroll the carpet and position it to suit the shape of the room. She's thrilled to see the pattern on it is very Aladdin with the overall colour tying in perfectly with the curtains. On the down side, the room smells even more like an unwanted inheritance. On the upside, the room is warming up. Or maybe that's all the physical work it's taken to get it to this stage.

"Wow! I'm going to have to vacuum in here."

"Something else we need to do is cover those." Mark jabs his thumb in the direction of the two skylights.

He's right; when Jennie stands under them she can feel cool air dropping from them. She's still thinking about how they could tackle this, when Mark grunts, clicks his fingers and leaves her still looking up.

He returns, staggering under the weight of the rickety ladder and a couple of large boards. The boards are painted white and have hooks in each corner.

"I've seen these in the cellar a couple of times and wondered what they were for. Then I spotted the eyebolts in the corners of the skylights."

With Jennie steadying the ladder, Mark hooks the first of the two boards into place, effectively closing off the skylight and any cold still seeping in. After the second board clips into place, extinguishing the remaining daylight is, the room plunges into a warm pinkish glow. It's more romantic than Jennie is comfortable with, especially given her proximity to one of Mark's thighs. She lets go of the stepladder as if it's on fire and moves away.

"Arrrgh! Effing hell. Grab the ladder, would you."

Jennie looks up to see Mark swaying dangerously above her; the only thing stopping him from coming a cropper, is jamming both hands hard against the ceiling.

"Oh, oh, I'm so sorry." Jennie grabs the ladder to stop it bucking from side to side.

Safely back on the ground, Mark glares at her, pushes the sides of the ladder together and picks it up.

"If you'll excuse me, I'm off to change my jocks!"

Jennie's still sniggering quietly to herself when walking back up to the studio, or rather her bedroom, after collecting the vacuum cleaner from the cupboard under the stairs.

It takes a lot of effort and emptying the bag more than once to get her new magic carpet relatively free from dust. Jennie suspects it won't be until she's done this three or four more times that it will be safe to sit on it. Even then, she doubts it will get off the ground.

By the time she's finished, she's been over every surface in the room twice and has also dusted off the paintings. She's not sure if it's because she's getting used to it, but the musty smell doesn't seem so bad either. She's happy to see her bedroom now has the luxury of those on the floors below, making her feel a lot less like Rose out of *Upstairs Downstairs*.

It's certainly taken a lot longer to sort her room out than she expected and checking her watch, she realises it's time to take all the paintings downstairs for Eadie to have a squiz. Looking at the paintings lined up on the floor, Jennie realises it will take a fair few trips to get them all downstairs. She'll have quads like Arnold Schwarzenegger when the exhibition is over.

She's on her third trip, when Mark pops his head out of his room. "What are you doing?"

"Sorry about the racket. Need to get all the paintings downstairs, so Eadie can give them the once over."

"I'll give you a hand."

"That'd be great." Jennie is thinking this is big of him given how miffed he'd been when he'd left with the ladder earlier. His next comment puts paid to this.

"Anything to stop the mouse convention."

"The what?"

Rather than answer, Mark steps onto one of the squeakiest boards and bounces up and down on it several times.

"Oh, right. Everything's leaning against the cupboards," says Jennie, moving toward the stairs.

Even from a floor down, she easily hears his bark of laughter when he sees the line-up.

With all twelve paintings safely down in the sitting room, every available surface is taken up. Eadie, Mark and Jennie look at the collection in silence. Occasionally Mark or Eadie open their mouths as though to voice an opinion, but shut them again without uttering a word.

Eadie breaks the long silence. "I wonder what David Michaels will think about them. He's due here at five."

A quick glance at her watch is all it takes for Jennie to be swamped by nerves. She's still not sure she should be doing this. It could go horribly wrong if she's found out. She's got less than five minutes before the gallery owner arrives. She can pull out and let Shit-Brown have his way.

"I don't think this is a good idea." She's already picked up three of the B&D acrylics when the doorbell rings.

"You put those down, young lady. You're not backing out now. We've come too far." Eadie's tone is forceful enough to stop Jennie collecting, although not forceful enough that she's prepared to relinquish the three she's already holding.

"Mark, get the door." Eadie also says this forcefully, resulting in Mark jumping immediately to his feet.

Jennie hasn't moved and is still holding the three acrylics, when David enters. Mark doesn't return, obviously having decided to leave them to it.

"So how have you got on?" says David.

"Splendidly," says Eadie, when it becomes obvious Jennie isn't going to answer.

"Excellent."

His head spins like that chick out of *The Exorcist* as he takes in all the paintings. The beauty of the watercolours is in stark contrast to the ghastly technique and content of the acrylics. Pulling a pair of glasses from his pocket, he slides them on and wanders over to have a closer look at one of the acrylics. "I don't think we can get away with this."

His tone is so full of doubt that Jennie tightens her grip on the three acrylics she's holding.

"Careful, Jennie. You don't want to damage them."

David looks around to see what Eadie is talking about and in so doing, spots the canvases in danger of being crushed by Jennie. He walks over and takes them from her, prying her fingers away one at a time to do so. He then props them on the couch and stands back to consider them. After some moments, he says, "You've still got work to do on these."

"I have?"

"They're not bad enough I'm afraid. No one's going to take them as being Shit-Brown's work in their current state."

"What do you think I should do?"

"Nothing major. Spend another half hour or so on each of them, making sure you over-egg the pudding."

"Over-egg the pudding?"

"Rupert doesn't know when to give in and leave well enough alone. He thinks more is more, so throws everything he can at them."

"Ah, right."

Jennie understands what she needs to do. It won't be easy

screwing up the acrylics even more than she already has, although easier than if it were the watercolours she had to sabotage.

"What about the watercolours?" Jennie twists her hands nervously while she waits for his verdict. She's proud of these and genuinely cares what he thinks of them. She knows Eadie likes them, but it's always good to have a second opinion.

"They're good, although maybe not as good as your first collection."

"I wasn't able to throw as much energy into them knowing they'd have his name on them. And why does he have to sign them? Can't I do it for him?"

"Because if you sign his name, you're the one breaking the law. Whereas if he signs your work, he's the one in the wrong," says the gallery owner.

"Of course!" says Jennie, feeling some small relief that she's dodged at least one crime.

"I've been meaning to ask you, how did you come up with the name Flushing for the acrylics?"

Jennie breaks into a broad grin. "Dad's a plumber."

When Jennie shows David Michaels to the door, he's still chuckling over her pseudonym.

"You've done well, young lady. And I promise, once this is over, I'm going to organise a solo exhibition for you."

"Oh, right." Jennie knows her response to this honour is half-baked, but she's feeling burned out as a result of all the work she's had to do for Rupert's exhibition.

"Only when you're ready, though. You need to get over this debacle first." David waves his hand airily toward the front room by way of explanation.

Back in the sitting room, Jennie grabs a couple of the acrylics, ready to take them up to the studio for their special RSB treatment.

"Promise me you won't deliberately ruin them," says Eadie, interrupting Jennie's thoughts on that subject.

When she doesn't immediately respond, Eadie follows up with an authoritative, "Well?"

Jennie swings to face the clairvoyant in the room. "I promise I won't ruin them. Well, no more than I have to."

"Excellent."

"I wish I'd never come up with this harebrained idea now."

"Rubbish. We need to take that little todger down once and for all."

36

The following morning, Jennie pulls her new bedroom curtains back as far as they'll go on all windows; while loads of light streams in, because the angled skylights are covered it means the room is nowhere as bright as it had been the day before. Even though her work this morning is designed to ruin the acrylics, she still needs light to achieve the correct level of bastardisation.

Looking at the wooden panels hanging on their hooks far above her, Jennie resigns herself to going all the way down to the cellar and grabbing the deathtrap of a ladder.

"Unless ... maybe I could reach one end with a broom and poke it."

Jennie stares up at the boards while she works through various scenarios in her head. No matter how she looks at it, all of them result in her being sconed by a board when it comes crashing down.

Taking the shade off her bedside lamp, she stands it on the table next to the easel. It helps but lighting the piece from only one side distorts it something chronic.

"Damn!"

Traipsing down the stairs she concentrates on various devices she could construct so she can pull the panels down as and when she needs to, without having to resort to using the ladder. She's still deep in thought when she walks through the kitchen on her way to the door that leads to the cellar. It's only when Eadie speaks, that Jennie realises she's sitting in her usual spot at the end of the table.

"Penny for 'em?"

"Sorry?"

"You're obviously stewing over something, if that wrinkled brow of yours is anything to go by."

"Oh," says Jennie, consciously unwrinkling her forehead. "I was thinking about how I could jury rig something to take those skylight panels down when I need to paint."

"Is the pole no longer in the cupboard?"

"Pole?"

"Yes, in the cupboard closest to the door, there's a pole with a hook on the end. That's how I used to take them down."

"Checking now."

Jennie swings back toward the hallway and hurtles up to the studio, ditching her coat on the way. Sure enough, when she opens the cupboard Eadie had mentioned the poles are tucked in at one end. One of them has a tube at the top designed for the other pole to clip into, making it long enough to reach the skylights. The second pole has a hook device at one end that takes Jennie straight back to primary school. She'd used something similar when she was room monitor and it had been her duty to open the louvres up by the ceiling.

"Bingo!"

The two halves of the pole clip together easily, enabling Jennie to reach the hooks on the boards with room to spare. She unhooks the lower end first, leaving the board hanging from the skylight by the two hooks at the other end. The board swings backwards and forwards before settling. Realising she can safely walk under it without beaning herself, Jennie leaves it hanging like that.

After she repeats this process with the second board, the room is almost back up to full brightness. The hanging boards do block a little light, but not enough for her to bother taking them down.

Putting the pole away, Jennie retrieves all her art equipment from the cupboard and sets it back up. With any luck she'll be able to ruin all of the acrylics by the end of the day. Then she can officially start her Christmas break.

She spends a productive, if you can call it that, morning reducing the standard of the acrylics to a level low enough that people will believe Rupert has painted them. Jennie has to work at this endeavour in order to achieve the degree of ruination required and even carries on through into the afternoon, finishing as the light fails. Who'd have thought stuffing up something would be so labour intensive? She's daubing on the last paint when she hears noise from below. Sam and Chris are home.

She rushes through cleaning her brushes and dashes downstairs, meeting up with Sam on the first floor landing.

Jennie throws her arms around Sam and squeezes hard. "I missed you so much!"

Sam squeezes back with as much enthusiasm. "Me too! About you."

The two of them are still dancing around in each other's arms when Chris staggers up the stairs. He has Sam's suitcase in one hand and his other is wrapped around the handles of at least a dozen carrier bags. The girls stumble to a stop and Sam rushes to help him by taking hold of the shopping bags.

"Christmas shopping?" says Jennie.

"Yeah, we had so much fun!"

Chris coughs hard at this comment, causing Sam to amend it. "Okay, so maybe it was only me that had fun."

Chris drops Sam's suitcase next to their wardrobe and disappears back down the stairs, presumably to collect more luggage. Jennie follows Sam into their bedroom as the girls keep chatting about everything that's been happening while she's been up North. Sam sifts through the carrier bags until she finds the one she's looking for.

"I got some amazing fabric while I was up there."

She opens the bag wide for Jennie to get a good look at it. The variety of textures and colours is kaleidoscopic.

"Wow!"

"Awesome." Sam finds another bag with the same logo on the side and takes the two of them into her sewing room. Jennie stands by while Sam upends the bags of fabric onto her big sewing table shaking them vigorously until they're both empty.

They're back on the landing when Sam stops in her tracks. "You're really embracing Christmas, aren't you?"

"I guess so," says Jennie.

It's only when Sam nods in the direction of the door to Jennie's old bedroom that she twigs what her friend is on about.

The faint strains of Snoopy's Christmas emanate through the door.

"Not me. Brenda."

"Brenda?"

"Yeah, with you guys due home, I gave her my old room and moved back up to the studio."

"Really!"

Sam's response, coupled with her eyebrows jiggling, is so chock-full of innuendo that Jennie squashes it immediately.

"Not on your blinking life."

"Shame. You two would be great together."

Leaving Jennie on the landing with her mouth hanging open, Sam wanders back into her bedroom, drops the empty carrier bags on the floor and then throws open her suitcase.

She systematically goes through her bag sorting her possessions into several untidy piles. Jennie still hasn't moved when Chris staggers past her with more bags.

"You okay?" he asks, returning to the ground floor to retrieve yet more stuff.

"I'm-I'm ..." Jennie doesn't try for anything more coherent than this.

Shaking her head to clear it of any stray thoughts about Mark, Jennie steps over to the door of Sam's room. The place looks like an explosion in a laundrette.

Jennie steps back when a pair of undies flies across the room in her direction.

"Doesn't he have a washing machine up North?"

"Not one that works and the laundromat was a hole."

Her suitcase empty, Sam shoves it under the huge four poster bed that dominates the room. She stows the bulging carrier bags under there too. Once she's put away all the shoes, toiletries and her few remaining clean clothes, the room looks reasonably tidy again. That is until Chris arrives with what Jennie hopes is his final load.

He drops everything in an untidy heap next to the bed. "That's the lot!"

Jennie looks at all the stuff heaped up around Chris's legs. "Did you leave anything up there at all?"

"No point paying rent to the boarding-house biddy if we're not there."

"Aren't you worried you won't get your room back?"

"Hah, fat chance," says Sam. "I doubt the old crone who owns the place has had full occupancy in over fifty years."

Sam corrals her dirty clothes into a neater pile and grabbing the empty fabric shop carrier bags, starts shoving everything into them.

"It must have been a nightmare bringing that lot back on

the train," says Jennie, eyeing the sheer amount of stuff in the room.

"That's the best part. We didn't need to," says Sam, jumping to her feet.

She grabs Jennie's arm, leads her through the sewing room, and then pulls back the curtains on the side window and says, "Ta da."

Jennie looks out into the night, but isn't sure what she's supposed to be looking that that is 'ta da' worthy.

"In the driveway," says Sam.

Jennie drops her line of vision and sees a VW Combi Van sitting squatly in front of the garage. It's hard to make out the colour in the dim light from the street lamp, but the reflections let her know that whatever colour it is, it's very shiny.

"Who does it belong to?"

"Chris bought it off another guy who's been on contract with Rolls Royce. The body's mint, but the engine sounds like someone's chucked a handful of bolts into a tumble dryer."

"Sam!"

Both of them clearly hear Chris bellowing from downstairs. Sam races out onto the landing, followed by Jennie at a slower pace.

"What?" yells Sam, over the balustrade.

"I've heard back from Italy," is shouted back up in response. Chris walks up the stairs for before adding, "They want to meet me!"

"You mean?" says Sam, standing strangely still, as though unable to believe this new development.

"Fiat!" yells Chris, before completing an impromptu dance around the landing, dragging Sam and Jennie along with him after a couple of circuits.

"That's amazing," says Sam, breathing hard after they've stumbled to a halt.

"When?" says Jennie, also puffing.

Chris pulls the crumpled letter out of the back pocket of his jeans and unfolds it. “Not sure. I flipped out after the first sentence.”

He skims his finger down the surprisingly long letter, before announcing “Second week of January.”

“We could take Harry,” says Sam, bouncing on her toes.

“That’s a brilliant idea,” says Chris, pulling her into a tight embrace.

“Who’s Harry?”

“The Combi van,” says Chris.

“Short for Harriett,” adds Sam.

“So, you’re planning on driving to Italy in Harry The Combi. With the engine that sounds like hardware in a dryer? That Harry?” says Jennie, unable to stop her look of scepticism

“Oh, ye of little faith,” says Chris, over the top of Sam’s head. “Mark and I will have her running like a top in no time.”

“Have who running like a top?” says Mark, walking up the stairs to join them.

Chris untangles himself from Sam and slings his arm around Mark’s shoulders. “Mate, have I got a challenge for you.”

Jennie surveys her bedroom, tidy again after the day spent ruining the acrylics.

With all the paintings stowed behind the couch in the sitting room, the room looks nothing like a studio. That is apart from the splatters of paint on the floor where the easel has stood. Jennie frowns at them, then walks onto the rug and looks down at it, checking how it sits on all four sides.

“That’ll work.”

Stepping off the carpet, she drags it over another foot and is pleased to see it covers the paint splatters without the rug sitting skew-whiff. Symmetry is everything to Jennie. She's nodding in satisfaction when Sam arrives, weighed down by an enormous eiderdown.

"Eadie thought you might need this."

Sam dumps her burden unceremoniously in the middle of the bed where it blossoms into even bigger puffiness.

"Yeah! It was still blimmin' chilly up here last night, even with all the curtains closed."

Jennie goes over to the bed and picks up a corner of the soft pink comforter, sniffing it experimentally. Rather than smelling of damp as she's been expecting, there's the faintest hint of floral.

Jennie spins to face Sam. "Where did she get it from?"

"I'm not sure. It was over a kitchen chair when I walked through from the wash house. She said I should take it up to you."

"If she's done what I think she's done, I'm going to have her guts for garters."

"You think it's off her bed?"

"I do," says Jennie, corralling the eiderdown to a point it's small enough that she can easily pick it up. "Come on, let's head down for a cuppa and I can grill her about it."

Jennie totters along the hall ahead of Sam and is about to start down the stairs when Sam pushes past her.

"Recipe for disaster. Let me go first."

Jennie is glad of this when she misses a step near the bottom and cannons into Sam. Luckily, neither of them is hurt because of the cushiony softness of the comforter that is close to engulfing Jennie. Damn thing has a life all of its own.

Safely on the ground floor, the two of them make their way to the kitchen. Sam swings into the room and holds the door open for Jennie, who forces her way blindly into the room.

Jennie's all ready to launch into Eadie about how nonsensical it is for her to give up her bedding, but the old lady isn't there.

"Oh."

"I'll make the cuppa. You find her." Sam waves Jennie out of the room.

Because of Eadie's lack of mobility, there aren't that many places for Jennie to look and so she stumbles her way back along the hall and into the sitting room. It's empty.

Dumping her feathery payload into the nearest chair, Jennie is dismayed to see a small piece of Lladro topple onto the floor from a side table.

She lets out a sigh of relief when, rather than shatter, it bounces gently to a stop. Thank goodness for lush carpet.

"Is that you, Mark?" Eadie warbles from the depths of her bedroom.

"No, it's me," says Jennie, walking through the wide open door.

She's all ready to tackle Eadie on the subject of bedding when she clocks the old lady is in bed and covered by a duvet that makes the comforter in the sitting room look threadbare. One hell of a lot of ducks must be walking around starkers if the fluffy monster that's close to swallowing Eadie whole is anything to go by.

"Are you not well?"

"I'm fine, dear. Just my joints are playing up with the cold weather and so I thought I'd snuggle in here for a wee while.

"Would you like a cup of tea? Sam and I are having one."

"That'd be lovely but I don't think my old hands are up to a cup and saucer today."

This bald statement saddens Jennie. She usually thinks of Eadie's affliction in terms of it stopping her from painting, but it's more far-reaching than that. Everyday life is sometimes a struggle, although Eadie never lets on if she can help it.

"Let me see what I can organise."

On her way back to the kitchen, Jennie retrieves the piece of Lladro, which is ironically of a girl feeding ducks, wrestles the comforter into submission and slings it over the newel post at the bottom of the stairs before heading to the kitchen. As she does so, she has to straighten every painting she passes. She's lucky the feather beast didn't knock half of them off the wall.

Walking into the kitchen, she finds Sam in the process of pulling a knitted cosy into place over the pot of tea she's made. "What did she say?"

"She was in bed under the biggest duvet I've ever seen. No way is she going cold."

"Isn't she feeling well?"

Jennie pulls her head out of the kitchen cupboard she's rummaging through.

"She's not actually sick."

Jennie opens another cupboard and rifles through its contents. When she stops and sees the look of query on Sam's face, she says, "Her joints are giving her grief."

She's onto her third cupboard before Sam says, "What on earth are you looking for?"

Jennie explains the trouble about Eadie holding a cup and saucer and missing out on her tea as a result.

"I thought if I could find a thermos and a straw, she might be able to manage those more easily."

"I know where there's one," says Sam. She walks over to the corner cupboard, opens the door wide and then gets down on her hands and knees. Reaching right inside toward the back, she disappears.

A muffled "Hah! Got it," follows.

She backs out of the cupboard and hands a small tartan-clad Thermos to Jennie.

Jennie removes the cup, unscrews the cap and sniffs inside before holding it up to the light so she can check out the lining. She's relieved to see that rather than the usual highly-smashable Christmas tree-ornament-style inner, this one is made of plastic.

"Phew, there's a relief." Turning to look at Sam, who looks to be au fait with the contents of the kitchen, she asks, "Do we have any straws?"

"Not exactly. But there's something that might be better."

Sam sifts through the contents of the third drawer down and pulls out a length of plastic tubing. Jennie's not sure what its original purpose was, but it's clean and perfect for sipping tea through.

"Tape?"

Sam finds some black gaffer tape in the bottom drawer.

"Excellent." Jennie rinses the Thermos thoroughly under the hot tap and dries it. Adding milk and sugar, she fills it to halfway with hot tea and, using a knife, gives it a good stir. She puts the length of plastic tubing inside, and then with Sam's help, tapes around the tube and over the top of the Thermos so that Eadie could conceivably knock it over without spilling a drop. It'll also help keep the tea nice and hot.

37

Jennie's nose sneaks out from the under the covers and she sniffs the air in her room.

"Smells like snow."

In truth, Jennie's never smelled snow before and so this is a wild guess on her part. But it does remind her of the smell from the depths of the Bambina-sized chest-freezer her parents have parked in their garage back home. She takes this as a positive sign.

Her hand snakes out from the warmth of her bed and lifts the bottom of the curtains. She doesn't want to commit to getting up if there's no snow. Unfortunately, the ice on the windows means it's impossible to see outside. She touches the window experimentally and is shocked to find the ice is on the inside.

"No wonder it's so darn cold."

Although it's not as cold in her room as it would have been if Mark hadn't managed to get the room's antique radiator working again. He'd sweated over it for hours and his language had veered from technical to atrocious in short order. Chris had taken pity on his mate and lent a hand and between the two of them, they'd sorted it out.

Jennie had been concerned when they suggested she leave the room when it was switched on for the first time. Other than some strange gurgling sounds at the beginning, the radiator had settled down and was soon hot enough to cook eggs on.

Going to bed the night before, the room had been toasty, so she wonders if the radiator might have given up the ghost again.

The icy quiet of the room is shattered by her small alarm clock chattering into life.

"Damn!"

She can't ignore it as there's a heap to get through if Christmas dinner is to be on the table at one o'clock as planned. She slams her hand down on top of the clock, takes a few hyperventilating breaths and then jumps out of bed. Before her body can register the cold, she drags on her dressing gown and stuffs her feet into her slippers. These are a tight fit given she hasn't removed her bed socks.

She breathes out experimentally, but the room is so gloomy she can't see if her breath is visible or not. She checks the radiator and is surprised to find it's still reasonably warm.

"It must be perishing out there."

Hoping to have a better view now she's standing, Jennie opens the curtains on the window overlooking the road. Luckily the ice is only halfway up the window and she's able to peer over the top. The street and roofs of the cars are shrouded in white. However, it's a heavy duty frost rather than snow. It doesn't look pretty. It looks hard and unforgiving.

Her gaze moves from the street to the window pane itself, and Jennie is alarmed to see the ice on the inside is glistening and there are tell-tale pools forming on the window sill.

"Yikes!"

Racing from her room, Jennie flies all the way down to the kitchen before scurrying way back up to her room, armed with a fish slice and a tray. She scrapes the ice off the inside of the front window and after opening the other curtains, gets to work on the window over her bed and the other overlooking the garden. One thing's for sure, she's moving her bed away from the big window. It's much colder there than in the rest of the room.

Her bedroom windows de-iced, Jennie has a birdbath of a shower rather than freeze to death and dresses in haste, ready for action down in the kitchen. Checking the shelf in the oven is sitting on the lowest rungs, she turns it on, cranking it right up to get the oven heated as quickly as possible. It will take a fair few hours to roast the Labrador-sized turkey currently taking up a whole shelf in the larder. There hadn't been any choice on where to store it as Jennie had doubted anything other than brute force and a tyre-iron would have wedged that turkey inside the fridge.

Retrieving the bird, she's concerned to find that it's cold to the touch. With the drop in temperature overnight, the larder is a fair few degrees cooler than the fridge. But there's an element of relief when she removes the giblets and they're squishy rather than rock solid.

"Thank goodness."

It takes a lot of experimentation before Jennie finds an oven dish and roasting rack big enough to hold the Christmas Emu and plonks the bird in it, breast side up. She dabs away with a kitchen towel to remove any moisture to help the skin go crispy, or so her mum had told her on the phone the night before.

After rubbing oil, salt and pepper into the skin and stuffing a couple of peeled onions inside the cavity, Jennie adds some broth to the pan. She then manhandles the not paltry poultry into the oven. It just fits, with the enormous bird wearing the oven like a metal straitjacket. On closing the door, she worries that one of its wings is dangerously close to the glass. She hopes it'll shrink as it cooks, otherwise they're in for truly crispy skin and one hell of a dirty oven.

With the turkey safely on its way to lunch, Jennie sorts herself out some breakfast. She's finishing off her second piece of toast, when Sam arrives.

Sam looks closely at the wall of flesh visible through the window of the oven. "You got it in whole! I thought we might have to attack it with a chainsaw."

"I thought about cutting it up, but apparently that can make it as dry as old boots."

"I reckon that's how it tastes anyway. How in God's name are we meant to roast the veggies?"

"We'll have to do them in the electric frying pan, because there's no way we're going to fit them in with that thing," says Jennie, nodding toward the oven.

In tandem with getting Christmas lunch ready for the household, Jennie puts together another package.

"What on earth is that for?" says Sam, seeing the pile of newspaper and tinfoil topped with a plastic plate.

"I'm putting together a lunch for Chicken George."

"Is he still living rough?"

"Yeah. I'd have thought he'd move into a shelter for the winter but I guess he likes his independence.

"He must be freezing, living in that glorified wood pile of his."

Jennie tries imagining it but simply can't process thoughts of what it must be like to deal with that sort of cold.

"I'm about done here. Do you want to find Mark and see if he can run me down there in the car? Otherwise, it'll be cold before I can get there."

"George? Are you around?" Jennie uses her chicken-coaxing tone and is rewarded when she hears the rustle of newspaper from inside the hut.

The vagrant is as cautious as always when he exits his rumpty and Jennie knows that having Mark standing right behind her isn't helping matters.

"Can you wait for me by the hedge? Or even better in the car."

"Hedge is as far as I go," says Mark, before retracing his steps through the crunchy ice-coated grass.

The farther away Mark is, the closer George comes to Jennie until she's able to hand over her package. After wishing him Merry Christmas she updates him on having seen Peggy.

"She's alive?"

"She was last time I saw her," says Jennie, not wanting to give him too much false hope. With the temperatures they've been experiencing of late, the chicken might well have a lot in common with her supermarket counterparts.

The look of elation that shows on George's face at learning that his beloved pet might still be alive is a Christmas present in its own right.

Bang on one o'clock, they all sit down at the table in the formal dining room. It's festively decorated and groaning under the weight of the food piled high in its middle. The effort put in by Jennie and Sam that morning has both of them feeling frayed around the edges. The others had helped out where they could, but the lion's share had fallen to the two girls.

Once they've pulled the crackers and put on their too-small paper hats, they compare cheap plastic novelties and then get stuck in. Any conversation is limited with all of them applying themselves to the enormous amount of food.

They're having a breather when Mark staggers to his feet and starts clearing dishes.

"Jeez, I'm so full I feel like I've polished off a family of hamsters," says Brenda, massaging her tummy, "including their cage and bloody exercise wheel."

Jennie looks down at her own stomach, shocked to see how distended it is. "Can we hold on dessert for a while? I don't think I could do it justice right now."

"We can't stop now. I've made pudding," says Brenda.

This is so out of character that anyone on their feet sits back down with a bump.

Jennie and Sam stare at each other through the candelabra sitting in the middle of the table. It only takes a second before both pairs of eyes are out like a snail's.

"You didn't," they say in unison, their minds going back to the only meal they'd ever eaten prepared by Brenda.

"Jeez, relax, would ya," says Brenda, pushing herself to her feet. "Eadie talked me through it."

"What did you make?" says Mark to Brenda's back, as she pushes her way through the swing door into the kitchen.

The word "Trifle!" comes back at them in slices through the gradually narrowing gaps left by the swinging door.

"Trifle?" Now it's time for Mark's eyes to open wider than nature intended. He looks pointedly at Eadie, sitting proudly at the head of the table. "Tell me you didn't?"

"Lighten up, boy. It's only once a year."

In response to the questioning looks from Jennie, Sam and Chris, he says, "Eadie's idea of a trifle is closer to a cocktail than a dessert."

Jennie thinks he's being a tad melodramatic when he stands and blows out all the candles, plunging the room into darkness. Jennie doubts she'll ever get used to the night in winter arriving mid-afternoon. There's a little weak light still coming in through the large windows that face the street, but not enough to eat without taking your eye out with a spoon.

"Sorry," says Mark, making his way toward the door where he flicks on the main light. "It's safer this way," has only cleared his lips when Brenda storms triumphantly back into the room, nearly giving Mark a frontal lobotomy in the process.

She's carrying a large bowl filled to the brim with one of Jennie's least-loved desserts. Sloppy sponge and custard doesn't do anything for her and the monster trifle Brenda has plonked on the table, looks sloppier than anything Jennie has felt duty-bound to eat to date.

"It's looking perfect," says Eadie peering at the blah-and-yellow concoction that's doing its best to sneak over the top of the crystal bowl.

Brenda slops out enormous helpings and passes them around the table. Jennie holds up her hand to reject her serving but at the look on Eadie's face, gracefully flips her hand over and takes the bowl from Brenda. With any luck, she can get away with a couple of mouthsful.

She has her spoon with a small glob of trifle poised in front of her mouth when Sam starts coughing and spluttering. Jennie is so busy looking at the now scarlet Sam that she isn't even conscious of putting the spoon in her mouth until the alcoholic burn hits.

"Delicious," says Eadie, managing to get another huge spoonful into her mouth. The old lady gobbles her way through half her bowl while everyone else is getting up the nerve to have a second spoonful. Even Brenda, who's a hard drinker, is slow to eat her pud.

"Glad you blew the candles out, mate," says Chris, swiping his napkin across his forehead.

"Lightweights," cackles Eadie, with obvious glee and what looks to be a second helping of the ninety-proof pudding in front of her.

Mark shakes his head. "This is gonna get ugly."

Jennie manages to force down three small mouthsful, before putting her spoon back in the bowl as quietly as she can. Eadie still clocks it though.

"Come on, Jennie," says Eadie, before polishing off her second bowl and looking hopefully at Brenda for a top up. "S'only oncer yee."

"It's, ah, it's lovely, but I'm so full." Jennie pats her tummy for emphasis.

The look Eadie gives her makes Jennie feel she's single-handedly killed off the spirits of Christmas Past, while Brenda is steering more toward wanting to force-feed Jennie the rest of the bowl. Jennie reluctantly takes up her spoon and powers through her plateful of gloop, shallow breathing to avoid the worst of the fumes. The liquid left in the bottom of the bowl when she's finished all the solids looks to be pure alcohol.

She's putting her spoon down, when Eadie pipes up, "You have to drink that, it's the best bit."

Jennie isn't sure if it's the champagne consumed with lunch or the incendiary device that Brenda's whipped up, but her temper flares.

"For God's sake, fine. I'll finish the bloody stuff." She slams her spoon on the table, picks up the bowl and swallows the dregs straight from the plate. Putting the bowl down again, hard, she's appalled at the sarcastic, "Happy now?" that escapes.

She needn't have worried, as rather than be upset, Eadie grins broadly. "Seconds?"

Brenda holds her hand out for Jennie's bowl.

"What the hell," says Jennie, passing it over.

"It's only once a year," say the three crones in unison.

Jennie slugs back three helpings in the end, egged on by Brenda and Eadie. Even in her fully cut state, Jennie is still aware of the looks she, Brenda and Eadie are receiving from the three at the other end of the table. Sam is laughing but incredulous and Chris looks mildly amused but Mark is veering between censure and something Jennie doesn't want to examine too closely. It makes her wonder if getting this trolleyed is a good idea, given how thinly veiled his sensual gaze is when he looks at her.

Once the crystal bowl is thankfully empty and the plates licked clean, Eadie claps her hands together. Wincing briefly at the pain caused by the momentarily forgotten arthritis, she carefully enunciates, "Time for charades."

Jennie is keen, so is Brenda, but there's a decided lack of enthusiasm from the others. Jennie's sure she hears, "If you can bloody walk," from Mark's direction but when she looks at him, his expression is neutral. Suspiciously so.

It's not until she's dragged herself to her feet, that she thinks he might have a point. It's only by slamming her hands down on the table that she stops herself from falling back into her chair. It takes a few more seconds to gain her equilibrium and feel safe enough to move away from the stability provided by the furniture.

Eadie is encountering stability issues of her own, but Jennie doesn't feel capable of providing the help so obviously needed. Luckily Brenda appears to have full use of her limbs and helps Eadie to her feet and through to the sitting room.

Jennie is safely in the sitting room when she hears Mark say, "No, no. It's okay, we'll clear up in here."

She's about to swing back into the dining room and rip strips off him when Sam jumps to her defence.

"Bloody right, too. We cooked. You clean."

Sam joins Jennie and helps her navigate her way to the sitting room.

Sinking ungracefully into the couch, Jennie waves in the general direction of the others, eschewing the favoured first spot, preferring instead the upholstered softness currently cuddling up to her. Brenda is on her third attempt at conveying the title of a movie that's also a book and a play, when Jennie falls asleep.

38

Morning arrives with remarkable speed and many recriminations. Jennie doesn't have any memories of staggering up to her room the night before and if the slime in her mouth is anything to go by, she missed brushing her teeth. She runs her tongue over them several times, which helps.

Keeping her eyes closed to avoid having to deal with the day and herself, Jennie rolls over to face the wall. Instead of encountering wallpaper, she bumps into another body.

"Huh?" Her voice manages to croak and break up even on such a small word.

Daring to open her eyes she's facing Mark, frighteningly close and smiling in a manner too intimate for it to be a good sign. When Jennie realises she's in his bed and not her own, she scrambles away from him, shame burrowing into every nook and cranny.

"What am I doing in here?"

"You threw up all over your bed and I couldn't be arsed changing the sheets at three in the bloody morning."

Jennie inches her way to the edge of the bed and flings the

covers to one side to make her escape. She rips them back over herself.

"You spewed on your pyjamas too."

Jennie looks wildly around the room. "Where are my clothes?"

Mark doesn't respond immediately, leading Jennie to say, "No wonder my mouth feels so awful."

It's a good approximation of how the rest of her feels too. The hangover isn't so bad, no doubt due to the number of times she'd apparently been sick. But her remorse and disgrace are all-consuming. She's wallowing in this when Mark mumbles, "Don't know why your mouth tastes bad, you bloody insisted on brushing your teeth."

"Thank God for small mercies," mutters Jennie.

"Yeah, I was surprised you'd bother, being naked and all."

Jennie pulls the covers over her head as if to hide from her disgusting behaviour. Her first sob takes them both by surprise; Mark scoots over and pulls the covers back so he can look at her. He then drags her into his arms.

The amount of skin on skin connection is more than Jennie's experienced since a few months before Steve passed away. He'd been so sick that any sexual feelings had been stomped on and then buried with him. At least that's what she'd thought.

Jennie's guilt is further spiked when her body reacts to Mark's, as if making up for lost time. The tears are falling fast now, mostly because Mark is being kind rather than trying to get his end away as she would have expected, although he's undeniably prepared.

His hand draws soothing circles on her back until the last tears have hiccoughed themselves away. Looks as though she's making up for lost time on the tears front, having cried more in the last couple of months than she had in the year or so prior to that.

"Nothing happened last night," says Mark.

At Jennie's look, he says, "Okay, I might have skimmed a boob, but that was it. And that only happened when you snuggled up to me."

He puts some distance between them, before adding "And I did check out your arse while you were bent over the sink brushing your teeth."

He's not far enough away to dodge the pillow that Jennie aims at his head; although it doesn't take him long to retaliate.

He gets a couple of good swings in before Jennie delivers a stonking one to the side of his head. It's hard enough to bust open the pillow and have foam chips flying around like large chunks of bread.

It's at this point that Jennie twigs they're both kneeling and nowhere hidden by the covers. She whips the half-empty pillow case up in front of her and steps off the edge of the bed. Her plan is to back her way out of his room and then on over to Vomit Central.

Mark has other ideas. "Oh, no, you don't."

Jennie can't help but squeal when he bounds off the bed, scoops her up and deposits them both back in the middle of a tangle of covers and foam chips.

His lips find hers and the kiss is glorious until her guilt comes back with a vengeance. Jennie rips herself out of his embrace, bounces off the bed and runs back to her room. That she does this buck-naked is testament to how she's feeling.

The smell in her bedroom is acrid and reminiscent of a public bar early on a Saturday morning and soon anything left in her stomach wants out. She only makes it to the toilet in time.

"Humiliation complete," she says miserably into the bowl.

The remainder of her Boxing Day is reasonably uneventful. Once she's stripped her bed and washed everything covered in second-hand trifle, Jennie crawls into it, hugging a pillow tight to stop herself from falling apart.

Her mind keeps going over her kiss with Mark and she, just as persistently, keeps shoving all thoughts of it to one side. But they sneak back in. Each time carrying a little more guilt.

Maybe if she hadn't enjoyed it so much, it would be easier to deal with. Problem is she'd enjoyed kissing Mark even more than kissing Steve and that's messing her up something chronic.

As a fresh bout of tears washes over her, she hugs her pillow hard. She shrieks when a hand is laid gently on her shoulder. She'd been so wrapped up in her own misery she hadn't even heard the door open.

She turns, ready to tell Mark to get lost, but it's Sam looking down at her instead.

"Scoot over," says Sam.

Jennie does, until she's hard against the wall to allow enough space for her friend.

"You once gave me a good piece of advice," says Sam.

"Oh?"

"Yeah, something about love being a rare and special thing and that I should grab it with both hands."

"Hah, this isn't love. I don't know what the heck it is."

"It might be different from what you had with Steve, but that doesn't make it any less special."

Sam grabs another tissue off the bedside table and hands it to Jennie who frees up her hands by throwing her current sodden one in the general direction of the rubbish bin.

"It feels wrong." Jennie knows this sounds lame, but is at a loss to explain it any better.

"You need to move on and you're not going to do that by constantly looking for a Steve lookalike."

Jennie can't help the sharp intake of breath at this

comment, setting off a coughing fit. "That's so mean. And it's not true either," says Jennie, her temper starting to ramp up.

"That's better."

"What's better?" says Jennie, her voice loud enough that Sam jerks her head away.

"You're starting to feel something again. I thought we were never going to see the end of the *Stepford Wives* routine."

"*Stepford Wives*! Why are you being such a bitch?"

"Because it's about time you rejoined the land of the living and stopped emotionally gagging yourself." With Jennie struggling for a response, Sam pushes on. "I thought when you got back into the painting, it'd shake something loose. But no."

"Is that really what you think?" says Jennie, once she gets a handle on her temper.

"Yep."

"Then you don't know me at all."

"Oh, please. I know you better than you know yourself. Do you think Steve would want you moping around like a bloody Italian widow for the rest of your life?"

"How dare you say that to me," says Jennie, shoving Sam out of the bed.

"Come on! All that's missing is the black outfit and the sodding donkey!" says Sam, from her spot on the floor.

Jennie stumbles out of bed and marches over to the door.

"Get out," she says, her voice vibrating with suppressed rage.

She gives the rage its head when she closes the door after her ex-friend, causing a picture to crash to the floor, its frame broken beyond repair. Jennie had been dreading Sam leaving for Italy and the possibility of her even moving there. Now, she thinks it's a good thing.

She's dressed and stomping backwards and forwards across her room muttering, "How dare she?" when there's a tentative knock at the door.

"Bugger off," screams Jennie, at the top of her voice. It feels so good that she follows it up by bellowing, "Go away and bloody stay away," at the door.

"I'll do no such thing, young lady!" says Eadie, from the other side.

Eadie? But how?

Jennie hauls open the door and nearly slams it shut, when confronted by Eadie being held aloft by Chris and Mark. She's still sitting on one of the kitchen chairs and has a large manila envelope in her lap.

"Sorry, I thought it was someone else," says Jennie, explaining her less than sterling welcome.

"Over there," says Eadie, to the boys as though Jennie hasn't spoken. They crab their way into the room and then gently settle Eadie and her chair on the floor next to the bed. "I'll call when I'm ready to go back down."

Once the boys leave, Eadie asks Jennie to close the door so they can have some privacy. Jennie doesn't like where this is heading. She's still riled over Sam's lecture and isn't ready to face another browbeating just yet. But when she doesn't comply fast enough, she gets a prompt from the little old lady.

Resigning herself to more supposed home truths, Jennie closes the door and sits on her bed. She may as well be comfortable while her character is assassinated.

Jennie knows the shock must show on her face when rather than pointing out her shortcomings, Eadie asks Jennie to complete an acrylic especially for her.

"Of course I will," says Jennie, relieved to be talking about something other than her emotional state, or lack thereof.

The brief from Eadie is explicit, as is the subject matter. Jennie can't help blushing as her landlady ticks off the content in a matter-of-fact way. You'd think they were discussing a still life and not something straight out of a torture chamber.

Eadie hands over the manila folder and Jennie looks through the photos and clippings. "Are you sure about this?"

"Most definitely."

"You realise we can't put this one in the exhibition." Jennie waves a yellowed newspaper clipping of a distinguished-looking chap wearing a judge's wig. "Isn't this libel, or slander, or something?"

"Trust me, Jennie. This painting will never see the light of day, but it's important that you complete it for me."

"Okay, I guess. Do I sign it with Flushing's signature, same as the other acrylics?"

"Probably best if this one is unsigned. And maybe if you could tweak the style somewhat so it looks different from the others."

"All right, I'll start on it tomorrow."

"So long as it's ready by the third of January."

"You're sure it's not going in the exhibition?" says Jennie, smelling a B&D rat.

Eadie's assurances on the subject put her at her ease and Jennie jumps up to open the door in readiness to yell for the boys to come and collect her guest. She's unable to believe she's dodged the elephant in the room.

"Now about this disagreement between you and Sam," says Eadie, before Jennie can call out.

"I'd prefer not talk about it," says Jennie, her voice bordering on prim.

"She's right, you know. Unless you believe in reincarnation, no two lovers are the same and to look for a replacement is to set yourself up for failure."

The pain etched in Eadie's face has Jennie's counterattack stumbling after a breathless, "But ..."

"He's a good lad. The wild ones always are."

"I'm not up to taming anyone!" says Jennie, exasperation driving the abruptness of her response.

"God, no. How bloody boring would that be?"

"But I like boring. I like things to be predictable. I already hate the idea of the exhibition. I don't need more drama."

The upheaval in her life has been giving Jennie more than a few sleepless nights and while she acknowledges that her newly-discovered temper getting the better of her is what's placed her in this mess, if she could start again, she'd make different choices.

"Oh, *pffft*. Drama is what makes life worthwhile. Otherwise, what's the point? I want to leave waves behind, not ripples."

Unable to deal with any further well-meaning homilies, Jennie grits out, "I'll go get the guys to help you back downstairs."

Anger wins out over her innate politeness, allowing her to leave Eadie sitting there while she goes in search of Chris and Mark. She's had a gutful of lectures for one day. After finding them, she grabs her winter coat from its hook in the hallway and leaves, slamming the door hard enough to rattle the glass. If she doesn't get rid of some of her rage, she'll explode.

Hours and miles pass before her rage simmers down to simply 'pissed off' and she's able to head back to the house. It's dark and she's like a block of ice when she finally sneaks in the front door. It's as though every light in the place is burning brightly. The place would be visible from the Voyager 2. "Bloody waste of power," murmurs Jennie, sneaking up to her room. She can't believe her luck when she gets there without running into anyone.

Because she knows it's only a matter of time before someone heads up to see if she's home, she neatly writes a small note and tapes it to the outside of her door.

"I'm fine, leave me in peace."

Hopefully, they'll respect her request.

She's been home a couple of hours before it dawns on her that the house is strangely quiet. Even up in the eaves, it's still possible to hear doors opening and closing, floor boards creaking and the murmur of conversations.

Her ears are scanning like radar when she hears a familiar scratching outside her door.

"What's he doing up here?"

Jennie unlocks and opens the door to find Charlie, who rather than enter, stays sitting. His gaze is glued to her face. The look is hopeful with a tinge of concern.

"Not you, too?"

Her words get him moving, but instead of strolling into her bedroom as she's been expecting, he walks down the hallway, looking over his shoulder every few steps in an open invitation to follow, yowling hideously when she doesn't move. It's loud enough to animate dead people and is sure to rouse anyone else in a fifty-foot radius.

"So much for hiding," mutters Jennie.

It only takes one step from her to silence the bloody-minded feline. Jennie follows him all the way down to the kitchen. On the way she encounters a lot of empty rooms; their doors wide open. She can't remember if they'd been like this when she got home. She'd been concentrating so hard on not making any noise that everything else had been muted, too.

That the door to Eadie's sitting room is also wide open, piques her curiosity, enough for her to risk a quick look inside. It's empty, although the half-drunk glass of sherry on the table next to Eadie's chair indicates the old lady can't be too far away.

"Strange for her not to finish the glass though," says Jennie to Charlie, as he turns circles in the middle of the hall. His sign for hurry up.

"Okay, okay," says Jennie, proceeding toward the kitchen.

It's the only place left and so she suspects that's where everyone is, although it's quiet enough. Jennie takes a deep breath before pushing open the kitchen door knowing she has to face them all sooner or later.

The kitchen is as empty as Charlie's bowl.

"So that's the big emergency?"

Charlie confirms she's on the money by doing a couple of quick kneads of the lino and blinking at her.

With his bowl topped up and the cat trying to chew and purr simultaneously, Jennie makes herself a cup of tea. She'd usually take it back up to her room, but the Mary Celeste qualities of the house have made her worry where everyone is. It's never happened before that everyone was out of the house at the same time, unless they were at a function and she knows that's not the case tonight.

She's sucking on the dregs of her cuppa when she hears the front door open and the chatter of multiple voices shatter the eerie quiet. She hears her name mentioned several times before the mob stumbles into the kitchen, with Eadie in the lead.

Their reactions on seeing her are overwhelming. Eadie and Sam burst into tears, Brenda lets loose a string of obscenities, while Chris simply shakes his head. It's Mark's reaction that punches Jennie's gut the hardest.

His express goes from utterly wretched, to spiralling relief, and then onto raging anger. His expression forbidding.

"What's happened?" says Jennie, her cup held forgotten in front of her.

It must be something truly awful based on the meltdown. It's Mark who answers.

"You selfish cow! We've been worried sick about you and here you are drinking tea like Lady Muck while we pound the sodding streets looking for you. We spotted that sodding chicken half a dozen times. But not you!"

"Huh? I went for a walk. That's hardly cause for ... this!" Jennie waves her hand toward them. "Hang on, you saw Peggy? Where?"

"You were upset when you left," says Eadie, gently lowering

herself into her usual spot at the table, ignoring Jennie's question about the chicken.

"I wasn't upset. I was mad," says Jennie, feeling her anger bubble to the surface again and forcing her to her feet. "Stop treating me like some Bloody! Fragile! Flower!"

Jennie isn't aware of her excessive volume and vehemence until the group as a whole take a step back and Mark holds his hands up.

"Whoa, tiger!"

Eadie diffuses the situation somewhat by calmly saying, "If only you could put some of that anger into that, ah, training piece we discussed earlier."

"What?" says Jennie, swinging on her. The look on Eadie's face is enough to have Jennie apologising. "I'm sorry, Eadie. What was that you were saying?"

"Your work. It's brilliant, but think what you could achieve if you harnessed this energy." Eadie flutters her hand toward Jennie, whose body is still in a fighting stance despite the recent apology.

It gives her pause to look at herself critically and she doesn't like what she sees. She doesn't like or understand this angry version of herself enough to want to infuse her art with it.

"Why not give it a try? It's not like the piece is ever going to see the light of day."

Jennie thinks on this, dropping back into her seat. She closes her eyes and tries to visualise what her anger would look like on canvas. Seeing the bold colours that flash across the inside of her eyelids, her breath quickens.

"Exactly, my dear," says Eadie.

Jennie's eyes snap open, and she's surprised to find that she, Eadie and Charlie are the only ones left in the kitchen.

"I'm so sorry about storming off. I didn't think you would all worry about me like that."

"Why on earth not? We all care deeply about you, Jennie. Some of us more than others."

"It was my first tantrum. I wasn't thinking straight."

39

Only a lot of grovelling the next morning gets Jennie back in favour with the rest of the household. She's still angry at their attitude on how they think she should live her life, but she's adult enough to realise that same life will be tough without a few running bridge repairs. The truce is tentative, but enough to move forward for the time being.

Psyche bruised and battered, Jennie tries to get her head around the piece Eadie has commissioned her to paint. Part of her is shying away from the project and the energy Eadie says Jennie could inject into it. Another part of her is intrigued. Art has always been a Zen-like exercise for her, with a meditative state being achieved rather than her purposefully trying to dredge up suppressed feelings.

Staring at the canvas sitting in readiness on the easel, Jennie realises she has enough time and supplies to have a couple of cracks at the B&D painting; she figures she's got nothing to lose if her first attempt doesn't work out. It might even be fun to go a little crazy.

Eight hours later, not including the world's fastest sandwich break and Jennie is glad she's wearing old clothes. Angry painting is very fast but very messy! The paint she's slapped on is thick and confronting, with every line chock-full of energy. It's unlike anything she's done before, apart from maybe finger painting at kindy. The style does nothing to soften the hideous content of the composition with the grimaces of the key players taking on a grotesque nature.

The wide eyes and slack mouths of the team of 'horses' are screaming at pleasure only achieved through pain; lots of pain if the size of the whip being wielded by the masked dominatrix is any guide.

It doesn't take a genius to know that this equestrian team is made up of the rich and powerful. As well as the judge's wig, uniforms and regalia feature in many of the old press clippings and photos Eadie has given her as references.

Jennie sweeps the hairdryer back and forth across the canvas in a calming motion. It's while idly watching the paint drying under the constantly moving sweep of hot air that she appreciates how calm she's feeling.

As soon as the painting is dry enough to move, Jennie drapes it carefully with a piece of old sheet and carries it gingerly down for Eadie to have a gander. Conscious of the need to keep this one under wraps, Jennie's progress is marked by moments of stillness to check no one is around, and then bursts of energy as she moves forward at speed. She arrives at the door to Eadie's sitting room where she listens carefully to check the old lady is alone.

Happy this is the case, she opens the door and enters, closing it behind her and standing against it to ensure no one can sneak up on them.

"Is that what I think it is?" says Eadie, her face alight with anticipation.

"Yep!"

"Well, let's have a look then!"

Now that it's time for the great unveiling, Jennie suddenly

feels nervous. The piece she's holding is unlike anything she's ever done before. It's a raw snapshot of a part of her soul that she's not so keen on and showing it to another person fills her with trepidation.

"Come on then." Eadie is close to bouncing in her seat and Jennie worries there will be some sherry spillage if she doesn't get a move on.

Heart in mouth, Jennie drops the cloth to reveal the painting to Eadie.

"Oh my god. On my god. Oh, it's, ah," Eadie splutters away, filling Jennie with dread.

"It's only my first go. I can paint another. We can burn this one."

Jennie's starting in on more excuses and solutions when Eadie holds her hand up to silence her.

"It's brilliant. It's your best work, ever. It's so, so ... alive!"

Looking up from the painting she's holding at her side, Jennie's shocked to see Eadie is crying.

"I didn't mean to upset you."

"Don't mind me. Just memories, that's all."

They don't have time to discuss this further. Hearing footsteps in the hallway, they both freeze. At Eadie's prompting, Jennie drags the piece of cloth back over the painting and rushes into the bedroom with it. Looking around wildly for a hiding spot, she eventually stows it behind the dressing table.

Jennie easily hears Mark's, "What on earth's wrong? What's upset you?" from her spot next to the bed and wonders whether she should simply stay in here until he leaves. He's sure as eggs bound to blame her for Eadie's tears.

Hearing the springs of the couch react to his weight she realises she can't stay hiding. Another scan of the room finds a book on Eadie's bedside table. It's the perfect excuse for her being in here.

"I found it," she says, walking back in and causing Mark's gaze to swing rapidly in her direction.

"Borrowing a book from Eadie," says Jennie, waving the tome around in the air next to her head like a guilty person.

After Mark's expression goes from anger, to confusion, to amusement, and then full-on belly laughter, Jennie thinks he might have lost it.

"Maybe not that one," says Eadie, a smile also playing around her mouth.

"Huh?" Jennie takes a proper look at the book she's holding, aware of her face flooding with colour. *The Kama Sutra*! It's hardly what you'd expect to pick up from an octogenarian's bedside table. Jennie drops it on the nearest chair as if it's toxic, which in her mind it is, then flees the room unable to cope with Mark's, and now Eadie's, laughter any longer.

She takes her anger out on the next available canvas but what starts out as a way to get rid of her rage, turns into something else entirely. While the completed painting has her in tears, it's one she's proud to sign with her own name.

Standing back to examine it, sitting on the easel and still a little damp in places, she spits out, "I challenge anyone to laugh at me now!"

She's consumed by her art over the next week. It's something she embraces because it stops her thinking about Rupert's forthcoming exhibition and her part in that. She works her way cathartically through all the canvases and any paint left in the studio to a background of punk music, designed to feed her anger. The final painting is particularly gloomy, painted as it is, in all the dark colours she's previously avoided.

After it's dry enough to handle, Jennie props it up against the cupboards with the others, in order of completion, and looks at them thoughtfully. Eventually satisfied that she's done as much as she can, she flips them around and leaves her room.

She needs a second opinion.

Her knuckles attack the closed door of Mark's bedroom. When he answers, she's polite albeit distant.

"Do you think you and Chris could carry Eadie up to my studio? I've got something she needs to see."

A questioning look flits across Mark's face and he opens his mouth to ask something, but closes it again. Following a short pause, he says "Sure," before hurrying down the stairs.

Back in her room, Jennie paces nervously waiting for her guest. A lot of huffing and puffing announces Eadie's arrival. She's safely ensconced in a kitchen chair as for her previous visit to this normally out-of-bounds area.

"I need you to look at something for me," says Jennie, without preamble.

"So Mark tells me."

"Can you put the chair down here, facing this way," instructs Jennie.

When they've done this, the boys stand, but don't move.

"Sorry, I only want Eadie to see these."

Jennie gestures toward the door, in what she's hopes is a polite manner. Chris is quick to comply, while Mark looks a little miffed and his surly, "Sure," confirms this.

"Sorry," says Jennie, closing the door on them.

"Why all the secrecy?" says Eadie.

Rather than answer, Jennie walks over and starts flipping the canvases outwards one at a time. She doesn't pause between them, worried if she stops, she won't be able to start again. With everything ready for Eadie, Jennie retreats to her bed and sits hunched over, examining the covers minutely.

While Eadie examines each of the paintings in turn, the silence in the room stretches, pulling tightly on Jennie's nerves. They ping alarmingly when Eadie finally speaks.

"Was he in a lot of pain?" says Eadie, her voice gentle.

"Not toward the end," says Jennie, looking at the painting of Steve's final day. "By then, he was in a coma and on enough morphine to kill a horse."

Silence reigns again as Eadie goes back to examining the paintings.

The longer it lasts, the greater the tension for Jennie.

Her scalp prickles when Eadie barks out an imperious "Mark, in here now!"

"What?" Jennie looks up, confused.

Of all the responses from Eadie going through her head, this is one she hasn't expected. She jumps to her feet when Mark opens the door.

"I don't want anyone else seeing them!" Jennie runs at the door, attempting to stop him coming in.

"You might not want him to see it, but he needs to. Mark, move her if you need to."

Hearing this instruction, Jennie swings toward Eadie. "What? Why?"

Any other words *oomph* out of her as Mark picks her up and throws her easily over his shoulder before walking into the studio to stand next to Eadie. "What am I looking at?"

"These, dear boy."

From her upside down position, Jennie sees Eadie gesture toward the first painting in her small collection where it sits huddled on the floor. Mark walks over to look at it, and then moves to the right. From her position hard against his back, Jennie can hear his breathing change as he works his way along the row of paintings. Reaching the last one, he gently puts Jennie down and drags her into a crushing embrace.

"I didn't know. I didn't know," he whispers into her hair, his breath warming her scalp and her soul.

The mood in the sitting room is relaxed. Eadie and Jennie are both reading while Brenda is painting her nails and managing to keep quiet apart from some off-key humming.

The atmosphere spikes when Mark thunders down the stairs. It can't be Chris or Sam as they're out buying bits and bobs for the Harry the Combi Van.

The door to the sitting room is opened forcefully, causing Jennie and Eadie to squeak and Brenda to spit out a couple of effings and blindings. She looks up from her half-painted nail long enough to throw a dirty look in Mark's direction.

"I'm off to the pub. Anyone?"

All three women look pointedly at the window, and the rain pelting against it, before giving him a unanimous, "No!"

Jennie hates it when the weather is like this. Any colour the city might have owned has been leeched away, resulting in a soul-destroying, monotonous blah.

"Suit yourselves."

The sitting room door shuts loudly behind him although they can still hear him whistling as he gets ready to head out into the grey day.

When they hear him say, "And what the hell do you want?" their heads snap up. Alert.

"Sonja?" mouths Jennie to Eadie.

A male voice mumbles in response, and their tension ratchets down a little.

The door to the sitting room reopens and Mark ushers in a dripping pile of tweed. It takes a second for Jennie to recognise who's holding it all up.

"And to what do we owe the honour of your presence, Rupert?" says Eadie, her tone implying it's anything but.

"I've come to collect my paintings. As agreed."

"Hah. Your paintings! That's bloody rich," says Mark, intentionally crowding Rupert Smythe-Brown against the door and looking menacingly at him.

"Yes, mine. I've paid for them," says Rupert, bristling. "Ergo, they're mine. Legally," he finishes smugly.

"Hardly the point though, is it?" says Eadie.

"Let's see them, then." Rupert taps his foot impatiently, although the depth of pile on the carpet takes the edge off this.

"They've already been delivered to the gallery for framing," says Jennie.

"But ... but, I said I'd pick them up today!"

"We saw the forecast and thought it'd be better to get them to the gallery while it was fine."

"Don't worry, you little wart," says Mark, leaning over their guest to further demonstrate the difference in their heights. "I said I was dropping them off on your behalf."

"When did you take them in?" demands Rupert, backing up.

"On Sunday. The gallery opened up specially," says Jennie, enjoying Rupert's mounting alarm.

"But, how?" splutters Rupert.

"Come now," says Eadie," do you really think you and your dear papa are the only ones in this town with influence?"

"Right. That's sorted that out," says Mark. "You were just leaving!"

Mark doesn't waste his breath by arguing with Rupert and instead grabs a handful of tweed and frogmarches the odious little twerp out of the sitting room, before shoving him, none too gently, through the front door. Mark dusts his hands together as though to rid them of something unpleasant before closing the front door and coming back into the sitting room. He sits heavily on the couch next to Jennie.

"I thought you were going to the pub?" says Jennie.

"I will, just want to give that little crud time to slink away. Can't very well throw him out and then walk up the road to the pub with him, now can I?"

"He's walking! No wonder he was so wet? Surely someone that rich would be able to afford a car, if not two or three."

"Doubtless he'd prefer no one knows he's visited this particular house," says Eadie. "Especially not his father's chauffeur."

Jennie's forehead wrinkles. "Chauffeur?"

"Yes. I doubt young Shit-Brown even knows how to drive," says Eadie.

Brenda, who has remained quiet, with her head down, for the entire time Rupert had been there, says, "We have so got to Salami Boy that little arsehole."

"Salami Boy?" say both Mark and Eadie in unison.

Rather than answer, and reveal some of Sam's past that her friend would prefer didn't see the light of day, Jennie says, "Do you think we should?"

"Hell, yes," says Brenda, carefully screwing the top back on her nail polish.

Both Eadie and Mark look at them in turn, waiting for a detailed explanation of what 'a Salami Boy' is.

But neither of them says anything and Jennie is relieved when the awkward silence is eventually broken by a clunky change of subject by Brenda. "Won't the gallery owner think it's strange the paintings aren't signed?"

"Not really. The gallery owner is in on the plan," says Jennie.

"Too funny, that means the little shithead will have to sign them at the gallery," says Brenda.

"Exactly! And if I know David Michaels he'll stall on that taking place until the eleventh hour," says Eadie, glee writ large on her face.

"Anything to add pain to the experience," says Jennie, before sniggering.

Mark looks at Eadie and Jennie in turn. "Remind me never to get on the bad side of you two."

Eadie and Jennie assume their most innocent expressions, causing him to crack up. "Right, I hear a pint of Guinness calling my name."

With his departure, the room once again falls silent, although this is broken by Eadie saying, "And don't think I didn't notice the change of subject there." She looks pointedly at Brenda, for all the good it does. Silence then reigns, until it's interrupted by Eadie's gentle snores.

Brenda gestures to Jennie that they should head upstairs and they leave quietly. It's not until they're sitting on Brenda's bed, along with Charlie, that they start talking again.

"How are you going to keep him away from the gallery on the day?" says Brenda. "Your whole plan is stuffed if he rocks up before the official kick-off."

"Not sure." Jennie looks up from stroking Charlie's head. "That's the only wrinkle still to be ironed out."

"Maybe that's where Project Salami Boy could come in?"

Jennie's concentration moves from Charlie to the problem at hand. "We've got until Wednesday to sort it out."

"I'm sure I can delay him on the night. I could probably tie him up for most of the day if I really tried," says Brenda.

Jennie suspects Brenda is talking literally here rather than figuratively.

Their planning session lasts a couple of hours with their laughter escalating as it progresses.

"But how are we going to get him to go with us? We can't simply turn up unannounced," says Jennie.

"Hmmm. Good point. Maybe we can phone and pretend to be from a knocking-shop and arrange to call around."

"Would a dominatrix do house calls?" says Jennie, continuing to examine their plan from every angle.

"It's not like we're going to beat the crap out of him in the front parlour," says Brenda, "just pick him up."

"True," says Jennie, warming to the idea.

"We need to find a place he hasn't used."

"Why? Wouldn't it be better if we pretended to be from one of his regular places?"

Brenda doesn't say anything and, instead, stares at Jennie, arms crossed, mouth twisted up at one side.

This allows Jennie to think through what she's said. "Oh, right. Too easy to check."

After thrashing through the details, it's decided that Brenda will be in charge of finding a dominatrix who is unfamiliar with Rupert. Brenda's sure that if she plonks down fifty quid on the front counter that she can get someone to ring Shit-Brown to set up the appointment. Better than her phoning and spooking him with her Aussie accent.

"How did you get on?" says Jennie, following Brenda into her bedroom later the next day.

"Give me a mo. My feet feel like someone's taken to them with a sodding cricket bat."

Sitting herself on the edge of the bed, Jennie waits while Brenda removes her patently inappropriate footwear. The soundtrack to this exercise is a series of groans interspersed with profanities.

"You should have worn sneakers."

"Sod off. I wouldn't have been able to get in the front door, let alone speak to a dom. Well, not without paying."

Jennie is still processing this when Brenda lowers herself onto her bed with a heartfelt sigh.

"I can come back if you like," says Jennie, although her anticipation is arming itself in readiness to kill her.

"Nah, you're all right. I needed to get off my feet." Brenda wiggle's her toes before pressing on, "It looks like Shit-Brown has been spanked by every dom on *both* sides of the Thames.

"Wow."

"Yeah! And while the little crud is happy to take his punishment, he's not so keen on paying."

"That figures," says Jennie, pleased she'd insisted he pay up front for the paintings.

"It's why he's had to go to so many different shops. I only needed that one name from that photo of Eadie's. Then it was like an effing B&D treasure hunt."

"Do we simply make up a name then?"

"No need. I was about to call it a day when I decided on one more."

The smug grin on Brenda's face has Jennie prompting her impatiently, "And?"

"And I hit pay dirt. Nothing pisses a dominatrix off more than one of her slaves doing a runner. Although I think she was more hacked off because she's back to doing her own housework."

Jennie knows the look on her face must match the lack of comprehension she's currently experiencing.

"The self-important little turd used to get dressed up as a maid and do her hoovering while she yelled at him."

"No!"

"True! Hey, maybe we could get him to pitch in around here?" says Brenda, seemingly alight to the possibilities. "I'd be happy to smack him around the arse if he missed a spot."

Jennie's gagging sounds are answer enough.

"Maybe not."

"So?" says Jennie, hoping to get Brenda back on track.

"Oh, yeah, right. So she's still so furious that she phoned him while I was there and said she'd forgiven him and was sending him a present to help celebrate the opening of his new show."

"What's she sending him?" says Jennie, agog.

"Us. Yah doofus!"

40

Staring hard in the mirror, Jennie checks her outfit for the umpteenth time. She's turning frequently enough that she resembles a bondage kebab, if there is such a thing. The black rubber outfit belongs to Brenda and Jennie's glad it's the middle of winter; otherwise she'd be sweating like a pig. The tops of her thighs, where the fishnet stockings don't reach the bottom of the dress, feel cold and somehow vulnerable. It's the first time Jennie's worn suspenders.

Brenda's black patent boots, with their cripplingly high stiletto heels, are figuratively designed for kicking shit. In this case Shit-Brown. Rupert Shit-Brown. The voice in Jennie's head is pure Bond.

Picking up a long sheaf of black silk, also courtesy of Brenda, Jennie briefly holds the dress up to check it over. She hopes the fabric is thick enough to cover all that rubber when it comes down to it. She folds it carefully, wraps it in a scarf and stows it deep inside her handbag next to the mask she'd made the day before. She grabs her heavy winter coat off the wardrobe door and drags it on. She feels a little better when it's all buttoned up, although she notices in the brief few steps it has taken to get over to the wardrobe that she squeaks when she walks.

Thinking she's as ready as she's ever going to be, Jennie mentally prepares herself to go downstairs to Eadie's sitting room where they're congregating. They're still hours away from the opening, but the plan is to have a few calming sherries at home before going out for a quick bite to eat. Jennie's stomach is so knotted, she's glad she and Brenda have their own plan.

She opens her door and shrieks at the sight of Brenda standing right outside, her hands held up as though in surrender. There's nothing submissive about her demeanour as she shoulders Jennie toward her bed.

"Sit down. I need to sort your hair."

"My hair?"

One of Jennie's hands strays toward her mop, which she pats, checking it's all in place. Brenda knocks her hand away.

"You can hardly pull off dom with hair like Shirley Temple's."

Without warning Brenda plunges both hands into Jennie's short auburn curls.

"What are you putting in it?" squeaks Jennie, horrified at how sticky if feels.

Jennie grabs at Brenda's hands to get them away from her head, but Brenda bats her aside again. She concentrates on twisting and pulling at Jennie's hair.

"Just as well I brought more," says Brenda, pulling a large tube from the pocket of the dressing gown she's no doubt wearing to cover an outfit similar to Jennie's.

The amount of gel she squeezes onto her hand has Jennie struggling to her feet.

"Brenda, I don't think that's—"

"Relax. It's going to look amazing."

By the time Brenda stands back to examine her handiwork,

Jennie feels like she's wearing a hat. Dreading the result, she jumps up to look at the disaster in the mirror.

"Wow!"

"Told ya," says Brenda, smugly.

Jennie touches one of the spikes experimentally.

"Don't do that! They're not bullet-proof like the real deal. We'd need soap for that."

"Soap?" says Jennie, her brow creased.

"Yeah. Apparently that's what the Punks use to make those big Mohawks stay in place."

Brenda and Jennie go downstairs together. Jennie's glad of the support as she's a little wobbly on heels this high. She leans against the wall next to Brenda's bedroom door, while Brenda nips inside to ditch the dressing gown and put on her coat. No overdress for her. She emerges, wearing a gorgeous full-length black velvet coat that shrieks money and oozes sex appeal. It buttons most of the way down, meaning it could easily double as a dress, which it might have to later.

Brenda squares her shoulders in readiness. "Right, let's get this show on the road."

"Coming," yells Sam, in response to this call to action.

She and Chris pop out of their room a moment later, ready to go. Sam comes to a staggering halt.

"What the hell have you done to your hair?"

"I, oh, I thought I'd try something different," says Jennie, consciously vague.

"You definitely achieved that," says Mark, coming down the stairs from his room.

"It looks brilliant. Come on you lot. Night's not getting any younger," says Brenda, putting a stop to any further discussion about Jennie's hair.

A quick glance at her watch makes Jennie's stomach clench tightly. She's torn between moving toward the stairs because she hates being late or running back up to her room and hiding inside her wardrobe.

With all of them are inside the sitting room, it's chocker. Jennie and Brenda opt to stand next to each other by the sitting room door. To Jennie's mind, it makes more sense to be in her coat if she's standing ready to leave than if she was sitting on the couch sipping a sherry. Because her coat doesn't button as far down as Brenda's, Jennie knows if she sat down on the couch she'd end up flashing her suspenders and her rubber outfit would be sure to squeak.

Making sure everyone is holding a full sherry glass, Eadie proposes a toast.

"Here's to a successful evening."

Before anyone can take a sip, Chris speaks. "How can you stop him coming back at you? Legally or otherwise."

Eadie raises her hand and stops the ensuing discussion. "Jennie and I have that covered."

"We do?" says Jennie, forehead creased.

"We do," confirms Eadie, holding up her glass to continue the toast.

The rest of the room's occupants raise their glasses in return, and then everyone takes a small sip.

Before anyone has time for a second sip, there's an impatient beeping from the front of the house. Jennie's nostrils flare as she tries surreptitiously to get in as much air as she needs. Brenda sends a sneaky wink in her direction before sculling the rest of her sherry.

"Right. We're off," says Brenda, putting her glass on the sideboard.

Jennie knocks back the rest of her drink, too. She'd like a second glass but the beeping out front is frantic.

"I didn't think we were leaving yet?" Eadie's face is creased in confusion and she looks to be readying herself to knock back the rest of her sherry in one go if she has to.

"Brenda and I have something we need to do first. We'll see you at the gallery at six-thirty," says Jennie.

The two girls leave the sitting room in a barrage of questions but don't stop to answer any. They don't have time and Jennie knows she wouldn't have the nerve to face down that particular cross-examination. For one thing, it might bring home the enormity of what she and Brenda are about to do and cause her to baulk. It's safer to keep moving forward.

It's only once their cab is speeding down the road to an address in Knightsbridge that Jennie undoes the buttons of her coat in preparation for removing it at their destination. While they quietly go over their plan again, Brenda drags a mask, along with an assortment of bits and pieces, from an oversized shoulder bag that would give the one Jennie's lugging around a run for its money. Seeing a pair of handcuffs slapped down on the seat between them, Jennie stares questioningly at Brenda.

"I'm lousy at knots," says Brenda, securing her mask.

Pulling up outside an imposing building that's held together by a multitude of columns, Jennie stays in the black cab while Brenda saunters up the front steps, already in character in case she's under scrutiny.

Jennie doesn't recognise the person who answers the door. The hired help obviously isn't buying Brenda's story as he shuts the door in her face and leaves her standing in the cold.

Brenda stays where she is, letting Jennie know it isn't over yet. A worrying five minutes of the cab's meter clunking away passes before the door opens again. This time, it's Rupert.

With the door at its widest point, Brenda shrugs out of her long black coat, and both Jennie and the cab driver gasp simultaneously. Jennie's outfit is positively habit-like in comparison. The driver gives her a measured look in the rear-view mirror and she manages to squawk, "Fancy dress."

In seconds, Rupert is on the doorstep next to Brenda. When

he grabs hold of her arse, she smacks him soundly and starts berating him.

Rupert's head drops and his body crumples in on itself. It's while he's in this submissive pose that Brenda throws her coat over one shoulder, grabs his tie and yanks him toward the cab. That she's close to naked while doing this doesn't seem to bother her although Jennie can hear the cab driver's breathing speed up.

Jennie ditches her coat and then lounges nonchalantly in her corner. Brenda and Rupert are right beside the cab when she realises she's missing the most important part of her disguise and has to scramble to get her mask in place before they arrive. She's vastly relieved her studded leather mask has been fashioned around a large pair of sunglasses, making it easy for her to slip it on.

Rupert's spots her and lurches toward her side of the cab causing her to shrink back, that one small sherry gagging to escape. A sharp rap from Brenda restores him to her control. He sits primly on the little fold-down seat opposite her and well away from Jennie.

Brenda then makes a real production number out of peeling off her sheer stockings. The first she rolls up and stuffs into Rupert's mouth, the second she uses to blindfold him. Once he's blindfolded Brenda and Jennie waste no time in getting their coats back on.

Jennie can see by the small tent forming in the crotch of Rupert's beautifully tailored trousers that he's not upset by developments. Anything but.

Pulling up at the end of a dark alleyway, Brenda helps Rupert out of the cab while Jennie takes care of paying the driver. The look he gives her while she's handing over a distressingly large number of notes, let's her know he's not buying the fancy dress line. She shrugs, and he shakes his head before roaring off into the night.

Jennie takes a second to get herself in character before walking down the alley to where Rupert and Brenda are standing next to a doorway leading into an innocuous concrete building. There's nothing glamourous about the back entrance to the gallery.

"Has he been bad?" Jennie hopes she's disguised her voice enough that their captive won't twig who she is. She's sure her East End accent is atrocious but, with any luck, good enough to pass muster. Brenda, who is also linguistically-challenged, has an accent that's wavering wildly between Cockney and Jamaican.

Jennie digs a large key out of her pocket and slides it into the lock of the heavy-duty metal security door. She's still amazed that David Michaels has agreed to their crazy plan. It's evidence of how annoyed the gallery owner is with Rupert.

The room they enter is empty but for a few cardboard boxes and some large shelves that sit hard up against the wall opposite the door. The room is dimly lit by a couple of naked bulbs. It's freezing inside.

"Strip!" demands Brenda.

The voice of command is such that Jennie's hands spring toward the buttons on her coat and Brenda has to slap her hand over her mouth to stop a snort of laughter from escaping.

Rupert doesn't move fast enough to do her bidding, so Brenda adds a forceful "Now!" that gets him moving.

With Rupert busy taking off his Harris Tweed, Brenda has a rummage in her handbag of tricks pulling out lengths of rope and then a riding crop, which she hands to Jennie, who immediately drops it.

There follows a pantomime of 'pick it up' from Brenda, which Jennie eventually does, although she's not happy about it. This isn't part of their plan.

Meanwhile, Rupert has removed his jacket and is holding it out, obviously wanting to hand it over.

"Drop it!" roars Jennie, surprising all three of them.

He does so and Jennie is astounded, but also delighted, at the surge of power that zooms through her body.

"Shirt!" she barks, finding it easier to mask her Kiwi accent by simply yelling one-word instructions at the little weasel.

Following a seven-denier-muffled, "Yes, mistress," Rupert meekly complies with her wishes, nearly garrotting himself when he removes his navy and white striped tie.

Feeling he's taking too long over the buttons Jennie adds an authoritative "Faster, you little maggot!" reinforcing her command with a hard, fast smack to his buttocks with the whip.

She looks at Brenda for confirmation that she's being realistic. The wide smile and slow nodding are all the answer she needs.

Rupert is now down to his trousers and a string vest. The sight of his breasts trussed up like Christmas hams has both girls trying desperately not to snigger.

Completely naked, apart from his socks, she and Brenda tie him up to the shelving. Laughter is now the farthest thing from Jennie's mind. A life of celibacy is currently winning out.

With no chance of him escaping, Jennie places her whip on the shelf next to a large pail and brush she'd left there the day before. Dragging on a pair of washing-up gloves, she pulls the lid off the pail to reveal a couple of gallons of cloudy white glue. It's her special recipe and guaranteed to give the superglue the thugs use to stick people to the walls of the Embankment a good old nudge in the adhesion stakes. She dips the four-inch-wide brush into the viscous liquid, then wipes it on the side of the pail to stop any drips.

She's unsure how to proceed. Up and down, or side to side.

More panto from Brenda has her slapping the brush against her willing victim's chest. Hard and fast.

The more she slaps him with the brush, the more willing

he becomes, which makes it both easier and harder to give his do-dads a good going over. Jennie's glad she hasn't eaten since lunch time.

Finished, she drops the brush back into the pail, before removing the rubber gloves, safely turning them inside out as she does so.

Brenda spins her finger over her watch and Jennie whispers in Brenda's ear, "At least ten minutes before you let him get dressed."

It won't be until he's getting ready for bed that he'll realise he can't take anything off. All going well, it'll be a couple of days before the horrible little man can strip again. That this will make ablutions problematic is a bonus.

With her part in proceedings over, Jennie retrieves the dress from her handbag and, after taking off her coat, slips it over her head. It drops into place covering everything up, although Jennie can see the tell-tale bumps of her suspender belt clips. Her hand is already on the sliding door at the far end of the room when there's a cough from Brenda.

When Jennie turns, Brenda points dramatically at her hair, before miming slick-back actions. Nodding, Jennie delves into her handbag and is relieved when her hand closes on her afro comb. She drags this through her gelled spikes until everything is slicked back and she has no doubts that she now resembles Eddie Munster. Still, this is better than Rupert recognising her distinctive spikes when he makes it into the launch.

At a thumbs-up from Brenda, Jennie slides open the door. She's closing it after her when she hears Brenda yell, "Shut up, you little scumbag," followed by the unmistakable sound of leather striking flabby buttock. Jennie's less pleased when she hears Rupert's obvious moan of pleasure in response.

With the sliding door fully closed and locked behind her, the hallway is plunged into darkness. She has a mental snapshot of it from when she'd first opened the door from the storeroom. Unfortunately, the photo is still in focus enough for her to know she can't blindly walk down the obstacle course laid out in front of her.

As her pupils dilate, she realises the hall isn't completely pitch black. The door at the far end is open a sliver, allowing a shaft of light to dissect the gloom. Jennie edges her way carefully forward and makes it to the other end without damaging herself or, more importantly, her expensive fishnets. Jennie had been relieved when Brenda had offered to sacrifice her stockings for the blindfold and gag at their planning session.

Jennie puts her eye to the gap and peers into the next room, relieved it's empty. The door squawks in protest when she pushes it open enough to slip through. She's tiptoeing across the room, when someone behind her says, "What on earth are you doing back here?" in a plummy voice.

It's a close call between peeing herself, having a coronary, or sending her large handbag skyward. Jennie's pleased when her body chooses the final option, although the handbag's contents scatter far and wide.

Spinning, she finds a young woman standing in front of a large industrial fridge, a bottle of champagne in each hand. While the accent might be upper class, the plain black dress screams hired help.

"I ... ah ... I," stutters Jennie, "I got lost on the way to the bathroom."

"I'll bet you did," says the woman, looking at the leather mask and a length of rope on the floor next to the Jennie's bag. "David doesn't like hookers on the premises."

This statement makes Jennie bristle, but instead of backing down as she usually would, she stands tall, stares down her nose at the little Sloane Ranger hopeful and crowds her until she's hard up against the fridge. "Excuse me! I'm not the one being paid by the hour!"

It's only when the woman's face pales that Jennie realises how scary she must be coming across.

"Scat!" says Jennie, pointing toward the door.

She's secretly relieved when the woman obeys because it's all bluster on Jennie's part. It's not until she's repacked her handbag and is out in the hall that it dawns how much she enjoyed putting that jumped-up twit in her place. "I could get used to this."

"Get used to what?" says David Michaels, coming up beside her unexpectedly and ratcheting her heart rate back up. "Sorry, didn't mean to startle you, was looking for more champers to keep up with that lot." He jerks his head toward the door leading to the gallery proper.

"Did he come in to sign the paintings?" says Jennie.

"Yes. Held him off until lunchtime today though. He was in a hell of a state!"

"Serves him right," says Jennie.

"Everything going okay?" says David Michaels, his head nodding subtly toward the back storeroom.

"As well as can be expected," says Jennie.

"Excellent," says David, before disappearing into the room vacated by Jennie.

Even with his backing, Jennie worries that the plan she and Brenda have concocted might not be so clever after all. She's torn between retracing her steps and putting a stop to things or joining the others in the gallery.

If she bails, Rupert will know she was involved. If she continues, there's a good chance she'll get away with it. Safety wins out and she goes in search of a coat check.

The crowded gallery comes as a shock following the relative quiet of the various back rooms. She scans the crowd, looking for Mark, who'll be the easiest to spot because of his height. She sees him on the far side of the gallery and swims through the crowd in his general direction. Jennie slips through the moneyed mob anonymously, relieved that their chatter drowns out her squeaky dress. It's not until she's closer to Mark that she can see the others standing next to him.

Jennie knows exactly when Eadie spots her, relief flooding the old lady's face. "Where on earth have you been? I was worried you'd changed your mind," says Eadie, when Jennie pulls up next to her.

"Just helping Brenda with a few things," says Jennie, being purposely obscure.

"What happened to your hair?" says Sam.

"Oh, ah, the spikes were drooping so I had to slick it back."

Sam fingers the material of Jennie's dress. "I like this. Is it new?"

"Brenda's."

Jennie can tell by how Mark's eyes widen that he's also keen on the dress. If only he knew what she had on underneath. Actually, the less she thinks about that the better.

They're making nervous small talk when David Michaels calls for everyone's attention. There's no going back now.

41

It takes several minutes for the posh chatter to subside enough that the gallery owner can start on his prepared speech.

It comes as no surprise to Jennie who had read it through with Eadie. The language David Michaels uses is particular in that it absolves him of any responsibility for the content of the exhibition. He's halfway through what is essentially a disclaimer, when comments start to pop up around the room.

"Come on old chap, unveil the damned things," comes gruffly from the back of the room.

David continues to stall until it dawns on the crowd that the star of the show is missing. The room is evenly split between those who think David should push on with the unveiling, presumably so they can get back to the buffet, and those who want to wait. Countess Harrow, Rupert's aunt, is the power behind those wanting to wait.

It becomes obvious that if they wait any longer, half the crowd will have moved on, so she relents, although she's extremely miffed about it.

David grabs hold of a corner of the black satin cloth

covering the panel farthest to the left and briefly looks in Jennie's direction, before expertly flicking the fabric clear. This reveals two paintings. The watercolour of the Victorian toy is on the left, while its graphic acrylic counterpart is on the right.

There is a smattering of polite applause from the optically challenged in the audience. Those able to see the content of the acrylic gasp, and then crowd forward in an effort to take a closer look.

"Excuse me, if you could all move back," says David Michaels, his arms spread wide as he herds them back behind some invisible marker.

He wastes no time removing the other five cloths, and then moves swiftly to the side for fear of being trampled. He makes his way over to stand next to Jennie and the others and they watch the ensuing *mêlée.*

"It's a damned shame Rupert isn't here," says David Michaels. "Wonder where the hell he is?"

No sooner has he uttered these words, than their attention is caught by movement on the other side of the plate glass window they're standing next to.

Jennie stares out the window horrified.

What on earth is he doing out there? And why's he still wearing the blasted blindfold? And the handcuffs! More importantly, why the hell is he still naked? His clothes should be firmly glued on by now.

They all watch in fascinated horror as he runs first one way, then the other. Jennie hopes he doesn't run out into the traffic, although what happens next will take longer to recover from.

Momentarily frozen, Rupert stands right next the window as though looking into the gallery. His now-flaccid bits seemingly stuck in the upright position.

Damn, that glue of mine is good.

Looking briefly to the right of Rupert, Jennie is surprised to see Brenda sauntering down the pavement smiling fit to burst.

Her arm is tucked safely through that of Martin McGowan, her elderly lover. With the merest of swerves, she swings her hip hard into Rupert's bum, helping him to make contact with the plate glass window. Jennie expects the little creep to move away, but he stays exactly where he is like some grotesque entomological specimen mounted on the glass.

He tries pulling back but realises he's stuck; he panics, whacking his head hard into the glass. This loud bang captures the attention of the crowd who turn as one to stare transfixed at the artist of the moment.

"You wouldn't happen to know anything about this, would you?" says Eadie, archly to Jennie.

"This?" says Jennie, nodding toward the bug on the windscreen that is Rupert. "No! Not this."

Essentially she isn't telling fibs. This bit hadn't been part of the plan.

"I hope his Prince Albert doesn't scratch the glass," says Mark, into the deathly quiet that has now descended on the gallery.

The only response to his observation are the sobs that erupt from Countess Harrow as she rushes over to stand in front of Rupert to preserve what's left of his dignity. Jennie suspects this might be a lost cause.

Jennie's looking down to avoid having to witness this sad spectacle when she becomes aware of a new pair of shoes having joined their little group. The highly polished brogues, with all their little holes, scream Saville Row, or wherever flash shoes come from in London.

"This has your mark," says a cultured voice.

This simple statement is so chock-full of venom that Jennie's head snaps up. She feels Mark bristling next to her.

Eadie's demeanour is suspiciously calm when she says, "Wallace Smythe-Brown, I have no idea what you're talking about."

Wallace Smythe-Brown? Rupert's father?

His face is scarlet with rage, blood pressure and what Jennie suspects is a drinking problem. She feels a small sense of relief when she realises he's not looking at her, but her protective instincts snap to attention when she clicks that the odious man is crowding Eadie. His pose intimidating.

"You old crone. You'll never let it lie. Will you?"

"And why should I?" spits back Eadie, finally allowing her annoyance to show.

This has the effect of Wallace becoming even more aggressive in his stance. When Mark's hand slams down hard on his shoulder and he's pulled away from Eadie, Smythe-Brown swings around to see who's manhandling him. He must see something in Mark's expression that makes him think twice about taking on that particular challenge.

He flings a spleen-filled, "This isn't over," at Eadie, before he storms off, immediately contradicting himself by shouting, "This bloody event is over. Finished! Everyone leave now!"

With a few exceptions, he's totally ignored although this doesn't stop him proceeding to rip the acrylics off the stands. There's no way this crowd will go home while there's still free food and wine on offer. It will take more than a naked chappie stuck to the front window to put them off.

By the time they collect their coats, Rupert's reputation is in tatters although there are sold stickers on all the watercolours and even a couple on the glass next to Rupert, much to Lady Harrow's disgust.

Wallace Smythe-Brown had been forced to buy all the B&D acrylics by David Michaels, although the owners of the lounges and saddlery that feature prominently had also been keen to get their hands on them. This has resulted in bidding wars, forcing Rupert's father to pay way over the odds for some of them and only adding to his already foul mood. Eadie thought he'd be heading home to have one of the most expensive bonfires since Guy Fawkes took on parliament.

Driving past the gallery on their way home, they see Lady Harrow is still stuck to the inside of the window as hard and fast as Rupert is stuck to the outside. He's no longer wearing his blindfold and is surrounded by policemen and ambulance crew all scratching their heads as to how to scrape him off the glass without leaving his bits behind.

As she sees this tableau, Jennie yells, "Mark! Stop the car!" She says this with enough force that the Jag screeches to a halt immediately, much to the annoyance of the driver of the car that nearly rear-ends them.

"You can't stop here. Pull up around the corner," says Jennie, leaning between the front seats and pointing furiously to a road a short way off.

With the Jag once again moving, Jennie drags the Polaroid camera out of her handbag and then wastes precious seconds looking for its strip of flash cubes, eventually holding it up triumphantly.

"Thank God, one left."

She clips the strip of bulbs in place on top of the camera, shoves her bag in Sam's general direction and then jumps out of the car before running back to the gallery as fast as Brenda's killer heels will allow. She doesn't bother with any David Bailey-style framing of the shot, given she has to sneak between Rupert and his saviours to take it. She simply pushes the button and is on her way back to the car with the photo still spitting out of the front of the camera, when she hears shouting behind her. She legs it, head down to hide her features.

"Go, go, go!" she yells at Mark, the moment her bum hits leather. They're moving before her door is properly closed. She looks nervously over her shoulder at the corner, but doesn't see anyone round it until they're hopefully too far away for their number plate to be still visible.

"Did you get it?" says Sam, looking at the square of black Jennie pulls clear of the camera.

"Hope so." Jennie flaps the Polaroid backwards and forwards to speed up its development, eventually sliding it carefully inside her coat where the air is warmer.

"What are you going to do with it?" says Sam.

"Haven't thought that far ahead yet."

"Would be funny as hell to see it make the paper," says Chris.

Jennie mulls it over for mere seconds before speaking. "Mark, can you swing by Fleet Street on the way home?" She knows they're in the general vicinity thanks to the few sightseeing trips she's managed to squeeze in between all the painting.

"Yeah, sure. Anywhere in particular?"

Jennie looks at the fully developed Polaroid. "*The Sun* offices I suppose."

Gluing Rupert naked to the front window of the gallery hadn't been part of the plan, but that didn't mean Jennie wasn't going to take full advantage of it.

"I can think of something better than that," pipes up Eadie from the front seat.

Jennie's about to her ask her to elaborate when Eadie tells Mark to pull over. They're across the road from an off-licence-come-post-office-come-general store.

Once he's turned off the engine and pulled on the handbrake, Mark turns in his seat and gives Eadie a stern look. "You want me to buy sherry now?"

"Of course not! But I should imagine Jennie can buy pen and paper in there," says Eadie nodding toward the shop.

"Great idea," says Jennie. She hands the Polaroid photo over to Sam who holds it delicately by one corner, her lip pulled back in disgust. Jennie roots around in her bottomless pit of a handbag until she finds her wallet in a side pocket.

Before long she's back with a pink flowery circa 1960s boxed writing set and a green ballpoint pen.

She's about to start writing a short note to accompany the photo when Eadie suggests it might be better if the note was in someone else's hand. In response, Jennie wipes the piece of paper furiously.

"What on earth are you doing?" says Mark, who's twisted around in his seat.

"Fingerprints," say Jennie and Sam, in unison, causing Mark to roll his eyes.

Jennie carefully slides the piece of paper over to Sam, who keeps sliding it over to Chris who's on the far side of back seat.

"Give me the box so I can lean on it," says Chris, resigned to playing scribe. He reaches up and flips on the interior light.

Jennie starts to dictate a note to him, but is stopped by Eadie.

"As amusing as it would be to see Rupert's pock-marked posterior make it onto the infamous page three nudie spot, I think we owe it to him to try for the front page."

Everyone in the car contributes to a list of 'tips' for the journalist. They're careful not to make any accusations, which leads to a lot more questions than statements. The only thing they don't include is his name.

Some of the suggestions from Eadie don't appear to have much to do with the current situation but when questioned, she enigmatically says, "This is a much bigger story than any of you suppose."

Chris folds the two sheets of paper, carefully holding them at the edges and slipping them into an envelope along with the Polaroid photo.

He scrawls the words BIG STORY across the front,

although these look incongruous next to the spray of flowers printed on the bottom left corner.

Holding it by the edges, Jennie slides the envelope into her bag. "Okay, let's find the *Sun* offices."

They're motoring along Fleet Street, when Eadie again tells Mark to stop. Rather than be outside the Sun newspaper's offices, they're outside what looks to be a wine shop.

"I thought you said you didn't need sherry?" says Jennie, anxious at the delay. "If we leave it much longer there won't be anyone still at the paper."

"Honestly!" says Eadie, indignantly, "The way you're all going on, you'd think I had a drinking problem."

Following an awkward lull, Mark says "So, if not for sherry, why exactly this place?"

"Because El Vivo is a popular haunt with journalists."

"I can't simply walk in there and hand it over," says Jennie, retrieving the pink envelope from her bag.

"No need," says Eadie. "The sexist owner of this place refuses to allow women in the main bar, so they're all stuck out the back at the mercy of slow table service."

"And?" says Jennie, pushing for enlightenment.

"It means any female journalists drinking in there will be missing out on all the big stories talked about in the main bar."

"Right," says Jennie, catching on. "I'll leave it on top of a cistern in the ladies."

Mission accomplished, Jennie leans back in the back seat of the Jag and a sense of peace settles on her as she watches a crisp and cold London slip by on the trip home.

They're close to home when Jennie spots the world's cagiest chicken. "It's Peggy!" she yells, loudly enough for the occupants of the car to cringe and Mark to slam on the anchors.

Jennie wastes no time in reaching the bird. She's surprised it hasn't done a runner as she did before. It's only when she tries to pick up Peggy that she realises the chicken is frozen to the pavement.

"Is there any water in the car?" Jennie yells, in the general direction of the vehicle.

She's close enough that she can hear the ensuing chatter, but too far away to make out actual words. She only knows they've heard her request when Mark stands next to her with a bottle of beer in his hand.

"Will this do?"

"Yes. Can you open it?"

"Yep!" says Mark, popping the cap off expertly with his teeth, as Jennie shudders at thoughts of cracked enamel.

She pours the beer around the chicken's feet and the bird stands in a lot of froth, smelling like a brewery, and when it shows signs of moving its feet, Jennie grabs hold of it.

"No way are you escaping this time, young miss."

"I don't think she understands you," says Mark, his voice full of laughter.

"You sure about that?" Jennie looks at the chicken, who in turn is giving Mark the evils.

Peggy enjoys being ferried around in a luxury vehicle if her contented clucking is anything to go on. In the short time it's taken them to execute a U-turn and make their way to Chicken George's domicile, the bird has settled down and is close to nodding off.

Jennie isn't sure what George's routine is but hopes he's still up. No electricity means there won't be any lights showing and using candles in a shack as flammable as this one, would be bonkers.

"George, are you there?" Jennie calls out softly, rearranging the chicken under her coat where she's stuffed it to keep it warm.

"Who's there?" His voice is deep, his tone threatening.

Because of her previous dealings with him, Jennie knows

the menace is for effect and more of a home security system than anything else.

"It's me, Jennie. I've got someone here who wants to see you."

And indeed it's true. No sooner had the chicken heard George's voice than she'd been scrabbling for release from the depths of Jennie's coat. The bird escapes seconds after George emerges.

To watch them running toward each other is both touching and vaguely comical. It's imagining it being filmed in slow-mo with a romantic soundtrack that reduces Jennie to crying with laughter.

"My baby, my baby," croons George, to Peggy, who is now held firmly against his chest, her head jammed hard into the side of the man's neck and clucking softly.

"You ever need anything, you let me know," says George, seriously.

The next morning Jennie tucks into a full cooked breakfast with the others. She knows her healthy appetite is the result of a huge sense of relief that the situation with Rupert is finally over. Her months of forging paintings for him are done and with luck she'll never have to speak to him again. If he has any sense, he'll be on his way to the continent by now.

They're going over the previous evening in detail, when Brenda walks in after presumably spending the night with her sugar daddy, given she's still wearing the velvet coat.

"So, how did he end up out front? Naked!" says Jennie to Brenda.

"Once I untied him, I couldn't simply let the little shit get dressed like you wanted. So I slapped the cuffs on and left him to it."

"Couldn't you have cuffed him in front," says Sam with a delicate shudder.

"Hah. As if," crows Brenda.

"But I still don't understand how he got out?" says Jennie.

"Hmmm. I might not have shut the door properly after me," says Brenda, before cracking up laughing. "Couldn't believe it when I saw him out in front of the gallery."

They bring her up to speed with what happened after she nudged Rupert into the plate glass, with each of them taking turns to continue the story. Every time the laughter gets the better of one of them, someone else takes up the conversational baton.

Even though the house is shaking with laughter, none of them can miss the loud and official banging on the front door. Jennie's laughter chokes to a stop, with the others following. The silence in the kitchen makes the hammering on the front of the house sound even louder.

"I'll get it," says Mark.

"I'll help," says Chris.

The two of them stride purposefully through the swinging kitchen door, leaving the females in the house listening hard and ready to bolt. The quiet that ensues is a little nerve-racking and eventually Jennie can take it no longer. "I'm going to take a peek."

42

Opening the kitchen door a smidge, Jennie looks into the hallway and is relieved to see it's empty. She opens the door wider but is disappointed that this still doesn't help her hear what's being said in the front room. There are deep mumbles but she can't make out more than the occasional word. When the word "bitches" jumps out of the general hubbub, she knows for sure that one of the visitors is Rupert. She'd recognise that plummy git's voice anywhere.

"Damn!" she hisses into the door, before turning to look at Eadie. "It's Rupert."

"No surprise there," says Eadie, getting awkwardly to her feet. "Let's silence that little todger once and for all."

She walks across the room and hooks her arm through Jennie's. "Ready?"

"Not really," says Jennie, wishing she didn't have to do this.

As they walk down the hall, the voices in the sitting room become clearer. It's obvious that there are at least four people in the sitting room.

"Wallace!" spits out Eadie, her bearing hardening into something military. "Come on. I'm going to enjoy this."

Eadie's grip on Jennie's arm tightens. Jennie suspects this has more to do with stopping her from escaping than any instability on Eadie's part. Jennie knows she can't pull away without hurting the old lady. But it doesn't stop her from dragging her feet as Eadie steers them purposefully into the sitting room.

Jennie stumbles to a stop when she sees Rupert. If the state of his forehead, nose and chin are anything to go by, he's recently been circumcised, too.

"Good God. I hope David managed to scrape all of you off the front window," says Eadie, causing Rupert to redden and his eyes to narrow.

"Shit-Brown feels he should get his money back," says Mark, his body language indicating that Rupert's nose is a gnat's whisker away from being bloody as well as stripped raw of its top couple of layers.

"I don't see why," says Eadie.

"Yeah. I provided you with six paintings. Exactly as you asked."

"Maybe you should be paying for the acrylics too," says Eadie to Rupert. "I hear they achieved some excellent prices."

Rupert's father splutters furiously, drawing Jennie's attention toward him. She looks at him closely, not altogether surprised to see his face is sooty in places, and is glad to know those hideous acrylics have been incinerated. She also understands why he'd looked familiar when she'd seen him at the gallery the night before.

"I'm going to tell everyone you painted those," says Rupert, spitefully. You'll be a social pariah," he finishes smugly.

"But if you do that people will wonder why I used your alias," says Jennie.

"And we'll stand firm and say you painted the acrylics and deliberately and maliciously used Rupert's pseudonym," says Wallace. "You'll be ruined."

Jennie is unable to fight the rage that springs to life in her chest. It's only quick work on Mark's part that stops Jennie's fist making contact with Wallace Smythe-Brown's strawberry-like nose. Mark's arms firmly wrapped around her middle, work like armour, so while she can't make physical contact, she doesn't hold back when telling Rupert and Wallace exactly what she thinks of them and their lack of morals.

After Jennie finally runs out of expletives, Eadie says to Chris, "Would you be so good as to collect the painting from behind my dressing table."

Chris looks confused, but immediately leaves to do so and is soon back holding a canvas. He's looking at it as he walks back into the room and his muttered, "Gross," leaves Jennie in no doubt as to exactly which painting he's holding. This helps dampen her rage somewhat.

"If you could prop it up on the mantle," says Eadie.

When Chris stands back after ensuring the large canvas is secure, the gasps from both Rupert and Wallace are loud, although not as loud as the tirade they direct at Eadie and Jennie.

There's a lot about ruination and calling the police. Rupert attempts to retrieve the painting, but Chris stands in his way. Rupert tries walking around him only to have Chris move to stop him. There follows some fancy footwork on Rupert's part which has Chris zipping from side to side like a goal defence in netball. Chris is more than a match for the much shorter man and eventually Rupert admits defeat.

With the netball action no longer blocking her view of the painting, Jennie can look backwards and forwards between it and the still fuming Wallace Smythe-Brown. Her artistic side is pleased at how well she's captured his ugly mug. After all, there's not that much difference between the expression caused by a scream of ecstasy and one of fury. Not that Jennie is happy to have seen either.

"I think you should leave now," says Eadie.

"Am I safe to let you go?" whispers Mark in Jennie's ear, making shivers work their way down her neck.

It's only when she nods subtly that he drops his arms, leaving her feeling strangely bereft.

"Not without that-that-that thing!" says Wallace, gesturing at the painting.

"Oh, no. I'm keeping that as insurance against either of you saying anything derogatory about *anyone* in this household," says Eadie.

Both Smythe-Browns are apoplectic with rage, their behaviour is threatening enough for Mark and Chris to escort them roughly from the house. When Rupert shouts out that Eadie had better start locking her front door, Mark helps him reach the street much quicker than he could have on foot.

With the threat removed, Jennie's rage dies down until all that's left is the shaking. "What if they do go to the police?"

"They can hardly go to the cops when Rupert's responsible for perpetrating fraud through extortion, now can they?" says Mark.

"And I'd say that painting is fairly good insurance," says Chris.

"You should move it somewhere else," says Sam, who's arrived with Brenda.

Brenda walks over to the mantle so she can take a closer look at the painting. "I don't know, I like it."

"Sam's right. You need to put it somewhere safe," says Mark.

"True," says Eadie. "I wouldn't put it past either of them to pay someone to steal it."

A discussion ensues on where would be a good spot to stow it, with the consensus being that it would be best if it were in another suburb, if not county. Before they come to a final decision, their ruminations are interrupted by another knock at the door. Because it's of a normal level, they know it's not the Smythe-Browns back for another round.

"I'll get it," says Brenda, before anyone else has a chance to offer. "Might be for me."

"Mark, put that away," says Eadie pointing to the porn on the mantle. "There are more than a few famous 'horses' amongst that lot."

Their visitor is David Michaels from the gallery and, after initial pleasantries, he gives them a run down on the previous evening. "Thought I'd better warn you that a reporter came to see me this morning."

"And what did he want?" says Eadie, her voice purposefully neutral.

Anxious to hear his reply, Jennie leans forward in her seat on the couch.

"*She* was trying to track down the star of last night's show although I think she was more interested in the action outside than anything on canvas."

"And?" says Jennie, leaning even further forward.

"I told her who it was. No reason for me to keep mum about that."

"He's toast," says Mark, dropping onto the seat next to Jennie. He nonchalantly slings his hand around her shoulders and pulls her back into the couch and hard up against him.

She stills, waiting for the usual feelings of guilt to nag away at her, but nothing comes, and instead she realises she enjoys the feeling of his support. Of someone having her back.

"Is that all?" says Eadie.

"No, I thought she might be interested in seeing some of his work, as background to her story."

"You mean my work!" says Jennie, fuming again.

"Yes, about that. I had to cancel the sales of the water-colours. After all, they're forgeries and it'd be illegal for me to flog them but I've got them in the car if you'd like them. In the meantime here's your cut of the acrylics."

David Michaels hands Jennie a folded cheque, that when opened out, has her smiling broadly.

"We replaced the watercolours with some of Rupert's god-awful stuff that not even his auntie would buy."

"Oh, dear," says Eadie, shaking her head.

"Yes. Going to be the shortest damned exhibition in history," says David, unable to hold in his shudder of revulsion. "We're taking everything down this afternoon, boxing it up and sending it around to his house."

"We're free and clear then!" says Jennie, relief flooding her.

"Not quite," says David Michaels, in a manner that makes everyone in the room stiffen in suspense. "I suspect that reporter will be like a dog with a bone over this. She muttered something about wanting to get the jump on the Old Boy Network."

Looking at the small suitcase that Eadie has loaned to her, Jennie worries that she won't be able to fit everything in. Sure it'll be easier to move than the beast, but it's killing her deciding what to pack and what to leave behind.

Packing all the art equipment had been easy, although she still needs to pick up a lot of supplies from the art shop on their way out of town.

She hears Brenda's panting and bitching about the stairs well before the girl herself arrives.

"Jeez, you need breathing gear to survive up here!"

Jennie removes a green jumper from the case and replaces it with a blue one of a similar design. "I'm used to it now."

With Brenda watching, she changes her mind and swaps the blue jumper for a purple one.

"Would it help you decide if I told you there was a reporter downstairs with Eadie?" says Brenda, casually.

"What!" screeches Jennie.

"Yeah. Eadie's playing the simple old lady card, but I don't think she can hold out much longer. You need to haul arse and get the hell out of here. The nosy bitch is asking questions about *you.*"

It becomes obvious that rather than this nugget speeding Jennie's packing, it has the opposite effect; Brenda spits out a few obscenities and shoves Jennie out of the way.

Brenda's a packing machine and has the suitcase full of mix and match outfits in minutes. Granted most of the stuff is black or denim but at least it'll all go together. Brenda is closing the clasps on the case when Mark cannons into the room.

"Ready?"

"I guess," says Jennie, in a panicked voice.

It's all too out of control for someone who likes to start packing couple of weeks before departure, ticking things off an extensively researched list as she does so. She and Mark tagging along with Chris and Sam on the interview trip to Italy hadn't been her idea and she still didn't think it was such a great one. For one thing, she still isn't sure how she feels about Mark, and thoughts of them being locked up in close proximity for hours on end has her heartbeat pattering away double-time. Never mind their departure date being brought forward because of nosy reporters.

"Great!" Mark grabs the bag of art supplies and her suitcase, and then hightails it out of her room and off down the stairs before she can voice concerns that she might have forgotten something.

Brenda herds Jennie in Mark's footsteps, grilling her on important details like has she got her passport, has she got traveller's cheques. None of this makes Jennie feel any better about their hasty departure.

They meet up with Sam and Chris on the first floor landing. Rather than being nervous like Jennie, Sam is bubbling with excitement. "Imagine it. Italy here we come!"

"Shhh," admonishes Mark, who's quietly making his way back up the stairs in giant steps to minimise the amount of creaking.

"Sorry," mouths Sam, although her energy doesn't subside in the least.

"Brenda, you sure you're okay with staying on with Eadie for a while?" says Jennie.

"'Course I am. I like the old bird and anyway, Martin will be tied up with family shit when he gets back to Melbourne. This suits both of us."

The trip down the stairs to the ground floor is preposterously slow and yet it seems they step on every blooming loose board in the process. They're sneaking down the hall toward the kitchen when there's a loud banging on the front door. Jennie freezes, weighing up her options of aneurism or accident. Before she can decide, Mark who's behind her, picks her up and carries her into the kitchen.

"I'll get it," whispers Brenda.

"What if it's Rupert?" says Jennie, quietly.

This theory is quashed when they hear "Miss Cadwalader? Ian Griffin, Sun Newspaper," yelled through the letterbox flap. Obviously the story has made its way out of the ladies-only room at El Vivo if a male reporter is sniffing around.

"Maybe we need to stay and held Eadie and Brenda?" Jennie inches her way back toward the front door.

"Bugger off. I can handle him. If he gives me any trouble I'll beat the crap out of him!"

Brenda's grin is maniacal and her response makes Jennie giggle.

"Come on, we need to move it," says Chris, opening the French doors out onto the garden.

Jennie's pace slows and she chews nervously on the inside

of her cheek. "I still feel bad about not saying goodbye to Eadie."

"Oh, no, you don't." Mark hustles her along from behind, giving her cheeks a gentle squeeze, and causing her to squeak in surprise. They stumble through the undergrowth at the back of the garage and then down the side, climbing over ladders, scaffolding, and mowers on the brink of extinction, in the process.

Mark helps Jennie into the back of the Combi, following her in. He takes the last luggage from Chris and stows it on the floor in front of them. The back of the van is now so jam packed with all their stuff that it's easier for Mark and Jennie to prop their feet up on the assortment of bags and boxes than it is to find space on the floor.

After Sam and Chris are safely in the front and all the doors are shut, Chris looks over his shoulder. "Ready?"

"As we'll ever be," says Mark.

Jennie isn't sure enough to formulate a response and Chris doesn't wait for one, instead firing up the engine leading to a sigh of relief all round when it starts first time. Letting his foot off the clutch, he allows the little bus to creep forward onto the street.

Rather than turning toward Chiswick High Street, he steers the bus around in front of the house and as they glide slowly past, they see Brenda standing in the doorway, holding the reporter firmly by one of his ears. She waves gaily at them with her free hand, before leading him out onto the footpath and twisting his lug hard enough to bring him to his knees. Looks as if the lady reporter in with Eadie is going to get the scoop after all.

"Italy, here we come!" yells Sam, turning the radio up loud enough to be heard over the engine and herself.

"It's going to be okay, you know," says Mark, a hand on

either side of Jennie's face in an effort to get her eyes to focus on him rather than darting around wildly as they have been.

Jennie pulls his hands away from her face. "It's-it's just that I like a plan."

Chris hits the accelerator to send them on their way, and Jennie is forced into the seat. With it still being set up as a bed, there's nothing there to stop her backwards momentum and she lands flat on her back

Mark wastes no time flopping down next to her. "I've been planning a couple of things myself." His dilating pupils leave her in no doubt as to where he's going with this.

She's still scouting around inside her head for an appropriate response when his lips claim hers, effectively blocking any words. That she allows their kiss to proceed from hesitant to fully-engaged at head-spinning speed is all the permission he needs to proceed.

"Get a room you two," calls Chris from the front, loudly enough to be heard over the music and the engine chattering away beneath Mark and Jennie.

Pulling himself away from her, Mark responds, "We've already got one."

Jennie can tell by the amount of laughter and cheering from the front seats that Sam and Chris are pleased by proceedings.

At the questioning look on Jennie's face, he says, "Back in a sec."

True to his word, he wastes no time in pulling himself upright, scrambling across all the bags and pulling the curtains closed behind Sam and Chris.

Jennie's smile falters when he proceeds to pull the side curtains too. Now the only view of the outside world is through the back window. Everywhere else is a geometric wall of green and brown.

She's seriously worrying when Mark crawls back onto the

bed and reaches for the curtain at the rear. He's leaning over her to accomplish this when Chris reaches what must be a roundabout. The resultant sideways momentum has Mark fully stretched out on top of Jennie, and she can't help but notice he's as hard as the mattress.

"Too soon?" he says, obviously having seen the flash of panic she'd been unable to keep off her face.

"We can't," says Jennie, waving her hand around hoping to draw to his attention that they're in the back of a Combi, stuck in London traffic.

"I don't know. I think the vibrations add a certain something."

Sandwiched as she is between Mark and the vibrating metal below the criminally thin mattress, she concedes he might have a point.

Her tentative smile is all the invitation he requires.

"What if someone hears," says Jennie, when their lips momentarily part.

Arching up high enough to execute a salute worthy of a boy scout, Mark solemnly vows to smother her screams when she climaxes. When he promises one for every roundabout, she's both aroused and alarmed in turn.

"Okay, maybe every country," says Mark, with a look that makes Jennie hope they're driving to Italy the long way around.

THANK YOU

For choosing my book from all those fantastic Chick Lit stories out there! It's readers like you who allow me to pursue my career as a writer.

Lastly, don't be a stranger. I'm mostly online at Twitter, but I'm also on Facebook, Instagram (so many sunset and cat photos) and Pinterest. Because my name is as unusual as it is, you should be good simply searching for that.

www.andrenelowauthor.com

ABOUT THE AUTHOR

Andrene's love of writing was instilled in her by her mother, although if her mum was still alive, she'd be smacking Andrene across the back of the head given the direction some of her writing has taken. Irreverent, cutting and reflecting her background as a stand-up comic, it's edgy with humour that's very dark in places.

Her That Seventies Series, which was relaunched in August 2017, comprises Friday Night Fever, Brush With Fame and Strapped for Cash. The series explores the wild ride the seventies was for anyone lucky enough to be young and single during this craziest of decades. Imagine a mash up between Sex in the City and That Seventies Show and you're half way there.

Andrene's currently working on a cozy paranormal mystery series about Frankie B, a jinxed witch with Bruce Lee moves and Dex, her Jack Russell familiar. Andrene lives in New Zealand with Jasmine, a neurotic, geriatric cat who should be bald given how much fur she sheds.

CPSIA information can be obtained
at www.ICGtesting.com
Printed in the USA
LVHW041628200819
628309LV00014B/1085/P